*MORE PRAISE FOR* NOCTURNAL ANIMALS

***previously published as*** TONY AND SUSAN

"A masterful example of narrative intensity and artistic control."
—*The Sunday Times*

"Brilliantly original. . . . Two thrillers in one . . . and each infinitely superior to most thrillers because they play for keeps. . . . Read it at your peril—in daylight, preferably."
—*Chicago Tribune*

"A thrilling narrative about reading, marriage, crises and revenge."
—*The Times* (London)

"A brilliant novel. . . . Astute, cunning and thrilling in equal measure."
—*The Independent*

"A thriller with the grip of a pit bull. . . . With its trapdoor narrative and its psychological sleight of hand, this is a novel of immense guile and unsettling velocity. Why Wright isn't better known is a mystery to me. He's brilliant."
—Rupert Thomson

"Manages to combine a truly first-rate thriller with some serious discourse about the relationship between reading and writing."
—The *Big Issue*

"Fiction seldom gets this good."
—*The Seattle Times*

"Creepy, illuminating, quite wonderful."
—Donna Leon

"An excellent book: gripping, well-written, structurally interesting."
—*The Guardian*

# NOCTURNAL ANIMALS

*Previously published as* TONY AND SUSAN

*Austin Wright*

HARPER PERENNIAL

*Nocturnal Animals*


Published by Harper Perennial, an imprint of HarperCollins Publishers Ltd

Previous editions of this book were published under the title *Tony and Susan*.

First published in the United States in 1993 by Baskerville Publishers Ltd.
Originally published in Great Britain in 1994 by Touchstone,
an imprint of Simon & Schuster Ltd.
Reissued in Great Britain in 2010 by Atlantic Books,
an imprint of Grove Atlantic Ltd.

First published in Canada by HarperCollins Publishers Ltd
in an original trade paperback edition: 2011
This Harper Perennial trade paperback edition: 2016



HarperCollins Publishers Ltd
2 Bloor Street East, 20th Floor
Toronto, Ontario, Canada
M4W 1A8

*www.harpercollins.ca*

Library and Archives Canada Cataloguing in Publication
information is available upon request

ISBN 978-1-44345-387-5

Printed and bound in the United States
RRD 9 8 7 6 5 4 3 2 1

# NOCTURNAL ANIMALS

# BEFORE

This goes back to the letter Susan Morrow's first husband Edward sent her last September. He had written a book, a novel, and would she like to read it? Susan was shocked because, except for Christmas cards from his second wife signed 'Love,' she hadn't heard from Edward in twenty years.

So she looked him up in her memory. She remembered he had wanted to write, stories, poems, sketches, anything in words, she remembered it well. It was the chief cause of trouble between them. But she thought he had given up writing later when he went into insurance. Evidently not.

In the unrealistic days of their marriage there was a question whether she should read what he wrote. He was a beginner and she a tougher critic than she meant to be. It was touchy, her embarrassment, his resentment. Now in his letter he said, damn! but this book is good. How much he had learned about life and craft. He wanted to show her, let her read and see, judge for herself. She was the best critic he ever had, he said. She could help him too, for in spite of its merits he was afraid the novel lacked something. She would know, she could tell him. Take your time, he said, scribble a few words, whatever pops into your head. Signed, 'Your old Edward still remembering.'

The signature irritated her. It reminded her of too much and theatened the peace she had made with her past. She didn't like to remember or slip back into that unpleasant frame of mind. But she told him to send the book along. She felt ashamed of her suspicions and objections. Why he'd ask her rather than a more recent acquaintance. The imposition, as if what pops into her head were easier than thinking things through. She couldn't refuse, though, lest it look like she were still living in the past. The package arrived a week later. Her daughter Dorothy brought it into the kitchen where they were eating peanut butter sandwiches, she and Dorothy and Henry and Rosie. The package was heavily taped. She extracted the manuscript and read the title page:

NOCTURNAL ANIMALS
A Novel By
Edward Sheffield

Well typed, clean pages. She wondered what the title meant. She liked Edward's gesture, reconciling and flattering. She had a sneaky feeling that put her on guard, so that when her real husband Arnold came in that night, she announced boldly: I heard from Edward today.

Edward who?

Oh, Arnold.

Oh Edward. Well. What does that old bastard have to say for himself?

That was three months ago. There's a worry in Susan's mind that comes and goes, hard to pin down. When she's not worrying, she worries lest she's forgotten what she's worrying about. And when she knows what she's worrying about, like whether Arnold understood what she meant, or what he meant when he said what he meant this morning, even then she has a feeling it's really something else, more important. Meanwhile she runs the house, pays the bills, cleans and cooks, takes care of the kids, teaches three times a week in the community college, while her husband in the hospital repairs hearts. In the evenings she reads, preferring that to television. She reads to take her mind off herself.

She looks forward to Edward's novel because she likes to read, and she's willing to believe he can improve, but for three months she has put it off. The delay was not intentional. She put the manuscript in the closet and forgot, remembering thereafter only at wrong times, like while shopping for groceries or driving Dorothy to her riding lesson or grading freshman papers. When she was free, she forgot.

When not forgetting, she would try to clean out her mind to read Edward's novel in the way it deserved. The problem was old memory, coming back like an old volcano, full of rumble and quake. All that abandoned intimacy, his out-of-date knowledge of her, and hers of him. Her memory of his admiration of himself, his vanity, also his fears – his smallness – knowledge she must ignore if her reading was to be fair. She's determined to be fair. To be fair she must deny her memory and make as if she were a stranger.

She couldn't believe he merely wanted her to read his book. It must be something personal, a new twist in their dead romance. She wondered what Edward thought was missing in his book. His letter suggested he didn't know, but she wondered if there was a secret message: Susan and Edward, a subtle love song? Saying, read this, and when you look for what is missing, find Susan.

Or hate, which seemed more likely, though they got rid of that ages ago. If she was the villain, the missing thing a poison to lick like Snow White's deep red apple. It would be nice to know how ironic Edward's letter really was.

But though she prepared herself, she kept forgetting, did not read, and in time believed her failure was a completed event. This made her both defiant and ashamed until she got a card from Stephanie a few days before Christmas, with a note from Edward attached. He's coming to Chicago, the note said, December 30, one day only, staying at the Marriott, hope to see you then. She was alarmed because he'd want to talk about his unread manuscript, and then relieved to realize there was still time. After Christmas: Arnold her husband will be going to a convention of heart surgeons, three days. She can read it then. It will occupy her mind, a good distraction from Arnold's trip, and she needn't feel guilty after all.

Anticipating, she wonders what Edward looks like now. She remembers him blond, birdlike, eyes glancing down his beaky nose, unbelievably skinny with wire arms and pointed elbows, genitals disproportionately large among the bones. His quiet voice, clipped words, impatient as if he thought most of what he was obliged to say were too stupid to need saying.

Will he seem more dignified or more pompous? Probably he has put on weight, and his hair will be gray unless he's bald. She wonders what he'll think of her. She would like him to notice how much more tolerant, easygoing, and generous she is and how much more she knows. She fears he'll be put off by the difference between twenty-four and forty-nine. She has changed her glasses, but in Edward's day she wore no glasses at all. She is chubbier, breasts bigger, cheeks rosy where they were pale, convex where they were concave. Her hair, which in Edward's day was long straight and silky, is neat and short and turning gray. She has become healthy and wholesome, and Arnold says she looks like a Scandinavian skier.

Now that she is really going to read it, she wonders what kind of novel it is. Like traveling without knowing what country you're going to. The worst would be if it's inept, which might vindicate her for the past but would embarrass her now. Even if it's not inept, there are risks: an intimate trip through an unfamiliar mind, forced to contemplate icons more meaningful to others than herself, confined with strangers she never chose, asked to participate in alien customs. With Edward as guide, whose dominance she once so struggled to escape.

The negative possibilities are tremendous: to be bored, to be offended, bathed in sentimentality, stunned by depression and gloom. What interests Edward at forty-nine? She feels sure only of what the novel will not be. Unless Edward has changed radically, it won't be a detective story or baseball story or Western. It won't be a story of blood and revenge.

What's left? She'll find out. She begins Monday night, day after Christmas, after Arnold has gone. It will take her three evenings to complete.

# THE FIRST SITTING

# ONE

That night, as Susan Morrow settles down to read Edward's manuscript, a fear shocks her like a bullet. It begins with a moment of intense concentration which disappears too fast to remember, leaving a residue of unspecified fright. Danger, threat, disaster, she doesn't know what. She tries to recover what was on her mind, thinking back to the kitchen, the pans and cooking utensils, the dishwasher. Then to catching her breath on the living room couch, where she had the dangerous thought. Dorothy and Henry with Henry's friend Mike are playing Monopoly on the study floor. She declines their invitation to play too.

There's the Christmas tree, cards on the mantel, games and clothing with tissue paper on the couch. A mess. The traffic at O'Hare dies in the house, Arnold is in New York by now. Unable to remember what frightened her, she tries to ignore it, rests her legs on the coffee table, puffs and wipes her glasses.

The worry on her mind insists, it's greater than she can explain. She dreads Arnold's trip, if that's what it is, like the end of the world, but finds no logical reason for such a feeling. Plane crash, but planes don't crash. The convention seems innocuous. People will recognize him or spot his name tag. He'll be flattered as usual to discover how distinguished he is, which will put him in the best of moods. The Chickwash interview will do no harm if nothing comes of it. If by rare chance something does come of it, there's a whole new life and the opportunity to live in Washington if she wants. He's with colleagues and old hands, people she should trust. Probably she's just tired.

Still, she postpones Edward. She reads short things, the newspaper, editorials, crossword puzzle. The manuscript resists, or she resists, afraid to begin lest the book make her forget her danger, whatever that is. The manuscript is so heavy, so long. Books always resist her at the start, because they commit so much time. They can bury what she was thinking, sometimes forever. She could be a different person by the time she's through. This case is worse than usual, for Edward coming back to life brings new distractions that have nothing to do with her thoughts. He's dangerous too, unloading his brain, the bomb in him. Never mind. If she can't remember her trouble, the book will paint over it. Then she won't want to stop. She opens the box, looks at the title – *Nocturnal Animals.* She sees, going into the house at the zoo through the tunnel, glass tanks in dim purple light with strange busy little creatures, huge ears and big eye globes, thinking day is night. Come on, let's begin.

## *Nocturnal Animals 1*

There was this man Tony Hastings, his wife Laura, and his daughter Helen, traveling east at night on the Interstate in northern Pennsylvania. They were starting their vacation, going to their summer cottage in Maine. They were driving at night because they had been slow starting and had been further delayed having to get a new tire along the way. It was Helen's idea, when they got back into the car after dinner, somewhere in eastern Ohio: 'Let's not look for a motel,' she said, 'let's drive all night.'

'Do you mean that?' Tony Hastings said.

'Sure, why not?'

The suggestion violated his sense of order and alarmed his habits. He was a mathematics professor who took pride in reliability and good sense. He had quit smoking six months before but sometimes still carried a pipe in his mouth for the steadiness it imparted. His first reaction to the suggestion was, don't be an idiot, but he suppressed that, wanting to be a good father. He considered himself a good father, a good teacher, a good husband. A good man. Yet he also felt a kinship with cowboys and baseball players. He had never ridden a horse and had not played baseball since childhood, and he was not very big and strong, but he wore a black mustache and considered himself easygoing. Responding to the idea of vacation and the freedom of a highway at night, the sudden lark of it, he was liberated by the irresponsibility of not having to hunt for a place to stay, not having to stop at signs and go up to desks and ask for rooms, lifted by the thought of riding into the night leaving his habits behind.

'Are you willing to share the driving at three a.m.?'

'Anytime, Daddy, anytime.'

'What do you think, Laura?'

'You won't be too tired in the morning?'

He knew the exotic night would be followed by the ghastly day and he would feel horrible trying not to fall asleep in the afternoon and getting them back on a normal schedule, but he was a cowboy on vacation, and it was a good time to be irresponsible.

'Okay,' he said. 'Let's go.'

So on they went, zipping along the Interstate through the slowly descending June twilight, bypassing industrial cities, bending slowly at high speed around the curves and over the long rises and descents through farm land while the sun sinking behind them flashed in the windows of farmhouses in the high meadows ahead. The family of three was ecstatic with novelty, exclaiming to each other on the beauty of the countryside in this declining day, this angle of light looking away from the sun with the yellow fields and green woods and houses all tinted and changed with ambiguous brightness, and the road pavement also ambiguous, silver in the mirror and black in front.

They stopped for gas in the twilight, and when they came back to the highway the father Tony saw a ragged hitchhiker standing on the shoulder of the ramp up ahead. He began to accelerate. The hitchhiker had a sign, BANGOR ME.

The daughter Helen cried in his ear, 'He's going to Bangor, Daddy. Let's pick him up.'

Tony Hastings sped up. The hitchhiker had overalls and bare shoulders, a long yellow beard and a band around his hair. The man's eyes looked at Tony as he went past.

'Aw, Daddy.'

He looked over his shoulder to clear his way back to the highway.

'He was going to Bangor,' she said.

'You want his company for twelve hours?'

'You never stop for hitchhikers.'

'Strangers,' he said, wanting to warn Helen of the world's dangers but sounding like a prig just the same.

'Some people aren't as fortunate as we,' Helen said. 'Don't you feel guilty passing them up?'

'Guilty? Not me.'

'We have a car. We have space. We're going the same way.'

'Oh Helen,' Laura said. 'Don't be such a schoolgirl.'

'My pals who hitchhike home from school. What would they do if everybody thought like you?'

Silent a little. Helen said, 'That guy was perfectly nice. You can tell, how he looked.'

Tony amused, remembering the ragged man. 'That guy who wanted to bangor me?'

'Daddy!'

He felt wild in the growing night, exploratory, the unknown.

'He had a sign,' Helen said. 'That was polite of him, a considerate thing to do. And he had a guitar. Didn't you notice his guitar?'

'That wasn't a guitar, that was a machine gun,' Tony said. 'All thugs carry their machine guns in instrument cases so they'll be mistaken for musicians.'

He felt his wife Laura's hand on the back of his head.

'He looked like Jesus Christ, Daddy. Didn't you see his noble face?'

Laura laughed. 'Everybody with a flowing beard looks like Jesus Christ,' she said.

'That's exactly what I mean,' Helen said. 'If he has a flowing beard he's got to be okay.'

Laura's hand on the back of his head, and in the middle was Helen, leaning forward from the back seat with her head on the seatback between them.

'Daddy?'

'Yes?'

'Was that an obscene joke you made, a moment ago?'

'What are you talking about?'

Nothing. They drove quietly into the dark. Later the daughter Helen sang camp songs and the mother Laura joined in, even the father Tony, who never sang, contributed a bass, and they took their music along the great empty Interstate into Pennsylvania, while the color thickened and clogged into dark.

Then it was full night and Tony Hastings was driving alone, no voices now, only the roar of wind obscuring the roar of engine and tires, while his wife Laura sat silent in the dark beside him and his daughter Helen was out of sight in the back seat. There was not much traffic. The occasional lights on the opposite side flickered through the trees that separated the lanes. Sometimes they rose or dropped when the lanes diverged. On his own side from time to time he would overtake the red lights of someone ahead, and occasionally headlights would appear in the mirror and a car or truck would catch up with him, but for long stretches there was no one on his side at all. Nor was there light in the countryside, which he could not see but which he imagined to be all woods. He was glad to have his car between him and the wilderness, and he hummed his music thinking coffee in an hour, while meanwhile he enjoyed his good feeling, wide awake, steady – in the dark pilot house of his ship with the passengers asleep. He was glad of the hitchhiker he had left behind, of the love of his wife and the funny humor of his daughter.

He was a proud driver with a tendency to be self-righteous. He tried to stay as close to sixty-five as he could. On a long hill he overtook two pairs of tail lights side by side blocking both lanes ahead of him. One car was trying to pass the other but could not pull ahead, and he had to reduce his speed. He got into the left lane behind the car trying to pass. 'Come on, let's go,' he muttered, for he could be an impatient driver too. Then it occurred to him the car on the left was not trying to pass but was having a conversation with the other car, and indeed both cars were slowing down still more.

God damn it, quit blocking the road. It was one of his self righteous principles never to blow his horn, but he tapped it now, one quick blast. The car in front of him zoomed ahead. He pulled forward, passed the other, slid into the right lane again, feeling a little embarrassed. The slow car fell behind. The car in front, which had pulled ahead, slowed down again. He guessed the driver was waiting for the other car to resume their game, and he pulled out to pass, but the car in front swung left to block his way, and he had to hit the brakes. He felt a shock as he realized the driver of the other car meant to play games with him. The car slowed more. He noticed the headlights of the third car in the mirror far behind. He avoided blowing his horn. They were down to thirty miles per hour. He decided to pass in the right lane, but the other car swung in front of him again.

'Uh-oh,' he said.

Laura moved.

'We've got trouble,' he said.

Now the car in front was going a little faster but still too slow. The third car remained far behind. He blew his horn.

'Don't do that,' Laura said. 'It's what he wants.'

He pounded on the steering wheel. He thought a moment and took a breath. 'Hang on,' he said, pressed his foot down on the gas, and zipped to the left. This time he got by. The other car blew its horn, and he went fast.

'Kids,' Laura said.

From the back seat Helen spoke: 'Bunch of jerks.' He had not known she was awake.

'Are we rid of them?' Tony asked. The other car was behind a short distance, and he felt relieved.

'Helen!' Laura said. 'No!'

'What?' Tony said.

'She gave them the finger.'

The other car was a big old Buick with a dented left fender, dark, blue or black. He had not looked to see who was in it. They were gaining on him. He went faster, up to eighty, but the other headlights stayed close, tailgating, almost touching him.

'Tony,' Laura said quietly.

'Oh Jesus,' Helen said.

He tried to go faster still.

'Tony,' Laura said.

They stayed with him.

'If you just drive normally,' she said.

The third car was a long way back, the headlights disappearing on curves and reappearing after a long interval on straightaways.

'Eventually they'll get bored.'

He let his speed return to sixty-five, while the other car remained so close he could not see the headlights in his mirror, only the glare. The car began blowing its horn, then pulled out to pass.

'Let him go,' Laura said.

The car drove along beside him, faster when he tried to speed up, slowing down when he did. There were three guys, he couldn't see them well, only the guy in the front passenger seat who had a beard and was grinning at him.

So he decided to drive steadily at sixty-five. Pay no attention, if he could. The guys cut in front and slowed down, forcing him to slow down too. When he tried to pass, they cut left to prevent it. He swung back into the right lane and they let him catch up with them. They pulled ahead and swung back and forth between the two lanes. They went into the right lane as if to invite him to pass, but when he tried they swung back into his path. In a surge of rage he refused to give way, and there was a loud metallic explosion and a jolt, and he knew he had hit them.

'Oh shit!' he said.

As if in pain, the other car backed off and let him by. Serves them right, he said, they asked for it, but oh shit, he also said, and he slowed down, wondering what to do, while the other car slowed behind him.

'What are you doing?' Laura said.

'We ought to stop.'

'Daddy,' Helen said. 'We can't stop!'

'We hit them, we have to stop.'

'They'll kill us!'

'Are they stopping?'

He was thinking about leaving the site of an accident, wondering if the accident to their car would sober them up, if it was safe to assume that.

Then he heard Laura. In spite of the pride in his virtues, he usually relied on her for the finer moral points, and she was saying, 'Tony, please don't stop.' Her voice was low and quiet, and he would remember that a long time.

So he kept going.

'You can take the next exit and report to the police,' she said.

'I got their license number,' Helen said.

But the other car was after him again, they roared up beside him on his left, the guy with the beard was sticking his arm out the window and waving or shaking his fist or pointing, and he was shouting, and the car got ahead of him and veered, edged into his path trying to force him onto the shoulder.

'God help us,' Laura said.

'Smash into them,' Helen screamed. 'Don't let them, don't let them!'

He couldn't avoid it, another bump, a slight one with a crunching sound against his left front, he felt the damage and something rattling, shaking his steering wheel as the other car forced him to slow. The car trembled as if mortally wounded, and he gave up, pulled onto the shoulder, and prepared to stop. The other car stopped in front of him. The third car, the one that had been lagging behind, came into sight and zipped by at high speed.

Tony Hastings started to open his door, but Laura touched his arm.

'Don't,' she said. 'Stay in the car.'

# TWO

That's the end of the chapter, and Susan Morrow pauses to reflect. It looks more serious than expected, and she's relieved, glad to see the firmness of the writing, how well Edward has learned his craft. She's in for something and worries on behalf of Tony and his family on that lonely highway amid such menace. Is he safe if he keeps the doors locked? The question, she realizes, is not what he can do to keep them safe, but what the story has destined for him. That's Edward, who has the power in this case: what he has in mind.

She appreciates the irony in Edward's treatment of Tony, which suggests maturity, an ability to mock himself. She's full of illegal questions, like whether that's Christmas-card Stephanie putting her hand so affectionately on Tony's neck, and whether Helen is derived from Edward's own domestic life. She reminds herself not to confuse Tony with Edward, fiction is fiction, yet noticing Tony's last name she wonders if Edward deliberately named him after the town where they grew up.

She wonders how Stephanie likes Edward the Writer. She remembers, when Edward told her he wanted to quit school and write, she felt betrayed, but she was ashamed to admit it. After the divorce she followed Edward's surrender of that dream through her mother's reports. She drew her own conclusions, the transformation through stages of Edward the Poet into Edward the Capitalist, thinking it vindicated her doubts.

From poetry writing to sports writing. From sports writing to journalism teaching. From journalism teaching to insurance. He was what he was and was not what he was not. Money would compensate for lost dreams. With Stephanie presumably behind him all the way. So Susan supposed, but apparently she was wrong.

She pauses to locate herself before going on. She puts the box on the couch beside her, looks up at the two paintings, tries to see them fresh, the abstract beach, the brown geometry. Monopoly bargaining on the floor in the study, Henry's friend Mike has a mean laugh. On the gray rug in this room, Jeffrey twitches, asleep. Martha approaches him, sniffs, jumps on the coffee table, threatening Dorothy's camera. What?

That menacing unidentified monster she remembers in her mind before she began to read. Has the book put it to sleep? Just keep reading. Paragraphs and chapters on a lonely highway at night. She thinks of Tony, the tall thin face with the beaked nose, the glasses, the sad bagged eyes. No, that's Edward. Tony has a black mustache. She must remember the black mustache.

## *Nocturnal Animals 2*

The driver's door of the old Buick opened and a man stepped out. Tony Hastings felt Laura his wife's hand on his arm, to restrain or give him courage. He waited. The other men in the car were looking at him from their windows. He couldn't see what they looked like.

The man ambled over, slowly. He was wearing a pitcher's warmup jacket, zipper open but fastened at the bottom, with his hands in the pockets. He had a high forehead, the front part of his head bald. He looked at the front of Tony Hastings's car and came over to the window.

'Evening,' he said.

Tony Hastings felt rage rising for what he had been through, but he was more frightened than angry. 'Good evening,' he said.

'You're supposed to stop when there's an accident.'

'I know that.'

'Why didn't you stop?'

Tony Hastings did not know what to say. The reason he did not stop was that he was afraid, but he was afraid to admit that.

The man leaned down and looked inside the car, at Laura and at Helen in the back.

'Hah?'

'What?'

'Why didn't you?'

Close by, the man had big teeth in a small mouth with a small receding jaw. He had bulging eyes over small cheeks and his hair stood up in a pompadour behind the bald front of his head. His jaw was working but his mouth could not shut. The jacket had an elaborate Y in curling script sewed on the left front. Tony Hastings was thin, he had no muscle, only a black mustache, his soft sensitive face. He kept his hand on the key in the ignition. The window was half open, the door was locked.

Laura spoke up, her voice strong. 'We were going to report it to the police.'

'The police? You're not supposed to leave the scene of an accident. The law says. It's a crime.'

'We have reason not to trust you on this lonely road,' Laura said. Her voice was louder than usual with an edge Tony recognized when she said drastic, revolutionary, or scared things.

'What you say?'

'Your behavior on the road – '

The man called: 'Hey Turk!' The doors on the right side of the other car opened and two men got out. They were not in any hurry.

'I'm warning you,' Laura said.

'Be ready,' she whispered to Tony.

The man put his hands on the half-open window, stuck his head in, and grinned. 'What did you say? You're warning me?'

'You stay away from us.'

'Why lady, we've got an accident to report.'

The other two men had a flashlight and were inspecting the front of Tony's car, putting their hands on the hood, leaning down out of sight.

'All right,' Tony said, thinking all right if you want the protocol of accidents we'll have the protocol of accidents. 'Let's exchange information.'

'You have information you want to exchange?'

'Names, addresses, insurance companies.' He felt a sharp nudge from Laura, who thought giving these thugs their name was a bad idea, but protocol is protocol, he knew no other way.

'Insurance companies, hey?' The man laughed.

'You have no insurance?'

'Haha.'

'I'm going to report this to the police,' Tony said. He heard the weakness in his voice.

'Right, we report this to the cops, right,' the man said.

'So, we'll go to the cops. Let's do that,' Tony said.

'Great idea, man. What do we do, go together? What's to keep you from running away? It was your fuckin fault, right?'

'We'll see about that!' Laura said.

'Hey Ray,' one of the men in front said. 'This guy's got a flat tire.'

'Aw come on,' Tony said.

Ray went around to see. The men started to laugh. 'Well what do you know?' 'Well sure thing.' Someone kicked the tire, they could feel the jolt in the car.

'Don't believe it,' Helen said from behind.

The three men came back to the driver's window. One of them had a black beard and looked like a movie bandit. The other had a round face and wore silver rimmed glasses.

'Yes sir,' Ray said. 'Your right front tire is flat, sure is.'

'Flat as a pancake,' the man with the movie beard said.

'It sure is flat,' Ray said. 'You must have busted it when you was shoving us off the road.' Someone cackled.

'It wasn't I, it was you who – '

'Hush up,' Laura said.

'Don't believe them Daddy, don't believe them, it's a lie, it's a trick.'

'What's that?' Ray said, sharper than before. 'You don't believe me? You think I'm a liar? Shit, man.'

He waved the other guys back. 'You don't got a flat, go on and drive. Start the engine and drive. Drive on it, damn you, drive away. Nobody's stopping you.'

Tony hesitated. He realized what the vibration had meant and the jiggling of the steering wheel when he was forced to stop after the second collision. He leaned back in his seat and murmured, 'God damn!'

'Tell you what,' Ray said. 'We'll fix it for you.' He looked around. 'Won't we, guys?'

'Ya, sure,' one said.

'To show you we're okay, we'll fix it for you, you won't

have to do a thing. Then we can go to the cops together, you and me, report our accident.'

In a low voice Helen said, 'Don't believe them.'

'You got tire tools, mister?' the man with the beard said.

'Don't get out of the car,' Laura said.

'No need,' Ray said. 'Use ours. Come on, let's get moving.'

The three men went to the trunk of their car while Tony and his wife and daughter watched with their doors locked, watched while the men brought out their tools, the jack, the tire iron.

'You got a spare tire?' the man with the glasses said. The men started to laugh, except Ray. 'You can't change a tire without a spare.' Ray was not laughing. He was not grinning. He looked in the window and didn't say anything. Then he said, 'You wanna give me the keys to the trunk?'

'Don't do it!' Helen said.

The man looked at her a long time, staring.

'Who the fuck do you think you are?' he said.

Tony Hastings sighed and opened the door. 'I'll open it for you,' he said. He heard Helen moan in the back, 'Daddy.'

And Laura saying softly, 'It's all right, just be calm.'

He got out and opened the trunk and lifted out the suitcases and boxes in the light of the flashlight held by the man with the beard, until they could get at the spare tire. He watched the two men get it out while Ray stood by. They put the jack under the front wheel, and the man with the beard said, 'Get them women outa the car.'

'Come on,' Ray said. 'Get them out.'

'It isn't necessary, is it?' Tony Hastings said.

'Get em out. We're fixin your tire so get em out.'

Tony looked in at his wife and daughter. 'It's all right,' he said. 'They just want you out while they fix the tire.' So they got out and stood close to Tony near the door of the car. He thought if these men were dangerous it would be safer to stay near the car. The men went to work raising the car on the jack and loosening the flattened tire.

'Hey you,' Ray said. 'Come over here.' When Tony didn't move, he came over. He said, 'You think you're fuckin hot stuff, don't you?'

'What are you talking about?'

'"What are you talking about?" They think they're fuckin hot stuff, don't they?'

'Who?'

'Them, your women, your bitches. You too. You think you're something special, you can bump a guy's car and run off to the cops in violation of the law.'

'Listen, you were playing some crazy games out there.'

'Yeah.'

Every so often while they worked a car or a truck went by, full speed. Tony Hastings wished one would stop, he wanted someone civilized between him and these wild men he didn't know what they might do. Once a car slowed down, he thought it was going to stop, he stepped forward, but something grabbed him by the arm, drew him back. Ray was in front of him, blocking the view, and the car drove on. A little later, he saw the flashing blue lights of a police car approaching. They're coming to rescue us, he thought, and he ran out toward it as it neared, coming fast. It did not slow down and he suddenly realized it wasn't going to stop. He waved anyway and tried to shout as it zipped by. He heard women's family voices shouting too, but the car was already sparkling down the road at a hundred miles an hour out of sight.

'There goes your cops,' Ray said. 'You should have stopped them.'

'I tried to,' Tony said. He felt defeated, wondering what other trouble had caught the attention of the police while his own remained unnoticed in the dark.

The men seemed to enjoy their work. They were laughing, and he realized one of them had worked in a garage. Only Ray was not laughing. Tony Hastings did not like the waiting expression on Ray's pinched chinless face. The man is angry, he said to himself, while his own anger had ravelled out in the strangeness of things. He thought, they are trying to show me they are not what they seemed to be. They are trying to show me they are decent human beings after all. He hoped that was it.

# THREE

Susan Morrow sets down the page. Quiet returns, here where she lives, with the sound of the refrigerator, the Monopoly-playing children murmuring and laughing in the next room. Here, in this wooded enclave of winding residential streets, all is calm, all is still. It's safer here. She arches, stretches, this impulse to the kitchen for more coffee. Resist. Have a green wrapper mint instead, on the table under Martha's tail.

Once she too drove all night, Susan and Arnold and the children to Cape Cod. Arnold is smarter than Tony Hastings, could he have avoided Tony's fix? He's a distinguished man, he could give those men bypass surgery for fixing his tires, would that protect him? He's also a grinning boy with dusty hair who makes questionable jokes and waits for your response. Tonight Arnold is in a hotel, she almost forgot from worrying about imaginary Tony, in a tropical bamboo lounge underground in the dark, having drinks with the medical folk. Don't watch.

Martha the cat studies her, quietly puzzled. Every night Susan sits like this, stalking the flat white page in the glare as if she saw something which Martha sees is plainly not there. Martha understands stalking, but what can she stalk in her own lap, and how can she stalk with face so relaxed? Martha stalks for hours too, with only her tail twitching, but when she stalks there's always something, a mouse or bird or the illusion of one.

## *Nocturnal Animals 3*

The man with the triangular face whose name was Ray, the mouth too small for his chin, the half bald head with the pompadour, stood with hands in his pockets and watched the others work. He tapped his feet on the ground like a dance. I mustn't forget this is the man who forced me off the road, Tony Hastings said to himself, not forgetting. The man kept murmuring, 'Fuck you,' like a song. Tapping his feet and murmuring 'Fuck you,' looking at Tony's wife and daughter standing by the back door of the car close together, as if saying it to them, and then at Tony, looking at Tony while he murmured it, as if to him. In a kind of tune just loud enough to be heard, 'Fuck you, fuck you, fuck you.'

'What are you looking at?' the man said.

'What were you trying to do, there on the road?' Tony said.

A truck was coming, it went by, loud. If the man answered Tony did not hear it. A car or truck would go by every three or four minutes, maybe more. As long as cars go by we're safe, Tony thought, wondering what danger he was safe from.

'Hot shot,' the man said.

'What?'

'Law-abiding driver.'

'What?'

'That all you can say, "what"?'

'Look here – '

'I'm looking.'

He could not speak, caught, not having prepared a speech for his emotions.

'What were you trying to do, there on the road?' the man said after a while.

'We're just trying to get where we're going.'

'Where a you going?'

Tony held back.

'Where a you going?'

'We're trying to get to Maine. We're just trying to get to Maine.'

'What's in Maine?'

Tony did not want to answer.

'What's in Maine?'

He felt like a boy resisting bullies.

The man stepped toward him. 'I said what's in Maine?'

The man came close enough for Tony to smell the onions with something sweet and liquory, his face level with Tony's, and though he was thin, Tony knew the man could destroy him. He took a step backward but the man closed the gap. It's the age difference, Tony said to himself, not adding that he had not been in a fight since he was a boy and never won one then. I live in a different world, he almost said to himself.

He didn't want to say he had a summer place in Maine.

The man leaned forward, forcing Tony to lean back. He'd better not touch me, he said to himself. The man took hold of Tony's sweater and pushed a little. 'What did you say was in Maine?' he said.

Let go of me, Tony ought to have said. 'Let go of me,' he said. He heard his voice frail like a small kid being tortured.

Her voice rang out loud in the night: 'Let my Daddy alone!'

'Fuck you baby,' the man said. He let go of Tony's sweater, laughed, and strolled over to the women. Terrified, trembling, trying to heat his cowardly blood to the required temperature, Tony followed. 'What's in Maine? Your Daddy won't tell me, so you tell me, okay? What you going to in Maine?'

'What's it to you?' she said.

'Come on baby, we're nice guys. We're fixin your tire. You can tell me, what's in Maine?'

'Our summer place,' she said. 'Okay? Satisfied?'

'Your Daddy thinks he's better than me. What do you think of that?'

'Well he is,' she said.

'Your Daddy is scared of me. He's scared I can beat the shit out of him.'

'You're a lousy little no good,' she said. 'You're a punk, you scum.' Her voice was high and frantic, like a scream.

The man took an angry step toward her. When Laura stepped between he pushed her aside. He put his hands on the girl's shoulders up against the car and instantly Laura was on him again, hitting him, clawing, pulling at him from behind, until he flung about and pushed so she fell. 'Bitch!' he murmured. Somehow Tony must have gotten in there too, with a leap of strength before the man's arm swung around like a crowbar and knocked him back. His nose felt hit like a crowbar, it stung. The man faced the three of them and snarled: 'Watch it, you sons a bitches, you got no call to talk to me like that.'

The men by the tire had stopped their work to watch.

When Tony Hastings saw his wife Laura fall, when he heard her little cry of shock and pain in the private voice he knew so well and saw her in her traveling slacks and dark sweater sitting on the ground and watched her laboriously turn to pull herself to her feet, he thought, bad, a bad thing is happening, like news of the breakout of war. As if in his whole lucky life he had never before known a really bad thing. He remembered thinking, when his cowardly blood exploded in his head, jumping on the man and being flung back by the man's arm like a crowbar: this is no childhood bully. Real people are being knocked down.

The man looked a grievance at him. 'Christ sake, we're fixin your fuckin tire,' he said. He walked over to the others. They were almost finished, tightening the bolts. 'And when we're done we see the cops about this here accident you caused.'

'We'll have to find a telephone,' Tony said.

'Yeah? You see any telephones around here?'

'What's the nearest town ahead?'

The others put on the hubcap. They rolled the bad tire back to the trunk of Tony's car and stowed it in with the jack.

'What do you want a town for?'

'To report to the police.'

'Right,' the man said. 'So how you gonna do that?'

'We'll drive to the police station.'

'Leave the scene of the accident?'

'What do you want to do, wait until another police car comes by?' He remembered, you already sent one away.

'Daddy,' Helen said, 'there's phones along the road. Emergency phones, I saw them.'

Yes, he remembered.

'They's out of order,' the man said.

'All they good for is breakdowns and repairs,' the man with the glasses said. The man with the beard was grinning.

'We have to go to Bailey, it's the only way,' Ray said. 'You can't get cops on them road phones anyway.'

'All right,' Tony said, decisively. 'We'll go to Bailey and report it there.'

'So how do you propose to get there?' the man said.

'In our cars.'

'Yeah? Which car?'

'Both cars.'

'Naw, mister. Don't try no fuckin business with me.'

'What's the matter?'

'How do I know you ain't going to scoot outa here, leave me holding the bucket?'

'You think we would not go to the police?'

'How do I know you wouldn't?'

'Don't worry. I mean to report this.'

'You don't even know where Bailey is.'

'You lead the way, we'll follow.'

'Hah!' The man laughed. Then he seemed to think a while, looking out into the night woods as if something had occurred to him. He thought some more and seemed for a moment to have forgotten them all, dreaming away about something of his own. He's crazy, Tony thought, the words sounding like news. Then the man returned. 'What's to keep you from fading away and taking one of them crossways to the other side?'

'You seem pretty good at keeping close to other cars,' Tony said. The man laughed again. 'Okay, we'll go first and you follow. We couldn't get away from you very well that way.' They were all grinning now as if these were jokes, and even Tony grinned a little.

'Fuck you,' the man said. 'You go in my car.'

'What?'

'You go with us.'

'No way.'

'Lou can drive your car. He's a law abiding citizen. He'll take good care of it.'

Helen groaned. 'No.'

'We can't do that,' Tony said.

'Why not?'

'I'm not going to leave my car in your hands, for one thing.'

The man pretended to be surprised. 'You're not? What, you think we're gonna steal it?' Then he said, 'Okay. You go in your car, the girl comes with us.'

A cry of alarm from Helen. She went to the car, but the man blocked her way.

'No you don't,' Tony said.

'Sure you will,' the man said. 'You'll come with us, won't you honey?' He put his hand on her plaid shirt over her breast, and they struggled a little.

'Tony,' Laura said. She was looking at him, and the man was looking at them both. Then she shouted: 'Leave her alone!'

'Stop it,' Tony said, fighting the quaver in his voice.

'She likes it,' the man said.

'I do not!' she said.

'Sure you do honey, you just don't know.'

'Tony,' Laura said again, quietly. He tightened his muscles, clenched fists, and stepped toward the man, but the man with the beard held him by the arm. He tried to pull loose. The man named Ray noticed and turned to Tony, releasing the girl. She broke away and ran down the road.

'Helen!' Tony called.

'Who's boss in your family?' Ray said.

None of your business was in his head but he said nothing. He was looking at his daughter running along the shoulder of the highway. 'Helen, Helen.' The man named Ray was grinning at him with his oversized teeth in his undersized mouth. About fifty yards away she sat down on a rock just off the edge of the shoulder. He could see she was crying. There was a moment of silence.

With a nod of his head Ray signalled to the others and they went over to his car and had a conference. Tony was aware of the night, of the coolness and the mountain clarity of the stars. Behind him the ground descended into black woods, he could not see into them at all. The opposite lanes were out of sight up the slope on the other side, concealed by trees.

When cars went by there they cast a white light in the trees like a ghost in the branches. The men in their conference were gesturing, excited, laughing, and Helen down the road was sitting on the rock with her head in her hands.

A car came along. As it approached Helen went to the roadside and waved at it frantically. It increased its speed and went by.

Then Laura spoke to Tony. 'Come on,' she said, 'we can pick her up down there.' She got into their car. But when Tony went around to the driver's side, he saw Helen coming back, and the three men standing between her and the car.

She had a stick in her hand.

Another car was approaching. She had come almost up to the three men's car and when the lights came closer she ran into the highway waving both arms and the stick over her head. The car slowed down. It was a pickup truck, and it stopped just short of her. The driver leaned over to the right side and looked out. 'What are you trying to be killed?' he said.

He was an old man in a baseball cap. They all went up to him except Laura, who was in the car. 'These guys – ' Helen said.

'It's okay,' Ray said. 'She's a little shook up.'

'It's not okay, ask my Daddy.'

'Eh?' the old man said.

'We need help,' Tony said.

'What say?'

'Flat tire,' Ray said. 'We fixed it for them.' He was nodding and smiling, his teeth like a rodent. 'Everything's under control.'

'Eh?' the old man said. 'She trying to get herself killed?'

Ray shouted at him. 'It's okay! Everything's under control!'

Tony stepped forward. 'Excuse me – ' he said. He heard Helen crying: 'Help us, please.' The old man looked at Ray, who was laughing and waving the tire iron.

'What say?' He cupped his ear.

'No problem,' Ray said in a loud voice.

'No no,' Tony tried to shout. Someone was dragging him back by the arm. The old man looked at the group of them. His face was bewildered and unhappy, but perhaps it was always that way. He looked at Ray's tire iron, hesitating. 'No problem then,' he said suddenly. His voice was testy, and he disappeared from the window, put the pickup truck in gear, and drove off.

Behind him, Tony heard Helen cry out, 'For Christ sake, mister!'

'What's the matter, baby?' Ray said. 'You don't want to mess with a deaf old man like him.'

There was a rush of motion, the men startled, Helen making a dash around them to the car, into the back seat, slamming the door. Another moment of silence, Ray holding Tony by the elbow, not hard, Laura and Helen waiting for him in the car.

'Okay,' Ray said at last. 'We go in both cars.'

The relief at last of the nightmare ending, tired of their game, which had gone as far as it could, they must have realized nothing more was possible. He knew they would not go to the police, but he didn't care, glad only to be free of them.

Except that Ray had him by the elbow. He moved toward the car and felt the grip tighten, hold him back.

'Not you,' Ray said.

'What?'

The real fear now, shock of the first nuclear warning in the war.

'We split up,' Ray said. 'You go in my car.'

'No way.'

He saw the action at his car, the man with glasses running to the driver's door, opening it just before Laura on the passenger side realizing too late what was happening could reach over to lock it, the man holding it open, bracing it where he stood with his foot in the car, while Ray was saying, 'You ain't got no choice.'

'I'm not going to leave my family.'

'I said, mister, you ain't got no choice.'

So now the coercion was overt. With Ray's two partners, one with his foot in the door of Tony's car, looking at Ray waiting for some decision or order what to do. The man thought a while. He released Tony and said, 'You go with Lou.'

When Ray went over to Tony's car, Tony tried to follow, but the man with the beard touched him. 'Better not,' he said. He had something in his hand, Tony could not tell what. Tony shook him off and went after Ray. He saw the man with his foot in the door reach inside to unlock the back, which Helen sitting there tried to prevent. He saw a struggle with Helen trying to bite the hand of the man with glasses, who got the door open and got in. He ran after Ray thinking I'll hit him in the back, I'll knock him down and get in the car, but something heavy sliced across his shins, he plunged forward and fell with hands and knees scraping the pavement, his chin hit, and he looked up and saw Ray getting into the driver's seat.

With a violent roar the car started up, then a shriek of the tires as it pulled onto the highway and sped away. He saw the horrified faces of his wife and daughter looking at him as the car rushed by, and he heard the rushed diminuendo of the car's speed as it went down the road, the little red lights shrinking and getting closer together until they were gone.

For a few moments then there was only the silence of the woods and some distant roar of a truck almost indistinguishable from silence, while Tony looked down the invisible road where all he loved had disappeared, trying to find some way to deny what the words in his mind said had happened.

The man with the beard, whose name was Lou, was looking down at him. He held the tire iron in his hand. 'Come on,' he said. 'You'd better get in the car.'

# FOUR

Susan is shocked. They have kidnapped Tony's family while she, helpless, anticipated everything. She resists, she should have prevented it. They should have got into the car when Helen ran up the road, driven off before the men could react, picked her up as they went by. They knocked him down, tripped him up. They blocked him just as Edward is blocking her. She watches Tony's car disappear down the road with its precious load and shares his shame and dread.

She wakes up in the warm small living room, the game in the next room, a long way from that roadside wilderness. She feels a gap, someone missing. Not Arnold, she knows where he is. It's Rosie, my child Rosie, where is she? The cold night shoots an icicle of panic through her heart, why isn't she here? But Susan Morrow knows where Rosie is, she's spending the night with Carol. So that's not it. As for Arnold in his bamboo underground lounge. Relaxing (not with Marilyn Linwood) with Dr. Oldfriend and Dr. Famous and Dr. Newcomer and Dr. Medstud after a day of papers and panel discussions.

She would like to know, do such terrible things actually happen? She hears Edward's answer: you read it in the papers every day. Her dear ex-husband has plans for us. She dreads Edward's plans, but she's not afraid.

## Nocturnal Animals 4

'You drive,' the man named Lou said.

'Me?'

'Yeah you.'

The peculiarity of a stranger's car, the wounded metal of the screeching door, the driver's seat with torn seat back, the floor pedals too close. The man handed him the key. Tony Hastings was trembling, frantic with haste, he groped for the ignition. 'To your right,' the man said. The car didn't want to start, and when Tony finally put it in gear it was long since he had driven with a manual shift, and the car stalled.

There was Lou beside him, the man with the black beard, not saying anything. When Tony finally got going he drove as fast as he could, with plenty of speed in this car, rattling and squealing in the wind, but he knew with despair that mere speed would not catch the tail lights of the other car with their big start.

The luminous green sign for an exit. He eased up. The second sign specified Bear Valley and Grant Center. 'This exit?' he asked.

'I dunno, I guess so.'

'Is this the way to Bailey? Why doesn't the sign say Bailey?'

'What you want Bailey for?'

'Isn't that where we're going? Isn't that where we're going to report?'

'Oh yeah, that's right,' Lou said.

'Well, is this the way?' They had come to the beginning of the exit ramp, and were almost stopped.

'Yeah, I guess so.'

A stop sign. 'Left or right?' The road was rural. There was a darkened gas station, and black fields merging into woods.

It took the man a while to decide. 'Try right,' he said.

'I thought Bailey was the nearest town,' Tony said. 'How come the signs mention Bear Valley and Grant Center and not Bailey?'

'That's strange, ain't it?' the man said.

The road was narrow, winding through fields and patches of woods, up and down hills, past occasional darkened farmhouses. Tony drove as fast as he could, hitting the brakes for unexpected curves, chasing a car he could not see, while the distance extended to miles and more miles. In all that time, he met no other cars. They came to a reduced speed sign and another sign, CASPAR, and a small village all dark, nothing open. 'There's a telephone booth,' he said.

'Yeah,' Lou said.

He slowed down. 'Listen,' he said. 'Where the hell is Bailey?'

'Keep going,' the man said.

A crossroads, a somewhat bigger road, a sign to WHITE CREEK, a cluster of garages and roadside restaurants and stores, all closed. 'Left,' Lou said, and they left that settlement behind too. A straightaway, then a fork, one road going down, they took the other, climbing again in hills and woods. 'There's the church,' Lou murmured.

'What?' It was a small church in a clearing with a little white spire. The woods closed in on both sides of the road. There was a light-colored car parked in a turnout on a curve. It looked like his car, then he was sure, by God. 'That's my car!' he said, and he stopped beyond it.

'Don't stop on the goddamn curve.'

'That's my car.'

Whatever it was, it was empty. There was a lane into the woods and a house trailer above among the trees with a dim light in one of its windows.

'That ain't your car,' the man said.

Tony Hastings tried to back up to look at the license plate, but he had difficulty getting the car in reverse.

'Don't back on the curve, for Chrissake!' Tony thought, I haven't met a single car on the road since we left the Interstate. 'That ain't your car. Your car's a four door.'

He looked. 'Isn't that?'

'What's the matter with you, can't you see?'

Looking, trying to see the car beyond the man sitting on his right, who was telling him the car was not a four door, asking him to look and see for himself – he recognized panic distorting his judgment and perhaps his eyesight, and he resumed driving.

A winding road making a slow ascent through woods, then descending to a T intersection without signs, they turned right to climb some more. The man asked, 'What made you think that car was yours?'

'It looked like it.'

'Ain't nobody in it. What you think, they went to a party in that there trailer?'

'I don't know what to think.'

'You scared, mister?'

'I'd like to know where we're going.'

'You fraid my pals ain't playing straight?'

'I'd like to know where Bailey is.'

'Well my pal Ray, it's best to humor him, you know.'

'What do you mean?'

'Here, slow down here.'

The road was straight, with a deep ditch and woods on both sides.

'Watch out, you gotta make a turn up here.'

'What do you mean, there's nothing here.'

'Here it is, turn here.' An unmarked dirt road, a lane into the woods to the right. Tony Hastings stopped the car. 'What's going on?' he said.

'You turn down here, like I said.'

'The hell with you, I'm not going down that road.'

'Listen mister. Nobody hates violence like I do.'

The man with the beard was leaning back in the passenger seat, arm over the seatback, relaxed, looking at Tony.

'You want to see your wife and kid?'

The road, the lane, dwindled quickly to a narrow track with a grass ridge in the middle. It wound around big trees and rocky outcrops in the woods, while the car jounced and squeaked over rocks and pits. I have never been in a situation resembling this, Tony said to himself, nothing remotely this bad. He had a vague memory of what it was like to be hijacked by neighborhood boys bigger than himself, a memory which he created in order to prove how different this was, that nothing in all his civilized life had ever been anything like this.

'What are you doing to us?' he said.

The headlights flashed on the trunks of the trees sweeping from one to another as they turned. The man didn't say anything.

Tony asked again: 'What are you doing to us?'

'Hell mister, I don't know. Ask Ray.'

'Ray isn't here.'

'He sure ain't.' The man laughed. 'Well mister, I'll tell you. I really don't know what the fuck we're doing. Like I said, it's up to Ray.'

'Did Ray tell you to bring me down this road?'

The man didn't answer.

'Ray's a funny fellow,' he said. 'You got to admire him.'

'You admire him? What for?'

'His guts. He does what he's got to do.'

'I'll tell you something,' Tony said. 'I don't admire him. I don't admire him one little bit.' He wondered if the man with the beard would admire his guts for saying this.

'Don't worry. He don't expect you to.'

'He'd better not.'

He saw a fox standing in the leaves, colored jewels in its eyes, caught momentarily in the headlight flood before it turned and disappeared.

'I don't think you need to worry about your wife and kid.'

'What do you mean?' There were waves of shock in everything tonight. 'What is there to worry about?'

'You ain't scared?'

'Sure I'm scared. I'm scared as hell.'

'Well I can see how you might be.'

'What's he doing with them? What does he want with them?'

'Damned I know. He likes to see what he can do. Like I say, you don't need to worry.'

'You mean it's all a game. A big practical joke.'

'It ain't exactly a game. I wouldn't call it that.'

'What is it, then?'

'Hell mister, don't ask me what he's got up his sleeve. It's always different. It's always something new.'

'Then why do you say I don't have to worry?'

'He ain't never killed anybody yet, that's all I mean. At least as far as I know he ain't.'

The nature of this assurance gave Tony still another shock. 'Killed! Are you talking about killing?'

'I said he ain't killed,' Lou said. His voice was very quiet. 'If you'd a listen to me, you'd hear what I was saying.'

They came to a clearing where the tracks of the road

disappeared into grass. 'Well well,' Lou said. 'Looks like we run out of road.' Tony stopped the car.

'They ain't here,' he said. 'Wonder if I made a mistake. Guess you'd better get out.'

'Out? What for?'

'It's time for you to get out. Okay?'

'Suppose you tell me why.'

'We got trouble enough already. Just do what I say, right?'

In the case of muggings, the wisdom is not to resist, give up your wallet, don't brazen it out against weapons. Tony Hastings was wondering about the opposite wisdom, at what point does nonresistance become suicide or practical acceptance negligence? Where in the events of the just past was the moment when he could have seized the advantage, or was such a moment still possible?

Two men in the front seat of a car: the one on the right tells the one in the driver's seat to get out, the other resists. The one in the driver's seat is in his forties, academic, sedentary, his mind sees many things, but he has not been in a fight since childhood and cannot remember winning one. The other man has a black beard, wears blue jeans, and seems sure of himself. The sedentary man has no weapons except his fountain pen and reading glasses. The man with the beard has shown no weapons either but seems to know he has the resources to enforce his will. Question: how can the sedentary man avoid being thrown out of the car?

'I'm just telling you what to do so we don't have to have no violence.'

'What violence are you threatening me with?'

The man with the beard got out of the car on the right. He came around the back to the driver's side. During the few moments it took him, Tony Hastings was marveling at his confidence that Tony would not drive off or run him down. Start up and go – his hand was on the gear shift, the engine was running. Of course he'd have to turn around in the clearing. A metal yelp, the door flung open, it was Lou standing there at his elbow: 'Out!' he said.

Tony looked up at him. 'I won't be left here.' It was still not too late, if he moved suddenly enough. The man had him by the arm, bulldog grip, Tony put in the clutch and tried to shift, but the man yanked, and Tony fell backward out of the car onto the ground.

'You'll get killed if you don't watch it,' the man said. He got in the car, slammed the door, jerked forward, made a couple of quick turns, then jounced back down the lane up which they had come. Standing in the grass, Tony watched the jolting wash of light flaring in the branches of the trees for a long time after the car was gone before leaving him alone in the stillness and natural dark of the night.

She puts the manuscript down. What a predicament, it gets worse and worse. Annoyed with Tony Hastings, yet what would she have done if it were she? Not be there in the first place, she says.

She wants to get up. Do something before the next harrowing chapter. She'd rather not move, though. Just keep going, see what's coming.

What's likely to happen to a man who has just been dumped in the woods, while thugs have run off with his wife, daughter and car? Impossible to answer without knowing the thugs, what they think they are doing. But this is fiction, which changes the question. It's a path going somewhere, made by Edward up ahead. The question for Susan, do I want to follow? How can she not? She's caught, just like Tony.

On the Monopoly floor someone farts. Henry's friend Mike snorts, hee haw, Susan looks, wonders. Sees her dear son Henry from the back, his broad fat behind, much too fat, poor boy. Her golden-haired Dorothy, a year older, slugs him on the arm.

Nothing fits right, everything is askew. I'd better go to the bathroom, Susan says. Whatever else she might add later, she can tell Edward he's got her hooked, anyway.

# FIVE

This is a deliberate interruption of her reading, for she didn't really have to go to the bathroom. She comes down the stairs out of darkness. The light is out in the upstairs hall, it requires the ladder from the basement. Not tonight. Across the room Henry lies on his back, sweater lifted, scratching his stomach, ruled out of the game, while Mike spots his marker around the board with a villain's laugh. Henry is crooning: 'Who cares, whooo cares?'

'Don't be a brat,' Dorothy says.

Martha has moved onto the manuscript, makes herself heavy when Susan tries to move her. Susan remembers a graceful stretch of summer highway, the road bending from one hill-side down into a valley of farms and up another long curve to a ridge of woods. Herself, she loves that wilderness, she loves the woody ridges and long valleys and comforting snack stops in small friendly restaurants off the highway, especially after the pounding long day of driving across flat Indiana and Ohio. It rests her soul. She remembers the singing in the car, Dorothy, Henry, and Rosie in the back, Jeffrey moving from one lap to another and Martha hidden below. 'Tell me why, Camp Hazelnut.'

Dump Martha, who shakes herself, offended, then dashes out to the kitchen. Susan remembers the lake, morning light flashing spider lines under the tree leaning over the water while Arnold and Henry wade out to the float, Arnold up to his collarbone, his red freckled shoulders soft and plump, holding Henry in the water by his two hands under the stomach, while the boy sticks his chin up like a loon and Dorothy submarines twenty feet further out.

She remembers Edward's cabin in the woods when he wanted to be a writer. Soft impressions. Short confessional poems with everything unsaid. Nostalgic sketches, loss and grief. Father deaths. Haunted harbor scenes. Melancholy sex in the pastoral woods. It was not easy to read Edward in those days.

This is different. She admits it, Susan, this capture is power over her and Edward wields it, whether she likes it or not. As she follows Tony Hastings down his trail of terror she knows she sees what Edward wants her to see, feels what he feels, without a trace of Edward's offenses as she remembers them. Edward stiff and nervous, prissy and cranky, has yet to appear in this lonely Pennsylvania landscape, where she and Tony face with him the unambiguous horror of what these evil men (conceived by him) are doing. There's no ground to quarrel with him yet, and she's grateful for that.

## *Nocturnal Animals 5*

Tony Hastings stood there a long time, looking where the car had gone, now all dark. The night was thick, he tried to see, vaguely aware of differences in the shadows, but he could not distinguish, he felt blind. My God, he said, they went off and left me. What kind of a joke is this?

Now the woods in the night were silent, he heard nothing. After a while the darkness began to clear, not much but some, clearer than before anyway. He was in a small open space between the trees, he could see the sky overhead. He saw a few stars, not many, not brilliant, not what they should be in the mountains. He could distinguish the treetops from the sky, but all below was still unpenetrated black, a curtain around the arena.

Surely they don't expect me to get out without a flashlight, he said. Some joke.

The silence began to sort out. He distinguished a remote process, not a sound but the copy of a sound, recognized as trucks on the Interstate, miles away. He could not tell whether the faint whistling noises were insects in the grass or in his ear. Around the arena the curtain yielded shapes. He saw tree trunks and open spaces between the trees. He could see a black hole where the car had gone. He could see the road.

What are you waiting for? he said. It was stupid to suppose they would come back. Actually he had never supposed it. The problem was clear, he had been dumped in the wilderness in a prank a college sophomore would think of, and he would have to find his way out. So much for getting to Maine in one night.

The only question was whether he could find his way in the night. No, that was not the only question. Since he could see now, he went into the woods where the road was. He subdued an impulse to run, too far to go. He steadied his pace, he walked.

The road crossed a narrow stream on a log bridge and then went on, winding through the trees, turning and turning back, up and down hills, past thick brushy places and open stands of pines. Laura and Helen were waiting for him in a police office in Bailey, wherever that was. Worrying about him, deserted by him. The thought drove him wild, how to get a message to them. I'm all right, I'm coming, I'm in the woods, you'd better get some sleep because it will take a while.

Eventually they'll send someone to look for him, but it will be hours before they realize the need, and no one will think of looking down a hidden lane like this.

They will never come for me, he said. I'm coming I'm coming. If he sat down to wait he would never get out. As if his life itself depended on this walk through the woods.

He slogged on, steady as he could. Steady was not easy because the track of the road was rough and hidden in the night, he stumbled on rocks, landed his foot in pits and irregularities, sometimes the trees closed in so that the road almost disappeared. He remembered nothing from the drive in. He came to a maze, strayed off, knew the straying from the spring of matted brush under his feet, found and kept the road only by the feel of his feet as he rebounded cautiously from one side to the other, hands out to protect his eyes. It would be easier to sleep too and wait for daylight. But he had so far just to get out of the woods, and then so far again, while Laura and Helen waited.

Insulted and grotesquely humiliated. Rage concentrated in his fists, steadied his pace, defied the blindness of his feet, his toes and heels. He catalogued the idiocies of hoods and punks, the kind who would play chicken with real cars on a highway and kidnap a college professor and dump him in the woods. Who think that sort of thing is funny. Manly. Tough.

Tony Hastings was insulted but refused to be humiliated. My name is Tony Hastings, he said. I teach mathematics at the university. Last week I gave three students F for the course. I gave great pleasure to fifteen others with the grade of A. I have a Ph.D. The law will have something to say to Ray and Lou and Turk. God knows I am a peaceful person, I dislike conflict, but if the law doesn't. Guys who play pirate on the road may find out from me what it is like.

Outrage stiffened him against the danger of crying. From childhood, where the big boys snatched his hat and pushed him into the brook and ran away while he clambered out. They shall find out what it's like.

Distance weights his feet, step by step stumbling to unravel the miles of driving rolled up between him and his destination. Time locks him in a cell and borrows from itself hours hidden from the world. If he permits the morning to come before he gets out, if he lies down and closes his eyes.

What if they decide they can't wait any longer? What if they think he has run away? He must get the message to them before they leave.

Steady, man. Speak to him, calm him down. There's nothing you can do but what you are doing. They will wait. Hope them some blessed sleep while you slog your way back.

Back where? That's the question what police station? which he said you have not been thinking very clearly about. Knowing full well they weren't waiting for him in any police station. Knowing all along but his mind deflected to other things. Now the reasons come. They won't take Laura and Helen to the police station for the same reason they left you in the woods. They left you in the woods because they were not taking Laura and Helen to the police station. What Tony Hastings knew all along but only now understood, injecting mercury into his veins shooting everything cold, turning rage to terror. For if they were not taking Laura and Helen to the police station, where were they taking them to?

Steady, man, he said. Nothing to do but what you're doing.

A few moments later he saw rays of white light through the woods ahead, rising and vanishing like someone swinging a flashlight. Then he heard a car, whining around the bumps and turns of the road. Yes, the car, they were coming back.

The stupid long joke was over, they were coming back – as he had known they would, if he had only had the patience – and all his rage and terror dissolved into relief. Thank God! he said.

The white flood approaching, making grotesque shadows of sticks and pikes up into the branches, contracted suddenly into a fierce white eye visible for a second before hidden again, a second which lit up all the woods around him, trunks, bushes, boulders, and Tony Hastings himself like lightning, and in the same instant illuminated a warning in his mind: Hide!

He ran to the tree which the lightning had shown, hurrying before the headlights could reappear, then dashed across a space to the boulder beyond, while the lightflood bounced behind an intervening outcrop. Then for a moment all the woods were lit again but only for a moment, for suddenly it was pitch dark and he heard the car stop, lights off. They saw me, he said.

He stood behind the boulder, fright beating inside him. Saw me in that first flash of the headlight, and now they are waiting for me to show myself. I was right to be afraid.

'Hey mister!' The voice was close, resonant in the trees. 'Your wife wants you.'

He held still. Wondered, could that be true? It ought to be, for if she wasn't there, where was she?

'Mister? Your wife wants you.'

The voice had the music of a trap in it.

'Mister?'

'Ah shit!'

The lights snapped on, the forest floor was illuminated like a movie stage, and he was concealed behind the boulder in its shadow. The car started, and after a moment went on up the lane in the direction from which he had just come.

It looked like his own car. He watched its silhouette before the wash of light cast upon the woods beyond. He peered, strained his eyes, are they there? He saw the two men's heads, knobs against the light, the two, just two, he was sure it was just two.

Yet he might have been wrong, it was hard to tell how much life was in that car, peering against the light while trying not to be seen. He stepped out to the lane, listening to the diminishing sound while the silence and clarity of the darkness gradually returned. What's the matter with you? he said. Why didn't you go to meet them?

He cursed himself for cowardice, then listened to the silence. Paralyzed, wondering, now which way?

# SIX

The brutal telephone invades her reading, violating Susan in the woods. It's Arnold checking in from his New York hotel, making her heart pound. Says he loves her, as if he thinks it necessary. Two minutes of awkward conversation with nervous pauses, strangers married twenty-five years. His interview is tomorrow. Write this down: The Cedar Hall Institute for Cardiac Research and Practice in Washington. Known as Chickwash. A directorship. When she hangs up, she's as shaky as a fight, though there's no fight she knows of. Should be relieved, right?

Meanwhile, Tony Hastings is alone on the grassy road in the woods, which a mere telephone call has caused her to forget. She sinks into the couch, tries to reenter Edward's woods, but she's still trembling from Arnold's call. She reads a paragraph and takes in nothing. She tries again.

*[Nocturnal Animals 5 (continued)]*

Think, he said. You're not thinking. Which way? Because if that was his car they were driving. And if Laura and Helen were last seen going off in it. And if Laura and Helen were in it now. Mister, your wife wants you.

Think. Why the guys in his car would be going to the same lonely place where they had left him. They were bringing his wife and daughter to meet him. He should have waited for them. Stayed on the grass back where he was dumped. Instead here, his craven hiding behind the boulder, his failure to come out and meet them. Laura and Helen waiting in the car for him to come, and he did not. And so they went on up the road into the deeper wilderness with their captors, betrayed, abandoned. Shame, then grief, as if he had denied them and lost them for good.

Go after them. Hurry. He looked where they had gone, whence he had come. It was impossible, he could not move. Wordless, like instinct, like the light that had flashed saying 'Hide.' You're crazy, he said.

Some words followed, explaining why he could not go. They aren't there, they said. You'd only be trailing Ray and Turk, back into their sadistic hands. You'd have it all to walk out of again. There were only two heads in the car, Ray and Turk.

So he turned and continued as he had. The road was easier now, broader with fewer holes and rocks, not crowded so close by saplings and brush. But he was dragging a heavy chain of grief that tried to pull him back. He argued against it. He said, if they had been in the car they would have called too. She would have said, 'Tony?'

He walked faster now, talking. Proof of the menace, he said, was how they tried to lure you in just now. Proof of stupidity too: did they think turning off the lights and engine would fool you into thinking they weren't there after the thunder and lightning of their approach?

He felt them behind him, silent in the dark. Catching up. It made him walk faster. It made him wonder why they had gone in there, as if the question had not occurred to him until now. It surprised him. Yes, he said, why? What is in that grassy spot to make one of them leave me there and bring the other two after?

Rendezvous? Stash? He looked for explanations, but his mind resisted the effort. Come back to get him? That was ruled out when they kept going after spotting him by the road. More questions followed, which he had not known were there. The question of what their game really was. To steal his car? Maybe there was a place in the woods where they intended to secrete the car until later. Okay, that's a theory, but why did they take you there?

Simple meanness, a sadistic thrill, that'll do it, he said. The sheer devilish fun of dividing a family and putting them down in the wilderness as far apart from each other as the night will allow. See how long it takes them to find each other. Something like that. There were worse possibilities.

There were. He knew that, he knew it well, it was the habit of his mind to know the worst case, the ultimate. His life was a scenario of disasters that never took place. Because, if it really was just Ray and Turk in his car back there, then where were Laura and Helen?

The foolish image of the police station was still in his mind, of his wife and daughter sitting at a table, drinking coffee, waiting for news, but no, it was another image, image of the trailer over the curve in the road in the woods, with the dim light behind the curtain in the window. It was hard not to cry in his talk, which was a kind of pleading now, like a prayer. If it is rape, he prayed, if it must be rape, oh God, let that be the worst, let it not be worse than that.

Echo to God: let them be mean and cruel if they must, but give them some restraint, some limit beyond which they will not go, even them, let them not be mad, not psychopaths.

He noticed the thinning of trees ahead, an open space, flat

and bare, realized it was the paved road, he was almost out. In a moment he was in the clear. He stepped onto the pavement and looked around. The road ran straight in both directions above the floor of the woods on both sides. He noticed a broken gate by the entrance of the wood lane, a white board canted diagonally against a post, and tried to fix it in his mind, thinking, identify the place, it may be useful. He turned to the left to retrace his ride with Lou, though he knew it would be a long walk before he came to any people. Then behind him in the woods he heard the car. He saw the distant approach of light once again in the trees. Once again the fright warning, hide in the ditch. He resisted. You must face them, you must ask them, he said. You must not be so intimidated. He stood in the road and waited. The car came out of the woods and turned right, away from him. He was disappointed and relieved.

Then it stopped. They've seen me, he said. The car turned around and came toward him. He waited by the road. I'll ask where Laura and Helen are, he said. I'll ask what they intend to do with my car. The car approached slowly, then suddenly it wasn't slow, the tires screeched, it was coming at high speed, the headlights spreading like jaws. He leaped blind into the ditch and landed in the knives while the car threw gravel at him.

The car shrieked and stopped. Around its red and white light a cloud of smoke rose and dissolved. A door opened. A man got out, stood at the edge of the shoulder, looked back, a shadow, indistinguishable. Tony Hastings did not move. He did not know if he could. The knives held him, branches, barbed wire. Thorns scratched around his eyes. The man walked a few steps toward him. He looked, it seemed a long time. He went back to the car. 'Fuck him,' he said, The words were far off and not said loudly, but Tony heard them clearly.

He was afraid they would turn the car around and find him with the headlights, while he was still unable to move. But the car U-turned away from him and passed above him gaining speed.

He wondered if he was badly hurt. He was scratched on the forehead and around the eyes, and the palms of both hands were cut. Something had gashed at his shin through the trouser, and something like a fence post had struck him in the gut.

He spread the barbed wire that held him, tried his legs, stood up. After a few moments he scrambled up the gravel. The road, the woods, the night sky hazy with only a few stars, everything was quiet with only the barely perceptible sound of trucks on the Interstate.

They were trying to kill me, he whispered. The thought cut through the surface layers of his brain into deeper hollows where he had never known a thought could go. He repeated it: really trying. And if they were really trying to kill me, he added. He did not finish. These must be the worst thoughts he had ever had, and all around him he saw the sleeping world, road, woods, sky, doom.

# SEVEN

The chapter break, Susan wanting no pause looks up to see where she is. In the next room on the floor, Dorothy with the golden hair flat on her back with arms up, dirty elbow. Breasts. Henry's friend Mike looks at her with slit eyes. Wish she would move, do something. The rasp in Mike's voice sounds like Ray in the book. In three years Dorothy goes to college. In New York Arnold in the bamboo lounge with who? Dr. Medstud?

*Nocturnal Animals 6*

He walked fast on the pavement because he knew if he did not, it would be this road forever. Empty dark and despite the black foliage on the trees, blasted. The road turned, it descended, the woods rose over. He came to a fork, which he could not remember from his ride with Lou. Guessing, he took the turn to the right, down the hill, not familiar. He heard a car laboring up. He saw the approaching light and stepped into the woods until it went by. It was not Lou's car, nor his own, but it could have been, and he thought it wise not to take more risks. Yet wise seemed like nothing in this ravaged world as he walked along, fugitive, afraid of cars and men, as if he had been exiled from his species.

Looking ahead, though. Where are you going? he said.

Police. What police? Bailey police. How will you find them? Telephone, first house. People. Anywhere with people.

Imagining a telephone booth, he felt in his pocket for coins. Okay. Please connect me with the police office in Bailey. Excuse me, my name is Tony Hastings from Ohio, I have a problem. Help! Whatsat you say? Help!

What telephone booth? It needs no telephone booth, any farm house will do. Excuse me, I wonder if I could use your telephone? Land sakes mister you scared me out of my growth cant you see its the middle of the night.

My name is Tony Hastings, I'm professor of mathematics at a university you never heard of. Sic the dogs on him, no strangers snooping round my place middle of the night.

As Tony Hastings while he walked, he tried to look ahead beyond his temporary problems. If it should be necessary to rent a car for the rest of the trip. A call telling Roger McAllen to wait a day or two before opening up the cottage.

Excuse me police please I'm calling to ask are my wife and daughter there? Whatsat you say?

Three guys, name Ray Turk and Lou. Ray has a hateful sneering face triangular not much chin, teeth too big for his mouth, half bald, smash him one. Consider the charges that can be filed. Kidnapping, harassment. Car theft? Rape?

Whatsat you say, start at the beginning for Chrissake. Excuse me Tony Hastings professor Ohio going to Maine driving at night, we ran into these guys on the Interstate, they took my wife and child, no it's not just a bump on the road.

Looking beyond this problem, jobs to do when we arrive depend on when we arrive. I might reconsider renting a catboat from Jake Malcolm. Oh foolish blind hope. Excuse me, I didn't mean to scare you, it's an emergency, may I?

No problems are temporary until they are over. All problems are potentially permanent.

The road was steep down and winding, he had no memory of having come up it. Sure now he had lost the incoming trail, probably at the fork. No point trying to trace it back, he had come too far, nor could he remember the turns they had made – and even if he did, where would it lead to? No village, any village would do, any police station if you can't find Bailey. Excuse me, if you could call the other police stations with your teletype computer telephone. Because though we didn't make a specific arrangement, a police station would be a natural clearing house, especially as that's where we were supposed to meet.

The road leveled out and the trees stopped on both sides. Black fields. Farm country, a valley floor, he could see the shadow line of a ridge at the other end. A car appeared, its lights approaching from a long way off. Tony Hastings dropped down in the ditch and waited for it to go past. Bangor me. He had passed up a hitchhiker years ago, or tonight, Helen's mistake, she wanted to pick him up. He never thought she would get such a lesson as this. A moment later another car. He was tired of hiding from cars. He thought all cars with headlights were enemies, but he also remembered he was still Tony Hastings. He was standing near a lane that went through an opening in a fence, prepared to run if the car slowed down, into the field full of what was probably corn as tall as he was. The car zipped by.

The big box shape near the road ahead was turning into a house, but his relief died because it had no lights, and he dared not be a stranger waking a sleeping family in the night. The road ended against another, somewhat wider. He saw lights down to the left. Maybe now, he said, at last.

He walked faster, strengthened by a vision of destination. It was a floodlight standing watch, high at the corner between barn and silo illuminating the yard between barn and house. The house itself was dark like the other.

He saw dim red and blue lights advertising beer in a window on the other side, but the window otherwise was also dark. He asked, might not a man in desperate trouble be excused for waking up a sleeping stranger if the trouble were desperate enough? But he knew people in lonely farmhouses kept shotguns for strangers at night (they might be Ray or Turk or Lou).

There were more houses now, after passing one he would see another, all dark except for their floodlit yards. He heard a dog barking behind an illuminated pig trough. He saw dark shapes like rocks in a field and realized they were cows. He noticed the improvement in his eyes. In a cluster of trees a bird started to sing, robin, and he realized the black sky was fading.

This weakening of dark meant dawn, the night was ending. It brought despair, the coming of light catching his nightmare like a photographer and making it real. It brought relief. The pacification of common sense.

Common sense, he said. Think how often you have feared tragedy because Helen was late coming home or Laura did not call on time. Remember the hurricane. Yet none of those disasters occurred, his father and mother lived out their lives, the family still consisted of Tony, his wife Laura, his daughter Helen.

Common sense, however. They banged my car and forced me off the road. They separated me from my family and drove off with them. They dumped me in a lonely place in the woods. They tried to run me down, which would have killed me.

He listened to the terrible news spoken in his head. They are dead, it said. You know they are dead. Repeated: Laura and Helen are dead. Those men have killed them. Common sense tells you that. You know it, you have known it all along, you knew it when you saw them drive off. The only question was whether they have been killed yet or that is still to come. If there was a delay, if there were still a chance to save them.

He looked at it deliberately, his memory, Laura in her traveling slacks and dark sweater standing by the car, Helen with the red kerchief around her head sitting on a rock down the road, both faces looking out the window at him as the car rushed away.

Now though the sky was still dark you could see distinctly the fields, the clumps of trees, the ridges around the valley, the houses and barns. The robins were singing in the clumps of trees. He saw a car approaching. Lights, people awake. No more hiding from cars, it seemed crazy now. Excuse me mister, the nearest village, police. There was a ritual for it, a proper gesture. He held out his thumb, and the car zipped by.

Another car in the other direction, he crossed over and held out his thumb again. No good. Then more cars. People up in the earliest dawn. The ritual gesture didn't work. When the next car came, a van a few minutes later, he waved his hands above his head: help, help. The van tooted its horn.

His head whistled, his ears noisy, the unslept night dredged holes in his skull. The cold lit yard was like the others he had seen, but in this house there was a light upstairs and another on the ground floor in the back. He stood there, heart pounding.

He stepped up to the little front porch. The door had a window, he could see through the curtain to a corner of the lighted kitchen in the back. He turned the knob to ring the bell, jangly loud. Started up dog barking just inside. A gaunt woman in an apron appeared in the kitchen, squinting. Stayed where she was. A man in a plaid shirt appeared beside her, white hair. He approached. He pulled the curtain back and peeked out. Said something through the glass. Tony Hastings could not hear through the barking of the dog.

Tony shouted, the words he had memorized. 'Excuse me sir.'

The wife was behind the man, she bent down, and the dog stopped. The man opened the door a couple of inches.

'Excuse me sir, I wonder could I use your telephone.'

'What for?'

'I've had an accident.'

The man was examining his face.

'Anybody hurt?'

'No. Well. I don't know. I need help.'

'Anybody with you out there?'

'No just me.'

'Well okay, come in I guess.'

They turned on the light in the vestibule. The telephone was on a table inside the front door. The dog was black and white and sniffed at him and wagged its tail while the woman held it by the collar.

'You do look kind of scratched up,' the man said. 'Where was this here accident?'

'I don't know,' Tony Hastings said.

'You don't?'

'I've been walking half the night.'

'Got lost, eh?'

'I'm a stranger here.'

'Well set down there. Get a load off. What happen, traveling alone, fall asleep at the wheel?'

'No no, my wife and child.'

'Wife and child,' the woman said. 'They hurt?'

'He left them at the car,' the man said. 'What you want an ambulance?'

'Not that,' Tony Hastings said. 'It's not that.' He groped for believable words to bring his nightmare into the world.

'Maybe you'd like to use the bathroom wash off,' the wife said.

'Maybe he'd like to use the telephone first,' the man said. 'They're waiting for him at the car.'

'Worse than that,' Tony Hastings said. 'I can't explain. It wasn't an accident. Not exactly. We met these guys. My wife and child.' Come on, mathematician, explain. 'They took them. I mean I've lost them.'

The man and his wife looked at him.

'Lost what?'

'My wife and child.'

'What do you mean, lost your wife and child?'

'We ran into these guys on the road. Thugs. Hoodlums. They forced us off the road.'

'Son of a bitch, these god damn kids,' the man said.

'It's hard to explain. They took my wife and kid. In my car. They took me into the woods. I've been walking half the night. I don't know where they are.' He felt the tears coming. 'I don't know how to find them.'

'Boy,' the man said. 'How could you let them do that to you?'

He shook his head, fought them back. The man and his wife looked at each other.

'Who should he call?' the man said.

'Hamilton?' the wife said.

'He aint gonna be up yet.'

'Rouse him out?'

'You wanta rouse him outa bed for this?'

'Who's Hamilton?'

'Sheriff.'

'Someone should be up at Grant Center,' the wife said.

'Think so? Don't do no business until eight.'

'Jail,' the wife said. 'Jail stays open all night.'

'Only the night guard. He can't do nothing.'

'Wake Hamilton then. What good's a sheriff sleeps all night?'

'State troopers,' the man said. 'They're open all night.'

'Why yes of course,' the wife said.

'State troopers. That's who I'd call if you was me.'

'Okay,' Tony Hastings said. 'How do I reach them?'

'Look up Pennsylvania,' the wife said.

'State troopers. Fine men, professionals. They'll help you. They're the best.'

'You make your call and then wash up,' the wife said. 'I'll get you something to eat. You must be worn out.'

'Sheriff don't do nothing anyhow. State troopers, they're the ones. The elite. The finest.'

It wasn't friendly, it was watchful and dutiful. She went into the kitchen. The man continued to stare at Tony.

'I want to hear what you tell them cops. I can't understand, you said they put your wife and kid in the car and drove off with them. What were they, threatening you with a gun?'

'No gun,' Tony said.

'Well damned if I can understand how you let em get away with it.'

'Damned if I can either.'

Yet he understood well enough, for it had happened to him. The hard thing would be how to make anyone else understand.

# EIGHT

Susan Morrow, following Tony Hastings along the country road in the murdering dawn, wonders if she can stand what's coming. Like Tony she assesses the possibilities. She knows what Tony does not, that there's another compulsion in these events, the hand of Edward creating destinies. What happens to Laura and Helen depends on the kind of story it is. So while Tony struggles for hope, the reading Susan considers Edward, preparing some unbearable thing. Yet even as she fears, she encourages him, saying, Good work, Edward, you're doing fine. She's on edge not only for Tony's sake but for Edward's, wondering how he can avoid anticlimax without disaster.

*Nocturnal Animals 7*

Tony Hastings indoors. He sat in the rickety chair by the telephone inside the door, while the old farmer looked up the state police number. Thinking what to say, he had been thinking half the night. He thought: I must remember Tony Hastings. Mathematician, professor, organizing lectures and making everything clear. Emulate Tony Hastings. Afraid the police wouldn't listen, if they didn't understand, crackpot, joker, bum.

Nameless, abject, a speck of survival out of the woods. Yet already it was better, indoors, the chair, the burr of the telephone bell in his ear, the old farmer and his wife looking on.

The dark voice said, 'State Police, Morgan speaking.'

Shock of having to speak, yet Tony Hastings was coming to life, organizing, who when where what why.

'Excuse me, my name is Tony Hastings. I'm a university professor from Ohio traveling through. I'm trying to find my wife and child. Mrs. Tony Hastings. Has she called in?'

Silence on the other end, Morgan trying to figure out, a bad start. 'What's your problem, professor?'

Come back to civilization, Tony. Who where when what why? Try what.

'We ran into trouble on the Interstate. I think my wife and daughter have been abducted.'

Another definite silence. 'You need an ambulance?'

'No, I need help, I need help.'

The silence was conspicuous. Start with what your audience knows, state police: 'We were traveling on the Interstate – '

'Hold on a moment.' He sank into the silence, not yet indoors, though excused for a second chance. He realized it was not necessary to say what he was afraid to say, though. Another man came on. 'This is Sergeant Miles. Can I help you?'

'Yes, my name is Tony Hastings.'

'Yes, Tony. What seems to be the problem?'

'We ran into trouble on the Interstate. I think my wife and daughter have been kidnapped.'

Again the silence, enough for Tony to notice.

'Okay Tony, relax. Let me have your name and address.'

Then, 'Your wife's name?'

'And where you are calling from?'

He looked at the old farmer. 'I'm at Jack Combs's house in Bear Valley.'

'Okay Tony, take it easy and tell me exactly what you think happened.'

Never mind the skeptical silences, the patronizing Tonies, the interjected you think, at last Tony Hastings felt safe, back in a world he knew, with organization and machinery and civilized hearts to take care and protect him from horrors. The curious old farmer and his wife, listening, were no longer not kindly, the house was warm, the growing light outside was already adding pale green to the spread of the field across the road.

He was back in the world with a story to tell, an invisible listener taking it down, and two others standing in the hall because there was no place to sit.

He began. 'Last night, sometime after eleven. Traveling on the Interstate on our way to Maine. We were attacked by another car and forced off the road.'

He told it all, it took him several minutes. He told about the bumping of the cars and how they had to stop. How the guys changed the tire and drove off with Laura and Helen in his car, leaving him to go with Lou in theirs. He told how Lou led him along many roads before taking him finally up the grassy track into the woods where he was put out. How he walked out alone in the dark and met the other car coming in but hid from it and how when it came out again they tried to run him down. And how he had walked miles to find a house, Jack Combs's, with a light on.

It was as if telling the story made him safe. The police had it, the danger was dispelled, he had come back from the wilderness to five thousand years of progress in a warm house linked by telephone to computer, radio, and a trained specialist. Nothing bad could happen now. In the warm farmer's house with its breakfast smell, despite the crazy thought that wouldn't go away saying, you haven't found them yet.

Sergeant Miles asked questions. What exit did you leave the Interstate? Tony could not say. Describe the three guys. He did that eagerly. Describe their car. That was harder. License plate? Do you remember any landmarks while you were riding with Lou? (He remembered the small white church. He remembered the trailer above the bend in the mountain road with the light in the window.) Are you sure they were trying to run you down? Could you find your way back to the woods road from where you are now? Oh it was good to be asked questions, he didn't know how much life he had lost until it was restored by them.

Finally the sergeant said, 'Thank you Tony. We'll look into it and call you back.'

'Wait!'

'What?'

'I can't stay here.'

'Oh. Hold on a minute.' The phone went dead.

He glanced at his hosts, who looked away. Strangers at the edge of a village in the early morning, good enough to let him make a phone call, can't stay here – but where can he stay, with his wife and daughter missing and his car gone and nothing but the clothes he wore and his wallet?

The phone clicked back to life. 'Tony? Tell you what. We'll send a man over, pick you up. You can wait here.'

'Okay.'

'Man will be over about a half hour.'

So they were coming for him, they would take care of him, the good police, comforting and fatherly. He wanted to rejoice, but the farmer and his wife were looking at him.

'I'll give you a bite to eat,' Mrs. Combs said.

She fed him well at the checkered kitchen table in the harsh light of the hanging bulb, while the husband went out to do the early morning barn work that had roused him to turn on the lights Tony had spotted. Her look was cautious, she did not respond to his thanks, and he ate in silence.

'Never went in for traveling, myself,' she said. 'People is different in foreign parts. Never know what kind you run into.'

He nodded, his mouth was full. Criticism disguised as sympathy, yes maam, he thought, but this happens to be your country where I ran into these people you never know what kind. Nevertheless, be grateful for the good police and the kind if cautious hosts.

By the time the police car came for him it was full daylight though the morning sun was still behind a hill. The car had an official shield on its side and a rack of lights on top. The lights were off. The policeman was a large young man with a small fuzzy brown mustache and a broad front. He looked like a childlike student who kept coming to the office last year to ask for help, Tony couldn't remember his name.

He said, 'I am Officer Talbot. Sergeant Miles told me to tell you there has been no report on your wife and child.'

The disappointment in that, he realized he was expecting to be notified any minute that Laura and Helen had called in. He thought, it's still not eight, most stores and offices are not yet open.

The big young student in uniform idled his engine and spoke into his microphone. The radio snapped in dark male machine voices. Officer Talbot looked serious, grim. He said, 'You sure you didn't have no prearranged meeting place?'

'Yes we did, the police station in Bailey. Only they took me and dumped me in the woods instead.'

'What's Bailey?'

'They said it was the nearest town. We were supposed to go to the Bailey police.'

'Ain't no Bailey I ever heard of. Ain't no Bailey police, that's sure.'

Bad, bad – although not really new, this news.

'That's what I was afraid of.'

They started up, the police car going in the opposite direction from where Tony had come. He felt unexpectedly afraid, as of leaving something behind. He lost track of this new journey immediately, he could not remember the turns nor the frequent villages they passed through. As if riding in this sealed protective car left the nightmare behind but at the same time destroyed the path back to it and therefore the way back to life. He remembered Miles asking if he could find his way back to where he had been from the Combs house and thought, should I have asked Talbot to help me retrace my steps? But he had not made the suggestion, lest there be something obscene about it.

The countryside was green and yellow, rolling and fresh in the morning light. The roads shone black in the sun. They sped suspended high on the sides of hills overlooking broad valleys full of fields and patches of woods, and they descended into woody groves and rode up curves and climbed long straight slopes and slowed for villages and passed clusters of farmhouses and sheds and fields of corn and other fields with cows and yards with pigs and sheep on the opposite slope and dark patches of trees on the tops of the hills. He thought, how beautiful this country if he had Laura to say it to.

The police station was a new one-story brick building surrounded by a chain link fence at the edge of a town. There were cows beyond the fence and a motel across the street. Tony Hastings followed Officer Talbot through a corridor and past a bulletin board and through an office with a counter into another office with two desks. The man at the desk in the farthest corner got up. 'I'm Lieutenant Graves. Sergeant Miles went home.'

Lieutenant Graves was a small man with round cheekbones

and a small chin like a cartoon squirrel and a black mustache that descended below his mouth on each side. His eyes or the shape of his face made him look a little like Ray in the night. I must not look at him, Tony said. He was afraid the lieutenant's face would obliterate the memory of Ray's. While Tony sat in the chair by the desk, Lieutenant Graves read the handwritten document on his desk. He was a slow reader and it took a long time. Then he asked Tony to repeat his story. He took it down on a pad of yellow lined paper, though Tony did not understand how he could compress it into so few laborious words. When the story was finished, he repeated the questions Sergeant Miles had asked. He sat a long time with his chin in his hand.

'Well,' he said, 'we've already put out an alert for the two cars. That ought to turn up something. Don't know what else we can do except wait.'

He looked at Tony. 'Meanwhile, you ain't got no car. You got a place to stay?'

'No.'

'There's a motel across the street.' He wrote something on a card. 'Here's the taxi number, you want that. Money?'

'I have credit cards. My checkbook is in my suitcase. That's in the car. All my clothes.'

'There's a bank on Hallicot Street. Opens at nine.'

'Thank you.'

'It's still early yet. Quite likely they went to sleep somewhere.'

'Where?' Tony said.

The lieutenant thought. Nodded. 'Must say it don't look too good, with nobody calling in. But you know what I'm thinking. Maybe they left them some place like they left you and it take them a while to walk out. Fixing to take your car no doubt.'

'That's what I've been thinking, too,' Tony said, meaning that's what he was hoping, not saying what he was thinking. The lieutenant was tapping his forehead with his pencil, as if he were thinking other things as well.

'You want to stay at that motel?'

'I guess so.'

'We'll call you if we get anything.'

Tony Hastings walked across the street to the motel. 'No car?' the fat woman said.

'It's stolen.'

'Well, no kidding! So that's what you were doing at the police. What can you give me for security?'

'Credit card.'

The motel smelled of plastic and air conditioning, the closed thick brown drapes made an unreal darkness in the room. He lay on the bed in his clothes and instantly the night was back with wind and a swirl of galactic clouds. Ray sitting on the radiator, laughing and saying, Don't take it so serious, man, we was only kidding. But that was a dream, for now he was awake and crossing the yard to the police station where he saw, newly washed and sparkling in the sun, his car, safely returned. His heart leaped and he went inside. Laura and Helen were on a bench in the hall, there they were, and they jumped up and ran to him, smiling with relief, hugging and kissing and saying, 'We're all right, they only wanted us to meet their friends in the trailer,' and Tony Hastings held them, saying, 'It's not a dream, is it? It can't be a dream because it's too real for a dream.'

The horrible loud telephone on the table next to his ear. He grabbed it to stop it, heart crashing.

'Tony Hastings? Lieutenant Graves. Bad news.'

He saw a broad net spread under the trees hung from several treetrunks to catch whatever might fall from the high branches.

'They found your car in the river over at Topping. Looks like they was trying to get rid of it.'

The strands of the net were gathered in white nodes, spots, dots, pulses, at wide intervals all across the field. 'What about my wife, my daughter?'

'Still no word.'

Catching fruit, bodies. 'They weren't in the car?'

'The car was empty. They're pulling it out now.'

He looked at his watch. He had been asleep a half hour, it was only quarter past nine. If that was Lieutenant Graves's idea of the worst in bad news.

'What do you make of it?' Tony said.

'Don't know what to make of it.'

A silence while they pulled up the net, rolled it in.

'Sir, we're turning this case over to Lieutenant Andes. He wants to look around. Can he pick you up in a few minutes?'

Tony Hastings's body full of sandbags. 'I'm ready now,' he said.

# NINE

If Susan wants to know what happened, she'll have to keep reading. She hears the Monopoly game breaking up. Harsh-voiced Mike yanks soft-breasted Dorothy to her feet, while fat Henry struggles up on his own. Through the living room into the hall.

'Good night Mrs. Morrow.' He has a sharp nose and a sharp chin, a white face and grinning mouth. In the hall Dorothy leans her elbow up on Mike's shoulder and grins sassily at him. Susan Morrow has a prudish streak, wishing whatever happens out of her sight so she won't have to say anything. Someone slams someone in the ribs. Ouf! you motherfucker. Snuffles and giggles in the hall, hey watch it. Susan Morrow does have a prudish streak: if your friends don't know what people don't say where.

From around the corner, nasal and loud, 'Good night, Mrs. Morrow, I had a lovely evening.' Hoot, hoo hoo. Susan needs another chapter, it's going to take a while yet. Tell Edward: you know how to draw things out.

## *Nocturnal Animals 8*

The police car in front of the motel office, a man in police uniform driving, another man on the right, this one in a plain brown suit. The man in the suit said, 'Tony Hastings?' He was wearing a hat and twisted his hand out the half-opened window so as to shake Tony's. Tony got in the back.

'Meetcha,' he said. 'I'm Bobby Andes. I look into things.'

'You found my car?'

'They found it,' Andes said.

'In the river?'

'Listen Tony, do you think you can retrace your steps, where you went last night?'

'I got pretty mixed up. I could try.'

'Let me be sure I understand,' Bobby Andes said. He was a fat man short in the front seat, but his hat was big and so was his head, and his round cheeks were shaded with the coarse pepper dots of his clean shaven beard. Referred to as Lieutenant Andes on the phone. 'Two of these guys went off in your car with your wife and daughter. And you were supposed to meet in the police station at this place called Bailey, which don't exist.'

'That's right.'

'And they called each other Ray and Turk?'

'Yes.'

'And you went with the other man in their car – the one they called Lou.'

'Yes.'

'How did you happen to split up like that?'

'I've been trying to figure that out ever since.'

'Did they force their way into your car?'

'In effect, yes.'

'In effect?'

'Well yes, they did. I'd say they forced their way in.'

'Your wife and daughter tried to stop them?'

'I'd say yes, they tried to stop them.'

'And you tried to stop them?'

'There wasn't much I could do.'

'They had weapons?'

'They had something, I don't know what it was.'

'You saw it?'

'I felt it.'

'Okay,' Bobby Andes said. 'Tell you what. If we took you back to Jack Combs's house, could you backtrack from there?'

'As I said, I could try.'

'Okay then, you try. Let's go.'

The man in uniform drove pretty fast, and Tony Hastings could not follow the route. No one spoke. They went through the back section of Grant Center, past gas stations and a used car lot with tanks of bottled gas, and a street of stately white houses and arched shade trees. Out onto an open road, straight in a valley of flat fields, rich shades of green, the sun high now and a pair of house roofs on the hill across the valley reflecting it like mirrors. The loudspeaker chattered with radio police voices, and Tony had no idea where he was.

Bobby Andes turned the sound down. He said, 'Let's get some other things straight. You say this guy named Lou, he drove you into the woods and left you there?'

'He made me drive.'

'But he made you go there and then left you?'

'Yes.'

'And when you walked out, you saw them coming in again?'

'Yes.'

'You sure it was them?'

'Pretty sure.'

'Which car was it?'

'I think it was my car.'

'With Ray and Turk?'

'I think so.'

'How do you know?'

'The look of it, the sound of it. I don't know.'

'Could you see them in the dark?'

'Not very well. They turned off the lights and stopped and called me.'

'What did they say?'

'They said, Mister, your wife wants you.'

'Why didn't you go to them?'

Though Tony was glad for the effort of explaining things, he didn't like how the lieutenant's questions forced him to cram it all into conventional tracks. He tried to think how to say why he hadn't gone to them.

'I was afraid to.'

'Do you think they were with them?'

'Who?'

'Your wife and daughter.'

The memory made him shudder. This was by a billboard with a cowboy on it, bright in the sunlight at the edge of a village. He said, 'I don't know. I didn't think so then.'

'Where did you think they were?'

'I thought if they were there she would have spoken.'

'But you had no theory where they were?'

Tony Hastings tried to remember what had been in his head. That they were at the police station in Bailey. That they were in the trailer by the curve behind the curtain in the dim-lighted window. That they had been left in another woody spot like himself. Or worse. He said, 'I don't remember what I thought.'

'All right. And then a little later the car came out again. What happened this time?'

'I decided to approach them, but they tried to run me down.'

'Where was this?'

'On the main road, where the lane came out of the woods.'

Bobby Andes had a notebook, he wrote something in it. 'So the one guy took you in and left you there. And the others came there, drove in and then drove out again.'

'That seems to be what happened.'

'What do you make of it?'

'I don't know what to make of it.'

'Well I think we had better find that road in the woods. Don't you?'

What did they expect to find? Suddenly, no not suddenly, he had seen it all along, but it was a new discovery too, Tony Hastings noticed the cave where his hope usually was, cold, blank, despoiled, a vacancy of future, as if these men were helping him to look for something that no longer was. It was retracing his empty steps that made him feel this, empty steps to the empty roads, empty woods, empty cars. A pretense of looking so you could say you had looked, you had tried. Since there was nothing else you could think of to do. It made you realize there was nothing else you could think of to do.

He wondered why they were stopped in front of this house – small, brick with white window trim, a dirt yard separating it from its barn.

'Okay,' Bobby Andes said. 'Can you take it from here?'

He thought, if he was this slow recognizing Combs's place in the bright morning, how could he recognize his track from the night? Despite its heavy engraving in the dreams he had not yet had time to have.

'I came down that road,' he said.

Tracking, in reverse. The queasy reiterating panic – 'Go slow' – because nothing was familiar, not even the general shape of the valley which he had built in his imagination out of vague night shadows. This valley now was close and bumpy, the road turned and turned back more than he realized, the farms were small and getting smaller, it bumped into the woods, sliced corners of them, yet every few moments his panic unpulsed in the sight of something he recognized, usually not until it was passing or passed and he was looking at it from behind, which was the direction from which he had seen it before – mailbox, broken fence, house with porch and tool shed, narrow bridge over stream.

The road climbed out of the valley into the woods, and he remembered the pull on his feet coming down. The trees were raggedy, he had not known that, and then they thickened and grew tall, a high forest on the sides of an endless hill, which he had not known either. They came to another road level along the side of the hill, intersection, what should have been a memory checkpoint though he did not recognize it. So they pulled up onto the level road and stopped, and then he remembered the turn he had made down and deduced the left turn they should make now.

A road came in from the right, higher up, the fork which he remembered from his unslept nightmares as the probable point of deviation from the original route with Lou, the route where the lost church and mountain curve and dim-lighted trailer were. It did not look like much of a fork now, the upper road narrower and turning up sharply, no wonder he had missed it.

All the while Laura and Helen were in his mind asking, where are you going? He tried to take them out of past and future, where they absent-mindedly occupied their usual places, chattering and joking, and put them into the actual present, the question being just where are you and what are you doing right now? He listened, trying to see or hear, and in the silence he heard their silence slam across the stillness like a thunderbolt and saw their still faces frozen in a crash of marble. He tried to bring them to life – after all, they must be alive somewhere after who knows what kind of traumatic experience like his own? – and postulated them continually just around the next turn in the road: there they are now! walking down the middle of the road, mother and daughter, jeans kerchief traveling slacks dark sweater. Why aren't they there? You never find what you're looking for when you're looking, or if you do, you call it a miracle. Another reason for dread, as if the mere hunting for his wife and child on these empty roads where they clearly were not were the surest way to assure they would never be.

'There!' Tony Hastings said. Sooner, much sooner than he expected: the broken gate, the diagonal white board, memorized to identify the entrance to the mountain woods road, which looked even less like a road now, a lane, a path, a pair of tracks.

They stopped. The lieutenant wrote in his notebook. 'That's where they took you, huh?'

Tony Hastings saw the ditch, the barbed wire, the bushes on the other side of the ditch, shallower, closer to the road than when he had jumped in the nightmare.

'Want to go in?' the driver said.

Bobby Andes looked at Tony. 'Any point in doing that?' he asked.

Tony Hastings frozen, paralyzed, unwilling, afraid. 'What would we be looking for?'

Bobby Andes looked at him again. He had hairs in his nostrils and the little pink nodes swam moist in the corners of his smeary eyes. 'All right,' he said. 'Let's check out the other sights of your journey.'

'There wasn't much to see,' Tony said.

They turned around, and for a second time Tony Hastings left the mountain drive, with a second sharp agony of partition from his love a prisoner there and he cowardly abandoning her. Begging her to understand why.

They stopped where the road from above joined. 'I lost my trail somewhere coming out,' he reminded them, 'but I think it might have been here.'

'Makes a difference,' Andes said. 'That road comes across the top of the ridge from the next valley.'

'If he came that way he probably got off at the Bear Valley Exit,' the driver said.

'Let's try it.'

The road wound up and in a few moments was going down. They went around a curve with an old white trailer in the trees just above. 'There's the trailer!' he said.

No car parked.

'Keep going, don't slow down,' Andes said. They were going fast and it was out of sight in a moment.

The trailer must have been stationed there for years, with young trees grown up all around, locking it in.

'You sure?' Andes said.

Then the small white church.

'That's the one I saw, I'm sure of that. I don't know if it means anything.'

'What happened, your guy stopped there?'

'No, I thought I saw my car parked there. He said it wasn't, and I could easily have been wrong.'

'We'll check it out.'

They came down into a village with a greenhouse which Tony Hastings recognized.

'Bear Valley Exit, more and more obvious,' the driver said.

There were signs to the Interstate, then the entrance ramp and the highway bridge crossing above. They pulled over again.

'Do you think you could find the place where you stopped?'

'On the Interstate? That would be hard.'

'Well it's a long shot anyway.'

'What?'

'Evidence they might have dropped, who they were, tracks, footprints, that kind of thing.'

'It was on the hard shoulder.'

'Yeah.'

They sat on the country road by the entrance to the Interstate. Bobby Andes was thinking. He said, 'They went in and when they saw you they turned out their lights and called you? What did they turn the lights out for?'

'Damned if I know. Maybe they thought they could sneak up on me.'

Andes laughed, without mirth.

'And they went in, and they came out again, and they tried to run you down?'

'Yes.'

He was tapping on his notebook. 'I hate to say this, but I think maybe we'd ought take a look up that mountain road.'

Tony Hastings clutched as if something fatal had been said.

'Go the McCorkle way,' Bobby Andes told the driver. He turned around and explained to Tony: 'We'll go the other way so we don't have to go by the trailer. If someone's in there and sees a police car twice.'

They went fast, a strong highway up the side of the ridge. It took Tony a long time before he could ask. 'What are you expecting to find up that road?'

'We'll find out when we find out,' Bobby Andes said. 'Nothing, I expect.'

# TEN

Upstairs, water running, Dorothy taking a shower. Susan Morrow thumbs ahead, trying not to see words, finds PART TWO not far ahead. How sad it is, she thinks. Sadness in the news to come, which nobody mentions but all expect. She gropes for the possible loophole Edward might have allowed, but finds none. Meanwhile, despite the sadness, she feels this energy and does not know if it's her own chemistry or the book, Edward in a state of excitement, enjoying his work? She likes to see Edward enjoying his work, it sparks her up. She awaits the horrible discovery her spirit deplores, she awaits it avidly.

*Nocturnal Animals 9*

The reason Tony Hastings was afraid to go back up that mountain driveway. There was no reason and hence no fear. An irrational residue of the night. No reason to be afraid now, he was safe in the back seat of the comfortable police car with two officials (representatives of the civilization which had taken him back) whose whole effort was for him, to help him get back what he had lost.

A newly built highway with cars, making a long sweep up the wooded ridge. At the crest was a curio store, pennants and carved wooden owls. The reason he was so afraid. No reason. They were simply checking out possibilities. Reason to hope, actually. If Laura and Helen had been in that car driving in, if they had been left there as he had been, if the intention was that they all three would meet there. They should have walked out before now, however. That was the trouble with that idea. Unless they had decided to go to sleep and wait for day. But even so, by now almost noon after driving all over the countryside, they should have walked out by now.

As they drove Bobby Andes asked friendly questions about his life. His work. His place in Maine. The happiness of his marriage. His only child. Bobby Andes's only child. Why Bobby Andes had only one child, it wasn't deliberate. I mean we didn't deliberately attempt not to have another child. Did you?

The car stopped in a straight stretch where the road was above the floor of the woods on both sides, except right here where. He had not recognized it because they had approached from the opposite direction. He did not know how they had got around to the other side. It would be the direction in which the men drove off after trying to run him down.

The reason Tony Hastings was afraid to go in gulped in his heart as the driver turned the car and bumped across the ditch past the broken gate into the woods. The reason was, it was too late, the sun approaching noon with driving around all morning, much too late to meet Laura and Helen walking out from there.

Since it was too late, there was no reason to go in.

'I just want to see what they've got in here,' Bobby Andes said.

'I didn't see anything but woods.'

'That was at night.'

'You think they got a still in there?' the driver said.

Andes laughed. 'Maybe there's a house.'

'They took me to the end of the road, I think. I don't think there's anything in there.'

Tony Hastings did not think there was a house, nor did he believe Bobby Andes expected to find one. The track was narrow, it turned sharply around dodging rocks and trees, the car jounced and banged, 'Jesus!' Bobby Andes said. The woods were light and airy, messy with chunks of underbrush and fallen branches. Trees grew up around boulders and rocky outcrops. Tony Hastings could not connect what he saw with anything he could remember, either driving in with his headlights flashing on the trees or coming out in darkness guided by the power of his dilated eyes to distinguish shadows. He looked for the outcrop where he had hidden while Ray and Turk went by. He saw several that could have served but none like what he remembered.

The reason Tony Hastings was afraid to go into the woods was the credibility it gave to his imaginings. That the lieutenant, Bobby Andes, thought it should be done. To be checked out, eliminated. The act of driving up this agony road, the strain with every minute doubled by the additional minute it would take to drive out – it made a reality of what otherwise would have been a mere ghostly dream. It turned the ghostly dream into a fact.

Driving in, he felt again the grief which made him want to cry last night. It slashed him for his failure when the men had called, for now he was sure they had meant to reunite him with Laura and Helen. Dead or alive. And if he had thought it wise to escape being killed, how stupid that wisdom seemed if they had been killed. And if they had not been and were in the car at the time, with still a chance, how much worse.

He saw the log bridge and realized the thinning of the trees ahead was the clearing. His heart tightened. Already, as they dipped down to the bridge and lurched up the steep short slope, he felt the pure deep relief of having seen enough to know nothing was there. The clearing opened out, it really was a grassy field, empty, with recent tracks of cars turning around.

'Uh oh,' the driver said.

'Oh shit, god damn it!' Bobby Andes cried out.

Tony Hastings did not know what the matter was, he was so relieved and disappointed to see nothing in the clearing, nothing of what he had either expected and feared or what he had hoped. He saw someone had been here, the red kerchief and dark sweater and pair of jeans draped on the bushes across the grass. When Bobby Andes moved his head, he saw the lovers naked under the bush, their naked limbs, asleep.

'Easy man,' Bobby Andes said. He wondered why they were so concerned about him. Already he was out of the car walking fast over to where the lovers lay, and Bobby Andes and the policeman were after him, running, someone trying to hold his arm as if he needed restraint. That was not the problem. He merely wanted to eliminate once and for all the grotesque assumption his officer companions were making, and even if they were naked make these lovers, boy and girl he could see, wake up so they could tell these men who they were not. Boy and girl, though which was which he was not yet sure, one lying on her back, the other close by, face down. It was possible, he realized as he approached, that they were dead, not asleep, that they might have been killed by someone. If so, that was proper business for his officer companions, not him.

It wasn't Laura and Helen because these two were naked and looked like children sprawled asleep, or stunned, knocked out on the head, in a coma, or possibly dead. He was walking fast, away from Bobby Andes who was trying to hold him back, because he wanted to make sure they were not Laura and Helen. He was not running because he knew of course they were not.

Only they were. That was why he was out of the car even before it stopped, he knew the instant he saw them, naked children asleep in the bushes, they were Laura and Helen, this was the meaning of the car coming in back here last night and the lesson of Ray and Turk and Lou, he knew it before he saw them, before he saw the kerchief on the bush, before he heard the cries of outrage of the two men in the front, he knew it.

Helen's kerchief, Laura's sweater and slacks. He was hurrying because he could not yet see their faces. They looked too small, children only, nor could he yet tell their sexes, which was the girl, which the boy.

They were inside the bush with crushed branches as if they had crashed and fallen there, and he could not see their faces, the graceful naked girl lying on her back with her head turned away, the bigger person lying close by face down, head down concealed by her shoulders so he could not see her hair, and his way was blocked by the branches. 'Easy man,' holding him.

'Let me see, let me see.'

The policeman holding him while Bobby Andes slashed at the branches with a knife, shoved through to the girl, where he knelt and lifted her head gently in his hand, he saw the face from the side, from an angle, still unsure. While Bobby Andes dropped her and climbed over her quick to the other, pushing her by the shoulder, trying to force her over, the dark hair, the thick black hair like Laura's, lifting her face.

He saw Laura's mouth half open like a cry, her cheeks and eyes contorted with pain, he recognized the cry, the cheeks and eyes, he recognized the pain, the frozen intelligence, the language, the years. There was Bobby Andes, contorted too, looking up at him, supporting her head for him to see. Bobby Andes, a stranger from the world. He plunged forward to look, if there was still a chance, if not too late, the vines grabbed him around the feet, he fell forward, he sagged into branches.

'Is this your wife?'

'Is she all right?'

The face was white, the eyes fixed. Bobby Andes did not answer.

# ELEVEN

Susan Morrow reads to a stop, shocked. You killed them, Edward, she says, you went ahead and did it. What she thought she couldn't bear. She feels stunned with Tony as if she had not seen it coming. A terrible sad crime, though she believes that if they had not died having come this far she would have been disappointed. Poor Tony, how much her pleasure depends on his distress. She has a notion that the pain the scene uncovers, incarnated in Tony, is really her own, which is alarming. Her own designated pain, old or new, past or future, she can't tell which. It's obscure because she knows that unlike Tony's her pain is not here but somewhere else, and its absence, made so vivid, is what makes the moment thrilling. Not sure what she means by this, she resorts to critical appreciation. Appreciate the narrative, details of discovery, irrationality everywhere, denial of the obvious, appreciate that. Later you can criticize if you object to the victimization of women, for instance – but not yet, first submit, appreciate, horrible though it be.

Next page: PART TWO on a blank sheet. So it's Part One we have been reading, putting Tony into a shape, like a bottle. Where do we go now? Whatever it is will be different, which makes a risk for Edward, like starting over. For that, she wishes him well.

Susan Morrow had intended to stop here but that's impossible. Besides, someone is still taking a shower. She must take a look at Part Two.

## *Nocturnal Animals 10*

The word in Tony Hastings's mind was no!, denial slamming up against the hard fact his mind had prepared him for. They walked with him back to the police car, holding him by the arm like an old man. He sat in the back seat with the door open, looking back. He listened to the police radio, loud voices and the trooper talking into the microphone making a report which he did not understand. He looked at the bushes with the clothes draped on them. He looked at what was under the bushes, which did not change, every time he looked they were the same, like the trees. With grasshoppers buzzing in the tall grass and a flycatcher with faint whistle darting from a branch into the still air. He looked away, at the policeman leaning into the front seat to speak into the microphone, at the tops of the trees on the edge of the clearing where he saw a hawk's nest, and he looked back at the bushes and saw them again, placed, established, a photograph.

There was only no! no!, his refusal to follow the movement of time through the intersection. End of future. Moment separated from moment, time moving away without his participation. No thought except no. Sorry, someone said, we can't touch them, we can't move anything until they come. Waiting, without wondering what they were waiting for, nor noticing how long, only looking again from time to time to the scene in the bushes, the same every time he looked. Bobby Andes and the policeman walked around the clearing, back and forth, looking at the ground, poking delicately into the brush, back to the car and out again. He could not remember afterwards if he walked around too.

The cars came as if there had been no wait at all, flashing their lights in the woods at midday, and the men jumped out and tromped the clearing, measuring and taking pictures. They lined up with their backs blocking his view, chattering like sparrows, and he did remember thinking, they're mine, my Laura, my Helen. He saw them working awkwardly with gray canvas, and when the view cleared, the clothes weren't there and neither were they.

He saw the wrapped cocoon carried out of the broken bushes on a stretcher. Then he saw the other one. He wondered which was which, lying side by side. He thought he knew, then realized he did not, and no way to find out except by asking someone, who might get it wrong. Thinking he ought to know, his own Laura and Helen, the thought knocked something loose in his throat, leaking down his cheeks like a child.

A young policeman said, 'Come, I'll take you back.'

'Where?'

He looked for Bobby Andes, the trooper, someone he knew.

'I'll take you to your motel.'

'What can I do there?'

Bobby Andes was reading from his notebook into a tape recorder. He noticed Tony Hastings. He said, 'You can go with George. I'll talk to you this afternoon.'

Tony Hastings pulled the world together. He said, 'Will my car be usable?'

'Tomorrow. I want to examine it first.'

'Can I have my suitcase?'

'George will get it.' Bobby Andes spoke to George: 'Tell Max he needs his worldly goods.'

The one Bobby Andes called George drove him back, the long trip out the terrible woods track like a gash in his mind, and fast on the country roads to his motel across from the police station.

Afterwards, Tony Hastings remembered him only vaguely, like a blond high school football player in a policeman's uniform. They did not speak. Tony Hastings stared at the repeating woods, two times in each direction, backdrop to dizzy thought. Afterwards he remembered the display of his thought upon the big deciduous trunks, the fallen branches, the rock outcrops with the radio police voices. The word No. He did not know what he was thinking, except that what had happened was the worst and the world was over. Nor what he was feeling, if he was feeling anything. Fatigue and lethargy. He wondered what he should do. He guessed there would be no point in going to Maine. Of course there would be no point, what was he thinking about? What would he do with August and the rest of the summer? What would he do with his car? What when the policeman left him at the motel? He wondered if his emotions required him to skip lunch, but he was hungry, whatever his emotions were, which he didn't know anyway. He wondered where he could eat lunch and what it would be like. He wondered what to do in the afternoon, and looked forward to his interview with Bobby Andes, which would be something, anyway. Then there would be dinner to think about. After dinner, the evening.

He knew his loss was heavy even if he didn't feel its weight, and he ought to tell someone. Of course he should, it was his privilege as one bereaved. Bereaved. He thought of his friends and wondered who to tell, intimates who would gather around in your hour of need. He could not think of anyone who would want to gather around, yet someone should be notified. Who? Probably his sister and brother. Of course his sister and brother. He was glad he remembered his sister. He was not so sure about his brother. But when he thought what to tell her, he didn't want to break the news, he did not want to deal with her shock, he did not want to listen to it.

Thinking about grief made him remember the wrapped cocoons, which was which, and the memory released his tears a second time.

He said, 'Would it be possible for someone to call my sister and tell her? Give her my number so she can call back.'

The look on George's face could not understand why if Tony wanted his sister to call him, he couldn't call her himself. But it was only his face, and he said, 'I guess so, sure.' He took the numbers which Tony had written on a slip from his notebook.

He began to wonder if he had made a mistake. The possibility that, distraught as he was and expecting the worst, he had not taken sufficient care in identifying them, had jumped to his conclusion too quickly. He realized he had looked only once. Long enough only to see what he had expected to see. The possibility of error grew like a fountain. Try it on George. 'I'm afraid I'm not absolutely sure of my identification.'

It took George a moment to understand. 'Yeah?' Annoyed. Tony was embarrassed. 'You'll have to look again in the morgue, anyway,' George said.

At the motel before leaving, George said, 'You want to cancel that call to your sister?'

'What for?'

'Until you're sure?'

Though he already knew this was a futile hope, the slightest possibility he had made a mistake, that his sister might be given false news he would later have to retract, paralyzed him. He didn't know what to say. The policeman waited.

'No. Yes. No.'

'Which?'

Wait, then yield.

'Go ahead and notify her.'

'You're sure?'

'Yes.'

In the afternoon he fell asleep on the motel bed in his clothes. Later a man from the police office took him to the morgue to identify the bodies again. Bodies. They were in a cold room with white tiles on the walls. Each on a separate table. The man pulled back a sheet to disclose the head. They were either wax busts, gray and green, or his dear ones, Laura depicted in an ironic angry smile and Helen in a pout that could have been playful but was not. No doubt about it.

They took him back to the station, where he had a talk with Bobby Andes. 'News,' he said. 'Report from Topping, someone else harassed on the Interstate last night just like you.'

'Same guys, probably.'

'Got a license plate.' Tony Hastings looked at him. 'Unfortunately, it's stolen from a car that had been junked.' Suddenly Tony Hastings realized that Bobby Andes wanted to catch the three guys. For him that would be the logical next step.

He apologized. 'If you don't mind, we'd like your fingerprints too,' he said.

'Mine?'

'No offense. We found some prints on the trunk of your car, which was sticking out of the water.'

He was pleased with that. He asked Tony to go over his story again. The highway harassing, the stopping and the flat tire, the separation of the family, the drive into the woods, the walk out, the whole thing. Bobby Andes was sympathetic, he kept shaking his head, and his sympathy grew angry as they talked. 'The rotten bastards,' he said. 'The filthy sons of bitches.'

He threw down his pen and leaned back in his chair. 'Your whole goddamn family. Can you imagine such a thing?'

Tony Hastings didn't have to imagine it. He was grateful for Bobby Andes's sympathy, though it surprised him, and he didn't know what to make of the anger.

'Beasts,' Bobby Andes said.

He said, 'I had a wife and kid, she divorced me. That makes no difference.' He took his hands and made a neck-twisting motion. His face was mottled. 'We'll get em,' he said. 'Count on me.' His hands went snap!

I appreciate your interest, Tony thought, but what good will it do?

Bobby Andes became businesslike. 'I'd like you to stay till tomorrow afternoon,' he said. 'We've got a warrant to check out the trailer, and we're going over your car for evidence. We might need you.'

'Okay.'

'We'll put out a call for witnesses on TV. Might fetch your old deaf man in the pickup.'

'What could he do?

'Witness. Who knows what he seen, if he's not too scared. You all right for tonight?'

'I think so.'

'You got a place to eat?'

'Motel, probably.'

'You like Italian food? Try Julio's.'

'Thanks.'

'Oh yes. Hawk wants to know what arrangements you want. Disposal. Funeral. You know.'

You know. Tony Hastings did not know. Funeral.

'Do I have to manage that?'

'Take your time, no rush.'

'I don't know any funeral people.'

'You could have it done here, then ship them out. I can recommend you somebody.'

Ship them out.

He took a taxi to Julio's and ate an Italian dinner alone, preceded by a drink. The drink reminded him of loneliness, and the dinner was good, which made it worse. He bought magazines to get through the evening and went back to the motel.

He got a call from Paula, his sister. She was upset. 'Oh Tony. How awful.' When he heard her say how awful, some old habit wanted to say, 'It's not that bad.' Catching himself, he said nothing. She invited him to come at once and stay at the Cape. He said he had to take care of the arrangements first. The arrangements. She said she would come for the funeral. Then he must come back to the Cape with her. Funeral. He was grateful. She asked how he intended to get home. He said he would drive, as soon as he got his car back. Funeral.

'Drive at a time like this? Do you think that's safe?'

He wondered about that. He said, 'I'm all right. You don't have to worry about me.'

She wished he wouldn't drive that long trip all by himself. She had an idea. She'd send Merton, send him tomorrow to keep you company on your trip back. She'd do it herself if it weren't for whatever it was.

No, he didn't want Merton. He didn't want anybody. He was all right, he could drive by himself. She mustn't worry.

Well if you're sure, she said. She would see him at the funeral. She would fly there and pick him up and they could fly back to the Cape together. Funeral. She promised to call his brother Alex in Chicago, as well as someone in Cincinnati to tell whoever needed to be notified. So I'll see you Thursday, she said. Notified. He spent the rest of the evening in the motel reading magazines, and when it was time to sleep, he slept.

Tony Hastings picked up his car at the police station the next afternoon. It had been dried out and cleaned. It was full of memory, but never mind that. Bobby Andes had more news.

'We got the cause of death.'

Tony sat down, waited for it. Andes not looking at him.

'Your wife had a fractured skull. She appears to have been struck, hammer or baseball bat. Only once or twice. Your daughter had a harder time. She was strangled. Suffocated.'

He waited for Tony to think about it, with more to say.

'She also had a broken arm.'

'You mean there was a struggle?'

'Looks like it.'

He was watching Tony. 'Something else,' he said. Tony waited. 'They were raped.' He made this sound like the worst news yet, though Tony was not surprised to hear it. He was surprised to hear it, though.

Bobby Andes brightened. 'I'll tell you one thing. Seems you were right about that trailer.'

'What do you mean?'

'Your friends took your folks there just like you said.'

'How do you know that?'

Hammer.

'We found your wife's fingerprint on the bedpost.' As if that were good news.

'Oh my God. What about Helen?'

'Not hers, just your wife's.'

'Well, whose trailer is it?'

Rape.

'Oh that.' Bobby Andes, knowing his business. 'He's clear. He lives in Poleville, uses it for the hunting season. The place had been broken into. Someone's been living in it.'

The news was dark and cold, Laura and Helen in the trailer. 'Damn,' Tony murmured. Struggle.

'Right. We got other prints too.'

'Where?'

'The trailer has a couple. Tell you something else. The prints on the car ain't yours.'

'Good,' Tony Hastings said. Good. Why did he say that? 'Have you checked them against the prints in the trailer?' Tony Hastings, detective. What good would that do?

'Too soon. It takes time, man. We'll have to check the prints in the trailer against the owner's, see if we can separate out. But I'm hopeful. The owner hasn't been there since last fall. It looks promising.'

'I guess it does.' Tony Hastings polite but reluctant to admit anything was promising. It was too late for that.

'We've sent them to be checked. You'll be hearing from me.'

Bobby Andes was pleased. To Tony Hastings it was all too late. It was long before he realized he himself might have needed to be cleared in the minds of the police by those stranger's prints on his car.

## TWELVE

Dark, Edward, heavy. With a last paragraph that could ruin the book. There's no doubt: it's risk time for Edward, an intersection, where to go. Whether to pursue the evil men and be a mystery, or pursue Tony's soul and be something else. Susan likes the problem in this chapter: what to do with the rest of the day when you get the bad news. What would she do if she lost Dorothy, Henry, Rosie? That's a taboo question she doesn't dare think about except by imagining Tony. Damned if she knows.

She foresees a possible objection she might make later (not yet) to Edward's raping those women before killing them. Crimes against women, a cliché she hates. It depends on what you expect of her, if you don't ask her to enjoy your sadism which would only be masochism for her. She always knew Edward liked violence despite his pursed lips. The violence of his restraint, his deliberate gentleness, his secretly angry pacifism.

She remembers giving him advice on how to write. How audacious that now seems. She said, you need to stop writing about yourself, nobody cares how fine your feelings are. He replied, Nobody ever writes about anything but himself. She said, You need to know literature, you need to write with literature and the world in mind. For years she was afraid she had killed something in him, and she hoped his turning to insurance meant he didn't mind. But this book looks like a different kind of answer. She wonders how much contempt or irony lies behind his choice of subject, and she hopes he is sincere.

This other memory comes up out of nowhere: boy and girl like brother and sister, longer ago, in the rowboat at the shore, while up in the house above the rocks, she can't remember. He flings a cigarette hiss into the water about something.

Bathroom free now, they say, with water probably all over the floor. One more chapter tonight.

## *Nocturnal Animals 11*

Tony Hastings, civilized, was raised by gentle people, intellectual and scholarly, mannerly and kind, his father a college dean, his mother a poet. He grew up in a brick house with a brother and sister and pets, they fed the birds and went to the Cape for the summer. He learned to hate prejudice and cruelty. As a young man he was courtly and considerate of women. He married for love and became a professor and bought a house and had a daughter and bought his own summer place in Maine. He read books, listened to music, played the piano, and had his wife's paintings on the walls of his house which was surrounded by a lawn with an oak tree. He kept a journal. Sometimes he suspected that being civilized concealed a great weakness, but since he could not conceive a remedy, he clung to it and took pride in it.

Before this thing happened, his great fear had been that civilization would break down and drop him in the rubble. Nuclear war, or anarchy, or terrorism. How terrible for mankind if all the labor of centuries were destroyed. His evening reading supplied alternative disasters: carbon dioxide turning all to tropics and desert, the sun blistering us through the disappearing ozone. And always the nearer possibility of getting caught in the machinery, as when cars crunch on the highway.

Now he thought, I have seen it. I know what's out there, the walls of Troy. In the shock of his loss, Tony Hastings knew the importance of remaining civilized, with a bomb behind his eyeballs that would blow up if he was not careful. The way was to defuse it with delicate ritual operations. The importance of remembering who he was, Tony Hastings, professor, resident of, son of, father of. Reciting his name as he walked along the road in the dark. Organizing words, constituting thought. Shaving carefully around his mustache. Preparing for what would be given him to feel.

He read magazines in the motel because it was important to keep his mind active. He resisted tears because it was important to have control of his face. He declined to let Merton drive him home because it was important. It was important to recognize the importance of things, for he knew now that everything important was important, nothing was more important than importance.

In the morning before his car was ready, he called the Frazer and Stover Funeral Home, recommended by Bobby Andes. He said, 'This is Tony Hastings. I don't know if the police have told you about me.'

The man had not been told. He had a singer's voice, kind and unsurprised. He said, 'I take it you don't want cremation?'

'I hadn't thought about it.' Not true. Tony remembered a year or two ago when Laura said, 'I assume we'll all be cremated when we go,' and Helen protested, 'Don't cremate me, for God's sake.' So he said, 'My daughter was afraid of cremation.'

'I understand,' the man said. 'We'll prepare the bodies and ship them to Cincinnati to handle the ceremonies at that end. Whom would you like us to ship them to?'

Tony had no idea. He didn't know where to have the funeral, either. They were not churchgoers, and he didn't know what to do. 'Don't worry,' the man said. 'We'll fix you up, one step at a time. It all works out in the end.'

After Frazer and Stover, Tony Hastings called long distance to Jack Harriman, who had drawn up Laura's will. It was identical with his, each left everything to the other. There wasn't much of interest to a lawyer, dresses and shoes, pans and kitchen knives, paints, canvases, easel. He fought off Harriman's expressions of sympathy. 'I just want to know what to do. Whether we have to seal off the house.'

Everything in his suitcase was damp, and he spread his clothes to dry on the empty second bed in his room. The next morning he had an early breakfast and paid his bill. He felt odd leaving without speaking to anyone, so he called the police office and said goodbye to Bobby Andes.

The car worked well enough and he had not forgotten how to drive. He headed out to the Interstate, conscious of being alone in the car. With the waterlogged bags of Laura and Helen like bodies in the trunk. A pang in leaving them behind, desertion. Not so, they will follow – on a plane or in a truck, he did not know. The day was preparing to be hot, the sky white, the wooded ridges and fields across the valleys attenuated, unbodied, pale and filmy. He drove fast but attentively. He said to himself, I am under unusual stress. Therefore I must pay attention to my attention and drive with care, and he drove with care.

The evil Interstate had regained its innocence. It was now a broad white track, busy with trucks and speeding cars trying to pass. He did not try to find the place on the other side where they had been stopped, and soon it was behind. He looked at the drivers of the other cars. Families, couples, single men, salesmen. He said, I have not been traumatized for driving on the highway. What happened to me was exceptional, one in a million. Most drivers here are ordinary people, and if I had to stop and wait for help I would be quite safe. I am not afraid of the cars passing me, for I know they are merely driving faster than I, just as I am driving faster than others.

He worked to keep thrusts of shocked thought from interfering with his attention. The emptiness of the car in places they had passed three days before. He came down from the woody mountains into Ohio farmland, the sky still white and the far fields faint in the thick air. He made regular stops for coffee, gas, meals, taking care not to stop where they had stopped before.

His mind was busy. Against the march of high-tension towers across a field to the smoggy horizon, he saw imprinted the curve of a road at night with the bearded man named Lou, and he saw his car parked in the turnout while Lou told him to drive on, that ain't yours, your car's a four door, and he knew by Laura's fingerprint on the bedpost that she and Helen were there at that moment, in the trailer among the trees with the dim light in the window, in the presence of two men named Ray and Turk.

He went through it again, while unconsciously passing trucks and exceeding the speed limit. They must have just got there. They were standing probably by the door while Ray gripped Laura by the arm and Helen looked around for a way to break loose, and Laura said, 'Let us go, you can't do this to us.' At that moment, they perhaps heard the other car going by with a surge of hope which died when the car went on, and in the window the faded ruffly curtain with rose blossoms and leaves, placed in the window by the hunter's wife, concealed the scene from the night.

Then he would force the following moment to ensue, wondering what overcame them, whether it was Ray using a knife on Helen's throat to force her mother to disrobe, or twisting Helen's arm until it broke to force the mother's compliance, or if there was a gun although Tony had seen none. 'They were raped,' Bobby Andes said, with a bed to imagine just below the flowered curtain, and a bedpost for Laura's fingers to grab, pulling up with all her strength against whoever was pushing her down. Screaming and fighting. Violent men – their clawed fingers digging into the soft shoulders of his wife, his daughter, forcing them down in terror on a bare mattress with violent springs, cramming hate into the warm love Tony knew and his daughter's unknown future.

Driving into the hot blaze of ill-defined afternoon sun, he did not want to know how they died, it would be easier to leave it blank like all the other blank spots in the history of the world. But he did know. These were not anonymous victims of the world but Laura and Helen, a blow to the skull, strangulation. Making it impossible not to recapitulate, Ray and Turk (and Lou too, probably, going back to the trailer after leaving Tony in the woods) smashing the hammer and squeezing the fighting little body against the wall, god damn I said shut up.

He arrived home early in the evening. He steadied himself when he saw the house, standing so still like a picture of life. The oak tree on the front lawn, the slope on the side with the lilac bushes and Mr. Husserl's house above. He braced himself again when he unlocked the door and went in and found it empty. The kitchen, cleaned up as they had left it, in the unlit living room Laura's two paintings on the wall in dim twilight. You knew it would be hard, he said, this is only to be expected. He brought in the waterlogged suitcases and dufflebags, took them up to Helen's room, dumped them on the floor. After a while he turned on the lights.

The telephone rang.

'You home?'

'Yes.'

'I saw it in the newspaper.'

'You did? Who's this?'

'You got home all right?'

'Yes. Who is this?'

No answer. He looked in the refrigerator. He would need milk and juice and bread for breakfast. He didn't want to go out tonight, he didn't want anyone to see him. To hell with it.

The phone rang again, Lisa McGregor of the *Tribune*, wanting an interview. He pulled down the shades. He sat in the living room, facing Laura's empty chair, not knowing what to do. He went upstairs and dumped his clothes, still damp, into a laundry bag. He undressed and went to the bathroom and found his way to the bed in the dark. He seemed to be in a narrow track, and everywhere he went, he was surrounded by the tangible absence.

The next day was deliberately busy. He went to Jake's Coffee Shop for breakfast, hoping nobody would recognize him. He called Bill Furman and had a long conversation, which made him feel more civilized, and he allowed Bill to take responsibility for arranging the funeral and spreading the word. While he was talking he noticed a colorful van parked in front of the house, in the shade of the oak tree. It was from a local television station. A smartly dressed young woman in a business suit came up the walk, followed by two men carrying equipment. She wanted a statement. She said, 'Are you in favor of the death penalty?' He said, 'I don't want to answer that question just now.'

Later he went to Lot Hill. Mr. Camel showed him a plot of ground on a slope facing the back fence and a row of back-yards. He stopped at the monument company, rock of ages, granite. He added up the costs indifferently. At home again, he swept the downstairs and stuffed his clothes in the washer and dryer. Clean sheets and towels for his brother in the guest room and his sister in Helen's room, thinking, this is civilized. I am doing things I never did before, which is good for me. At the airport he met Paula, who embraced him and wept, and they stayed on to meet Alex's plane. In the house that night, they were their parents' three reunited children, though separated by adult life for so long they felt like strangers. Still, people in the house, talk in the kitchen, made a difference. The future was like a newborn wild beast, which their talk domesticated. What kind of life would Tony live now, should he keep the house, how well could he take care of himself? Paula made plans, she bought supplies, she interviewed Mrs. Fleischer. There were drinks and then dinner, which Paula cooked, and there was a lot of memory and nostalgia. They agreed that after Tony's visit to Paula at the Cape, she would come back in September to help him dispose of things. He would go to Alex in Chicago for Thanksgiving and to Paula again in Westchester for Christmas.

In the front row at the Unitarian Church, he sat insulated between Paula and Alex while the sunshine streamed through the windows. A lake into which the violent memory sank and violent motion ceased. Sunshine with music and quiet voices. In front, two strange oblongs, side by side, covered with white cloth. Tony Hastings vaguely aware the church was full of people, people peeking to get a look at him. Colleagues. Friends of Laura, he not sure who. High schoolers, friends of Helen's. Shaking hands afterwards.

People he knew and people he didn't, crying and embracing. The tide rushed through him, and he cried too.

The next morning he and Paula closed the house and flew to the Cape. After taking off the plane flew over the city. The air was clear, the streets and blocks crisp and distinct. He looked for the small green patch of Lot Hill, but he was rising away from them in a capsule, and perhaps it was not Lot Hill. The ground shifted and he couldn't tell, it was or it wasn't. Then it was white cotton clouds and all the world as sea.

Ray said to Lou, you fuckin sonofabitch you let him go, now he'll tell, and Lou said how the hell was I supposed to know, and Ray said, Hey mister, your wife wants you, and Paula said, 'We'll have a good time at the beach, won't we?'

The writer's economy, using what you know: Tony lives in Cincinnati, like Edward. It gives Susan an odd feeling of knowing something she shouldn't know. Never mind. That's enough for tonight, Edward old friend. What's there to say? This book has her in its grip, she can say that truly. The long slow plunge into the evil night and Tony trying to brace himself by being civilized. The notion that being civilized conceals a great weakness. With that tension or irony, taut cold surface, she can't tell whether it reflects a sadness her own imagination has contributed, or emits a sadness of its own. The irony makes her think of Edward, which interferes with the sadness, for Edward's irony always did make her uneasy.

She puts the manuscript in the box, and even that seems like violence, like putting the coffins into the ground: images from the book moving out into the house. Fear and regret. The fear is mirror to the fear with which she started. Then she was afraid of entering the novel's world, lest she forget reality. Now, leaving, she is afraid of not being able to return. The book weaves around her chair like a web. She has to make a hole in it to get out. The web damaged, the hole will grow, and when she returns, the web will be gone.

Once she has left the book, living room to kitchen, refrigerator, lights, going upstairs, Tony settles in his pages. She recalls as if it were a long time ago, ages, the vague terror she had felt about Arnold away, but it seems remote now, like Arnold himself. It's Edward on her mind. Childhood things revive. When we two sat on the porch looking across the river to the Palisades while the younger kids played hide and seek, and we talked about topics of importance, like brother and sister. Then what?

He went off to school. And met her again years later in graduate school. Why, you've been childhood sweethearts all along, her mother exclaimed, ignorantly.

So what went wrong? Her mother forever asked without asking. Was it that Arnold appeared, no more than that? But there must have been something wrong with Edward, for no one can believe Susan Morrow would simply trade him in for a better model. What evil thing did Edward do?

The official registered explanation. There never was but one thing wrong with Edward, it says. His personality. After all the old grievances had been weathered away, his personality remained. Only the most intimate would know, because on the outside he was fine: responsible, considerate, reliable. Shy. Modest. Nice. You have to live with him day and night. That's when you'll find him getting in your hair.

Edward was prissy. He was prim. He was fussy and neat. He pursed his lips. He tapped his foot. He said to the traffic cop: What seems to be the problem, officer? He refused to watch television in the late evening. When they were fifteen, out in the boat with the big Maine house up on the shore, they were idling, going nowhere, and he asked her not to drag her hand in the water. No one was rowing, and still he asked her not to drag her hand. He was like that from the beginning and was probably born that way. Isn't that true, Stephanie?

She wished she hadn't thought of that. She didn't want to think of Edward's pursed lips while she was trying to do justice to his book.

# FIRST INTERLUDE

# ONE

Every night before descending into her mind, Susan Morrow performs rituals. Dog walk, kitty kitty, lock doors. Three children safe with a nightlight for the stairs. Teeth and hair, bed light, make love sometimes. Roll away from Arnold to the right, puff the pillow up, wait.

Tonight differs because no Arnold. Freedom, the possibility of something wild. She puts the wild impulse down, and makes tonight like the others, except that instead of turning right with her back to Arnold, she sprawls left, enjoying the husbandless state in the husbandless space. A horrible thought occurs to her about Arnold in New York, but she puts that down too.

Then like every night she waits for her mind, rumbling under the door in the floor. She puts her head into the pillow and waits. Biological sounds distract her, heart changing speed in her ear. Breathing unsettles her. Sometimes the intestinal lab works late, preparing a shipment to disturb her sleep. Speech from the day liquefies the hard surface of her mind like waves in a windstorm. Time to batten down, pack her plans and arguments. She stows *Nocturnal Animals* for the night.

The storm she waits for begins when the words in her head start speaking on their own. They come up through the trap door, people talking without her. Her mind is down there, and she hears the voices in the rooms with the flimsy partitions. This moment is scary because the danger is unknown. Her mind surges up and sucks her down, expanding then into a world, and though the country is familiar, she is a visitor. Each night she revisits places she has visited before and meets people, changed since her last visit. She's ashamed of her faulty memory, knowing what she can't remember is more important than what she can. With her orders in a sealed envelope which she has lost, she wanders, feet bare, legs paralyzed, she loses her footing and sails into the air, or struggles up the hill to meet the class already half through its hour, or sees her kindly dead father and asks if he minds being dead, or lets some quiet student sit on the desk with his hand approaching her crotch which he will never reach – while she tries to avoid the death room.

White morning assaults her with a moment of absolute blankness. She's expelled into the empty day. When she recognizes the blue flowered curtains in the window and the maple branches with a thin line of snow, the door in the floor has slammed shut. If she retains a fragment of dream, it will blow away unless she can chronologize it and put it into words. Yet chronology and words kill it. The story that remains is no dream, and the dream remains uncaught, contiguous to the other dreams below the door, constituting one great unbroken lifetime dream all through the oblivious day, to be continued on her next visit down.

Meanwhile, in the empty cool morning light, dreamless, Susan Morrow, lacking at first even her name, gradually constructs the new day. Tuesday. Eight. Arnold gone, the convention in New York. Wake up to that, suddenly, real life like an alarm clock. The sharp memory of Arnold's reassuring call last night, and what it really means. It means that in New York, Marilyn Linwood, receptionist, either is or is not having an affair with him. Organizing records in his hotel room. Marilyn Linwood waits for Susan to wake up: this prim young woman in her thirties, professional, neat tweed suit, glasses, hair pinned back, careful little face. Secretive, the perfect telephone girl. Some of whose secrets came out at the staff picnic: yellow bikini, bronze hair flowing loose, white thighs a shade too thin. Who's that? Dr. Gaspar said. Patronizing. Is that our Miss Linwood?

Things have changed since Susan gave up jealousy. She wakes up again, remembering. Liberated by a decision not to think, accepting the unknown for peace and not having to know if it needs to be accepted. Making for good marriage, stable and steady after sixteen years of doubt.

Return to the day, up you get, Susan. Let the kids sleep because it's the Christmas break. What must I do today? You must do the laundry, Jeffrey to the vet. Shovel snow? Look out the window to see. By the time she is out of bed with her robe on to look at the snow (only a thin coat on the ground, which will disappear soon), Susan Morrow is restored without a gap. The new day stitches across the night's wound as if her conscious life were continuous.

She does the following things during the day, along with other things. She showers, dresses, wakes the kids, gets breakfast, drives to the Burridges' to pick up Rosie. Gathers the week's laundry to the machine in the basement, makes beds, goes to the supermarket for margarine, lunch meat, and milk. Lunch for three children and herself. To the library to return books, then pick up the living room, carrying Rosie's presents upstairs, also Henry's and Dorothy's who were supposed to do it themselves. A break at the piano, Bach inventions. Back to the basement to exchange laundry loads. Ham in the oven, run the dishwasher, set the table. Her day mind, which knows nothing of her other mind, is full of what's not there, but knows where everything is: Rosie upstairs with Carol, Dorothy outside, Henry with Mike, Arnold in New York.

And Edward. A long hook-up from the past, grabbing her by the mind. All day she keeps wondering, why am I thinking about Edward? His memory reverberates out of slumber like a dream, it flashes like birds tree to tree. It comes too fast, flits away too quickly. To keep it, she must chronologize it just the way she chronologizes her dreams. This kills it too. Her dead memory of Edward was stored in bound volumes years ago, while the new living Edward flies around outside uncaught.

# TWO

When Edward and Susan were fifteen, his father died of a heart attack, and her father and mother took him in for a year. His real mother was in an institution, and his stepmother, who had just divorced the father, wanted nothing to do with the son. He had cousins in Ohio who took him later, but her parents took him first so that he would not have to leave Hastings High. There were negotiations and long distance calls and financial compensation, but she always thought it most kind of her parents.

There was no particular reason to take him in. They were neighbors. Edward's father would ride the commuting train to New York with her father. He came to dinner from time to time. He was a mild amusing affable man who played the violin on the side.

They lived on Edgar's Lane, a street with comfortable suburban houses under the trees, Edward's house at the top of a curving flight of steps down where the street dipped below the overhanging branches. The street was historical, there having been a Battle of Edgar's Lane in Revolutionary times.

She hardly knew him before his father died, or if she did, she did not remember. They walked to school on the Aqueduct, a level grassy path between the backs of the houses, separated from them by a fence and a wide swath of grass. The Aqueduct maintained its level on embankments across all the natural dips in the land, and wherever it crossed a street people walking had to pass through wooden gates from the old horse days.

His father died on a sunny day in May. On the afternoon of that day, Susan was on the Aqueduct with Marjorie Grabel, the grass unmowed on either side, the path still damp but not muddy. Edward was a hundred yards ahead, indolent with his bookbag, chewing blades of Aqueduct grass. Behind her, Susan's younger sister and brother lagged, avoiding her. At that time Edward was a skinny kid with yellow hair, thin neck and squinty eyes like a water bird with long legs, and he was too shy to be liked, though Susan did not realize it was shyness but thought it was innate maturity compared to which she was only a child. They came up Edgar's Lane under the trees. Edward went up the steps into his house. Marjorie turned left at the corner, and Susan went home, with Paul and Penny keeping their distance behind.

A few minutes later he was at the door of her house, his mouth working, trying to say, Get your mother. Then she followed her mother and Edward running down the street, even her mother running. They ran up the steps beside the rock garden to the house, stucco and timbered, her mother stopping to get her breath, while Susan caught up, asking what the matter was. She stayed outside while her mother and Edward went in. Afraid because she had never seen a corpse, she waited on the stone parapet by the front door, with its box of pansies and its view down the street. After a while people arrived, going into the house past her. A fat man puffing up the steps asked her, Is this the place? Her mother came down and told her to go home. By going home she missed the covered body removed on a stretcher, and only later regretted not having seen it.

That night, Edward came to dinner at her house, and she

remembers questions. Do you know your stepmother's address? No grandparents? No uncles and aunts? Do you know anything about your father's finances?

They put him in the room on the top floor, where he had a view over rooftops to a section of the Palisades across the river and a smaller patch of the river itself between trees, where sometimes in the summer if he was lucky he would get a glimpse of the day boats going by.

No one dreamed that anything would develop between Edward and Susan. He said, Let's have an understanding here. You don't want me in your house, and I don't want to be here, but what can we do, so let's shut up about it. You stay out of my room and I'll stay out of yours.

He said, So there'll be no confusion later on, just because I'm male and you're female doesn't mean anything, agreed? You won't expect me to ask you for dates and I won't expect anything from you. We just happen to be boarding in the same house.

Less generous than her parents, she did not want him there, because it took away the family's privacy. When he first made those remarks she was glad, thinking it cleared the air. Later when he repeated them she was annoyed. When he continued to say them, she felt really angry, but by then she was angry with him about everything, so she didn't trust her judgment.

He lived with them for a year. When no one invited her to the spring dance he politely took her. They studied together and did well in school. He went with them in the summer to Maine. There were peaceful moments she hardly noticed. He never mentioned becoming a writer.

## THREE

After that year, Susan did not see Edward again until Chicago, eight years later. She was entering graduate school. He was already there, studying law. Her mother told her to look him up, but she did not want to.

She felt lonely and sad at this university where she went without friends, knowing no one. She was leaving behind a boyfriend named Jake, who took offense at her going away and promised to be unfaithful to her. She lived in a women's dormitory and had classes in a massive gothic building with thick walls and narrow leaded windows, a building entered from an arched vestibule like a culvert, through which the wind blew. She listened to the message of the architecture in the stone halls, the whispers of the professors keeping their voices down, the wary manners of her fellow students keeping their distance. Intelligently, she tried to distinguish the annual sadness of autumn (the gray buildings a shade whiter as the leaves came down) from her personal sadness (Jake, or childhood, or Susan the free) and both of these from the cloistered intellectual sadness, surrounded by the incendiary ghetto said to be dangerous.

Somewhere in this busy monastery was Edward. Her antagonism had disappeared in nostalgia, but she made no effort to look him up. Instead he found her, accidentally. She was on 57th Street going to the bookstore when she heard behind her: Susan, wait up! How fine he looked, changed, poised, tall and magnificent, Edward holding out his hand: I knew you were here. Dressed up, coat and tie, glasses sparkling, he grasped her elbow, steered her into Steinway's. Come have a Coke with me.

Two former children meeting after childhood, their chief care is to prove they are no longer children. This makes them friendly and civil, super-polite. Inquiries about mother and father, brother and sister. Genteel boasts of new sophistication plus rehearsed propaganda to explain our life decisions. No memory how awful things used to be. He was studying law, she English. He lived in an apartment, she in the dorm. His gratitude: I have never failed to appreciate your parents' kindness.

He showed her around, met her for lunch at the Commons, tested with her the other community eating places: Ida Noyes, International House. He pointed out the secondhand bookstores, took her to the Oriental Institute and the Museum of Science and Industry. He taught her how to get downtown on the I.C. and introduced her to the Art Institute and the Aquarium.

She was astonished by his change, which could be either a new layer or a peeling away. He said it: I'm not the brat I used to be. He was courtly, polite, chivalric. This was before chivalries went obsolete, and his was so careful it got on her nerves: walking on the outside of the sidewalk, holding doors open, holding her chair, the trite old things. Yet she thought it wonderful. Blame it on the earlier antagonism. She had such a memory of his old manner that when his rudeness was replaced by civility, civility looked like glamor.

The most interesting change was his new astonishment in everything. Sharp contrast to age fifteen when he knew all and was conspicuously bored by every wonder and outrage they saw. Now he was all wonder and outrage. He was amazed by the city, the university, the traffic, the blue of the lake, the haze of the steel mills, the dangers of the ghetto, the wisdom and knowledge of the professors, the complexity of the law, the glories of literature. For a while this puzzled her, since it seemed to reverse the normal order in which innocent wonder precedes jaded boredom. No doubt at fifteen he had preferred to hide his astonishment because it seemed more grown up. Now at twenty-three it was policy instead to be if necessary even more surprised than he really was. On the whole she liked this, though later she got sick of it too as she perceived how practiced it was.

Despite his fine outer manner, she soon discovered he had suffered a crippling injury: his heart was broken. He had been engaged to a girl named Maria, who had jilted him and married somebody else. Jilted: a good old-fashioned word. He did not seem heartbroken. He seemed vigorous and enthusiastic about the future. But heartbroken was a secret state, which she could share. It occurred to her she was heartbroken too, on account of Jake, who was retaliating for her career choice by a program of worldwide travel and picking up girls. She and Edward could be heartbroken together. It gave them something to talk about, and it protected them from each other, like brother and sister: no need to worry about hearts since their hearts were broken.

Chaste and platonic, this was the deceptive situation that led to Edward's seducing Susan, or Susan's seducing Edward, whichever it was, the ultimate result being the marriage which made necessary their divorce. To be heartbroken means to have a story, and their stories brought them together, as they told them over, repeating and enlarging, Edward more than Susan, since she didn't have much to say about No Good Jake. He talked and she listened, with queries and advice, both knowing pretty well that it was not the story or Maria that mattered but the acts of telling and listening. This went on into the winter. She cooked dinner for him in his apartment, a sisterly thing to do, and they talked about his wounds until three. An engagement to marry. A flighty girl, too young to be tied down. He agreed with everything Susan said.

Looking back from the superior present, Susan sees that Edward's heartbreak was only the current local manifestation of his normal condition as he always encouraged her to see it. The notion that he had always been and always would be subtly hurt by life and was always gallantly trying to make himself strong. Why he was any more hurt than anyone else she never questioned then. There were enough specifics to make it sound good. The death of his father. The loss of his home with no one to take care of him except her own father and mother. Jilting fit right in.

She spotted a gap in his story, the question of sex, which he dodged as unimportant until the dodging made it important. She asked him outright: Did you have sex with her, Edward?

He was shocked by the question, but it came out: he had not had sex with Maria, because he had not had sex with anyone. He was twenty-three years old, competent paternalistic Edward with jacket and tie removed, admitting this strange inexperience. Actually, it did not seem as strange then as it would twenty-five years later after the revolutions. (They didn't call it having sex, either. They called it making love or sleeping together, whether or not slumber was involved: her question really had been, Did you sleep with her?)

There were several possible explanations for Edward. Courtesy and respect, his fine sensitive old nineteenth century genes. Unless he was just a child in gentleman's clothing, afraid to grow up. Or some difference in the internal compass, a matter of what later jargon would call Sexual Orientation.

Edward's virginity stimulated her curiosity and made her talk. If his secrets were gone, she had no right to hers. She blabbed. He was shocked again, as disturbed as if she were the heroine of a nineteenth century novel, and his gloom when he said, I'll have to get used to that, irritated the hell out of her. Rather, it irritates the remembering Susan, who can't remember if she was irritated then. She was temporarily inspired by zeal for the principle, not exactly worth a crusade but enough to motivate her, that Sex is Natural. The result maybe of her recent battles with Jake. What she saw in Edward was the opposite conviction, Sex is Unnatural. Sex is Natural was Susan's pre-feminist feminism: it turned her against big breasts, pornographic beer and cigarettes, the double standard for men and women, the equation of romance with lust, and Jake's notion that there was a difference between good (dark) and bad (blonde) women. (What Jake's belief meant for Susan was that while romantic love required her to yield to him, her doing so constituted a flaw in her character which relieved him of obligation.) As for Edward, believing Sex was Unnatural was the natural consequence of his astonishment with everything (everything was unnatural). He could not believe real people did the things they wrote about and his imagination embellished.

So she decided to educate Edward. It popped into her head one drizzly afternoon on the museum steps. She said without thought, Edward, get someone to teach you the facts of life.

I know the facts of life.

The idea stuck in her head, and it had serious consequences, because the outcome, which would certainly have deterred her if she had known, was that Edward married her. At the time, she thought it would be educational and healthy for both of them. Sex is Natural, Edward. It doesn't mean a thing. Even you and I can do it, and no one else need know. This was early spring, when the campus was wet and the young branches sparkled with a residue of rain, and the gray buildings looked freshly washed under the pale skies. I can slip into your apartment, and no one will see, and when I go back to the dorm, neither my mother or father nor Jake or Maria nor your professors will know a thing.

What a crazy idea. That must have been another Susan because the real Susan remembers being annoyed by such thoughts. She remembers trying to analyze out of existence her fascination with what Edward had become: the combination of his acquired childlike eagerness with his innate jaded primness. She remembers trying to scorn to death her wicked curiosity to see what this correct and careful Edward would be like in the grasp of something uncontrollably intense and physical in himself.

The plot summary of Susan's memory says she made up her mind to seduce Edward and then went out and did it. The detailed text says otherwise. She gave him hints without any idea what the hints were about. Affectionate impulses. Along the street in the rain, patting and cuffing. Flirty things. She punched him in the chest when he came out of the library. In the University Tavern she came up behind him and put her fingers over his eyes. At dinner in the Commons, after a hard day and before a night of labor with a paper to write, where they ate in silence, her gaze settled on his light hair loosely disheveled, his tired eyes staring vaguely, and she felt a surprising old warmth for this strange young man strangely dear to her, whom she would like to take care of. She did not know she wanted to seduce him.

Was he interested, or was he not? She only thought she was looking in him for signs, whether he was attracted or repelled. At the University Tavern where they had a beer, she said, Let me live with you, Edward. He laughed, resisting by turning it into a joke, and she laughed too, thinking that's what she meant.

She initiated conversations about censorship and pornography, psychoanalysis and the three stages of development – oral, anal, and genital. She discussed homosexuality in Plato, and the naked athletes in the Olympic Games. She showed him the analysis she was writing about 'To His Coy Mistress.' She broke out in the middle of that, I keep forgetting you're a virgin, and he blushed and hemmed.

She didn't intend anything serious, she thought, she was just trying to shake him out of his complacency. On a warm spring day they went to the Forest Preserve to look for migratory birds. They had a good nostalgic talk about family life, life in Hastings, and his future. As a lawyer he intended to take civil rights cases no one else would handle and give free legal aid to the poor. She thought what a good man he was, which made her proud as if she had made him good. Then back to the university, late and dark, where he invited her to his apartment for coffee before taking her home. As they went up the dark stairs, and he unlocked the door, and they entered the room, and he turned on the light, she experienced an unbearable excitement of the present tense, the dazzling immanence of now, which was full of her presence and Edward and all life concentrated, making her want to scream or sing. He heated the coffee and set out cookies and went to the bookshelf for his bird book, and they sat shoulder elbow arm and thigh while he looked up the American redstart and warblers they had seen. And all the while present time hummed with presence until she could hardly stand it, and she heard a voice saying, Go ahead, it's all right now, and then her own real voice whispering a suggestion into Edward's ear.

Then was heartbeat time for both of them, tremble and shake, his large eyes staring too close for focus, his voice hoarse: Do you mean it? The belated caution and sanity of her reply: Only if you want to. And his deep wow: Oh grateful God.

There was a single light on his bed table which cast its glare downward and suffused elsewhere through the room. She was wearing a soft pale green sweater, a plaid skirt with pleats, white socks. Underneath, a white bra and white pants. Emerging from these, she was thin and lanky, her cheeks were pale, with no glasses in those days, and her hair hung lightly down her back. She was worried about the smallness of her breasts until she saw the wonder in Edward's eyes. He was even lankier than she. His ribs showed in his chest, his thighs were thin, his sex was chunkier than any other part of him. The room was chilly and they both shivered and kept shivering.

In the bedroom he gasped and grunted and puffed and roared. Be frank, Susan, she enjoyed it too, a lot more than she was to enjoy some of the repetitions later. He bore down on her and rocked and yelled in a loud voice, You great wonderful thing, I can't believe how wonderful you are. Afterwards, he thanked her for her generosity.

A long naked conversation followed, while they idly fingered each other. He told her a secret he had not told anybody else. He had taken up writing, he told her. He had poems and stories and sketches, and two notebooks already filled.

# FOUR

Edward and Susan: how wonderful, her mother said, like marrying back into the family. This was 1965, in chilly March, no change in plans: they kept up their studies, only now Susan lived in Edward's apartment. They assumed it was happiness.

Susan can remember some of that happiness if she tries. For twenty-five years she has not tried, preferring to consider it an illusion, thereby protecting Arnold and her children. She had no wish to dismantle her disillusionment.

What she remembers now is not so much happiness as places where happiness occurred. Happiness was intangible, place made it visible. There were places in the summer, and there was Chicago. For Edward-happiness she remembers only summers, and of the two Edward summers, only the first, which they divided between her parents' old house in Maine and his cousins' borrowed cabin in upstate New York. The Maine house, which goes back to childhood, overlooked a cold harbor with pine trees. It had gables and screened windows and a screened porch around, and it stood over the steep grass down to the rocks. She remembers Edward in the rowboat, for they went out in it when they were fifteen and again when they were married. She confuses the memories somewhat. She remembers Edward the child in the rowboat trying a cigarette and throwing it into the water. She remembers him talking about his stepmother, who divorced his father before the fatal heart attack, and she felt ashamed to see a boy cry.

The other house, his cousin's cabin in upstate New York, was more primitive. It was in the deep shade of trees by a small river in the woods. It had a screen door and a main room with unfinished walls and exposed timbers, and two small back rooms. She remembers Edward writing with his typewriter under the table lamp while she tried to read by the same lamp in the Morris chair, and she's not sure if that was happiness or not. They went swimming, running without clothes out the door into the river. All that screwing. Enjoying the contrast to their hostile past, pretending they were still fifteen in the Hastings house, breaking the rules. Then back to the obligations of the present: having finished sex, they wrote a letter to her mother and father signed Susie and Edward. Childhood sweethearts, her mother would say, just like brother and sister.

Memories of happiness in Chicago are harder to find. Edward's apartment, where they were so busy. Papers and exams to prove how their minds had been professionalized, dredged and rebuilt. As students in different fields, they respected each other's needs and stayed polite. They finished the first year on their scholarships with help from her father. Later, because Edward did not want to depend on her parents, she taught freshman English in a city junior college. With an interruption or two she has kept that job ever since. When Edward resigned his scholarship in March, her job was their only source of funds.

He resigned his scholarship because he had quit his studies. He could have waited until summer when the scholarship expired, but since he had stopped studying, he thought it more honorable to stop the scholarship too.

He gave up the law to become a writer. This surprised Susan because she thought he should first find out if he could write. But Edward was sure. In long talks he explained his decision and clarified their future and her role. Her father came to Chicago to talk him out of it, but Edward said the strength of his writing compulsion, by preventing him from studying for his exams, proved law school was a mistake. It was other people who wanted me to study law, Edward said. It was I who wanted me to write.

When Susan learned he had been writing all the time, she wondered why he never showed her any of his work. He explained he wasn't ready because it was still baby stuff. He asked her support, and she stood by him. It was a time of idealism. Her secret alarm was selfish and bourgeois (she had never worried about being bourgeois before). Her expectation of a comfortable house, children, all that, and of pursuing a scholarly career with Ph.D.: that was bourgeois. Do writers make money? she asked anxiously, having heard most poets and fiction writers support themselves with other jobs. Who needs money? Edward said. With your job, which does provide a salary, we'll scrape by. She would teach, he would write. He would dedicate his books to her, without whom none of this etcetera.

Her father on his visit gently asked. Do you really want to give up so much? But what am I giving up, Daddy? she replied. Brave, determined. What else am I good for? What about your plans, your two years of graduate school? I'm utilizing that, she said. I couldn't have got this job without it.

The second summer of their marriage, they stayed in Chicago so she could earn more money teaching summer school. Now she read his writing, some of it. He told her to be absolutely frank, but she learned it was better not to be. His poems were short and casual, pieces of nostalgia, memories of places or states of mind, fitted to a word or two. Also some little sexy poems about how amazing it was to screw her, anticipation, performance, and recovery. He had certain phrases for her, especially her soft shallow breasts, which annoyed her. She had a suspicion she could write just as well, if she wanted to. Later she cultivated this thought because it enabled her to regard Edward as a phony, which helped put him behind her, but at the time it was a heresy against the faith she needed.

Poems and sketches. He stopped showing them to her. She hoped it wasn't because of anything she said. He talked of larger projects. He had been working on a novel but had not mentioned it because it was so unfinished. It was pretty long. She gathered it was autobiographical, with twelve hundred pages so far, and had brought young Eddie up to the age of twelve.

During the second autumn of their marriage, he got rather crabby. Things were not going well. He was working on a project requiring special concentration. What project? she asked. A new novel, a long poem? He wouldn't say because he worked better when nobody was looking over his shoulder. It was a mistake to show your unfinished work. I need to go off by myself, he said.

Without me? He needed to go to the river cabin where he could write undisturbed. What am I supposed to do? Susan said. You have to teach, he said. You have a contract to fulfill.

It's hard for Susan to remember the mood of her acquiescence and even harder to transcend her later scorn. How could she give in so meekly? But since he wasn't unfaithful sexually, she agreed to stay behind. He went off and called her every second night. She wrote letters to her parents making the best of it, boasting of their unconventionality, Edward wrestling in the wilderness, and what a great life. Unfortunately, he came back gloomier than ever. It didn't work, he said. He'll have to start over again. Start what? But it was too private for words. Not until later did she register her official verdict: Edward the phony, herself gullible fool. The only good thing about that October, she would say, was that it enabled her to meet Arnold. He was a hospital intern living in an apartment upstairs. His wife had a nervous breakdown and had to be hospitalized. In the end, everybody except Selena would later say, the whole episode was a blessing for them all.

But twenty years of marriage (no idyll, to be sure) allow Susan to wonder with an open mind what sticking with Edward would have been like. If she had stayed with him, she'd now be Stephanie. With due allowance for Rosie and Dorothy and Henry, Susan is no longer afraid to ask if life as Stephanie would necessarily have been any less wonderful than life as Susan.

Once she asked him why he wanted to write. Not why he wanted to be a writer but why he wanted to write. His answers differed day to day. It's food and drink, he said. You write because everything dies, to save what dies. You write because the world is an inarticulate mess, which you can't see until you map it in words. Your eyes are dim and you write to put your glasses on. No, you write because you read, to remake for your own use the stories in your life. You write because your mind is babble, you dig a track in the babble to find your way around yourself. No, you write because you are shelled up inside your skull. You send out probes to other people in their skulls, and you wait for a reply. The only way to show you why I write, he said, is to show you what I write, which I'm not ready for.

She thought it sounded just fine. He made it look like a necessity of life. She was afraid, though, lest he be insufficiently nourished by what he could actually write. When she heard he had given it up to sell insurance, she hoped he had found some way to make insurance equally nourishing.

One thing bothered her about his creed. If writing was a necessity of life, what would her Freshman English students do? Or herself. Except for letters, an occasional diary, some reminiscences in a notebook, she was no writer. How did she survive?

Well, she was a reader. If Edward couldn't live without writing, she couldn't live without reading. And without me, Edward, she says, you'd have no reason to exist. He was a transmitter, spending his resources, she a receptor who became richer the more she received. Her way with the chaos in her mind was to cultivate it through the articulations of others, by which she meant the reading of a lifetime with whose aid she created the interesting architecture and geography of herself. She had constructed over the years a rich and civilized country, full of history and culture with views and vistas she had never dreamed of in the days when Edward wanted to make his visions known. How thin those visions seemed compared to the lands she had seen. Generously, in the years since then, she has wished him a good education. Now along comes *Nocturnal Animals.* Whether it shows an education is unknown, but at least it's a vision and he's making that known, and Susan is glad for him.

All through the day as she works about the house, Susan looks forward to reading tonight. She has discarded her contempt for Edward's folly, which was no more than her own. Take his book frankly and be glad of it. If the Edward who wrote it seems more intelligent and better than the Edward she knew, no reason to be surprised. She looks forward to meeting the new Edward on Friday, twenty-five years of maturity added on. But be prepared for him not to shine. Though some writers as people seem nicer than their books (you like them fine but not what they write), others are not so nice, selfish or surly, though their books are attractive, intelligent, and full of light.

Yet to tell the truth (Susan's truth), the Edward of this book is still concealed. Hidden in the intensity of Tony's case, like police invisible behind the spotlight. That won't last. When Tony, having tracked down his disaster and found his murdered wife and child, steps off the common ground of his misfortune and into his personal Tonyness, then will Edward appear? Susan thinks what to say until then. So far, only this: You begin well enough. If you can't keep it up, at least you have this. Which is a relief, Edward, you can't imagine what a relief.

# THE SECOND SITTING

# ONE

It's late before Susan Morrow returns to her book. She sits on the couch with the last two hours crashing in her head, of Dorothy trotting down the steps with Arthur to his car, Rosie hunting for her Christmas horses, Henry upstairs with the enormous sound of Wagner at full strength – not rock for Henry but Wagner that she makes him shut his door and lower the volume. She finds the manuscript on the coffee table under the Monopoly board, which someone has dropped with thousands of dollars and green houses and hotels strewn about. She relaxes, closes her eyes. In a moment she will extricate it from that abandoned wealth. In a moment she will read.

Her mind resists focus. If young Arthur, rosy cheeked, is really the nice young fellow he pretends to be, shy, not looking you in the eye, incipient madness, insane boy killer. While Martha settles down on the Monopoly board, money and all, hotels poking her belly, and all that world of Tony underneath. When Susan slips her hand in, Martha spills to the floor, taking modern civilization with her. Murl you, Martha says.

Susan puts the unread manuscript in the box on the couch, finished pages in a pile next to it. Looks for her place, marked by a piece of red and green Christmas paper. She thinks. Tries to remember Tony who lost his family in the woods. Not ready yet. Wrong mood. She dreams a little, thinking herself into Tony. Dreaming, comparing his case to hers, what kind of novel would Susan's troubles make? How much more terrible his are, except that hers are real, his imaginary, made up by somebody – by Edward. His are simpler too, stark questions of life and death, in contrast to hers, which are ordinary, messy, and minor, complicated by uncertainty as to whether they rate as troubles at all. Troubles are the homeless, people ravaged by poverty, war, crime, disease. Is Marilyn Linwood a trouble? Whose affair with Arnold ended three years ago but might still be going on. Susan doesn't know if it is, honestly, she doesn't. And won't ask. Not after all their talks and the understanding reached, according to which Linwood has no significance, since this marriage, Arnold says, is strong enough to withstand all rival attractions. Not something to bother a marriage counselor about.

Dreaming on brings up floating Mrs. Givens, and through her Mrs. Macomber the professor's wife who sued Arnold for malpractice because her husband got a stroke after heart surgery. Whose anger and bitterness (understandable in human terms) made Susan cringe, responsible by virtue of wifehood for Arnold's hand with the scalpel and the clamps and precautions in an operating room she has never seen. Doctor's wife equals doctor, which Arnold takes for granted while she relies on his estimate of himself. Such a good surgeon, brilliant, skillful, careful, trustworthy. She knows without having to ask that poor Mrs. Macomber's suit was ignorant if not malicious or frivolous, and that's what she told nosy Mrs. Givens. If the wife doesn't believe her husband is right, who besides the husband ever will? The truth is, Susan doesn't know how good a doctor her husband is. Some people admire him: patients praise him, a few colleagues, certain nurses, but what does she know? He works hard, takes it seriously, studies. He never seemed especially bright to her, but his reputation must be good or he could not have become a candidate for Cedar Hall

(Chickwash). Patients die. He says it can't be avoided and takes it stoically. Sometimes when he talks about dead patients she wants to cry, though they are only strangers, for someone ought to cry besides those who have an interest. But she doesn't cry lest it look like a criticism which she has no right to make.

Enough. This is time she's wasting, unhealthy. A whiff of self-pity, like body odor. The book will restore her, that's what it's for. She looks at the page on top. Puffs on her glasses, tries to remember. Tony Hastings, the crime, the clearing with the mannequins. And more: the return home and the funeral. At last she remembers, he's flying to the Cape with Paula his sister. She wonders what new things will happen to Tony Hastings, now that his family is dead, already written in those still unread pages.

## *Nocturnal Animals 12*

Tony Hastings did not want to recover. He kept energy low to avoid the danger. He came to the Cape so as not to argue with Paula about going to the Cape. Merton met them in a station wagon, touched his arm, long face in his beard, expressing the inexpressible. Tony saw the intent, and realized he didn't like Merton. He never had, which was a surprise because he had always liked Merton. He didn't like the kids either. They sat in the back seat, solemn so as not to get shushed.

They drove through scrubby sandy woods. The flat middle land of the Cape, you could tell from the pale mist in the sky that the sea was near by. Paula and Merton talked. He saw Peter and Jenny trying not to be caught staring.

The house was in the woods a half mile from the bay. A

dirt driveway with grass in the middle climbed up from the road. They gave him the same room he had occupied with Laura. From the window you could see over the tops of the trees to the bay dazzling blind in the afternoon sun beyond the line of dunes. The room smelled of pine, the floors were gritty with sand.

They went to the beach, deserted in the late afternoon. A sharp breeze blew off the bay from the west, and it was chilly. In their bathing suits Peter and Jenny put their sweaters on. 'Aren't you going swimming?' Tony Hastings said with effort.

'Too cold!' Jenny said. Peter had a frisbee, and he and Jenny tossed it back and forth, to avoid having to talk to him. They didn't know what to say because they were afraid to ask about the big thing they knew about him. The wind chopped up a ragged surf. The beach showed remains left by the crowd that had been there, the big rusted trash can was full with papers and plastic food cartons blowing out of the top. A large seagull walked on the sand, gawky with orange legs, an evil eye, a vicious beak. Another came down out of the sky and hung in place on the wind two feet above the sand with great motionless wings, looking things over. Remnants of a sandwich. Empty egg carton. Someone's sweater, half buried in the sand.

'I'm shivering to death, let's go home,' Peter said.

Plenty of animated conversation at dinner that night. Tony Hastings knew he should take part if he could keep track of what it was about. Later he thought, I'm a dead log, I should try harder, I mustn't forget who I am.

In the morning he slashed off his mustache, which disgusted him. The beach was bright. The air was fresh, the bay green and calm, the water warm, and the children swam long. He swam with them for a while, and wondered if it was doing him good. He noticed a query on Jenny's face as she came up out of the water, bubbles in her face and soggy hair, looking at him and diving away. He knew what she was thinking. She was remembering Aunt Laura the underwater swimmer who used to prowl like a submarine among the surface waders, nibbling and dunking. Or water cavalry with Uncle Tony and Aunt Laura. He thought, if they ask, I'll play horse, but no one asked.

Since he felt little pleasure in either water or land, he came out soon and sat on a towel. When the children returned, he made an effort. 'Would you like to walk to the inlet?' he said. It was hard to ask questions like that, for words sat on his chest like lead.

They walked toward the inlet. Now (he knew) they were thinking of last year's walk, Aunt Laura looking for shells and pebbles, Uncle Tony identifying shore birds, Helen digging out the little holes in the wet sand, wondering what was down there, a clam, a crab? Silently he defended his pain, refusing to care about pretty stones or delicate crab shells, indifferent to sand dollars. He did not want to distinguish gulls from terns. The sand was thick around his feet. The children walked quietly. Then Peter muttered something to Jenny. She ran ahead and he threw the frisbee to her. They broke loose, circling with the frisbee the rest of the way, while he marched on.

He spent two weeks at the Cape, trying to be depressed without being uncongenial. Paula said, 'Tony, you have every right to be depressed.' She suggested he go to a psychiatrist when he got back.

When he got home two weeks later, arriving in the empty house alone in the afternoon, this house absolutely and only his own from now on, he found a letter waiting from Grant Center.

Thought you would like to know a fingerprint on your car matches one found in the trailer. Plus, another on your car has been identified as belonging to Steven Adams formerly of Los Angeles. He has a record in California, stolen car, with acquittal on a rape charge. Enclosed please find a picture, face and profile, of said Adams and would appreciate if you can identify him as any of the people who attacked you and your wife. An A.P.B. has been sent out for him.

No one has responded to our call for witnesses.

Looking forward to hearing from you promptly, will let you know further developments.

Robert G. Andes

The picture trembled. Mug shot, front and side, a gaunt man with long black hair, full black beard like a prophet. Tony Hastings stared, trying to see into it. Who? Crooked nose, sad eyes. Not Ray, not Turk. He tried to remember, warding off the keen disappointment, Lou's beard, Lou's hair? Lou's beard was not so long, his hair different, though Tony could not remember how, and the eyes in the picture flashed nothing. This was a picture of no one he had ever seen. He tried to imagine Ray with a beard, but the picture made it hard to remember what Ray looked like without one.

The letter stirred motion in him, a desire to punish. He thought, What difference does it make whether they catch them or not, yet at night he had murderous thoughts. They made him bite his lips and bang his fist on the sheet. But he forgot to answer the letter, and after a few days he got a telephone call from Bobby Andes. He heard the voice weakly, a poor connection.

'Did you get my letter?'

'Yes.'

'Well?'

'What?'

'Do you recognize the face?'

'No.'

'No what?'

'I don't recognize it.'

'Aw shit, man.'

'I'm sorry.'

'God damn it, man. This is the guy whose fingerprints are on your car. What do you mean, you don't recognize it?'

'I'm sorry, I don't.'

'Ah hell.'

Depressed though he was, Tony Hastings did what was necessary to stay alive. He cooked his breakfast and made sandwiches for lunch. He went to cheap restaurants for dinner. Sometimes when he felt less apathetic than usual he cooked his own. He went to his office, but it was hard to keep his mind on his work and he came home early. At night he tried to read but he could not concentrate, and he spent most of the time watching television. He could not concentrate on that either and usually did not know what he was seeing. Once a week Mrs. Fleischer came to clean and do the laundry. In between, the house got messy, newspapers and books and dirty dishes. He was impatient for the summer to end so he could resume teaching, though he was not eager to teach.

One evening, having decided it was time to get ready for his fall classes, he went to his study and tried to think where to start. But his thought went in other directions. He wanted to perform a ceremony, but he could think of none that would do. He went to the window, but all he could see was his reflection in the glass. A person outside could see in better than he could see out. He turned off all the lights, so that the house was completely dark. Why am I doing this? he asked. The dim illumination from outside, from the streetlamps and the neighbors' houses and the glow in the night sky, came in through the windows and cast patches and shadows on the walls. He went to the side window looking up at Mr. Husserl's house all lit up, and around to the other windows, the black night over the bushes and choked gardens. He walked around the darkened house from room to room, looking at the night outside and the patterns it made inside.

Then he went out. He walked up the street to the shops. He looked in the windows at people in the restaurants, the open stores, Walgreen's, Stu's Deli, the lighted windows of the closed stores, the hardware store, the bookstore. He went into the park down a slope under huge trees, so dark he had to hold his hand in front of his face against invisible branches. Why have I come out here? he asked.

They must have thought of it while fixing the tire. When they went over to Ray's car and had a conference. Let's take them to the trailer, have a ball. What about him? Shit guys, we gotta get rid of him. Okay, here's what we do. *Separate* em. Him in one car, the dames in the other. Him you take, Lou. It's dangerous, man. Shit boy, everything's dangerous.

He tried to remember, the iron which they used to change his tire. Was it lying on the ground when they finished? He could have picked it up. With the tire iron in his hand he could have prevented Ray and Turk from getting into his car. He could have held it in front of him with two hands. If he had to, he could have swung it and hit Ray on the head.

In the park he lost the path. He saw a light through the

lacework of the trees and used it to guide him back to the sidewalk. The light was a sign in a beauty shop, closed for the night. He was trembling, and his face was scratched.

In the darkened house he sat looking out. Take me back, he said. Start over, *undo* this thing. Change one moment, that's all I ask, then let history take its course. Stop me at the trailer where I did not stop. Stand me by the car door to fight Ray and Turk, give me that, no more, just one link in the logical chain. Pick up the Bangor hitchhiker, listen to the sweetness of my daughter for the man with the flowing beard, idiot father.

The house was an empty tank full of grief. Their empty ghosts floated everywhere they were not. Not the box of jewelry left open on the dresser. Neither the drawers nor the closets where her dresses hang, where he fingered their textures. He wrapped her heavy gray sweater around his head. Sentimental and pious, he watered the hanging plants she had left in the vestibule. Pick up the blue and white china. Not using the Hitchcock chairs, nor the electric can opener in the kitchen. Nor typing a letter at her old rolltop desk in what she does not call the sewing room though she does no sewing there. Nor her easel, her crazy palette, unframed canvases against the studio wall.

How detached are her two big paintings in the living room, the one all pale blue like an early morning misty seascape, the other hues of pink and orange, serene and constant, ignorant of future force and rape and hammer. Helen's stupid stuffed panda, symbol of sentimentality with calculated big glass eyes and oversized head, does to him what it was made to do where it sits on the bed in the room full of the house that Jack built.

In the morning he waited to hear the sound of water in

the bathroom. He expected to hear the screen door and the footsteps on the walk starting off to school. He wanted to say good bye when he left the house but she must have gone upstairs. When he came back in the afternoon, she would be painting in her studio, he would listen at the foot of the stairs. The afternoon advanced, he was waiting to hear the other one come busting through the screen door. After dinner he would wait for her so they could go for their walk.

He plotted these rediscoveries of absence so they would come as pulses of surprise, to maintain the steady flow of grief. They enabled him to realize it again, over and over. He would deliberately forget and then restore the order in which things happened. The strange oblongs covered by white cloth in the church were later than the canvas cocoons carried out of the bushes, which were later than the mannequins in the bushes. These came after they were driven off in the car in the night, which was later than anything that ever happened in this house. Nothing in this house was more recent than what happened by the road, nothing is newer or fresher than their death. The last you ever saw them, Tony Hastings told himself with astonishment, would always be their scared faces in the car driving down the road.

He talked it over with her. He said, The worst moment was when Ray and Turk forced themselves into the car with you. That was pretty bad, she agreed. No, he corrected himself, the worst was when I first saw something in the bushes and realized it was you. She smiled. He said, I wish you could tell me your part of it. So do I, she said.

The other one clumping down the stairs at night, two at a time, thump crash at the bottom, letting the screen door slam. He asked, what should I do with her things, the stuffed animals, the china horses, I need your advice. I know, she said.

## TWO

Upstairs poor old fat Henry plays *Siegfried's Funeral March* too loud like rock. Turn that down, Susan Morrow yells, then hears the telephone, which is Arnold calling from New York again. She returns to the manuscript after the call, full of the sound of Arnold's elation. It jams her reading and obliterates Tony Hastings, wipes him out. The news is Chickwash, and Arnold's elation is Susan's dread, though he does not know it. If they must leave this home for the advancement of Arnold's career. The question sharpens her eyes, makes her look at her life from this spot on the couch. Wallpaper, mantelpiece, pictures, stairs, banisters, woodwork. Outside, a lawn, maple tree, streetcorner, streetlamp. She has friends here: Maria, Norma. To take her children out of school for Chickwash's sake. They'll be upset, they may cry forlornly, boyfriends girlfriends and bestfriends lost forever. So may Susan, who said nothing about this on the phone to Arnold, lest she be guilty of selfishness and petty domesticity. She's had enough of asserting rights and feeling bad afterwards. She has no wish to quarrel with Arnold.

He assumes she'll abide by his decision. He may even think they arrived at the decision together. They'll talk about it. She'll ask the questions he expects her to, to help him decide what he's already decided, telling him what's on his mind, reminding him of his interests. She'll weigh his love for the surgeon's art and his care for patients against prestige and the power to do good on a national scale. If she doesn't like it, she won't tell him lest it be taken as an attempt to influence him against his best interests. She'll mention the children and their interests, but if he says children can adapt and speaks of the advantages to them of a Washington environment and a successful father, she'll support him of course.

His voice like a high school kid. Virtually promised me the job, he said. Isn't that great? It's wonderful, dear, she said. We must talk it over, he said, we must consider what's best for all of us, you and the children too, I won't accept it without consulting you. All the angles. He made suggestions on how to consider all the angles.

There was more than that in the call. A bad moment, some question she asked which was not a proper response to her husband's triumph, realized too late. It passed, an error, leaving a soil of worry after the call ended. A feeling of disaster averted, though a danger still remains of bogging down in thoughts. Stop, Susan tells Susan, let it be. It could have been worse. The evening is for reading, and to continue that she must wipe herself out of her mind.

Tony Hastings instead. He grieves, apathetic, obsessed, and she wonders what she is supposed to make of him when he turns off the lights and looks out. He's become a character, complicated by that hint of Edward's irony threaded through the style. She wonders if she'll lose touch with him, if his woe slips into self-pity. She hopes the novel does not prolong his depression, for who wants to read about a depressed protagonist? She tends to be impatient with depressed people, more than Edward, perhaps. She remembers Edward's own depression when he was trying to write, before their marriage failed.

In the rowboat, on the pebbly shore, with the hiss of Edward's cigarette, she remembers (even earlier) his refusal to forgive his long institutionalized mother. When Susan defended her, he tried to splash her with the oars. While now and for twenty-five years every month Arnold has sent a fat check to keep Selena foaming in her luxurious cage in Gray Crest. Susan remembers how he used to say to her with astonished joy, Thank God you're sane. After all these years he's used to her and doesn't say it any more.

## *Nocturnal Animals 13*

In September Paula came to visit. She came to give things away and throw things out. She went into Laura's closets and Helen's room, packed up clothes and jewelry, went over letters, paintings, photographs, toys and stuffed animals. Then she left and the semester began. Colleagues and students returned. That was good, though questions having nothing to do with math still intervened. Mister, your wife wants you. Raids on his thought while he lectured or talked to students. And this new habit of turning off the lights and looking out the windows at night. He would look at the dark branches and light squares in the houses and the dim glow of the sky and feel the spacious darkness in the house like a cave, especially exciting when a person went by, unaware of being watched.

He supposed he was recovering. He went to a party given by Kevin Malk, head of Tony's department. At the Malks' parties they played games. Charades: Tony pitched in, contributing titles to be acted out: 'The Sunny Side of the Street' and 'The Decline of the West.' He himself acted out 'Nocturnal Animal House' and was surprised by the vigor of the applause.

He drove Francesca Hooton home. She was alone because

her husband, a lawyer, had gone to New Orleans. Tony had always liked Francesca. She taught French, was tall and fair and had a pretty face with fine features and gold in her hair. In the old days he sometimes wondered what if they had both been free. Now he was uncomfortable, because he was an escort, and because of the possibility this was an opportunity, which he did not want in the confusion of being stricken and bereaved. She sat beside him in the car, wearing an elegant light tan dress. 'Have they got any leads?' she asked.

'The police? Not that I know of.'

'Aren't you angry?'

'Who at? The police?'

'Those men. Don't you want them caught and punished?'

'What's the use? That won't bring Laura and Helen back.'

He realized immediately this was bravado, while she said, 'Well if you're not angry, I am. I'm angry on your behalf. I want them killed. Don't you?'

'I'm angry enough,' he murmured.

At the foot of the stairs to her second story apartment, she said, 'I don't suppose you want to come in.'

He felt a wild leap inside and said, 'I'd better get home.'

In his darkened house he described his evening to Laura. We played charades, he said. I was the life of the party. Then I took Francesca Hooton home. She wants me to be angry and want revenge, but I don't want to be distracted from you. She also expects me to have an affair with her, but I refused. He turned out the lights and went around again looking out from the dark into dark, saying, I won't forget. Nothing can make me forget.

He walked stiffly from class to class like a man with a cane. A graduate student named Louise Germane who had soft wheatcolored hair came to his office and said, 'I heard what happened, Mr. Hastings. I want you to know I'm sorry.' He pinched his smile and thanked her. When she left, he said, I must expect to be lonely, my hair will turn white. He decided to write a history of his marriage. He thought writing would make him remember. He was afraid of losing the sense of presence, the vital feeling that the past was still part of the present.

He gathered specific memories to prove things: the Tolstoy evening to show her intelligence, the beach trip to demonstrate her vitality, the jokes and puns which he had such difficulty remembering to confirm her wit, the kitchen discussions about the Malks to show her judgment, the famous evening walk to Peterson Street to reiterate her generosity and kind heart. His memory was recalcitrant, it did not like to be forced. He tried to liberate her from the frame on the table, her eyes frozen into a smile by the photographer, her hair in a fixed wave over one side of her forehead. He looked away and waited for memory to ambush him. It ambushed him often but not when asked. To expose himself to ambush, he recapitulated old habits: she drove him to the university a hundred times on her way to the gallery, liberating a nice moment at the gallery when she asked his advice. Once she ambushed him with a vision of her walk coming up the street to the house, real as life, swinging her arms. How she swung them – but every memory that ambushed him became fixed. He developed a store of images, while memory ambushed him less and less.

Then he got better. He spent three hours at a faculty meeting arguing passionately for two promotion and tenure candidates. Only when he left the building with Bill Furman in the snow just beginning, did he remember he was bereaved. He had forgotten for three hours. Nor did the returning memory, recalled by the empty house and the snow, bring the shock it used to. This happened often. In the classroom or reading, he would realize he'd been working for hours without remembering his life wasn't normal. Life goes on, he would say. I can't grind my teeth all the time.

This was the first snow of the winter. Tony drove through it with Bill Furman, thick flakes swirling around the car in a strong wind, the streets slippery and dangerous. He expected the snow to revive his grief because it was burying the place where they died. He could think of it falling in the woods: a winter they will never see. The snow was peaceful, though. Later he watched it from his house. Once again he went around and turned off the lights. He watched the stream of flakes in the light of the streetlamp. He thought of snow on the mountain track in the woods. And in the clearing, covering it up. He took off his shoes and walked around in his socks. Light reflected by the snow from the streetlamps and city sky came in the windows of the big house and illuminated the empty rooms. He thought how free he was in this house alone, his solitary ownership in the darkness lit by the spooky outside glow. As he had done on those earlier nights, only now feeling quite sane, he went from one window to another, looking up the hill to Mr. Husserl's house, and to the lawn and snowy oak branches and the garages and fringed cars parked, with a feeling like ecstasy.

When he asked Laura about it, she said be glad you're alive. Watching the snow filling the front lawn and street, he became conscious of his body, which had been ignorant of grief from the start. The only constant, his need to sleep and shave, brush his teeth, eat and drink and release his wastes. Watching his eating habits so as not to feel greasy, gaseous, or bleak. Wearing clean clothes, underwear, shirts, shoes, and dirty clothes to Mrs. Fleischer to wash. And now with snow, an overcoat, muffler, cap and gloves, and if he walks out tomorrow he will stamp his feet to restore circulation. He noticed his cock, strapped in, disturbed by the night feeling, which made it move a little, like a ballet dancer impersonating the dawn. That was the only part of his body with a grief of its own, sullen in his pants. But if ever it tried to sprout, he need only remember, like admonishing a dog, and it would shrivel and withdraw.

Yet it had always had independent thoughts. Even in the good days of his marriage, there was always this doggy part of him noticing things, Francesca Hooton and the student Louise Germane and the girls in bikinis with leopard spots at the beach. Always this muffled little anarchic hope which he disclaimed, as if it had nothing to do with him.

Now, though, he thought deliberately about women he knew. Francesca Hooton. Eleanor Arthur. Louise Germane. Sex, not love. Love was out, the idea of another marriage inconceivable, but sex he could imagine. But there was a problem in every case. Francesca was married, and though her lawyer husband traveled a lot, Tony didn't want a mess. Nor did he trust her signals. Eleanor Arthur's signals were plainer, and he guessed her husband wanted her to be as free as he, but her nervous edges made Tony edgy, and he could not forget how much older she was than he. With Louise Germane he felt easy and comfortable, but she was a graduate student, and it was not good to get involved with them. Since no one suitable was available, he resigned himself easily.

A few days later the fair haired Francesca Hooton took him to the bookstore to help him get presents for Paula's children. He liked her reticent smile and implicating eyes. Later he accepted a dinner invitation from George and Eleanor Arthur, buffet, a large group. He sat on the edge of the couch with Roxanne Furman talking about the department, glad Eleanor was too busy as hostess to pay attention to him. Shortly before Christmas he got a card from Louise Germane, a tactful note in elegant handwriting. It recalled his suspicion, merely academic when Laura was alive, that she had a crush on him.

He had Thanksgiving dinner with his brother Alex's family in Chicago and managed not to cast gloom over the table. At Christmas he stayed ten days at Paula's suburban house, twenty miles from New York. He liked Merton now, and could not remember why he had disliked him before. He went for walks with the children on the snowy suburban streets, he put on ice skates with them and watched as they tried their new skis on the hill slope above town. In his bedroom at Paula's, in the northwest corner of the house, not much bigger than the bed, with a bookcase full of Paula's books, he felt as if he were starting a new life. The room had new blue mountainy wall paper, it smelled of clean sheets, it looked out on a slope with bare trees. He made a plan.

He left on Thursday after New Year's, going into New York on the train, refusing to let Merton drive him to the airport. He had a notion to resolve the sex question now, before going home. Once he was alone his nerves tightened up like electricity sparking in his chest. He felt it in the train along the river's edge. His breath was tight as he signed the register. The hotel was shabby, near the center of the city. He said to himself, My name is Tony Hastings, professor of mathematics. I live elsewhere. I have been through a bad experience.

I will eat dinner in an expensive elegant place. He found a restaurant in a fancy hotel but had no appetite nor patience for the long waits between courses. After dinner he went out, timidly moving through the crowds, glancing at the sleazy windows, like a hunter trying not to be seen. He thought Ray and Lou and Turk are here, hidden in the crowd, they'll see me. Record shops, food joints, pawn shops, arcades. He said, I am a sexual creature like anybody, but his mind was full of mugging and being rolled. Twisted into a kink in his mind. He went to a bar and surprised himself (though it was what he had planned to do) by sitting next to a woman on a bar stool. She was in her thirties, she wore a black dress with white flowers and a white bow, she had a round face and looked scared.

'Hi,' she said.

'Hi.'

'You got a name?'

'Tony. What's yours?'

'Sharon.'

She let him take her home in a taxi. He was nervously astonished by his success, since he had a deep fear of strangers and had never before picked up a woman in a public place. He was still afraid and wondered if he was going to his death, but her own anxiety relieved his fear somewhat. On the way she said, 'In case you're wondering, I'm not a prostitute.'

He wondered if that meant she would turn him away at the door. She said, 'I'm a working girl, I work in a department store. I'm a singles.'

On the stairs she said she liked to meet new people, but most of the men she picked up were creeps. He hoped he wasn't a creep. She hoped so too. She was forcing herself to talk. He noticed she was shivering. 'Are you cold?' he said.

'Not really.'

She had a flat three flights up. When she got to the door she took a deep breath as if to force her shivering to stop. She glanced at him apologetically. 'I get nervous,' she said.

He tried to put his hand on her shoulder. She slipped away, then grabbed his hand and pointed to his ring.

'Cheating on your wife, I see.'

'My wife is dead.'

She fished in her purse for the key and let him in. She told him to be quiet, her roommate was asleep in the other room.

Her own room was small. It had picture postcards on a bulletin board above her bed. She had an open wardrobe with dresses in it.

'What did she die of?'

'She was murdered.'

He sat on the bed and told Sharon about it. She sat motionless on the other chair, looking at him without expression. He told the story first in summary fashion, the main events. Then, though he didn't mean to, he got into detail. He went back to the beginning and described it step by step. She stared at him blankly, listening.

'Gee mister,' she said. 'You're giving me the creeps.'

He was describing the mannequins in the bushes, and suddenly he identified the look on her face, staring at him while he talked. Terror. She was a stranger, but he was a stranger too.

He stopped, shocked himself. It was not the conjured visions of Ray, Turk, and Lou she was terrified of.

'Sorry,' he said. 'I get carried away.'

She was looking around the room, like measuring distances.

After a moment he said, 'Do you want me to go?'

'Yeah,' she said. 'I guess you better.' Shivering again.

Once he was out in the hall she looked relieved. She leaned against the door, ready to push it shut if he changed his mind. 'Did I scare you?' he said. 'I didn't mean to.'

'Shit,' she said. 'Listen, I'm real sorry for your wife and kid, okay?'

He went down the stairs, relieved too.

On the way back to the hotel, Ray and Turk and Lou were in the street, in the shadows of doorways, the subway, watching him, while the big eyes of Sharon absorbed Laura and Helen into herself. She was killing his memory, defiling them.

So he brought it back. In the trailer Ray commanded them to strip. Turk held his knife to Helen's throat while Ray forced Laura on the bed. Then Helen's turn. When Laura yelled and charged, Ray smashed her in the head. Mother! Helen screamed. Screaming and crying, her mother destroyed on the floor, while Ray twisted her arm until it broke.

Something like that. Damn them to hell, Tony Hastings said.

## THREE

Susan puts the manuscript down. What's bothering me? she says. As she watches Tony groping in the sordid city for sex, she wonders if this will continue to be a story for her. When Tony was in the woods, horror transcended gender. But the struggle to recover manhood is different. Tony looking for a sex object: she gets no thrill from that.

What's bothering her is something else. Reading pushes through the sea like a swimmer. The creatures of Susan's daylight mind, animals of land and air, sink into it, converted into dolphins, submarines, fish. Something bites her while she swims, a small toothy shark. She needs to drag it into the air where she can see. While Tony Hastings grieves, it bites.

When the sea recedes she's back to Arnold on the telephone. She remembers a reproach. I wish you hadn't asked that, he said.

What did she ask?

At some point in the conversation he suggested commuting to the Washington job. Let her stay in Chicago with the kids, and he could fly home weekends. She remembers – by a process of association: commuting, which would mean two homes for him, which implies –

The question he reproached her for was whatever it was. He asked why she wanted to know, and she said something. That did not satisfy him, he probed, she resisted, and he said, You're asking about Linwood.

I didn't say that, she said.

She heard his impatient intake of breath. You did ask. So I'll tell you. It hasn't been decided. It's an opportunity, and she has a sister in Washington. I thought you understood. I wish you hadn't asked that question.

He wished she hadn't asked that question.

There's nothing to do but drop it back into the sea. Back to Tony, who gives the poor singles woman the creeps. She wonders if Edward invented Tony's grief by imagining how he would feel if something happened to Stephanie, if that's how he did it.

## *Nocturnal Animals 14*

When Tony Hastings returned home in the afternoon, there was a note in his mailbox from the local police, please call.

'Please call?' the woman said. 'Let's see. Hastings, you? Andes, Pennsylvania, call immediately. Would that be it?'

Could be. 'I don't know who you're supposed to call in Andes,' she said.

'Andes is a person.'

He called the number and got someone named Muskacs, who said, 'Andes ain't here.'

He left word and hurried to the pizza restaurant so as to be back by eight. The call came promptly.

'Hastings? I been trying to get you for three days.'

'I went to New York for Christmas. Visiting my sister.'

'A trip, huh? And now you gotta take another one.'

'What?'

'I want you to fly to Albany New York tomorrow, meet me.'

'What for?'

'Good news.'

'Tomorrow?'

'We'll pay. There's a plane you can meet me the airport at noon.'

'I have a class tomorrow.'

'Cancel it.'

'What's it about?'

'I just want you to look at some guys.'

'Identify them?'

'That's the idea.'

'Is that the good news?'

'Could be.'

'You think these are the ones?'

'I don't think anything, Tony, until you tell me what to think.'

'How did you catch them?'

'Can't tell you. Tell you later.'

Tony felt a growing thrill: Ray, Lou, and Turk, face to face.

'I have that class tomorrow. It's important.'

'More important than this, man?'

'I'll see if somebody can take my class.'

'Now you're talking. Get this. I want you to call U.S. Air, check in. We've made your reservation. Go in the morning, back tomorrow night, all in one day. I'll be driving there and meet you when you arrive. Can't complain about that, can you?'

Tony Hastings flew to Albany. He felt a growing fright as he stared out the window into the featureless milky sky. The flight attendant gave him ginger ale and a plastic bag of peanuts. He munched, recapitulating the idea of revenge, reminding himself what it was about. Justice, retribution, to end the sentence. What Bobby Andes expected him to feel. The joy of looking them in the eye with the shackles on them and saying, Your turn now.

They would look back into his eye. Was that what he was afraid of? Try to remember. The scene had been rerun so often, replayed so many times, the print was blotched, color faded, touch and taste dulled. But he was going back to it, to the very time. Try, you must remember.

The man across the aisle in the plane had a black beard. He also had a suit and tie and a clipboard in his lap. He looked like Lou except for his clothes. There was a man with glasses and a briefcase in the back who looked like Turk. The man in a jump suit with earphones on the tarmac in Pittsburgh had a triangular face, teeth bigger than his mouth, like Ray.

They will look at you, but why should you fear? They will be captive, under restraint. Bobby Andes will take care of you.

As he walked through the carpeted tunnel out of the plane, Tony Hastings wondered if he would recognize Bobby Andes.

He remembered Bobby Andes as short, fat, with a large head and smooth shiny cheeks shaded with pepper. He knew the man approaching was Andes, not because he recognized him but because Andes was supposed to meet him. Strange around the eyes, quickly ceasing to be strange, he remembered those eyes and thick lips, and it was the simplified remembered picture in his mind that had been wrong. In another moment, as they walked together through the long passageways toward the exit, the simplified picture was gone, the strangeness obliterated.

'We're going to Ajax,' Andes said. 'That's twenty miles from here. The meeting's at two. It won't take you five minutes. Then you can go home.'

'You want me to identify them?'

'Just say if you recognize anyone. If you do, you can sign a statement.'

'You got all three?'

'Never mind what we got. Just tell us who you know.'

'How did you catch them? Fingerprints?'

'Never mind, I told you. Afterwards okay. Beforehand nix.'

They drove out of the city, through fields on a fast two-lane road. Ajax was a factory town on a river. They went to an old brick building with concrete pillars. Up an old staircase under a stained glass window. In the room, a tall white haired man with a used face. Bobby Andes introduced. 'Captain Vanesco, Tony Hastings.'

Captain Vanesco was polite. They sat at a desk. 'Lieutenant Andes has told me your case,' he said. 'Do you feel intimidated by these people? Is there any reason you might hesitate to put the finger on anyone?'

As a matter of fact – but Tony was ashamed and said, 'No.'

Vanesco said, 'The people we are interested in are prisoners. They will not be released if you identify them.'

Bobby Andes said, 'Listen Tony, your testimony is damned important. Do you realize that?'

'Yes.'

'We don't have hardly anything else. Do you realize that?'

Vanesco said, 'Not all the people you are about to see are suspects. We do this to give the suspects a fair shake. If you can pick them out from others that strengthens identification.'

Tony was uneasy. He said, 'A lot of time has passed.'

'I understand.'

'It all took place at night.'

Vanesco said, 'Are you saying you didn't get a clear look at their faces?'

'I think I did, but it was dark.'

'I understand. Here's my advice. If you're unsure, pass. Because if you recognize someone it comes with a click, gestalt, do you know that word? Only don't pass too quick. Sometimes it takes a while for the click to come. The person might look like a stranger for a few minutes before he focuses and clicks. So if you're unsure, wait for the click.'

They went out and down the stairs to a room like a classroom. They sat in the front row.

Vanesco said, 'We're going to show you four men. I won't tell you how many are suspects. I want you to look and if you recognize anyone, from anywhere anytime, tell me.'

'When do I tell you?'

'As soon as you're sure.'

'Before they leave?'

'Don't worry,' Andes said. 'Nobody's killing you here.'

Tony Hastings pushed back in the classroom chair, trying to relax so as to breathe. He remembered the shivering Sharon climbing to her Village flat. A door opened and a policeman came in followed by four men. They stood in bright light in front of the blackboard. Tony Hastings looked at them bewildered.

The first man was big. He wore a red T-shirt stretched tight around his chest and had a round droopy face with blond fuzzy hair and a small mustache. The second man, not so big, wore a checked flannel shirt and had a bony face, calculating eyes, a blond forelock down his forehead. The third man, about the same size as the second, had glasses with large black frames, sparse dark hair and a bushy black mustache. He wore a jump suit and his face was puffy. The fourth man was short and scrawny. He wore an old shabby suitcoat without a tie and had silver rimmed glasses. Tony Hastings did not recognize any of them.

He sat a long time studying them, trying to remember. The men with their hands behind their backs grew restive, shifting weight from one foot to the other. The two with glasses looked at some mystic vision above his head in the back of the room. The blond man with the bony face glared as if trying to figure out who *he* was, while the big one with the droopy face darted furtive glances around the room. Guilty – but no one Tony had ever seen.

Faced with this unfamiliar four, Tony could no longer remember Ray or Lou or Turk, though their images had burned in his living thoughts for six months. He tried to bring them back. Could Ray have been as big as the big blond man? Never mind the mustache, could he put on so much weight in six months? Or the man with the bony face? Gradually he brought back to mind a rudimentary Ray, recovered the bald forehead, restored the triangular face, the big teeth in the small mouth. And the large intimidating eyes. So Ray at least was not here. What about Lou, who had led him down the woody road and forced him out of the car where the bodies of his wife and daughter were soon to be dumped? What would Lou look like if his black beard were shaved off? Rule out Lou. What of Turk? He remembered Turk's glasses, but not dark framed like these. If Turk grew a mustache? Tony Hastings was beginning to sweat. He had not paid enough attention to Turk, shadowed by his more vivid companions.

He thought: the man with the dark framed glasses might be Turk. He began to see familiarity in him, as if he had known him once. A long time ago. But not definitely, not with the click Vanesco needed. Though Tony Hastings thought he knew that man, he could not remember Turk. All he had left of Turk was a generic image, man with iron rimmed glasses.

He heard Bobby Andes breathing heavily beside him. One of the men in front muttered, 'Jesus!'

The bony man said, 'If it takes you this long to decide, it's no case.'

Now Tony was sure the man with the dark framed glasses was Turk. On the other hand, he could not remember Turk, therefore he could not be sure. Since making a false identification was worse than making none, he sighed and said, 'I'm sorry.'

Bobby Andes hissed. 'Take them out,' Vanesco said.

Bobby Andes flung his clipboard on the floor. 'For God's sake, man!' he said.

'I'm sorry.'

Vanesco was mild. 'It's all right. If you can't be sure, it's better to pass.'

'There goes our whole shittin case,' Andes said. To Vanesco: 'This means I can't have him, right?'

'That's up to you. If you've got the evidence.'

Bobby Andes said: 'Fuck!'

Tony said, 'There's a faint possibility – '

'What?'

'There's one guy who just might, I couldn't be sure.'

'You want to bring him back, bring him back!'

'Wait,' Vanesco said.

'I'm not sure, that's the problem.'

'One? Bring em back!'

'Wait,' Vanesco said. 'Which one, Tony?'

'The third one, glasses and mustache. If he's changed his glasses and grown a mustache.'

Bobby Andes and Captain Vanesco looked at each other for a long moment.

'Which one would he be? Ray? Lou?'

'I'm not saying he is. I'm very unsure. If he is one, he'd be the one they called Turk.'

'Turk.'

'And the others?'

'The others are out.'

Vanesco asked, 'Would you be willing to make a positive identification of this Turk?'

'I said I can't. I can't be sure. The only thing makes me think he's Turk is you brought me here to identify them. You have some reason for connecting them with the case.'

Vanesco and Bobby looked at each other. Vanesco shook his head and said, 'Not enough.'

Going out the door he put one hand on Bobby's shoulder, the other on Tony's, like a father. 'Think of it this way. It's a start. You'll have to develop more evidence.' To Tony he said, 'Don't feel bad. It's hard to form an image in the dark.'

Bobby Andes drove Tony Hastings back to the Albany airport. He was angry. 'You sure let me down, baby,' he said. They drove for miles along the valley floor saying nothing.

'I couldn't be certain,' Tony said.

'Yeah.'

Bobby Andes said, 'The guy you said "might" be Turk. Would you like to know who he is?'

'Yes.'

'That's Steve Adams, boy. That's the guy whose fingerprints were on your trunk. That's the circumstantial fact, he put his fucking hands on your car, and you never saw him before.'

Steve Adams, man in the picture: long hair to the shoulder, beard like a prophet. They sure do change. The original Turk so little distinguished that Tony could remember only the generic glasses was much more ordinary than either of the Steve Adamses.

Maybe Steve Adams's fingerprints had been put on the trunk at some other time, by a pump man in a gas station.

'Want to know the rest?' A sneer in Andes's voice.

'Yes of course.'

'They was three guys trying to make off with a car from a used car lot. One got away. Fingerprints turn up this Steve Adams, wanted by me. If you'd identified him, they would have extradited him to me.'

Later Bobby Andes broke another silence. 'How can you develop more evidence when the witness don't cooperate?'

'I do want to cooperate.'

Let him out at the departure doors. 'I doubt if I'll see you again,' Andes said. 'I don't see much future in this case.'

Tony Hastings bent down to the car window, wanting to shake his hand, but Bobby Andes drove off too quick. In the plane Tony felt sure: the man in the dark rimmed glasses was Turk.

# FOUR

Bathroom. Susan Morrow puts the manuscript down, goes upstairs. Music fights in the house. Through the closed study door, American commerce, a teary male voice trying to sell her little daughter the joys of cars and beer. Upstairs, *Parsifal*, ceremonial, exotic, music as perfume.

'Rosie, go to bed!'

Pursuing the murderers, a new direction in Tony's story, a complication. Susan's glad of that. She sympathizes with Tony's difficulty identifying Turk, and the scene embarrasses her as if it were her fault. How people recognize each other fills her with wonder. She confused the man selling storm windows with her neighbor Gelling, yet knew Elaine at the airport even though she has turned into a sphere. Back in the living room she knocks Martha off the manuscript again. There's another uncomfortable undertow below her reading, residue of suppressed thought, or else it's the same one still. She wishes it would go away.

## *Nocturnal Animals 15*

Tony Hastings was in bad shape. Trying to figure out the telephone call last night at three. The voice said, 'So this is Tony Hastings is it?'

'Who is this?'

'Nobody. I just wanted to hear your voice.'

People were avoiding him. He overheard. Jack Appleby in his office: 'It's gone on long enough.' In the coffee room, Myra Lopez, 'He thinks he deserves special consideration.' His friends had discovered how much his acceptability in their houses had depended on his wife's grace and charm. He knew what they were thinking. Without her he was a dark absence. The students mocked him behind his back. The girls avoided his eyes and watched his moves, ready to slap a suit on him. He looked up *pariah:* a low caste Indian with a turban chained next to the goat in the yard with the ragged castaway on the beach.

They were blaming him but wouldn't say so to his face. How easily he has recovered. That charade party at the Malks. The way he hangs on, sullen and morose, as if singled out by God. Didn't you wonder about his story, why he didn't resist?

By now it was March. He shouted at the student in his office. 'I told you at the beginning of the quarter. If you want to file a grievance, file a grievance.' The student was an athlete. He had a T-shirt with a 24 on it. He had large angry eyes and his head was bald except on the sides. He had a small chin. He strode out saying, 'You'll hear from me,' and Louise Germane came in to deliver papers she had graded for him. She must have heard something, or perhaps she had not. She said, 'Mr. Hastings, are you all right?'

He said something, and she said, 'I know what you're going through. Are you getting any help?'

'You mean a shrink? No one knows what I'm going through, and I don't need graduate students to advise me.'

Oh, she was sorry, but Tony Hastings, less angry than he sounded, sent her away. Then he was ashamed. Play actor. Poor Louise Germane, probably the only student left who liked him. He had fixed that, all right. He hurried out to look for her.

He found her in the coffee shop. 'I want to apologize,' he said. 'That was stupid of me.'

'That's all right, Mr. Hastings.' The tall girl, her wheat colored hair, loose flowing, the relieved smile. She said, 'I want you to know, if there's anything I can do. We're pulling for you.'

Her looking eyes, sea blue, yearning to be interpreted. He accepted a long idle coffee talk. Allowed himself to talk about Laura. He noticed the glaze coming over her face but kept on talking. She said, 'Thank you for telling me. I appreciate it.'

He said, 'Tell me about yourself.'

She spoke of brothers and sisters, he didn't follow, his concentration not so good. He asked why she was in graduate school. She told him.

It occurred to him her plans were naive and silly, and he said, 'What are you going to do when the world blows up?'

She looked at him in dismay. 'You mean, the bomb?'

'The Bomb. *It*. The rain. The scorch.'

She was bewildered. 'Maybe it won't blow up.'

Ha! Tony Hastings shook his head and smacked his lips and leaned back in his chair and told her. He told about the white peacekeeping missiles with the future of the world in their skins, warheads with a city in each, and programmed retaliation for after the people are dead. He spoke of the sun-blast that shoots through human flesh like a grid. He said *preemptive strike* and *lead time*. He told how after the blast comes the fire and then the fallout for those beyond the fire, and then the heavy blackout clouds, and he said *nuclear winter* and *blackened cinder*. 'You think it won't happen?'

She said, 'The cold war is over.'

He felt cold superior rage. 'You think so, do you? The rest of the world is coming. Arabs, Pakistani. Third World. Everybody will have it. You think they have no grievance?'

She said, 'I'm more worried about the greenhouse effect.'

But she wasn't worried enough. He pointed at her: 'The world is dying. The diseases are advanced, the death twitches have begun.'

She said: 'Anyone might die in an accident tomorrow.'

He attacked: 'The traditional knowledge that others will live on after you is not like the knowledge mankind is dying and everything anyone lived for is wiped out.'

Mild civilized Tony Hastings: crank, crotchet, curmudgeon. Easy to sizzle. Sometimes he sizzled all day. The morning paper at breakfast full of outrage, editorials, letters, stupidity, prejudice. On a particular April morning he saw a neighbor boy taking a shortcut through his yard behind Mr. Husserl's house. Tony Hastings ran after him. 'Hey you!'

The kid stopped. 'I thought we could go through.'

'You're supposed to ask permission. Ask for permission.'

'Can I have permission, mister?'

Wave him on. The garden was brown, new green poking up through sticks. The weeds were coming. They were on the march, and soon Mrs. Hapgood would be too, telephone calls and complaints. Someone forgot to put a notice of the faculty meeting in his box. To the secretary, calm: I'd just like to know who was responsible. It was Ruth who distributed the notices. Did I miss you? she said. You're sure it's not shuffled in with your other things? Control yourself back to the office.

The softball hit the windshield. His brakes screeched. He opened the door, ran out, grabbed the ball out of the gutter before the boys could get there.

'God damn it, you could kill someone.'

'Can we have our ball please?'

He slammed the door and locked it, remembering. Five boys gathered around, violently trying to hold him prisoner by standing in front of the car, while they banged on the hood pleading and bullying. 'That's our ball,, mister.'

He started the car, tried to edge forward. What held him? If it was a question of violence, his car could run right over them. Their violence depended on his pacifism. He inched forward, pushing them back. What right had they to assume he was law-abiding, or to take advantage of it? They stepped aside, all but one, white faced, who pushed his hands against the front and retreated one backward step at a time as the car forced him on. His face as furious as Tony felt, lips pressed together, eyes hot. Then he too gave way, yelled, 'Son of a bitch,' and banged the window as Tony roared by. Zipping into the next block, Tony watched in the mirror. Their ball. Expect more telephone calls tonight. He opened the window and flung it out. The boys in the mirror chased it among the parked cars.

Calm down Tony, take it easy. The house was church, where he prayed his ghosts to restore his soul. Worship service. He put his books on the table and went to the shelf in the living room where he kept the album. Prayer book. He leaned back in the chair and closed his eyes. Tableau. She sits on the couch, he in the chair, Helen on the floor leaning against the coffee table, saying 'You did? No kidding?'

Bible lesson. 'Then I began to wonder why I found myself talking to him every day as we came out of class and suddenly I realized he was waiting for me, and I was thrilled.'

Helen amused. 'You sound like a couple of kids.'

'We were a couple of kids.'

Tradition. 'Your father is the steadiest of men. That's worth something over the long haul.' Praise Daddy.

History. The spirit of inquiry, giggling. 'You know what I mean? It's absolutely impossible to imagine you two as lovers.'

'Your Daddy is very loving in his way.'

Mystery. The question Helen wanted to ask but did not want answered, which she never asked because not to answer was as much an answer as an answer.

Ritual. April a year ago on bikes after dinner. Signs of the coming, buds, new birds. Daughter leads the way, changing the route each evening, different turns around different blocks. Daddy goes last, guarding the others through the quiet streets, alert when a car goes by, tense when they come out to the main street between the parked cars and the traffic. When they get home it's dark. Homework time, no television tonight folks. Peace now, all dangers have been left behind.

The steadiest of men, loving in his way, taking coffee in the coffee shop, waved to Louise Germane in a booth with a student named Frank Hawthorne. He did not like this Hawthorne, it displeased him to see her with him, he wondered how to tell her. Frank Hawthorne had a greasy face and a dirty beard, his hair was tangled and bushy, his eyes looked out like an animal in the weeds, lips bulged through his beard like internal organs oozing through an open wound. He remembered Hawthorne's cheating case, hushed up to improve his character. Also the pigeon case: two guys with a baseball on the slope below Tony's office, Hawthorne standing by. 'Gimme that,' Hawthorne says, then hurls a fast ball into a flock of pigeons, which would have killed or maimed if it had hit. A girl complains, 'Don't do that. I like them.'

'Dirtier than rats,' Hawthorne, the virtuous murderer, says. In the coffee shop Tony Hastings wondered how to warn Louise.

So he asked Francesca the next time he saw her. She smiled at him. 'Why bother? If he's a skunk, she'll find out.'

'None of my business, you mean.'

'Unless you have other business you're not mentioning.'

That was at lunch. He said, 'I've been irritable lately.'

'I've noticed. Do me a favor,' she said. 'Don't get involved with a graduate student. You don't need that.'

'What do I need?'

There was a moment while she looked at him. The look grew long, it meant something. Serious, no smile, blue eyes speaking. It passed and she was smiling again in her usual way of partial implication, balanced complicity. He thought, I missed something. I have just been told, and now it is too late.

But he ate lunch with her regularly in the Faculty Club. Her look, reminiscent and kind. He thought: She is my only friend. She remembered him as he was. She knew he didn't want to be this way. He looked at her and thought, lovely, beautiful.

So he said, 'Today's Thursday.'

'What about it?'

'You're free this afternoon.'

'So?'

Spaghetti, curling on her fork, she avoided his eyes. Leap. 'May I take you somewhere in my car?'

Mouth upturned receiving spaghetti, she wiped tomato sauce off her elegant mouth. 'Where?'

'Anywhere.'

'All right.'

That's all. They drove to an overlook above the river, where they could hear the trucks below the bluff. They looked at the view, near another car with a couple looking at the view, and he felt a sexual surge generating steam like nothing he had felt in nine months, not even his night in New York.

He talked about the carbon dioxide shield, the growing warmer, the coming desert under the cancerous sun. He saw his eloquence carrying him away. He saw she was bored. He thought, I'm not a nice person any more, and his sexual feeling died.

He took her home, wondering if she would invite him in, but she did not. She thanked him for the afternoon, and he saw no magic in her routine eyes. She went up to her house, and a little girl came out to greet her.

He drove off abruptly enough to make the tires squeal. Stopped hard for the light, screech, then dashed into the intersection. Feeling something, he did not know what. He went out to the expressway, buzzed ahead of the car in front of him, slipped back and forth one lane to another. Blasted his horn at a car in the middle, nudging him along until he could get by.

When the wildness settled, he drove home and rested in his living room. What was this, Laura still refusing to let go? It seemed like something else. As if he needed a ceremony to return Tony to Tony. He imagined a primitive god, male and savage.

The image made him laugh, but the laughter had no feeling, and the next moment he had this overwhelming conviction that no thought of his had any feeling. He saw all his recent behavior on a screen with light shining through, disclosing emptiness. His wild driving on the road an hour ago, a display to conceal something he did not have. The revelation spread, it delved into the past, all the way back to the catastrophe, and all it found was counterfeit or fake. Phony feelings acted out. It frightened him, not for the abyss but for what would happen if anyone found out, thinking, This is something no one must know. A secret. In the late afternoon inside his house, he looked for his soul and saw only white indifference beneath the calculated displays of grief and, as that became wearisome, irritability and rage. He recognized the privileges grief had given him. What no one knew was how he had fooled them. He was an artificial man, fabricated of gestures.

He paced around the house totally free. A vague anger led him to his desk, where he typed out the following note to Bobby Andes:

> Just to say I'm now certain the one I couldn't identify was Turk. I hope you are not easing up your hunt for those men. I promise to cooperate in every possible way, for I am more determined than ever to bring them to justice.

# FIVE

The next page has a notice: PART THREE. Good. A change, Susan Morrow's had enough of this. She wonders if Edward expects a compliment on the internal organs oozing through the beard. Perhaps the pariah with the turban and the castaway goat was something he forgot to revise.

How far can she read tonight? She looks ahead to calculate. Right now we're about midway, should finish tomorrow. Take a break.

'Rosie, bed!'

Tiny voice upstairs. 'I yam in bed, Mama.'

Jeffrey wants to go out. She opens the door, lets him go. Not supposed to, but it's late, no one will know. Keep out of trouble, mister. She goes to the kitchen. Snack, a Coke? The kitchen is cold, temperature dropping outside. In the study she hears the voices of a television sitcom, nobody watching, someone left it on all evening.

She feels bruised by her reading and by life too. She wonders, does she always fight her books before yielding to them? She rides back and forth between sympathy for Tony and exasperation. If only she didn't have to talk to Edward afterwards. If you say Tony is going mad – or turning into a jerk – you need to be sure Tony is not really Edward.

Now he's Tony the artificial man. She wonders about that. Generally Susan is skeptical about words like hollow and superficial. Is *she* hollow or full? Damned if she knows, but she doesn't want someone else deciding for her. If Edward is condemning Tony through Tony's own voice, that's old judgmental Edward again. When he judges she resist. But she also has a notion of a fairer second reading, later when the soreness has eased and everything is past.

In any case, Part Three. Something has ended. Is it Three of Three or Three of Four? If three, a sonata: A B A. What would that mean, back to the woods? If four, a symphony? Statement, funeral march, scherzo, finale. We have a crime, a victim, a reaction, and a so far unsuccessful search for the killers. She thinks, she thinks: will Tony Hastings be destroyed or redeemed? A bad happy ending would ruin everything, but it's hard to imagine what a good one would be.

## *Nocturnal Animals 16*

When Bobby Andes did not answer his letter, he sent another.

> Repeat: I hope you are actively pursuing these men, not just waiting for something to fall into your lap. I hope you urged Ajax to pressure Adams to name his accomplices. The case warrants the attention of police nationwide, and I hope you have made the proper moves towards getting such attention. This is a matter of utmost importance to me. I hope you do not regard it as routine or insoluble.

In his car driving home late on a flowered May day, he lectured to himself. Other drivers thought he was cussing the traffic. He said, It's not the clotty rush hour nor drivers tailgating. Not boys throwing softballs at cars. Not the evil editorials of the morning papers, nor greedy students trying to get away with something, nor disgusting Frank Hawthorne. Not even greenhouse or nuclear war. There's but one crime, one evil, one grievance. It was you who did it to me, no criminals or devils but you. Everything else is distraction.

He thought, if Bobby Andes finds the letter provocative that's all right. If it annoys him, so much the better. Two weeks passed, and he realized again there would be no answer. Tony Hastings in pain, waiting for word from a detective in Pennsylvania who had the care of his health and hope of rescue in the month of May. The green of his yard was bright and full of yellow, the green weeds invaded the old brown. There were bright sky days, lawns mowing, gardens digging, but not Tony Hastings, resisting with last summer's business. He preferred the night, when you couldn't be seen looking out the darkened windows.

Since he knew what he wanted, he could wait. Be less disagreeable to innocent people. He pointed it out to Francesca Hooton at lunch. 'I have been blaming a lot of wrong people. I know whose fault it is now.'

'You've finally decided to be angry?'

Alone in his big house he talked on, perfecting a rage. He said, You think it's easy to become Tony Hastings? It takes forty years. It needs loving mother and intellectual father, a summer place, lessons on the back porch. Sister and brother to fence temper and create sensitivity to others' distress. Years of reading and study and wife and daughter to force pain into habit and make a man.

But it's even harder to become Laura Hastings. Assembled in the long accumulating day by day as Laura Turner, by Meyer Street and Dr. Handelman, with Donna and Jean, the lake in the mist and the death of Bobo and the studio, Laura

Hastings is not completed but just begun in her forty years of life. Laura Hastings is (was) not the life she lived but the forty years yet to be lived, as promised.

Beasts, do you think it easier to replace Helen Hastings? Hers is the longest lifetime of all, fifty to sixty years just begun, extracted from the outgrown child by the growing world, from the original Laura-Tony germ to sleepy song and Little Golden Book, momdad and doggie love with notebooked poems to the unbreakable contract of a grownup Helen-in-the-world.

Nothing, beasts, is harder to build or more impossible to replace than the unlived years of these three. Not your cars, your cocks, your sleazy girlfriends, your own ratty little souls. Tony Hastings imagined those cars, cocks, girlfriends and souls. He lived among them, looking for words to make his hatred overwhelming. A story, an account sufficiently degrading. Of stupid grown men who got this notion from movies or television and school bullies of how to be a man by pushing people around. Let's go out on the road and scare the squares. No more teachers' dirty looks, let's get the prissy girls and the tight-assed schoolmoms, give em a taste. If you get in trouble, knock them off. Tony Hastings looked for words adequate to his rage. Vile, wretched, cowardly. Low, vicious, despicable. Not evil: that word gave them too much dignity. The words he sought were lower and worse than evil. With such rhetoric he tried to replace the soul he thought he had lost.

The telephone in the afternoon: as he went to it he already knew what it was. He heard the harsh distant voice materializing his thought, 'I'm calling Tony Hastings, is this Tony Hastings?' He was right, they were both right. 'Andes, here.'

He heard. 'You want to identify somebody else?'

'Who is it?'

'I ain't telling. I ask if you want to tell *me* who it is?'

'When? Where?'

'Soon as you can come. Here. It's Grant Center this time.'

So he prepared for another trip. Not to fail this time. This time I'll see and know who it is, Ray or Lou or again Turk. Going overnight, he packed his bag wild with excitement, took one plane and stepped off another, a little commuting one, at a small airport in a valley. Bobby Andes was waiting behind a fence. He got into the car and they drove past fields and woods and under the edges of hills. Return to the land of terror.

'That was a couple insistent letters you wrote,' Andes said. 'You really want them guys?'

'What happened?'

'You tell me first. You going to mouse out on me again like before?'

'I meant what I said in my letters.'

'How come the change?'

'It's no change. I want those guys caught.'

'You don't want to give no false identifications, you know. I'll tell you what we got. We got an attempted holdup of a supermarket in Bear Valley Mall just before closing time. We got one guy caught and one killed. We got one guy got away, just like the other time.'

'How did that happen?'

'I'll tell you. There was three guys, dumb jerks, two in the store, one in the car outside. They don't see the manager in the back. The cashier puts her hands up like they say, the manager comes down the aisle with his gun, yells, "Drop that gun!" The idiot turns and shoots without looking, hits the Wheaties boxes, Wheaties shower. The manager shoots back.

The manager's a good shot. Got the guy in the chest, knocked him down, out of contention. They operated on him in the hospital. Twelve hours later he died.'

Tony Hastings quiet, wondering who died, not sure if good news or bad. 'What about the others?'

'Wait. The other guy in the store, he runs. The manager runs after him. He tries to get into the car, but a cop comes tearing around the corner. Manager calls, cop shouts warning, guy in the car starts up, other guy never does get in. The cop shoots out the tire, the driver of the car surrenders, but the running guy gets away.'

'How did he manage that?'

'Disappeared. Took off running when the cop started to shoot, ducked behind a car somewhere, I don't know. Not enough manpower to follow, don't know where he went.'

Tony asked, 'What do you want me to do?'

'See if you recognize the guy we caught.'

'You want to tell me why I might recognize him?'

'Later, later.'

They were coming back to where it began, the fields and hillsides, still in early green infiltrating the brown and gray winter that had fallen between. He recognized nothing until they drove into the police lot with the motel across the way.

'You might take a look at the corpse too, though it's not strictly necessary,' Andes said. 'We know who he is.'

'Who?'

'Steve Adams. The one you called Turk.'

'Turk? Dead?'

'Know him by the fingerprints.'

'I thought he was in jail in Ajax.'

'He jumped bail. So I'm told.'

Tony Hastings was trying to figure out the difference in

Bobby Andes's appearance. It was his loss of weight, grooves around his mouth and nose and under his eyes where it had been greasy smooth before.

Tony Hastings checked in across the street. When he came back, Andes said, 'I guess you'd like a lineup like the other time.'

'I thought that's what I was here for.'

'I could take you to see him and ask you who the hell he is, but I guess you'd prefer the lineup, more up and up.'

'Whatever you say.'

'Go get some coffee. If we're going to have a lineup I need to round up some guys.'

There was something not wholly serious about the lineup when they finally got to it. They had it in the office with the desks. They put Tony at one of the desks. Six people came in from the side door and stood in a row in front of the counter. It was a moment before Tony realized this was the lineup. The first of the six was a woman in brown who had been sitting a few minutes before at the desk where Tony sat now. She was giggling. The second was a policeman in uniform, trying not to grin. He looked familiar, and Tony wondered if they were trying to trick him by disguising the suspect. Later he realized this was the policeman named George who had brought him back from the crime in the woods on that day. The third and fourth people were handcuffed to each other. One was a heavy man with yellow hair, dressed like a garage mechanic, the other was an old man in a dirty open-collar shirt. The fifth and sixth were also handcuffed. Both wore beards and plaid shirts. The beard of one was brown and full. He looked independent and intelligent. The other's beard was black and clumsily trimmed. His eyes groped around the room in confusion, and Tony

Hastings watched in amazement as the unknown face turned like merging binocular images into a face he knew.

He knew by the eyes which had looked at him differently in the night, and the mouth in the beard also different then. He watched the man looking around the room, not knowing why he was there, who had not yet located Tony at the desk, whose eyes then passed over Tony without recognition, not noticing how intently Tony was staring trying to be sure. Testing him now against the woods and the car, superimposing him upon the stored memory, seeing him by the tire with Ray and Turk, in the car beside him as he tried to slow down at the trailer, and in the woods, his distinct words, Out! You'll get killed if you don't watch it!

At last the man noticed Tony staring at him but still did not recognize him. Blank, puzzled. But Tony knew him. Not sure how glad he was, afraid of what being glad could lead to, he whispered to Bobby Andes, 'Yes.'

Andes loud. 'Yes? Yes what? You know somebody?'

'The one with the beard.'

'Which beard? They're two beards there.'

'The one on the end.'

'The man with the beard on the end. The red plaid shirt. The blue jeans? You've seen him before?'

The man with the beard, shirt and jeans was looking at him now, perplexed.

'That's Lou.'

'Lou who? Who's Lou?'

'Lou's the one who drove me, who made me drive his car when the others went off in mine, who made me drive into the woods and left me there.'

'This guy? He don't seem to understand. Lou. Hey, you! Is your name Lou?'

'You know my name. I told you. What's going on?'

'You ever see this man before, Lou? Think carefully. You ever see him?'

Lou staring at Tony. Tony unable to tell if some slow recognition was appearing in the stare. 'No.'

'You sure?'

'I don't know him. Who is he?'

'Tell him, Tony. Tell him who he is.'

'Last summer, you – he – '

'This man?'

'This man and his friends forced us off the road on the Interstate. Then two of them forced their way into my car with my wife and daughter, and this man – '

'This man here? Lou?'

'Yes, Lou, made me drive his car and took me into the woods where he made me get out. Later my wife and daughter were found dead at the same place.'

'What say to that, Lou?'

It was all fear on Lou's face, obscuring whatever recognition there might be. He said, 'I don't know what you're talking about.'

'What do you know about this man's wife and daughter?'

'I never saw him in my life.'

'What do you know about Ray and Turk?'

'Never heard of them.'

To Tony: 'Just one thing now. Are you sure this is the man?'

'Absolutely.'

'Would you swear to it in court under penalty of perjury?'

Tony's breath. 'Yes.'

They took him to the morgue, where they uncovered a waxy gray face with stubble. Eyes closed, no glasses, the nose like a beak, mouth in a grimace, it could have been anybody.

Tony could not imagine this person awake. He had no memory of Turk to mesh with him. He could not even recall the faces of Turk he had been unable to identify in Ajax and in the picture.

'It's hard,' he said. 'I guess it's Turk.'

'You sure?'

'Yes,' he said.

Bobby Andes took him to dinner. He was elated. 'Good man,' he said. 'We got him now.'

Exhilarated. He coughed and coughed. 'We're going to charge him with murder.'

'You got enough evidence?'

'We got you, and we got fingerprints. We're going to check hair samples.'

He ran over the case. 'This Lou, it's his prints on the trailer and the car. That's why I wanted you to look at him.'

'Then he did go back to the trailer after leaving me.'

'Looks like it. Probably he went back and told them where he left you, and that's why they went back with the bodies.'

'To get me.'

'I'm betting your friend Ray was the third in our holdup.'

'The guy who escaped running?'

'The description fits.'

'What happens next?'

'We'll work up the case against Lou. You'll have to come back, you prepared for that? Meanwhile, I'm gonna find Ray.'

Tony Hastings returned home the next morning with shaky joy, the face of Lou, which he thought he wanted to spit in, looking at him with frightened eyes.

## SIX

Looks like we're going to chase crooks, Susan says, with Part Three to mark the point. We've killed Turk, caught Lou, and are after Ray. Good. The crime hangs over this story like a poisonous cloud. It needs to be washed away, which can't be done, Susan believes, without going after the perpetrators. Lou's discomfiture just makes plainer the need to get Ray.

Yet something odd is happening. That facetious police lineup. Tony's identification of Turk in the morgue. What's Edward doing with these hints of sleaze? Complicating the simple division between bad Ray and innocent Tony? It makes her queasy, wondering if she can keep her balance as she follows.

She's queasy too about Tony's little tribute to wife and child, more mannered than usual with its compressed phrases and sparse oddly chosen details. The quease slides into Arnold. She wonders, if he praised her like that, what odd detail would he elevate? As for Edward, she remembers the rowboat in the harbor when he was depressed. He said, I'll descend into oblivion. No one will ever know what I saw or thought. She said, *I'm* in oblivion now. No one knows my visions and thoughts, either. He said, You're not a writer. It doesn't mean as much to you.

### *Nocturnal Animals 17*

He told Francesca Hooton at lunch: 'We got two of them. I identified one and they killed the other.'

She said, 'You're glad?'

'Damn right.'

'They killed one. You're glad of that?'

'Yes.'

'What do you want them to do with the one they caught?'

'Lou? I want to see justice done.'

'What would that be in this case?'

Tony Hastings was not prepared for the question.

'Death? Should he get the death penalty?'

It occurred to him this was a political question. He had always avoided political discussions with Francesca because of her crazy right wing slant. He said, 'Lou's not the important one. The bad one is still at large.'

'Should *he* get the death penalty?'

He thought if Francesca knew his mind, she might think they had killed the principle in him that opposed the death penalty. He admitted, 'I don't know what punishment I want.'

She said, 'You do want them to suffer, don't you?'

The idea made him bite his lip the way he used to as a child. He said, 'I'd like them to have what they did to me.'

'Their wives and daughters killed.'

'No, I don't want that.'

'They themselves should be killed.'

'I suppose so.'

'Like Turk. Are you satisfied how Turk was killed?'

'Turk wasn't important. He went along with Ray.'

'You're not answering my question.'

'I don't know. He was killed in a holdup.'

'So he got what he deserved and you are satisfied.'

'Maybe not. It wasn't a punishment. He didn't know what he was being punished for.'

'You'd like him to know?'

'I'd like them to know what they did. I'd like them to be shown exactly what it was they did.'

'They know what they did, Tony.'

'They don't know what it means.'

'Maybe they do. They just don't care.'

'I'd like to make them care.'

'Repent? Say how sorry they are?'

'I'd like them to know exactly how awful a thing they did.'

'Tony, is that possible?'

'I suppose not.'

'Is it even what you want? Say Ray did learn that. He'd be a different person. Shouldn't he then go free?'

'He mustn't go free.'

'He knows he hurt you, Tony. Count on it, he knows.'

'I'd like to hurt him back.'

'Hurt him. But not kill him?'

'Kill him too. Both.'

'Both? It's not enough for him just to suffer?'

'I'd like him to suffer the agony of dying.'

'Ah. Torture?'

'I would like him to know he is dying and I'd like him to know why. That's what I mean by agony.'

'Would you like to kill Ray yourself?'

'I'd like him to know he is dying because of me.'

'Aha.' She smacked her fist into her hand. 'You *don't* want him to understand how bad he was. You don't give a damn about that. You want him to know he can't hurt you like that and get away with it. Because of who you are.'

'He can't do that to me and get away with it.'

'Now you're talking.'

Her gold-edged hair hung down one side of her face as she leaned on her hand, her eyes eager and beautiful on his behalf.

'I remember Helen lecturing Laura and me what a primitive emotion revenge is. We made a fine distinction between revenge and justice, and I remember how civilized we thought we were.'

'You were civilized. It's Ray who's not.'

'That puts a burden on me,' he said.

'It does if you think it does.'

The latest call came to his office. Louise Germane was there, she had just come in, he wondered what she wanted. He knew the voice: 'Andes here, can you pay us another visit?' He never did find out what Louise had wanted.

This was June, and Tony Hastings was free to travel, his third trip back. He drove his car, taking all day. The next day he sat with Bobby Andes in the top row of bleachers on the first base side, sandlot baseball on Sunday afternoon. The home team's white uniforms had CHEVROLET on their shirts, the visitors in gray wore the name of Poleville, a town fifteen miles up the valley. The outfield stretched to a row of houses beyond a wire fence. Above them was a bluff with trees, and the valley spread in a broad plain on both sides. Cars on the highway watched on the third base side, and when someone got a hit the horns blew.

Wearing a hat and dark glasses, Bobby Andes dropped cigarettes through the boards to the dead grass while the sun glared on his haggard face. The wind was blowing. A dark rain cloud with black undersides lurked over the two round hills across the valley. The sun shone around the black undersides.

They were watching home player number 19, who was sitting on the bench below them, not playing. Tony could see only the back of his uniform from time to time between the heads of fans in the first row. Number 19 was jiggling, fidgety. He was yelling out to the field. Once he turned and grinned up into the bleachers. Not close enough to recognize, his tanned face in the sun with tiny white fisheyes. His name was Ray Marcus, and someone had named him a frequent companion of Lou Bates and Steve Adams. The lieutenant was sure he was Tony's Ray because of the description. The possibility gave Tony chills in the sun.

With no one sitting near, Bobby Andes told Tony about it while the game dragged on. How he got the tip from the guys at Herman's, after questioning Lou and getting nowhere. Herman's, a bar in Topping, thirty miles up the valley from Grant Center. This Lou is a dumb ox, with one strategy: keep your mouth shut. Excellent detective work revealed that Lou came from California with Steve Adams, but nothing would make him tell who the other guy was in the Bear Valley holdup. As for your case, it couldn't have been him because he was in California.

Bobby Andes told about Lou's wife in California who hadn't seen him in a year and a half with good riddance. That was fine detective work too, finding her, though it provided no useful information. Meanwhile Lou was living in Topping with a Patricia Cutler, who was almost as dumb and stubborn as Lou although not quite. Her slightly higher intelligence led her into revealing things Lou's rocky stupidity kept hid, like the helpful admission they were *not* in California last year. And when Bobby Andes told her she wasn't a wife and therefore not protected from giving testimony, she did remember a jerk they went around with, real creep, but not his name nor what he looked like, for he never came around and she never saw him. Which might be true, for he seems to have had his own life separate from theirs.

According to Andes, that didn't matter, because he had what he needed. A good detective knows his people. Lou and

Turk were known in the village, though no one cared to have known them well. They were remembered at Herman's, with gossip, including a rumor about a place in the woods for pickup women which Patricia Cutler did not know about. Which Bobby Andes detective figured was probably your murder trailer before it got notorious.

As for this Ray, first there was a source at Herman's who remembered seeing a third guy with them, and then others remembered. With the folks at Herman's cooperating (because the people around here are peaceful and respect the police and regard these guys as foreigners bringing evil from outside), someone finally showed up who knew your guy's name, which is Ray Marcus from Hacksport, and here we are. Which for Lieutenant Andes pretty well closes the search, even before you take a look at him. Even the god damn name. He told about poking around Hacksport, where Ray Marcus was well known. Work as an odd job man, now in the tool factory, formerly and more usually a miscellaneous assistant, sometimes to the electrician, sometimes the plumber, with a short record of minor offenses. Breaking and entering, assault, a fight in a bar. One rape charge, which the woman dropped the case. And nobody wanting to admit being his friend.

Bobby Andes told how he took a peek at Ray in the factory. Not a bad match to both your description and the guy in the holdup. No fingerprints, but we knew that before.

'I wonder why there weren't any fingerprints,' Tony said.

'His hands were probably on your wife. Hell man, we're lucky to have the ones we do.' He said, 'Does he look familiar?'

'I'll need a closer look.'

'Plenty of time.'

Bobby Andes full of details. He said, 'I assume in the used car case this Ray was not involved. This Lou, maybe.'

'Used car case?'

'Ajax. Where you couldn't recognize Turk. Though you recognized him dead easily enough.'

'I was nervous. He looked different.'

'Yeah, yeah. I'm thinking your Lou might have been the guy who got away in Ajax. The black beard. I'm thinking this Lou and Turk decided to travel a bit and that's what they got into. More bad company. Why do you suppose they came back here? Because of Patricia or because of Ray? It looks to me like Ray has been here all along.'

Tony calculated. This was thirty miles from Bobby's office. It was fifteen miles from the place in the woods where they had taken him. Predators travel far in the night.

A gust of wind came up, blowing dust from the infield across the pitchers' mound and to the benches, stopping the game so the players could wipe their eyes. The shower on the two round hills had disappeared beyond the ridge. Overhead the bright clear sky, and more dark clouds over the other ridge.

In the seventh inning Marcus, number 19, entered the game, out in right field. Someone shouted at him, he grinned back, he did a dance step. He moved his hips in a hula, his face dark and tiny under the beak of his cap.

A ball came his way, he was lazy getting to it, the batter took second. Someone booed. He held up his middle finger, the boos were louder. He caught an easy fly, someone exaggerated a cheer. In the bottom of the ninth he waited in the batter's circle for his turn to bat. 'Let's go down to the backstop and get a closer look,' Bobby Andes said.

They worked through the small crowd to a place behind the backstop. Watched number 19 as he wiggled his legs, kicked and dug at the dirt, swung his bat and pointed it at the pitcher. His teeth and his eyes, tiny spots of white in his ruddy face.

The right type, you could say that. He took a ball and three strikes, not swinging at anything, and with each call said something to the umpire. Tony Hastings tried to see his expression. The man went back to the bench, shouting to someone in the bleachers. He stood for a moment with his bat in his hand. His words broke through a sudden silence. 'Fuck you, asshole.'

From behind the backstop, Tony Hastings watched him in profile as he sat on the bench and took a swig of water with a dipper from the bucket. He took off his cap and ran his arm over his head. The high forehead, the bare front half of his head.

'Looks like him,' Tony said.

'You sure?'

'I'd like a better look.'

'Wait.'

The game ended, the crowd loosened and spread out, fans merged with the players and began to disperse. Tony Hastings followed Bobby Andes into the cluster around the Chevrolet team. Bobby Andes had a baseball. He went up to the Chevrolet pitcher.

'Mr. Kazminski, would you mind autographing this here ball for my son?'

Kazminski, tall, young, surprised, laughed and said, 'Why shore, I'd be glad to.' Tony Hastings looked at Ray nearby. He was standing alone, looking out vaguely at the road, his glove hanging at his side, his cap in his hand. He was chewing, his adams apple went up and down. He looked as if he didn't know what to do. He stood there a long time, Tony looking at him. He turned around. Tony saw directly into his face, their eyes met for a flash, a shock for Tony, but Ray remembered nothing. He looked at the cluster around Kazminski, spat on the ground, and turned away. He walked slowly toward the road by himself.

'Well?'

'That's him,' Tony Hastings said.

# SEVEN

Caught in the excitement of closing in on Ray, Susan at the chapter break has almost forgotten her caution back there when Tony was discussing the death penalty with Francesca. On the question of revenge, Susan's own answer is simple: I'll kill anyone who harms my children. Send me to jail. Tracking down Ray is exactly what she wants, it thrills her. She hopes she's not being manipulated into some ideology she doesn't approve.

*Nocturnal Animals 18*

They watched Ray Marcus get into his car down beyond third base, a dirty green Pontiac, fifteen years old. 'Let's see where he goes,' Bobby Andes said.

They had come in Tony Hastings's car, parked near by. 'I'll drive,' Andes said. There was congestion where they turned out to the main road, Ray's car stopped ahead. They followed him into Hacksport with two cars between. They waited while he parked at a package store and came out with a six-pack, and watched without moving as he drove on two blocks, then turned right. 'He's going home,' Bobby Andes said. 'Let's go.'

They came to where he had left his car by a hydrant on a narrow one-way street parked with cars all the way down. Number 19, he walked on the left sidewalk with the six-pack and his baseball glove. There was a row of small white two-family houses along the street. Andes drove up beside him, with parked cars between. He leaned out the window. 'Hey Ray.'

Ray looked at him.

'Where you going?'

He stopped, said nothing.

'What you doing?'

He stood there behind the intervening car, staring.

'Come here, I want to talk to you.'

'What about?'

'I want to ask you some questions.'

'Fuck you.' He turned and went on.

'Hey look at me. Don't make me come and get you.'

The man stopped again. 'Who the hell are you?'

Bobby Andes held up a plastic case with a piece of paper in the window. His other hand was in his coat.

From a distance Ray squinted at the document Bobby Andes held. He looked around. He shifted his feet. 'What's that?'

'Come and see.'

He came, slowly, between the cars to Bobby's window, bent over, took a look. He took a new look at Bobby Andes in sunglasses, at the grim face under his hat. Tony Hastings watched Ray, closely, closer than he had ever been.

'What's it about?'

'A few questions. That's all. Get in back.'

'What for? I ain't done nothing.'

'Didn't say you did.'

'Ask me here,' Ray said.

'In the car. Okay?'

'Okay okay!' He shrugged his shoulders as if he were humoring Bobby Andes and opened the back door of Tony's car. Bobby Andes stepped out and got in the back seat with him.

'You drive,' Andes said to Tony.

From the back seat, Andes directed Tony where to go. They went down to the end of the street.

'Where you live, Ray?' he said.

'Right there,' Ray said, looking at a small white house with two doors and two mailboxes on the porch. He craned his long neck to look as they passed. Suddenly Tony felt sorry for him.

'A few questions to help us out,' Andes said. 'Turn right, Tony.'

They drove two or three blocks in Hacksport and came out on the main valley road where the sign pointed to Topping 10 and Bear Valley 25 and Grant Center 40.

'Live alone, Ray?'

'What's it to you?'

'It don't matter.'

'I live with someone.'

'I know you do. You live with a woman.'

'So why do you ask?'

'You married?'

'Hell.'

Bobby Andes laughed. Tony driving could not see Ray's face. He was conscious of the large white baseball uniform in the back seat. All he could see in the rearview mirror was his baseball cap. He felt an ugly responsibility: that man the substitute right fielder, picked up and tortured because of me.

'The reason I want to talk to you, we got a friend of yours in Grant Center, maybe you can help us with him.'

No word from Ray.

'Name of Lou Bates, he's in jail, maybe you heard. Two

friends in fact, only one's dead. Steve Adams, you know him.'

'Never heard of either of em.'

'That's funny,' Bobby Andes said. 'You sure you never heard of Lou Bates?'

'Don't know nobody by that name.'

'Maybe you know him by a different name. Think about it. At least you heard what he's in jail for.'

'Nah, what's that?'

'You hear about the holdup at the Bear Valley Mall supermarket? You musta heard about it, the guy getting killed.'

'Why are you asking me? I never heard none of it.'

'Like I say, that's strange. There's a bunch of folks says you and those two was good friends.'

'What folks?'

'Folks. You know a place in Topping called Herman's?'

Long pause before Ray said, 'Yes.'

'You know it? Good. You hang around there a lot?'

'Not a lot. Some.'

'You hang around there with other guys?'

'That doesn't mean I know who they are.'

'No? They's folks say you was hanging around at Herman's with these here Lou Bates and Turk Adams. You know anything about that?'

Another long pause from Ray. 'Is that who they was?'

'You want me to believe you don't know who they was?'

No answer from Ray. Silence in the car, wind blowing by the windows, the long straight road through new green fields in the valley floor between ridges. Heading for Topping, then Bear Valley, with Ray. Tony Hastings must not forget his hate, this man in his head for almost a year.

Ray said, 'What do you want from me?'

'For the moment, just some questions.'

'I ain't done nothin.'

'I ain't said you did.' Another windy silence. Tony could hardly hear the question: 'What would you have done that you say you ain't done?'

'Wha-at? You trying to trap me or something?'

Bobby Andes laughed again. 'What kind of trap could I set, Ray? How could I trap you if you ain't done nothing?'

'It's dumb.'

'What?'

'You're asking dumb questions. What do you want to know? Go on, ask me.'

'I just want to know what you know about that holdup your friends was involved in. If you heard anything, I mean. Or know anything. Only you say they wasn't your friends, only maybe you know them under a different name. So what do you say, Ray?'

Tony Hastings listening longed to hear an opening in Andes's questions, yet he felt uncomfortable about what was going on. Conscious of the baseball uniform and the right fielder wiggling his hips at the crowd, while he tried to remember a man in the woods.

'I don't know nothing about it. They didn't consult me.'

'You did know them?'

'If they was the guys at Herman's, I must of. Slightly.'

'Under a different name.'

'I don't remember their name.'

'Okay, now we have established you're a liar – '

'I ain't no liar. Why do you call me a liar, goddammit?'

'Forget it. I notice a reluctance on your part to tell the truth. There's no reason you shouldn't know Lou and Turk. Lots of people knows them wasn't in that holdup with them. Only *one* of their friends was in it.'

No sound from Ray.

'You any idea who that was?'

'Not me.'

'No rumors, no nothin?'

No answer.

'*I* heard a rumor,' Bobby Andes said.

'Yeah?'

'Some folks is telling me you was the third party.'

'I thought you said it wasn't me.'

This pity Tony was feeling for Ray, it shocked him. He tried to remember. For example: Mister, your wife wants you.

'I never said that, did I? I never said it was you, I never said it wasn't.'

'Hey,' Ray said. 'Are you questioning me?'

'Why yes, that's what we're doing, ain't it?'

'You ain't read me my rights.'

'You know your rights, Ray.'

'You're supposed to read em to me.'

'I read you your rights. Didn't I, Tony?'

Did he? Here's a jolt, if Andes expects Tony to play along.

'Hell. It ain't legal.'

'You've heard them before, Ray, you know them by heart. Any you want me to repeat?'

'It ain't legal. I'm supposed to have a lawyer.'

'Informal questions, Ray, you're helping me out. I haven't charged you with anything yet. If you want a lawyer, we'll have to take you to Grant Center and book you for something.'

'Looks like we're going to Grant Center anyway.'

'Right now we're just driving around. What do you want a lawyer for if you ain't done nothin?'

'Damn right I ain't done nothin.'

'I'll get you a lawyer when we get to Grant Center.'

'You said we wasn't going to Grant Center.'

'Changed my mind. Since you got rights on your mind.'

Pity for a man who slammed his car off the road, muscled Laura and Helen into a trailer, dug a hammer in her head, but now is just a dumb jerk outclassed in cat and mouse. Tony Hastings tried to rebuild his villainy, find the devil in him.

'Aw come on, man, you don't need to take me to Grant Center. I'm answering your questions, ain't I?'

'Well I don't know. Seems like I don't know no more about that holdup than I knew before.'

'It's sure a mystery, ain't it?'

'Well frankly Ray, I don't think it's no great mystery. Nah, I got most of the facts pretty straight. Tell you what. There's something else I'd like to ask you about. You recognize this car?'

'What car?'

'This. The one we're in.'

Tony Hastings felt a chill in his ribs. His ugly responsibility for having brought the man here, which he would now have to face. Either that or some cat glee in getting closer to the point. Both, probably.

'This car? What should I recognize this car?'

'It ain't familiar to you? It don't remind you of nothin? It don't take you back?'

'Nohoo man, why should it? It may be taking me somewhere but damned if I know where.' Joke. Think scum, Tony said. No compassion.

'You don't remember driving it?'

'What is it? Was this mine? I never had a car like this.' Clearly he did not remember it.

'How about the driver?'

'What?'

'The guy driving, my friend Tony there. You remember him?'

'I can't see him. Make him turn around.'

'Stop the car, Tony.'

Tony Hastings slowed and stopped on the gravel shoulder by a long straightaway. He felt the heavy thumping strokes of his heart, with shocking lustful fright, and other things. And a test to take he had forgotten would be so frightening.

'Turn around and let him see you.'

A truck roaring shook the car with a blast of wind. Tony turned around. The man in his soft white baseball uniform with CHEVROLET on the front, the face under the beak of his cap. The eyes looking out at him, the small mouth with the teeth too large. What he remembered but not quite like this.

'Who's this guy?' Ray said.

'You don't remember him?'

'Can't say as I do.'

He was chewing, a barely visible motion of the jaw, while he stared at Tony, wary, unrecognizing. Tony saw everything, the bulge of his eyes, the red beads in their corners, the little red veins in the eyewhites, as well as nose, nostrils, hair in nostrils, the crookedness of the two front teeth, one protruding, chipped – looking at him, waiting for him.

'You remember him, Tony?'

'Yes.'

'Refresh his memory.'

'I remember you,' Tony said.

'Tell him where it was.'

'Last summer, on the Interstate, near the Bear Valley exit.'

Ray's eyes looking at him, staring, waiting.

'Tell him what you remember he did.'

Looking at Ray's eyes, Tony did not know if he could say it. He tried. 'You killed my wife and daughter.' He was conscious of the tremor in his voice, like a lie.

He saw the slight widening of the man's large eyes, the chewing quietly stop, no other change. 'You're crazy man. I never killed nobody.'

'Tell him the whole thing.'

'You and your buddies on the Interstate. You forced us off the road.' The audible rasp in his voice, the quaver of being forced to speak.

'Tell him who his buddies were.'

'Lou and Turk.'

'Remember that, Ray? Remember horsing around on the Interstate, playing chicken with other cars?'

Ray's voice very soft. 'You're crazy man.'

'You made us stop and we had a flat tire. Lou and Turk fixed it. Then you and Turk got into my car with my wife and daughter and forced me into your car with Lou.'

'What then, Tony?'

'Lou took me up in the woods and kicked me out. I had to walk back.' Thinking the man's enjoyment of humiliating me, and does he enjoy a second time behind his careful locked mask hearing me confess it now?

Voice stronger now, asserting things, turning humiliation into vengeance. 'Then you came back to the woods in my car. You called and tried to lure me into a trap. You went on to where Lou had left me. When you came out later you tried to kill me with my car.'

'What did you go back there for, Ray?'

'You're crazy man.'

'Tell him what we found there, Tony.'

'You tell him.'

'Do I need to? You know, don't you, Ray?'

'You're crazy man. I don't know what the hell you're talking about.'

'The bodies of my wife and child, which you took back there and dumped.'

Image of the two white mannequins followed by the two wrapped cocoons, bringing back a sudden memory of old grief, clouding Tony Hastings's eyes with wetness which the man could see. He noticed, it must have touched his lust through the mask, and for one moment Tony saw a smile, not much but enough, the same smile he had seen last summer, sadistic and contemptuous then – just enough to ignite Tony's almost forgotten rage and blast pity out of mind. The mask was back again but too late for Ray.

'You're the one,' Tony said. 'I know you.'

'Whaddaya say, Ray?'

'You're crazy man.'

'Okay, let's go to Grant Center. I think I'll book you.'

'You're making a mistake, man.'

'I don't think so, Ray.'

Driving to Grant Center, Tony Hastings did not look back. He bit his lip, a childhood habit to hold together the organization of his nerves. He was full of angry joy, and he drove fast.

# EIGHT

Susan Morrow reads on, no pause here, elated by this capture of Ray, looking forward to what will come. Feeling good, she would like the enjoyment of a good fictitious rage.

*Nocturnal Animals 19*

Thinking into Ray. The man locked surly in a cell across the street, Tony Hastings not sleeping in the cold motel, full of the words behind Ray's dirty little smile. Drawing them out: I remember you. You're the fella let us drive off with your womenfolks. If you can't take care of them better than that.

He went back to the police station in the morning, had breakfast in the cafeteria with Bobby Andes. Andes's eyes were blood-streaked, the deep grooves in his face pulled the skin back from his teeth, fury and frustration had cut deep around his eyes and nose. He carried the tray like an old man, with a limp Tony had not noticed before. His skin looked like tarnish.

'Shit,' he said.

'What?'

'I said fuck.'

'That's what I thought you said.'

He leaned over his scrambled eggs, shoving in with his hand what spilled from his mouth. When he got to his third cup of coffee, he leaned back in the plastic chair.

'Now,' he said. 'I want to take your friend Ray on a little memory-jogging tour. I want you to come too.'

'Where to?'

'The sightseeing spots in Bear Valley.'

He felt some dread. 'You need me?'

'Yes.'

'What for?'

'It might do him good.'

Tony Hastings guessed Bobby Andes had some other purpose too, but could not think what it might be.

The guard with his pistol, whistle, and keys unlocked the steel outer doors and cell door and brought out Ray Marcus, wearing green army fatigues, no hat, his baseball uniform gone. He had the bald forehead Tony Hastings remembered.

'You again,' he said.

'We're taking you for a little ride.'

They went to the big tri-colored police car with bulbs on top and a painted shield on the side. The policeman Tony remembered as George got into the driver's seat with Tony beside him, while Bobby and Ray got in back.

'Where are we going?'

'Sightseeing.'

Ray looked at Tony. 'Why's he coming?'

'He's got an interest in this case.'

'I don't want him. You can't bring him.'

'What's the matter, Ray? I can bring anyone I like.'

'You can't bring him. He's prejudice. He tells lies.'

'Sorry Ray, there's nothing you can do about it.'

'You'll lose your case that way.'

'So much the better for you, eh Ray?'

George driving, they came out to the main valley road and headed back whence they had come yesterday. Andes said:

'Speaking of rights, Ray, I want you to know I got a tape in this car. It's hearing me tell you this.'

'Great.'

'We're going back to some places you may remember. You can help by telling about them. If you don't remember, Tony does.'

In the front seat, Tony leaned against the side and watched Ray and Bobby in the back. Ray was clicking his tongue like a school teacher, shaking his head how immoral this was.

'If you think I can tell you something about who killed this guy's wife and brother, you're wasting your time.'

'Brother, Ray?'

'Whatever it was.'

'Daughter, Ray, daughter. How could you confuse a daughter with a brother?'

'How the hell should I know what it was?'

'That's not as clever as you think, Ray. In fact it's dumb and I'm ashamed of you. Why, it's good as a confession.'

Ray holding himself in, eyes looking around. 'Whaddaya mean, good as a confession? What are you talking about?'

'It's stupid, Ray. It's stupid to make out you're dumber than you are.'

Ray looking away, out the window, in a sulk.

'You know damn well it was wife and daughter. You didn't have to be there to know that.'

Out the window. 'I never noticed. I don't pay much attention to the papers.'

'You didn't need the papers, Ray. Tony told you yesterday.'

'I didn't pay much attention to that neither.'

'And in our interview last night, I must have mentioned daughter twenty times.'

'All right, all right, daughter. You take me for an idiot?'

'Calm down Ray. We're not out to get you.'

'Like hell you ain't.'

'It will go easier for both of us if you tell us the truth.'

'I'm telling you the truth.'

'Both of us, Ray. That includes you. You cooperate, we get you better terms.'

'Better than what?'

'Better than what you'll get if you don't.'

'I told you why it couldn't be me. What more do you want?'

'You sticking to that story?'

'Christ, how could I stick to it if it's true?'

'Tell Tony. You expect him to believe it?'

'I don't give a fuck what he believes.'

'I do, Ray. He believes you murdered his wife and kid. Tell him what you say you were doing that night.'

'You tell him.'

'I forget. Already I've forgotten what you said.'

'You bastard.'

'Tell me again, Ray. I've got the tape. Maybe it will help me remember.'

'I told you, you got it on the other tape. I was with Leila. All night, you know what I mean. Watching television, Braves over Dodgers six to four. Look it up, damn you. A couple of beers, then bed, woowoo. Ask Leila. Have you asked Leila?'

'Don't worry about that.'

'You'd better ask her. It's your job to ask her. It ain't fair to me if you don't.'

'Like I say, Ray.'

They turned to the right, a black road into the woods, which began to climb the mountain, turning back and forth. Tony remembered it, the turns, his breath coming short.

'I have a question about your alibi, Ray. What night did you say that was?'

'July nineteen, I told you. You can look up the baseball score if you don't believe me.'

'You're sure it wasn't the twentieth or the twenty-first?'

'I know when it was.'

'Let me tell you my question. My question is where you was the night of the twenty-sixth? Last year, July twenty-sixth.'

Ray confused. 'What are you asking? It wan't that night.'

'No. I just wonder if you remember where you were that night.'

'Hell, that's a year ago, man.'

'Well how come you remember the night of the nineteenth if you don't remember the night of the twenty-sixth?'

Discomfort. Muddy eyes, scared. He thought of something. 'Maybe it was my mama's birthday.'

'Was it your mama's birthday, Ray? We can look that up too, you know.'

Hesitate. 'I said, *maybe* it was, I mean it might of been. It could just as well of been. But it wasn't.' He thought again. 'It was in the papers. That's how I remembered.'

'You'll have to explain that to me.'

'I mean, we saw it in the paper next morning. Leila and me, we saw how this guy's folks was killed, and we said, How interesting, and what was we doing when that happened, and we was watching the ballgame and afterwards we was in bed.' Suddenly Ray looked at Tony. 'I'm sorry you lost your folks, man, that's a shame. But I didn't have nothing to do with it, believe me.'

'The paper next morning, Ray?'

He thought. 'The morning after that.'

They passed the white church and a moment later went

fast around a curve where the trailer was still in the woods above the ditch. The sight shocked him in the chest, and it occurred to him to watch Ray, who glanced at it, you could see the glance and the pretense not to notice and the settling in his face right afterwards. Thinking into Ray, who was thinking you're such wise guys you don't even know where it happened. Tony looked at Bobby Andes whose eyes were watching his prisoner's eyes.

They came to where the other road went down the hill, where he had gone down that night, and in another moment turned up the drive into the woods. The road seemed first broader and then narrower and wilder than Tony remembered, with the grass high in the middle and green bushes leaning into the track to scratch the car, and sharp turns around boulders and trees and gullies. Almost a year had passed since this place located itself in Tony's mind, and it was hard to believe he had only been here twice. Since then, the leaves had fallen into it, the branches had gone bare, the heavy mountain snows had covered it and new green had appeared on everything, the scrub and undergrowth and all the high branches. All this green was new, a different growth from what he had stumbled through and recapitulated after, and it reminded Tony of the bleeding green agony of his grief, forgotten, left behind in the time between, the shame making everything since then a masquerade of neglect or a long foolish hibernation in the locked house of his living.

He heard the feigned stupidity of the voice in the back seat, 'What's this place?' He remembered the tyranny of the same voice in the woods: Mister, your wife wants you. He looked again at the face looking out the window at the trees, he stared at it trying to force the eyes back to him, compel them, look at me. He realized that Bobby Andes was looking not at Ray but at him, with a slight grin, just a suggestion of one.

It was Tony, not Andes, who said, 'You know this place.'

Now Ray did look at him, a long stare before he said, 'Honest to God I don't.' Not stupidity now, though. Now the voice was unmistakably ironic, and the stare was not stupid or confused. Tony Hastings was looking at his enemy as if no time had passed, and he did not have to think into Ray because the words were clear by themselves: What's this, man, you think you've got me? Why fella, you and your cops, you're just digging a hole for yourself because you ain't got a case, only your word which won't stand up in court without nothing to back it up.

They came to the end. New meadow grass covered all where the police cars had been. Tony saw the deep loss in the bushes of what he did not see. 'Want to get out, Tony?' Andes said.

All right, yes. He went over to the bushes, where he remembered having seen. As he approached he was suddenly aware of the danger of finding something belonging to them, overlooked by the police and left lying all winter. The possibility frightened him, he thought he should stop but he couldn't stop. He stood next to the bushes and realized he did not know exactly where it was. Bobby Andes took him by the elbow. His eyes were shining.

Tony Hastings went to the window and looked down at Ray in the car. 'I want to know,' he said. 'Were they already dead in the car when you brought them, or did you kill them here?'

'I didn't kill nobody, man.' The voice was soft and mocking.

'Nothing to say to us, eh, Ray?' Andes said.

'I'm telling you, you're wasting your time.'

Tony Hastings did not think so. He was more and more aware of power he had acquired to do whatever he liked. They left the place and drove out. When they got to the road, Tony pointed to the ditch and said, 'That's where you tried to run me down.'

Ray was grinning all the time now, enough for Tony to see but not Bobby Andes. If you ain't got sense to get out of the road. What was you doin in these parts anyway? I thought you was going to your summer place in Maine.

They turned up the hill road and down the other side of the ridge, and at the curve George pulled onto the gravel by the trailer.

'Now what,' Ray said.

'Care to look inside?' Bobby Andes said.

'What for?'

'Let's just take a look.'

They all went, Tony lagging, an unexpected shock. George the policeman held Ray by the arm and Bobby Andes took a key and unlocked the door. Tony in fright, about to see this place constructed so often in imagination, but unprepared, must he go in yet? Bobby Andes switched a light inside, the light drew him on. The walls, which he had imagined draped with a print cloth like the curtain in the window, were blank and gray. There was a small stove by the door and a bed with brass bedposts where the fingerprints must have been and a trashbox full of newspapers.

'Raped them on the bed I presume,' Andes said.

'I never raped nobody.'

'Come on Ray, we got your record.'

'God damn, the charges were dropped. I never raped nobody.'

Tony went to stand in front of Ray next to the bed. He was surprised how small it was, like a cot with bedposts. And Ray a shade shorter than he was. 'I want to know, Ray,' he said. 'The exact story of what you did to them.' He was surprised at the pressure of his words like steam driving him.

'You'll have to ask somebody else, man.'

'I want to know what they said. I want to know what Laura said and what Helen said. I have no one to tell me but you.'

Looking at Ray's face close, the bloody eyes, the teeth too big, the ironic grin. Why man, that's private between them and me. You was out hiking. If you ain't got the sense to come out of the woods. It's none of your business, man.

'I want to know how you killed them. I want to know if they knew what was happening to them. I want to know, damn it.'

Naw you don't, man, someone like you brought up with your antipathy to violence and fighting, it might make you sick to the stomach.

'What they suffered, Ray. I want to know if they hurt. I want to know what they felt.'

You don't want to know that now, you know you don't.

'Answer me, bastard.'

'Mister, you're out of your mind,' Ray Marcus said. The voice that said Mister. Why shit, fella, you ain't got no cause to complain. I thought you were done with them.

The eyes went on talking. I told you she wanted you. If you'd a come when we called. If you can't care for them better than that. Hell, I thought I was doing you a favor.

The face was in front of him, the small hard chin like a baseball with a gash in it, the misshapen teeth, the leer. That, and quick think, if he could, yes he could, by surprise before they could stop him, with all his strength, and *that*. Bobby Andes grabbed Tony by the arms pulling him back. 'Easy, easy.' George had his gun drawn, then reached down to where Ray was sprawled on the floor against the stove. There was blood on Ray's face, his mouth a mess. One second. Then Ray lunged up from the floor and George snagged his arms, twisting them behind, buckling him over, and Bobby Andes got between. Handcuffs, quick. Ray with his hand on his mouth, blood all over.

He was yelling at Tony. 'Oor gonna get hooed man.'

'What's he saying?'

'He's saying you're gonna get sued. Don't worry. He ain't gonna sue nobody for a while.'

'You're all gonna get hooed.'

'Ill advised, Ray. Look what you get for trying to escape.'

'Ethcape? Thit, man.'

Ray handcuffed to George, Andes patted him on the shoulder. 'It's all right, Ray, we'll get you a dentist. You got his tooth, George?' He gave Ray a handkerchief.

They went back to the car. 'I'll drive now,' Andes said. George and Ray, handcuffed together, got in back, Tony sat in front as before. Bobby Andes looked at him, his eyes gleaming.

'Pretty good,' he said. 'I didn't know you had it in you.'

Tony Hastings, who couldn't remember ever hitting anybody before, felt extraordinary. Wild and exhilarated, with righteous wrath fulfilled.

Susan Morrow smacks her fist into Ray Marcus's face and knocks him down against the stove. Ho.

She puts the manuscript down. It's time to stop for the night, though it seems murderous to quit now. Another painful interruption like divorce, required by the discrepancy between the laws of reading and the laws of life. You can't read all night, not if you have responsibilities like Susan. And if you must stop before the end, it might as well be here.

Sometime during her reading Dorothy and her friend Arthur came back from their date, well behaved, respecting her curfew. They've been watching television ever since. Upstairs a

Wagnerian sound continues behind a closed door, Tristan equating love and death.

She goes to the bathroom exhilarated with the feel of slugging Ray, whatever her reason, which may not be identical to Tony's. What did she mean a while ago by the enjoyment of a good rage? Who, exactly, is she raging at? Nobody? Susan, who loves everybody, her heart pours out to all.

So she remembers: we're moving to Washington. Are we? The question has been covered over, encysted like an insect in a cocoon, swathed in the silk of her reading. It will re-emerge soon enough, and then she'll have to think about it.

Should she tell Dorothy and Arthur to knock it off? She quells a theatrical impulse to scold them for wasting their youth in front of a television set. Television and going to Washington and socking Ray are mixed in her mind, as if it were the television set she wanted to smash. So she imagines an alien visitor asking what's the difference between Dorothy gaping at television and herself gaping at a book. Martha and Jeffrey her little pets who think it queer to see her stopping there transfixed. She wishes she didn't have to keep proving that it's her ability to read that makes her civilized.

# SECOND INTERLUDE

# ONE

Wake up now. Light, blank square, window, the door in the floor shuts off the retreating mind. Gap without mind before another mind, bright and superficial, greets her with temporal data: Good morning Susan it's the day of the week, hour of the clock, dress and address your schedule for the day.

This mind is full of order and regime. Yet for a while a receding world still dazzles like the frost lines on the window, where everything is connected, Edward, Tony, Susan's various minds, one leading to another and back, the same and interchangeable. As the dazzle fades differences reappear and once again Susan is the reader, Edward the writer. Yet she retains a curious vision of Susan as writer, as if there were no difference.

That's interesting enough to stop her in the kitchen after breakfast, pausing with a dish in each hand, trying to figure out rationally what it means. She observes herself. She sees words. She talks to herself all the time. Does this make her a writer?

She thinks. If writing is the fit of thought into language, everybody writes. Distinguish. The words she prepares to speak, that's speech, not writing. Words not meant for speech, that's reverie. If Susan is a writer, it's for other words neither speech nor reverie, words like these now: her habit of generalization. Her way of composing rules and laws and descriptions of things. She does it all the time, crating her thoughts in words stored for later use. She makes another generalization: it's saving words for later use that makes writing.

Susan's writing aspirations have always been modest: letters, an intermittent journal, a memoir of parents. An occasional letter to the editor on women's rights. Once no doubt she craved more, as she also craved to be a composer, a skater, a supreme court justice. She gave it up without regret as if what she gave up was not writing but something else, less important.

She needs to distinguish between the writer she refused to become and the writer she always was. Surely what she refused was not writing but the next step, dissemination: the adaptations and publicity required to induce others to read – an extensive process summed up in one word, publication. As she works about the house on this bright but darkening day, threatening snow, Susan thinks that's too bad, because in giving up publication she gave up the chance to be part of a writing conversation, to read the consequences of her words in other words from out in the world. And too bad in a vanity way, thinking of Edward (who started it all), since she knows her mind is as good as his, and if she had devoted years to the practice of a skill, she could have written a novel as good as his.

So why didn't she write? Other things had a higher claim. What? Husband, children, teaching Freshman English in the junior college? Susan needs another reason. Something in the publication process that subtly repelled her. She saw it in the old days when Edward was struggling. And felt it when she tried to write herself. Dishonesty, some subtle falsification, forced on her, it seemed, by writing for someone else to read. An uncomfortable lying feeling. It infected then and still infects even her most modest efforts, her letters, her

Christmas card messages, which lie no matter what she says or does not say.

The presence of the other person – that's the cause. The other person, the reader, contaminates what she writes. This reader's prejudice, taste, mere otherness, controlling what she may say like a Hollywood producer or market researcher. Yet even the unpublished writing in her soul has a misfit between itself and the sentence she can say it in. The sentence simplifies. If it does not simplify it's a mess, and she bogs in the additional vice of obscurity. She creates a clear sentence by lopping, exaggerating, distorting, and sealing over what's missing like paint. This gives her such an illusion of clarity or depth that she'll prefer it to truth and soon forget it's not truth.

The intrinsic dishonesty of writing corrupts memory too. Susan writes her memories into narrative. But narrative does not flash like memory, it's built across time with cells for storing the flashes that come. It transforms memory into a text, relieving the mind of the need to dig and hunt. Remembered Edward is such a text, and early Arnold and her marriage, established through many writings long ago. Obliged now to reread these old texts, she can't help rewriting. She's rewriting now, as hard as she can, trying her best to bring back an illusion of memory alive, because the orthodox narrative is totally dead.

# TWO

Susan should have known when she first consented to read Edward's book that it would have some such effect. Should have foreseen it would bring him back alive, as if no twenty years had passed. And bring with him also the divorce and early Arnold and other questions she would rather not think about. But could she have foreseen such excitement, combined with alarm? She doesn't understand the alarm. It's out of proportion to the cause. She wonders if the story itself, Tony's case, is acting on her in some hidden way, separate from the revival of Edward. There's a threat somewhere, but she doesn't know what it is or where it comes from. She tries to find it by researching her memory while doing physical labor about the house.

The situation was this: while Susan was married to Edward who was going insane with writing, Arnold was married to Selena going insane with a carving knife. The problem for Susan rewriting a memory is how to get from that arrangement of marriages to the present one.

Six apartments, two on each floor across the stairwell. Susan and Edward lived in 2B, Arnold and Selena in 3A. There was a lawn in back inside a fence, with one tree and two picnic tables. There was a picnic, hamburgers, and boiled corn in a pot over the charcoal grill. Susan and Edward had never met Arnold and Selena. Arnold was an anxious young intern at the hospital, who had terrible working hours but was free that day. Selena was the most beautiful woman Arnold had ever seen. She had raven black hair, sea blue eyes, artificial lashes, snow white skin, her smile was both radiant and vibrant, her voice soft and gentle, and she flirted with the gentlemen, ladies, and children like a princess of cats. She was tense as electricity. Arnold on the other hand was big and bearlike and worried, and he hovered around Selena bringing her hamburgers, Cokes, marshmallows. He was respectful and bewildered when Edward boasted of quitting law school to become a writer, and he gazed at Susan in a vague pleasant way. He had dusty short curly hair, a T-shirt, dusty hair on his thick arms, and dusty eyebrows. He worked in the hospital emergency room and was shocked by his experiences, which he described in a shocked voice, while Selena approached the children like the beautiful wicked witch, and Edward glazed over.

After that they met often on the stairs, Arnold and Susan-Edward, though never Selena. Susan never saw Selena, though sometimes she heard an operatic soprano upstairs.

Selena was hospitalized in October, middle of the month Edward was spending alone with his typewriter in the woods. That was convenient: one wife and one husband go away, leaving the other pair to discover each other. Neither had entered the other's mind, however, and Arnold's immediate problem was to get the knife away from Selena. Sunday afternoon. Susan all by her lonely self was watching a football game, which is embarrassing to admit because she never watched football, but she was too distracted to read, and she was furthermore ironing and happened to see a touchdown scored just when she tuned in. So she watched the football game with memories not of Edward but of Jake, who used to take her to games every Saturday and slip his chilly hand inside her coat in the bleachers. She remembered this just when the rapid knock on her door, nervous enough to alert her, introduced her to her future. This was Arnold, big and scared like a child asking her could she come upstairs and help with Selena who was having a spell? Not knowing Selena had spells, Susan recognized emergency and rushed up with him and only later remembered how life with Edward also began with an emergency.

Locked in the bathroom with the carving knife. Be careful what she might do with it, Arnold said. Causing Susan to grab a weapon, which turned out to be a broom. The fixed memory of her first entry into Arnold's apartment shows her carrying a broom in both hands, prepared to fend off the knife of a crazy woman who happened to be the most beautiful Arnold had ever seen – although Susan actually didn't learn she was that until later, when he would tell her more times than necessary.

As they came into the apartment, with the cold sun streaming through the lofty windows and the doors open, Arnold called out, Selena, Susan's here, can you come out to see her?

Susan who? The concealed voice was a metal screech behind the bathroom door in the vestibule, no operatic soprano today. I'm going to the bathroom for Christ sakes. Susan *what*, the neighbor? Did you go get her, you rat?

Come on, Selena.

Let me finish.

Arnold to Susan, aside, I called the hospital. They're sending someone. The door opened and Selena came out. Blue jeans and dirty white T-shirt, hair disheveled, beauty haggard. Unaware of the knife in her hand while Susan held her broom.

Hi Susan, how are you?

Arnold: What's that in your hand, Selena?

(Oh shit.) Arnold, you ought to be ashamed exposing your

wife to such humiliation, bringing in a stranger to witness our troubles. (Excuse me Susan.) I wouldn't do that to you. I wouldn't bring some man to watch and laugh at you.

Nobody's laughing, Arnold said.

Not to my face, they're not. Susan, I apologize. I apologize for Arnold. I'm just working in the kitchen and I don't see why I can't pick up the knife, it's just a carving knife. Don't you pick up knives in the kitchen, Susan Sheffield?

Come on, Selena, Arnold said.

What Susan remembers best through the years is Selena's voice when the ambulance men arrived, non-operatic and bitter: So that's what you're up to. I might have known.

Big worried Arnold, living by himself while his wife was hospitalized, with his terrible working schedule, Susan felt sorry for him. Down the stairs ten-thirty at night, going to work in the emergency room: she stuck her head out to ask how Selena was doing and if she could help. No one on the scene then guessed this was the married couple of the future.

What to do? In line at the grocery store checkout behind her, he explained, a few items to cook himself something to eat. Selena? Maybe she'll come home next week. She saw the simple friendly bear expression on his face and translated it into a haunted one, shadowed by its indeterminable future with a Selena wielding the carving knife on a periodic basis with years of calling the ambulance men, to leave for a while and then back home to the remains of the most beautiful woman ever seen, until her fondness for the carving knife grew up again. Full of sympathy, Susan thus diverted herself from a writing husband who would be going off with equal periodicity to great works under the spell of the wilderness angel.

That poor man cooking himself something to eat before those emergency nightmares: well, Susan was kind enough to invite him to dinner. You ask, did Susan have any consciousness, there in front of the old passionless cashier, of impropriety, the wife of a man lost in the woods cooking for the husband of a woman lost in psychiatry? This was one of those nodal points in a history, which because of its consequences people like Susan look back to.

Is it wrong, when your husband is away, to do a good deed for your temporarily wifeless neighbor who would otherwise cook for himself or go around to Gordon's for a bite? There are two sides to the question. One is what your neighbors think. Susan felt free to ignore them, remote in their own lives, even their names almost forgotten since the summer picnic. The other side is what you yourself think, with two options. One, not to think anything. Out of perfect innocence changes will arise that no one need foresee. Certainly Susan made an effort toward such absence of thought. The other option was to go ahead and think. But that means something exists to think about. Her reasoning was that it was an issue only if she and Arnold thought it an issue. Obviously they did not think so, since this was only a natural neighborly service: good neighbor, girl scout, useful friend. Plain roast beef, browned potatoes, brown and serve rolls, frozen peas. Face to face at the little dining room table she shared with Edward. Talk about Selena and Edward. Life in the emergency room. His schedule, to be up all night and tomorrow with killing hours. They scarcely knew each other. She was trying to figure out what he was really like, and how he got tangled up with a woman like Selena. If he got tangled because she was the most beautiful, what did that say about him? She was thinking he's a rather simple oaf, albeit a nice oaf. She encouraged the wine-leaked sadness that seeped out of him as they talked, full of mother, father, brothers, sisters, and old hopes from before the time he realized the problem Selena had brought. Reconciling himself to being unable to provide his parents with grandchildren of his own – that kind of sadness. And to periodic hospitalizations, that kind. And to a certain fear, since carving knife equivalents would continue to appear. All this he had to put up with, as she encouraged him to talk.

No thought of you and me. Edward was coming back in two weeks: he was creating his future as a writer. Arnold listened without much attention. Edward's problems were remote from him.

Yet it was not quite an ordinary dinner after all, you must admit. The candles were a detail she hadn't intended. She put the flowers (hibiscus) from the kitchen on the centerpiece and brought out her grandmother's silverware and the good china, trying to think, this is just a good natured neighbor guy in a fix who needs to eat before going to work. Then five minutes before his arrival, with the meat nearly finished, she was overwhelmed by the bleakness of the room under ordinary light, its need for some flickering darkness to conceal the simplicity of things. It was not just simple, this room no different from what it was in her meals with Edward, but it had now a conspicuous absence which made it look barbarously naked, and the only image she could conceive to make up what it lacked was candles. The candlesticks were a wedding present used just once, which she dusted off and filled with a pair of candles from the drawer.

Yet even by candlelight Susan Sheffield and Arnold Morrow retained their disguises, she the wife of and he the husband of. Still, she felt this high pitched noise in her hair or neck or solar plexus, making the moment extraordinary. Electricity, like Selena at the picnic, Selena with the purring cat's voice, whose matter seemed fully convertible to energy in the Einsteinian sense: $e=mc^2$. Selena the electric, altered into Susan the electric, as if Arnold were a transformer, thinking how easy to be free, what delicious things could be done in Edward's wonderful absence if you were the kind of person who did such things. Susan was not that kind. Susan was Susan, from Edgar's Lane, teacher of Freshman English, well organized, coherent, grammatical, unified, with margins on all sides, always ready to revise and improve herself. This Susan had delicious wild thoughts full of mountains and forests and floating streams, with fish on the wing and birds at sea, thoughts concentric and phallic, with penis hunting in the mists and cave exploration in the hermaphroditic clouds, but they were only thoughts, unacted, unuttered, the absent underside of Susan the Good.

Nothing happened that a witness listening or a tape recorder under the table could have reported to Edward or Selena. Despite which, by the time Arnold left for his nightly encounter with blood and bones, heart attacks and mutilations and decapitations, Susan was pitched so high she could hardly stand it. We've got to do this again, she said to herself, knowing something she wanted now, though still not allowing herself to think it. As he stood by the door, he grateful and bearlike, she asked, Will you come again night after tomorrow?

She went to bed trying to remember what it was like to love Edward. The next dinner she served Arnold was resolutely austere and functional in the bare electric overhead light, but she had no resistance later to what Arnold wanted to do in the double bed that belonged to Susan and Edward, while Selena was breathing hard trying to sleep under restraint in her hospital room, and Edward in his wooded cabin was getting depressed trying to find himself. When Arnold later went back to another night of crisis, Susan belatedly tried to grieve.

# THREE

Susan and Arnold, later so respectable, committed adultery in the gaps between her teaching schedule and his emergency duties. First in Edward's bed, the dark back room with alley beyond, full of books and magazines, with laundry hamper, orange crate, small TV set. Later in Selena's, the tall window with blowing curtain looking over rooftops, the closet open with airy dresses and lingering perfume.

When that young Susan on Edward's bed saw Arnold Morrow's alarming penis suddenly come into view with swollen purpose, she heard a gong in her head. She heard another soon after, when she decided to let it in. Gong, her head said, goodbye Edward. There he goes. Shocked by what kind of person she was. It had never occurred to her her marriage was in jeopardy.

She did not mean it to end. It was over and not over. Edward would come back and never know, and Arnold would return to Selena, and Susan was henceforth an unfaithful wife. Against the electric joy of the new, she went bang against the wrong she was doing. Edward aggrieved, their hopes betrayed – if he knew. She was a jaded woman now, with a secret. She asked Arnold, who had it all figured out.

Who's going to tell, he said, you? He had a philosophy according to which sex, vastly overemphasized by people attaching their egos to it, had nothing to do with his responsibilities to Selena (whom he would never abandon) nor hers to Edward. Arnold was especially down on jealousy, the stupidest of all emotions, nothing but property and power thinking they're love. That's my philosophy, he said while they lay open on the sheets, chatting in the sweaty afterglow.

She remembered having used the same argument (sex is natural) to rouse Edward. That was different. It led to marriage, for one thing. Yet already in this little taste of crime or nature (whichever), she had glimpsed a better life. Even before Arnold showed her his alarming thing, she thought: if I were married to him. For two weeks, during that casual ego-free affair, she compared Arnold's superiority to poor old Edward.

Thick muscled, plump in face, dusty haired, a mesomorph unlike ectomorphic Edward, he was easier and more natural. His manner was calm, his temper serene (so far). He was unpretentious, intelligent without being intellectual, would doubtless be brilliant in his field and attractively stupid in everything else. She welcomed his non-intellectuality, his deference to her mind. (Later, when the question of marriage appeared, it was easy to talk him out of his philosophy, which he abandoned without argument, a cheerful concession to her brain. So she thought, anyway.)

She felt gypped. Envious of Selena, who didn't appreciate what she had, which was available to Susan only on a rental basis. As she went about her work – teaching, paper grading, grocery shopping – she was so charged by electricity transferred from Selena that she dreaded Edward's dull return like Cinderella turned back into a prairie dog. The glamor of Arnold's magic sex, not that he was such a great lover, just the auspices or the situation or whatever – well, it's hard for contemporary Susan to remember why Arnold seemed so glamorous.

Feeling bad for Edward, she tried to remember why she

loved him. This is even harder for contemporary Susan because once she married Arnold it was important to make Edward's memory as disagreeable as possible. She remembers trying to rebuild him like a knocked down castle, stacking together chunks of time and place memorialized by love or something – a castle soon to be knocked down a second and final time. She remembers remorse, as if she were rebuilding not just Edward, but Edgar's Lane or her childhood or her mother, or something like that.

What went wrong? Susan could not divorce Edward and marry Arnold simply to validate a sexual adventure. She had her grievances. She hadn't counted on his becoming a writer, giving up everything so that she could support him with her teaching. She hadn't counted on his going off for a month to find himself. She had lots to be pissed off about, Susan, if you need reasons.

On the other hand, contemporary Susan remembers how, to preserve the status quo, she found and cuddled a frail feeling like a live or maybe stuffed small animal: Edward's dearness. Like what she has cuddled when needed in more recent times: Arnold's dearness. Since Arnold's dearness looks very much like Edward's, the two animals are perhaps the same and ought to be called Susan's dearness.

Arnold and Susan planned an orgy before Edward's return, but it fell through because of a change in Arnold's schedule. She spent the evening cleaning the apartment. She had to get back into an Edward state of mind, and it was better to be busy. She was also near panic, because they had no plan to meet again, and she didn't know what their future was supposed to be. They had forgotten to discuss it.

Then Edward came home. He called from a road stop out

of town and arrived at dinner time. Glad to be back, poor Edward, lovely Susan. They had a drink and ate together, while she wondered if he had enough ESP to detect the deep change in their marriage. The unfaithful wife. He didn't. He was depressed, he had been depressed before he went, he was still depressed. The woods had failed him. Her heart sank. He talked so much it was hard to sympathize, though she tried harder than ever before. He had accomplished nothing. He had thrown out all the work he had done in the cabin. What? Not literally, he had the pages in his suitcase, but he had thrown them out of his mind.

All evening as she listened to his complaint, she wondered what would happen if he knew. He was too preoccupied to notice. They went to bed. She was alarmed by her new preference for Arnold's way, gentler and slower than Edward's effortful puffing, while she kept trying to prefer Edward and revive love, because what else could she do?

She never saw Arnold now, not even on the stairs. No messages either. A week later she realized Selena had come home. Concealing her nervousness, she told Edward about Selena's carving knife. She had to, lest it become a public event. He was mildly interested.

She decided the lack of word from Arnold meant the affair was over. She was confusedly angry about that, but utilized her anger on Edward's behalf. She devoted herself to his problem. He appreciated that. It wasn't that he wasn't a writer, he explained, it was only that he was going too fast. He needed to go through a juvenile period. She tried to give advice without hurting his feelings. His feelings were easily hurt. He got very emotional and dependent. He dug up his old things and asked what was wrong with his style. His subject matter. Be frank, he said, and she tried to be, to explain what irritated her. That was a mistake. You don't have to be that frank, he said.

In her heart (contemporary Susan sees this) she wished Edward would give up and settle down to something real. Not that writing wasn't real, but she thought Edward was caught in a romantic dream for which he was not fitted. At heart he was as bourgeois as anybody else. He had a logical and organized mind, she could imagine him having excellent success running something, whereas writing seemed to be an infection of his ego, picked up somewhere, stunting his growth. She tried not to think such thoughts, which made her feel hypocritical as she gave him the encouragement he craved. Once when he had asked her to be brutally frank, she tried to tell him. She raised the question whether he had enough talent for what he wanted. Do you *have* to be a writer? she asked. That was a mistake. He reacted as if she had suggested suicide. You might as well ask me to blind myself, he said. Writing was like seeing, he said, not to write was blindness. She never made that mistake again.

A note from Arnold to her office: 'Just to tell you, Selena knows. No problem, everything under control.'

Selena knows. This raises questions. Did Arnold tell, or did she guess? Was there a fight? Would Selena have new notions for her carving knife? What should we make of the fact that this was Arnold's only word to her since Edward's return?

The news increased the likelihood Edward would find out. She and Arnold might keep a secret, but Selena had no reason to. While Edward sat at the table as if in disgrace, obsessed with failure, Susan wondered what Selena would do when the mood came. She wouldn't even have to tell Edward for the news to spread like a disease in the ivy trails reaching even to recluses in a state of depression.

To forestall the shock of a sudden discovery by Edward with its grief and loss of faith and her own embarrassed humiliation, she ought to confess in advance, so as to put the confession in her own terms. A volunteered confession would assure him it was over. Brief lapse in your absence, the stress of loneliness, telling you voluntarily so you'll know you can trust and believe me. It won't happen again.

Time passed. It's easier to plan such words than to say them. With no sign from Arnold, she wondered if it might blow over. They met Selena on the stairs. Susan and Edward coming in, Selena out. Selena looked fiercely at her, differently at Edward, thoughtful. It left Susan gasping. What's the matter? Edward said. The heavy grocery bags they were carrying.

How to tell him, break the news? What was she afraid of? Of hurting his feelings? Aggravating his depression? Driving him to suicide? Come on, Susan, don't be so merely virtuous. Of losing him? Of losing face, more likely. Her status in the house. The new light he would see her in. Not to speak of the plain uproar, the anarchy the raw emotion would release.

At least you should know your position in advance. She meant to cleave by Edward. Love him, reassure him, be humble. The direct approach, picking his most vulnerable time: on the bed beside him without clothes, curling her hair around her nose, he relieved by the distraction from his obsession. Edward love, I have a confession to make. Not that direct. Ease up to it: Edward dear, suppose you had a wife who. Nor that.

Indirect, to smother him with so much love he would know before the words came out that she couldn't possibly be saying anything bad. To come up behind him at lunch, put her cheek next to his, saying, Edward my sweet, how much I love.

The best way would be by accident when you are in the midst of something else. Day after day, she watches Edward, realizes as he talks, chews, holds his head, groans, belches, that he *still* doesn't know. The big change is yet to come, the consequences yet to be revealed.

The best way to confess is to be already angry about something, so you'll have the momentum of your grievance to carry forward against his hurt. And that's how it finally did happen: in the midst of a discussion about writing – which was the only thing they talked about nowadays. She said, God, I wish you'd stayed in law school. His reply: When you talk like that, it's like you were unfaithful.

She snapped: You haven't the slightest idea what that would be like.

Edward full of emphasis: It couldn't be worse.

It couldn't? And so she told. Not rancorously, for as soon as she saw her opportunity, her mood changed to humble and sad. All the same, she told and ended by saying, It's all over though, it has no future, I was not in love.

Edward the child. His staring eyes, which she had never seen so large. His meek questions: Who? Where? Do you want a divorce? Was it worth it?

He groaned, stretched, walked around the room, experimenting with reactions. What am I supposed to do? he said. How am I supposed to behave?

That's what she remembers. He did not get angry. He kept asking her to confirm she didn't want a divorce. He didn't dare ask if she loved him, so she said it without being asked.

Contemporary Susan thinks her confession perked him up. A respite from his depression. The next time in bed he seemed to enjoy thinking about the unnamed lover in the air. He was tactful enough not to ask for comparisons. She figured she had broken down a wall whose presence she had not noticed until it was gone. Now we know each other better, she thought. Not so romantic, weaker than we thought, which is maybe good to know. Her marriage would be stronger, she thought, believing she was glad of it.

# FOUR

There's a gap in the saga of Susan's official memory, almost a year between Edward's return from the woods and her marriage to Arnold. When she looks back, she finds the time blank. It could not have been totally without event. There must have been daily drives to the college with snow scenes and slushy streets. Also grocery shopping, cleaning, and cooking for Edward. And moods and arguments, movies, a friend or two. She remembers the apartment: dark walls, tiny kitchen, the bedroom with books on the floor and view of the alley.

The reason for the blockage is that the period was about to end in revolutionary change. Arnold would replace Edward with new laws, values, icons, everything. The new regime rewrites history to protect itself, burying Edward's time like the Dark Ages. It takes Edward's return to remind contemporary Susan of what is hidden and challenge her to rewrite the old saga through imaginative archaeology.

Rereading the saga, Susan would like to know if it's the light of later times that makes that interval look so dreary, or if it really was that way. How dark were the Dark Ages? She did her work and wondered. The saga notes change in Edward. Nervous and caustic, edgy with an increase in the irony level. Odd ugly jokes. Reading the paper sneering at the politicians, letter writers, editorialists, advice givers. Criticizing and ridiculing her colleagues, without quite identifying her with them.

According to the saga, he stopped talking about writing.

Surprising, though Susan doesn't remember being surprised. No more complaints or requests for opinions. Secretive, not even admitting that what he was doing in his study was writing.

What the saga ignores, but Susan now remembers, is Edward's silence about her affair. He never blamed her, not overtly. Never asked her to explain, after his first tentative questions. Avoided asking for love. Cautious, as if afraid of her.

She has no problem remembering Arnold's talk, one of the scriptural centers of the saga, though it's hard to remember where or when they could talk, since after Edward returned the affair supposedly stopped. She thought it was over. But Arnold did insist on talking and she found ways, listening to his urgent low whispering voice in the office she shared with the other composition teachers: Dear Susan, how good, intelligent, wise, who alone could make him feel like a human being again. Hair-raising anecdotes about Selena, rage and jealousy, the carving knife, pills, pliers. Clothes out the window, her broad brimmed hat sailing like a frisbee across the street. Who went out naked at night, brought back by the police.

In the narrative Arnold asked Susan for comfort and help. He was fed up. He wanted to know the right thing, what his duties were. What did Susan say? Only what she ought to, of course. Throw the question back to him. With two sides to it. His side is the release from obligation when love is dead with no children, and the woman he married no longer exists. The absurdity of sacrificing his chances for personal happiness to a crazy woman unable to appreciate it. Selena's side is the cruelty of abandonment when she is ill, confined, helpless, and alone. Selena banks heavily on the vow about sickness and health. But Jesus, Arnold would say, if she's going to be in a loony bin the rest of her life. If not, hard times and fight fight fight.

Asked to mediate, Susan tried to keep a third side out of the case. It's up to you, she would say, like a heroine in Henry James. Sometimes he would explode. He was not made to be celibate, it was not his nature. Did Selena realize that? Do *they* realize it? Who's they? Susan asked. You, he said. He compared her case to his: You happily married with your comfortable husband and love and sex and your sane mind and his sane mind and sane conversation full of love love love, and nothing to worry about. She refused to deny it.

One secret leads to another. Because they couldn't meet where they lived, they used her office phone for messages, trusting a friend of Arnold's who had a room or else meeting dangerously in secluded corners of the park or in deserted offices after classes, and Edward took her late arrivals for granted. The old saga recreates Susan's dilemma, caused by not knowing what kind of narrative she was in. A wife resumes an affair with her married lover. Though the husband knows of the earlier affair, he does not know about this one. And though the lover wants to be free of his institutionalized wife, he hasn't done anything about it, nor has he decided what his obligations are. Susan is therefore once again an unfaithful wife. What is the future if you are an unfaithful wife? Is this transitional to a new life, a step in the dismantling of Edward? Or is it a permanent concession to weakness, one infidelity after another? The issue is hard because she is a person loyal and true. If she is to remain Edward's wife, even though unfaithful, she ought to defend the Edward castle, protect its icons. If this is transitional, she should dismantle the castle without delay, tell Edward the truth and cut the ties. Love, love. Arnold talked of love. But he seemed happy with things as they were, and Susan did not know what to do. No doubt she was full of strong feelings, though the narrative remembers only the dilemma.

According to the chronicle, the renewal of her affair caused her to divorce Edward so as to marry Arnold. But when Susan looks now, she sees herself unable to make up her mind, never making it up until others made up theirs. She can't remember how many discussions she and Edward had, how many turns and vague decisions quickly cancelled, before it was settled. She remembers his silence, which she thought was for the failure of his writing, and she feared he was thinking of suicide. When she came home from her adventure full of exotic guilt, she felt ashamed of her joy while he was so miserable. There was an evening when Edward thought she was checking research papers in the library. And a night during which she heard him sighing and groaning as if he wanted her to notice. In the morning they got up, took turns in the bathroom, got their breakfast, ate together without speaking. They sat silent over coffee, Edward staring out over the enclosed yard to the back of the bookstore in the rain. The first words he spoke were sudden: I finally understand what's wrong. I expect too much from you.

She said something conciliatory, but he was going another way. Shut up, he said, I'm giving you advice. You should get a divorce, the sooner the better. No one has the right to expect what I expect of you.

The talks that followed were full of confusion. They made decisions and changed their minds often during the next few weeks, which were full of rhetoric and paradox. No one knew where anyone stood. Things went around. Gradually, though, as they kept returning to the point, it simplified. The official cause was her failure to appreciate his writing, which he kept insisting was serious, really serious. You don't esteem me, he would say. You don't *see* me. But since Susan in her heart had always thought Edward's commitment to writing was temporary, she did not take such complaints seriously. She assumed the real cause was her affair with Arnold, shown in Edward's reluctance to mention it, as if jealousy were beneath him.

So they divorced, Edward-Susan, Arnold-Selena, to remarry as Arnold-Susan, and, later, Edward-Stephanie, while Selena stayed in the mental hospital. Officially, the divorce was amicable. They were polite and did not dispute the ownership of things, but there was a moody cloud. Speech was hard, especially after she moved out. When they met in the divorce court, though there had been no quarrel, she felt as if it had been all quarrel.

In its place, a new romantic idyll, the second in Susan's saga and the last. New embodiments of the old forms reduced the triteness. Indiana Dunes. Brookfield Zoo. Museum of Science and Industry. The freedom to be seen in public. Gifts, jewelry and clothes. It was a relief not to judge his work and to look forward to his prosperity. The only drawback was his philosophy of sex and again, possibly, an insufficient consideration of what he expected from a wife. She asked him to revise the sex philosophy. No problem, he said, replacing it with a doctrine of fidelity and truth. As for his marital expectations, she learned these through trial and error.

Although it was a time of joy, Susan cried a lot. The narrative always has difficulty recovering feelings because they have no outer effects, but crying is an event which the narrative can describe. She cried for the honest Susan she would have to rebuild. She cried for her mother and father, for Edward at fifteen, the hours in the rowboat, the myth of childhood sweethearts, and the struggling artist life. She cried when her mother came to Chicago to persuade her to give Edward a second chance and said he would always continue to be her foster son.

She cried lest Arnold not divorce Selena and cried for Selena when he proved her wrong. She cried for Selena's crying, and for the doctor who said Selena would never get out and the lawyer who obligated Arnold to support her the rest of her life.

Susan did not usually cry much, but this was an emotional time. The old crying Susan was still a child. The maturing Susan who married Arnold was wiser, but not much, as she entered her second marriage expecting to rectify the mistakes of the first. The contemporary Susan admits rectification occurred, not because Arnold was better than Edward, but through the force of time. It came about. Arnold was different, but much the same, and Susan would never know if the same rectification might not have occurred if she had stayed with Edward – just as she assumed a comparable rectification for him with loyal Stephanie.

But that makes no difference. What the matured Susan knows is this: however it began, in what shady manner or under what clouds, with whatever deceptions and betrayals in good or bad faith, what they have created is a world. That world is hers and must be protected. Sometimes still she can remember imagining a different world. She went to graduate school thinking she would earn a doctorate. She might have been a professor, taught graduate students, written books, chaired a department, gone on lecture tours. Instead she teaches when there's a slot for her, part-time, auxiliary, not for the money, not for the career, but for the exercise. She might have been, but it annoys her when people like Lou Anne in the English Office speak of her sacrifices, feel sorry for her and blame Arnold like a tyrant or slaver. For though she never knew for sure whether it was by choice or default (it happened so gradually), this is what she has become: the mother of the family. The family is Dorothy, Henry, Rosie, and it's Arnold and herself, and she is the mother. It's the one thing in her life she knows is important, no doubt about that. Like it or not, it's who I am, she says. She knows it, Arnold knows it. It's what they know together.

They settled this for good three years ago with the Marilyn Linwood understanding. Their implicit agreement, never quite put into words, established by the events as they occurred. That Arnold remained, that he continued to act the parts of husband and father, that after enough had been said nothing more was said, proved the point, which is that Linwoods come and go. In the long run they mean nothing at all.

She stands by him, that's what it is. She never thought of it in those words. She always thought of herself as healthily selfish taking care of her interests, but it's true, isn't it?, she stands by him and always did. Not because he is Arnold but because once in the past she settled down to become his wife. And then the world turned into a crystal around them. She stands by him through Linwood in the same automatic way in which she stood by him in the Macomber malpractice suit, just as she'll accompany him if he goes to Washington (selling house, severing kids from school and friends, everything) for the advancement of his career. She'll do it, of course she will.

It's not just that they, with their children, house, car, dog, cat, engraved checks and writing paper, have created an institution like a bank, it's that the world is cold, lonely, and dangerous, and they need each other for shelter. This book she's reading knows about that. Tony in his plight should appreciate how fiercely she clings. He should. Yet this makes her uneasy, for she mistrusts Edward's book. She doesn't know why. It nudges a certain alarm in her, a fear whose object she does not know but which seems different from the fear in the story itself, something rather in herself. She thinks, if Edward intends, through Tony or in some other way, to shake her faith in her life, well – she'll resist, that's all. She'll simply resist. There are things in life the reading of no mere book can change.

# THE THIRD SITTING

# ONE

Susan Morrow returns to the book after a hard day's work. Cleaning up, the vacuum cleaner, wrapping paper, gadgets and toys upstairs. An hour paying the bills and another on the phone talking to Maureen about everything except what's on her mind.

Dorothy and Henry are skating with the Fowlers. The snow is falling, the roads could be dangerous coming back. Rosie watches television in the bedroom, keep the sound down, dear. Jeffrey on the couch: off, mutt, you know better than that. The nostalgia of pizza burns the corners of her lips.

Susan Morrow opens the box, pours the manuscript upside down on the coffee table looking for the red placemark. She puts the finished sheets face down in the box, the unread ones in a pile on the coffee table. The new pile is smaller than the used pile. Susan foresees the moment when there won't be enough space for what should happen. She anticipates the disappointment of the end, waiting for her, already typed into that pile.

She sits with her lap pages, trying to remember. Tony Hastings lost his family to thugs in the night. Looking at the last page last night, she finds him smashing Ray Marcus's tooth in the trailer. She remembers her righteous wrath. Before that, Tony and Bobby Andes picked up Ray in a baseball uniform and before that Tony identified Lou Bates after failing to identify Turk.

That all this was written by Edward makes her feel ashamed. She picks up the pages, prepares to go on.

## *Nocturnal Animals 20*

There will be a trial for Ray Marcus and Lou Bates in Grant Center as soon as we get the case together. You'll have to come back for that. Mr. Gorman, the district attorney, will be in charge. That'll be another two months at least.

Firm at the magistrate's hearing, answering Mr. Gorman's questions, looking straight at Ray, who looked straight at him. Bruised face. Mister, you're gonna be sued. No you're not, holding firm with lawyers and juries, the American flag in the corner and the press.

He heard himself singing through the wind blasting the open windows as he drove home. Released. June on the highway, the bright young fields, rich dug earth, horses and cows plowed into the roots of what we eat with a thick shitty smell.

Sing sing sing, Christopher Columbus. I did it. His knuckles still hurt, he hadn't noticed it at the time. There was a raw gash where the skin must have ripped on the snag end of a tooth. He enjoyed the pain for its reminding value.

Going home to a party, driving faster than ever before under the big June afternoon sky with its cool warmth bringing wind and fair weather clouds, zipping ahead of trucks and Cadillacs and Volkswagens. Without taking anything away from his love, it was time for Tony Hastings to resume his life, he sang. Having fixed what was troubling it. Touched the untouchable, knocked him cold. Released the unreleasable, smashed the bottle to let the boat out, exquisite Tony. Speedy Tony, clever about speed traps, no cops caught him today. Made it to the house with plenty of time. Naked in the shower, noticing himself, filling with hope. Two parties, in fact, the faculty party at the Furmans and the graduate student party, with a personal note from Louise Germane, 'Hope you can come.' The parties were in conflict.

He put a bandaid on Ray's last bite. Dressed for the Furman party, regretting the need to choose. The choice reduced his swelling hope, whatever that was, which he didn't know. A desire to say something important to someone. What, to whom? He tried to adjust his expectation to the Furmans' party. Francesca Hooton? He glanced about the house quickly before he left, smoothed the bedspread, put a clean second towel in the bathroom, then chided himself for a fool.

Malks, Arthurs, Washingtons, Garfields. Francesca Hooton was standing by the porch door, a glass in her hand, with her husband. He had forgotten she had a husband. All the guests stood around with glasses in their hands, on the screened back porch and outside on the lawn and garden in the nine o'clock June twilight. Exotic evening, light that won't die, lights in house windows shining still, fireflies, that sort of thing. Everything reminded him of Laura. The lights and fireflies reminded him of her. Standing around with drinks.

He wished he had gone to the other party. He tried to remember what the important thing was he had wanted to tell Francesca before he discovered she had a husband. The only thing he could think of was the news they had caught Ray and he personally had slugged him. It seemed full of meaning, which all dribbled out like an untied balloon when he came out on the screened porch and saw these good friends whom he knew so well, and realized what talking would be like.

In the garden Eleanor Arthur talked about something, and as she talked she drifted slowly to the other end toward the edge of the dark ravine. He felt obliged to follow her drift. She was talking about teaching math as against teaching English, which was her job. She tried to make an argument about it. He had no wish to oppose her on this or any subject, but she was annoyed that he would not quarrel. So she tried to make an argument on why he wouldn't take a stand on things. When he wouldn't argue that either, she tried to make an argument, though full of sympathy, that he was still crippled by his bereavement, and when he wouldn't oppose her on that either, though he had been telling himself all day it was no longer true, she talked about church groups, the Nature society, and sympathetic friends who were only waiting for him to ask. With his hands clasped behind his back and his head lowered thoughtfully, like a cow, or a bull, he tried grazing his way back to the door but still she remained planted like a stake to which he was tethered, until he got the idea of getting her another drink. He came back with Francesca, and then something got into him, and he told them about Ray.

'I lost control of myself and knocked him down.'

Eleanor Arthur was delighted. 'The murderer? Well bless you, I bet that made him think about what he had done.'

Not likely, he thought. He looked at Francesca, searching for a message across the maze of others. Her eyes were still bright, but he could not guess what they meant. He felt stupid, his powerful experience a shallow party boast. He felt ashamed, while Francesca looked at him with Laura's eyes.

He decided to go to the student party. He waited for the buffet, so as not to be impolite, then said goodnight to Francesca Hooton and Gerald and Eleanor Arthur and Bill and Roxanne

Furman, and he stepped out into the balmy June evening a few minutes before midnight and hurried to his car under the fresh leafed maple tree, wondering if there was still time.

To the third floor apartment of an old house, a narrow street, he had to park three blocks away. He could hear the music as he approached. Suddenly anxious again, another foolish thing, what interest could he have in these young people with their loud music, what was there to prefer here? The answer was Louise Germane. Of whom he knew nothing. Did Louise Germane have a boyfriend? Lover? Nothing. Only the flattering things she used to say to him and the personal note she had added to the mimeographed party invitation.

He climbed up the narrow steps into a jungle of noise. The door at the top was open, the room loud and crowded. His colleague Gabe Dalton leaned against the doorjamb with his pipe, his beard, a plastic cup of beer in his hand, lecturing to a group of three, avid and respectful. Inside, members of his seminar: 'Hey Mr. Hastings. Beer in the kitchen.'

Glad of Gabe Dalton, to make him feel less out of place. He was speaking with great pipe-wielding beard-fortified authority about first one thing and then another. Snowing the kids. He touched Tony on the arm, not to interrupt the monologue, with a lot of unspoken meaning, such as, Good to see you coming out of your cave, pal. Tony looked around, disappointed. He went into the kitchen and found Louise Germane.

She was leaning against the refrigerator, talking to Oscar Gametti and Myra Slue. She saw him and waved. How colorful she was, tall, a blue and red T-shirt, a blue scarf holding back her wheat hair. 'Get you some beer.'

The beer barrel in the corner, she pumped it up and handed him a cup. The kitchen was quieter than the rest of the party. She was glad he had come, as if she believed it. Oscar Gametti asked him a question, and he began to talk. The students stood around politely and just like Gabe Dalton he talked, with growing ease from the position of his greater age and knowledge, about national politics and mathematics and the Department of Mathematics. He thought how respectful they were, looking up to him with admiration.

He noticed what small bumps Louise Germane's breasts made in her T-shirt. He wanted to talk to her in a different way, to say something different. She listened with interest, eagerly, he thought, her eyes seemed to glow at him. He wished he could detach her from the others. He wondered how. He wondered how she had come, how she planned to leave, whether he might, for example, take her home. If he could offer to, in a natural way without shocking her or attracting the attention of others.

He began telling his story, the whole thing starting in the night on the Interstate. He guessed they all knew it already, but he had never told it to students before. He heard himself doing it, he could hardly believe it, and he felt ashamed telling it, but he could not help it. He told it as plain as he could, with diffidence, but he left out no important facts. He told it like something everybody should know, like a lesson about the world. Their expressions became serious, they shook their heads and looked dismayed. He watched Louise Germane's large awestruck eyes, looking as if she wanted to kiss him.

After the narrative, Myra Slue said, 'It's time for me to go home.'

Tony said, 'Me too, probably. Soon.' Then, not too loudly, 'Can I give anybody a lift?' Myra Slue did not hear, the others were turned and talking elsewhere. He looked directly at Louise Germane. Repeat, to her: 'Can I give you a lift?' The kinship eyes and face that wanted to kiss veiled its pleased surprise.

'Why, thank you,' she said, hesitating and adding, 'I came with Nora Jensen.'

He allowed his disappointment to show. She said, 'I'll go ask her.' Like an afterthought, 'I'll meet you downstairs.' Like an intrigue, a scheme to conceal. His heart jumped. As she went off to find Nora, he noticed her suppressed little grin. His dignity reeled a little. He said goodnight to Gabe Dalton still holding forth at the door, and went downstairs by himself, where he waited for Louise Germane, wondering if she really would, while his heart leaped raggedly.

# TWO

The space in the text is not a chapter, but Susan Morrow pauses, blocked by something. Anticipating the sex scene she sees coming. Not sure she wants it, unless she can keep Edward out of it. Nervous Edward, whose sexual imagination in real life was not great. She's irritated with him. His snobbish picture of the faculty party. She likes faculty parties herself, thinking academic people more intelligent and cultivated than most. She's irritated by Tony too, shocked when he tells the students his tragedy, irked by his male preference for young Louise over Eleanor. With a question about the ethics of faculty-student screwing, if he or Edward has thought of that.

What's ailing her, obstructing her reading? Rosie hangs on the telephone, talking to Carol. If Arnold is trying to call from New York: Never mind, let her talk. Susan hopes he doesn't call. The thought surprises her, why should she hope that? She's afraid of his call for no good reason and suddenly realizes she's afraid of his return too, tomorrow – tomorrow? – wishing she had another day to get ready. She imagines him bringing her some frightening gift. Some gift that is no gift, deadly. What would that be? She doesn't know, it's a lump of thought in her head, amorphous and opaque like coal.

She detects outside an alteration of city sound caused by falling snow. She hears it covering the car, which she will have to scrape clean tomorrow, and the sidewalk she will have to shovel – she or Henry. She's caught by the strangeness of what she's doing, reading a made-up story. Putting herself into a special state, like a trance, while someone else (Edward) pretends certain imaginings are real. A question for another time: What am I really doing? Am I learning something? Is the world better, Edward, because of this cooperation between you and me?

Tony's world resembles Susan's except for the violence in its middle which makes it totally different. What, Susan wonders, do I get from being made to witness such bad luck? Does this novel magnify the difference between Tony's life and mine, or does it bring us together? Does it threaten me or soothe me?

Such questions pass through her mind without answers in a pause in her reading.

*[Nocturnal Animals 20 (continued)]*

He waited at the bottom of the steps, where two students stood smoking. Louise Germane was slow, she did not come. He imagined Nora Jensen saying Come on, I'll take you, and wondered if Louise could reply, But I *want* Mr. Hastings to take me.

Meanwhile others came down. Gabriel Dalton, still talking to two guys who followed. Nora Jensen herself, with Myra Slue but not Louise. He wondered if Louise had slipped away, fire escape, back stairs. He began to despair, before he saw a thin legged person at the top coming down, talking to someone further up, the jeans and laced shoes, the red and blue T-shirt, yes, Louise Germane. She looked at him eagerly, he thought she was going to take his hand. 'Complications,' she said.

He walked with her to the car, the other students watching them, drawing conclusions. She walked fast with long strides.

'What complications?'

'Nothing important.' She said, 'I appreciate this.'

'My pleasure.' He noticed the pleased look on her face. He let her into the car and she leaned over to unlock his side. She sat with hands folded in her lap and sighed, a mock sigh, he thought. 'What's the matter?'

'Jack Billings wanted to take me home too. I had to tell him I was going with you.'

Tony Hastings was alarmed. 'Would you rather have gone with him?'

'It's too late now.'

'I didn't mean to take you from your friends.'

'Don't worry.' He wondered, is Jack Billings her lover? 'I wanted to go with you.' Adding quickly, 'If you don't mind.'

He thought, this is Louise Germane, a stranger, and I am driving her home. He tried to think what the ban was. She sat beside him like an intimate member of the family. Does she think she is Laura? There's no law against giving her a lift, a politeness, a favor. But does *she* think I am merely giving her a lift? The students watching us leave will think we are lovers. But since we are not lovers. Unless Louise Germane herself thinks we are.

He wondered, what is this imperative thing I have been wanting to tell her? Do I know what I am doing? What if she invites me in? The ban again. He wondered, does it look as if he is trying to *seduce* Louise Germane? Would she think so? If so, she should be more wary, make excuses, evade. So perhaps she expects it of him. Is it possible she is trying to seduce *him*?

'Here we are,' she said. The question was desperate, that

is, What question? It was a long white house going back, six mailboxes on the front porch. 'Would you like to come in?'

He groped for why he must not. 'It's not too late?'

Her face in shadow. 'I'd be honored if you did.'

'I'll have to find a place to park.'

Probably she didn't mean to seduce him, she merely meant to offer him coffee, in which case he need not worry about the ban. They parked a half block up the street, and walked together downhill to her apartment. The rough sidewalk, shoulders bumped. The windows in her house were dark, the hallway lit. She checked her mailbox: GERMANE. He followed her upstairs, stood beside her in front of the scratched piney door while she looked in her purse for the key, his raggedy heart wild.

It wasn't the adultery, because Laura was dead. It wasn't the mourning, because eleven months had passed, and life cruelly demanded to be lived. It wasn't the child she was, because she was a grown woman of her generation, who at twenty-eight or thirty had probably had more lovers than he at forty-five. It wasn't the crippling, because the wound the loveless singles lady could not heal had now been healed. It wasn't the graduate student, because she had finished her courses and he had just tonight vowed never to have official authority over her again.

They went in. The living room was spare, a couch, a table. She turned on a light by the sofa, and put on a jazz piano record. She had a poster of Montmartre. He sat on the couch, broken down inside so that his bottom almost hit the floor.

'Wine?'

She sat beside him on the couch. Their knees pointed up like peaks. Whatever he wanted to tell her, now was the time. Probably it had to do with the events in Grant Center, but he had already told his story at the party, and still it was unsaid. As if the story had a secret commentary attached to it, reserved for her. So secret even he lacked the code. Other than that, all he could think to say was that he had been transformed from something into something else. The news was tremendous but vague.

If he could convey to her the emotional force, the prismatic meaning, that was gathered into the act of hitting Ray. 'I really slugged him,' he said.

'You don't know what it means to have you sitting here in my own place, Mr. Hastings.' Eyes in the subdued light, the face that wants to kiss. Student infatuated with teacher, sure enough, a good thing she is no longer *his* student.

She took the blue kerchief off her head and shook her hair loose, wild all around.

'I've often thought of inviting you here. Since your bereavement, I mean.'

He said, 'You're a good friend.'

'I want to be your friend. I don't want to be just a student. Does that annoy you?'

'Not at all. I don't think of you as a student, I think of you as – ' Fill in the blank, he thought, I can't do this by myself.

'As what, Tony?'

'As friend.' Which you already said. (She called you Tony.)

'I thought you were going to say, woman.'

'I was going to say it.'

She was looking at him solemnly, speaking slowly. He felt as if he was play-acting, she too, in spite of the tension. She stopped looking at him, then looked at him again and said, 'Does that mean you want me to sleep with you?'

Catch your breath, man, this was faster than expected. 'Is that what I mean?'

'It's not?' Her eyes were big.

'Perhaps it is.'

'Perhaps?'

'Well yes. I mean it is.'

'Do you want me to?'

'Yes.'

Quiet now: 'Me too.'

She said, 'There's one problem.'

'You don't have any – ?'

'Not that. I'm not certain Jack Billings won't come over in a little while. I'm not sure I've seen the last of him tonight.'

'Would he want to sleep with you?'

She nodded.

'You're lovers?'

'He thinks we are.' She opened her hands, empty. 'I'm sorry. I just never thought I'd have a chance with you.'

So that was the ban. 'I shouldn't intervene.'

'I want you to intervene.' She considered. 'Let's take a chance. If he comes I won't let him in. I'll tell him I'm sick.'

He had an idea. Why not? 'Would you like to go to my house?'

'Hey. Great idea.'

Quick, before Jack Billings comes. She ran to the bedroom, brought out a white robe, looked about hastily trying to decide what to take, couldn't think of anything except a toothbrush. 'Hurry,' she said, as if Jack Billings were already at the door.

A car was going by slowly when they came out of the house. 'Jesus,' she said, 'that's him.' The car went on.

'Why didn't he stop?' she said.

He remembered the woods.

'He looked right at me.'

'I don't want to make trouble for you.'

'Please don't worry. It's not your problem.'

In the car she said, 'I'll explain to him tomorrow. I'll think of something to say.'

He thought, Is there trouble in this? Do I want to be responsible for a break between Louise Germane and her lover? Do I know what public stance to take?

Louise Germane came into his house in the middle of the night. He turned on the lights. She looked around happily. 'I've always wanted to come here. Even before your wife died.'

She stood in the middle of Laura's living room, looking at Laura's paintings, the piano, the bookcases, sofa, chair, coffee table. Violating Laura by not being her. She was not his wife, nor his daughter, he hardly knew her, yet he wanted to take hold of her like an intimate, a member of his family. The paradox made him dizzy.

She said, 'I want you to show me everything.'

'Now?'

She laughed, stepped up to him full front to front, and said, 'Tomorrow will do.' Then the kiss itself, the first one, already probing, this young person whom he once considered timid, but who knew all about this kind of kissing, better than he, probably. She pressed her middle and lower parts against him and leaned back to look at him, and said, 'Where do we go for the festivities?'

'Upstairs?'

'Master bedroom? Great, let's go.'

He felt a certain irritation. They went upstairs. At the door he turned on the light and stopped. Laura's ghost. Tony was surprised, for he thought she had lifted the ban, but here she was, still not ready to leave the room. He looked into Helen's room, also barred, and then the cool neutral guest room.

'Let's go here.'

The festivities. She crossed her arms and pulled off her T-shirt, then they undressed, looking at each other all the while, her triumphant smile no longer secret. She was thin, her hips cast a shadow over the hollow of her thighs. She touched his cock, this girl who had been his student.

Muffled laughs, murmurs, nuzzles, tickles. Her body was as familiar as if he had known her forever. Go there, it's okay, I wish you would. I never dreamed I'd be doing this with you. Not to rush things, but the time began to swell, it filled and could not be delayed, and he leaned over Louise Germane, maneuvering to find her, and then he was there. He thought how good to be back.

In his own guest room, under the hairy bone while she clutched, he became aware of someone watching in the doorway. Jack Billings, ousted. The ceremony was moving into its wild stage, the gauge rising. It wasn't Jack Billings, it was someone in the other bed, while the color changed, sunset blazed on the snow, the solitary skier released to fall raced downhill on the fiery snow and dropped below into the late gray shadow. In the other bed someone was being raped by a man with his back turned, whom Bobby Andes was hitting over the back with a stick. Then Tony Hastings, even as he drew the last rich gold from Louise Germane, felt himself dividing, rising like a spirit from his twitching body to tug at the raping man in the other bed but being a spirit unable to touch him.

It was as quiet in the room as the funeral had been. She was stroking the back of his head. The people were quiet, perhaps they were gone. He looked at the other bed and discovered there was no other bed. There was Louise Germane, sweet and vulnerable, smiling vaguely like a child just waked up, and he relieved she was still alive felt tender toward her. He was confused by the violence they had just been through and the shock of seeing there was no other bed. It seemed to mean that the two beds were the same, in which case the man raping the woman was himself, which they were trying to stop, and the spirit of himself trying to intervene was only a spirit.

He was disappointed, for though he knew the time with Louise Germane had been good in itself, it was not a time in itself, for the case was not closed. He asked, 'Will you spend the night?'

'I thought that was already settled.'

In the middle of the night he wanted to wake her up and tell her, hey, remember when she seduced him in the blueberry field behind the house in Maine? When Helen was bike riding with her friend, he and Laura went out with a couple of blueberry baskets. She in shorts and a flimsy shirt, a warm sunny day, absolutely still, he heard her laugh behind him, turned around, saw her with her blouse open and her hands hooked in the waist of her shorts, pushing them down. 'Hey man,' she said, 'what say?' and afterwards a buzzing in the silence on the prickly ground. 'Relax,' she said in his ear, 'no one ever comes here.' Then the water, chasing her running down to the rocks where she dove in naked and he behind, the bitter cold, quick in and quick out, and, 'Jesus, we forgot our towels,' running up to the house with wild stinging skin. Laura the athlete, her arm-swinging walk. Skating in winter, he went with her sometimes to the rink to watch her pirouettes and figures, where she would teach him though his ankles were weak and he had no aptitude. Once she went on a skating trip with her friend Mira to the northern part of the state and was late coming back. He lay awake until five in the morning and she still hadn't come, and he thought the car had smashed on the highway ice. Not her fault, she had a good reason for not calling, now forgotten. Nights in the dark to tell Louise Germane about. Usually the worry was Helen, while Laura and Tony pretended to be asleep though each knew the other was awake, before Laura would sit up in bed and say, 'Isn't that child back yet?' Marriage and worry, Louise. When the doctor discovered the abnormal tissue in a routine test, they had to wait through the step by step of elimination before they could celebrate with a Chinese dinner, their future free and clear at last again.

Thinking for Louise, if you marry, you will worry. But when she died, the worries ceased, which you might consider a relief. He looked at Louise Germane, a big lump in the bedclothes, and thought: let's marry you when we get straightened out.

# THREE

The next page marks the beginning of PART FOUR. Since there's no room for a fifth part, it's four movements, a symphony, and we're three quarters done. The shape of the book should be clear, but Susan still can't predict what's in it.

There was a blueberry field behind the house in Maine, where Susan and Edward went picking with their baskets. No sex, though. It was not she who opened her blouse or pulled down her shorts or said, 'Hey man.' Does Edward writing wish she had? She's uneasy about the sexuality in his novel. The notion that slugging Ray unfurled Tony's cock. The vision of rape and struggle while making love to Louise. Is Tony's sex full of rape and death because he was traumatized by Ray, or is that what Edward now believes sex is? If she could talk to Stephanie and ask.

She would tell Edward that Arnold denies violence in his cock. He never wanted to rape anyone, can't conceive of sex against a woman's will. Susan Morrow believes him. She wonders, do men really differ, like tribes, the gentles and the roughs? What's violent in Arnold is meted out in a different arena: in ritual steps, washed hands in rubber gloves, tray and scalpel, measured pressure and delicate cut, concentration and control.

In their version of sex, she comes in after her shower, door shut, bedlamp on, Arnold reading in bed. Undisciplined children loose in the house, television downstairs, Nilsson immolating Brünnhilde through a closed door upstairs. Her short nightie, perfume sweetening her neck and ears. She stands near where he reads. He looks gravely at her knees, puts his book down. His hand, sensitive, moves up the back of her leg, the undercurve of her buttocks before going around to the front. She likes to see her husband the great surgeon's distended cock, his eyes boylike before the ballgame, and she loves his stubbly head against her cheek, his projection inside her.

While it's happening, sometimes she pretends they are making love for the first time as they did when Selena was in the hospital, or, revising history, on an early date as teenagers. Sometimes they are divorced but still friendly after an accidental meeting in a restaurant, or they are on a beach at night, or unmarried adventurers sailing around the world in a sloop with the steering gear set, or a pair of movie stars going restless to his house after having just filmed a nude scene, or they are the nude scene itself getting out of hand in front of the stage crew. Or they are political leaders on the sly after the summit protocol, Ronald Reagan and Margaret Thatcher. She does not tell Arnold, who assumes it's the excitement of his own thick presence.

Such thoughts make her strangely sad, as if it were all finished. Not so, she scolds herself, stop that. Read, read. She likes this book tonight. It feeds her well. She wonders how someone so self-absorbed as Edward could disperse so easily through a story and take her so out of herself. The book makes her feel better about him, at least she hopes it does.

## *Nocturnal Animals 21*

Bobby Andes called again. The telephone rang Tony Hastings out of the shower before his second date with Louise Germane, forcing him to sit at the phone by his desk with a towel around him, dripping water. Watching the couple in shorts across the street, washing their bright red car.

The voice on the telephone said, 'I got some news you might not like.'

Tony waited for it. Static, the tiny dead words, the bad news: They're letting Ray Marcus go. Who? Ray Marcus, that's Ray, *Ray*, they're letting him go. 'What do you mean, they're letting him go?' Tony said.

He heard the voice explaining, Bobby Andes, thin and nasal through the wires, saying they're dropping the charges, dropping the case. Mr. District Fucking Attorney Gorman, that's who, dropping the charges, insufficient evidence.

Tony was wiping his head with the towel, his idle penis exposed in his lap, his wet hairy legs, and across the street the girl in shorts with perfect fair legs leaning over the roof of the bright red car and polishing it dry.

'He needs corroboration,' the voice said.

When the girl leaned far enough, the back of her shorts lifted over the edges of her buttocks.

'What did you say?'

'Well at least you had the satisfaction of socking him in the teeth.'

Other voices on the line, a woman laughing.

'It's politics, Tony, that's what it is.'

In the silence the girl turned the hose on her boyfriend, who threw a sponge at her. Louise Germane expected him at six.

The voice of Bobby Andes, stretched thin over miles of countryside, wanted Tony to make another trip to Grant Center.

Tony tried to resist. 'It takes ten, twelve hours to drive there,' he said. 'I can't keep going back.'

He heard Bobby Andes saying, 'I want you here as soon as possible. Marcus will try to leave the state. Get a head start, spend the night in a motel.'

The military peremptory, not to speak of the intrusion on his privacy, on Louise Germane, on Tony's bewildered showered penis at rest in his lap. 'I have a date tonight.'

Noise.

'What?'

'If you're satisfied slugging Ray Marcus in the jaw. You find that an adequate punishment.'

So Tony said he would come, but not until tomorrow. He thought, there is no reason to be upset, and I am not upset yet. I will be upset later on, though. I will be shocked and I won't be able to get it out of my head, later on.

He wondered if he would be angry. It was an affront. He said, You would think they would give at least equal weight to my word against Ray's and let the jury decide. You would think my status in life, not to mention I was the victim, would give me credence, with that record in his background.

So he started the next morning in the early sunlight at six, and drove with the memory of his abbreviated night with Louise Germane, their second, in which he brought her back to the house and she helped him pack, and he tried to keep his mind on her and enjoy her and keep down the fear. The alarm clock woke him at four-thirty to the shock of having been asleep while something terrible was happening. He woke her beside him, and they had breakfast in the kitchen and he took her back to her apartment, leaving her with puffy eyes in the cheerful birdsinging six o'clock sunlight, where she intended to go back to bed and get the rest of her sleep.

He watched her wave sleepily, then followed the empty streets to the Interstate, which took him out into the flat countryside with mist on the fields. Once she was gone, the fear he had been fighting took over, an invasion. Something terrible is going to happen. A disaster coming. He wondered how he could stand it the whole day ahead with nothing but to drive and drive.

The long tiresome trip began to unfold, which had become so familiar, every detail in the same slow order, step by step, with each curve ahead opening to another vista with no surprises, farmhouse to farmhouse, bridge to bridge, woods and fields, all day long. With the shriek of the wind, the pounding and constant presence of tires that could explode and engine that could burn out and shell that could rattle apart. Impatience rewoke with every mileage sign and back to sleep with the gentle curving of the road. The journey sheltered him for the time, hypnotizing him against its own dangers and keeping all else at bay.

He tried to understand what he was afraid of. He supposed it was Ray. Ray free, vicious, hunting him down to finish what he had failed to complete last summer. Mister, your wife. With additional motivation for the smashed tooth. Later in the morning the fear took a new turn. Ray would go after Louise Germane. Of course, that's what he does, destroying me through my women. All the more need for speed, to intercept before he slips away.

Passage through a city and the need for coffee took his attention, and when he was free again, Bobby Andes was there, screened through the girl leaning over the roof of her car, the back of her shorts above the edges of her buttocks: 'If you're content with hitting Marcus in the jaw.' Trust him, he had something up his sleeve. Tony thought, It's not just Ray. He was afraid of Bobby Andes. What, his moral harshness, his contempt? Something nasty, not yet clear, which could get him in trouble if he didn't spot it in time?

After lunch no explanation seemed adequate to his discomfort. He felt delinquent in some duty. He had contracted an enormous debt, the due date had passed and foreclosure was imminent. It haunted him, I owe something to somebody. It was not financial. It had to do with Ray Marcus or Bobby Andes or Laura and Helen. Possibly Louise Germane, though unlikely, she being too new. It grew dim again. It was like a ghost, supernatural. Something terrible is going to happen. Something terrible has happened. One, the other, or both.

It would be even worse if something terrible was happening right now. Happening because something terrible did not happen. Mr. District Fucking Attorney Gorman has determined there was no case. Because what Mr. Tony Hastings saw was not enough. His identification of Ray, the three guys in the woods, the crime, was judged to be no identification, no Ray Marcus, no three guys in the woods, no woods, no crime. Tony Hastings mistaken. It made him want to howl. If they don't believe me, who am I? If what I remember is not good enough, what am I remembering? Where did it go, my life, what have I been doing since?

In the late afternoon, in the rolling country of eastern Ohio after another coffee, his mind cleared and the world seemed ordinary again, though not without the feeling he had simply locked up the haunting question in a room and would be hearing from it again. He asked himself the rational question, Exactly what is the purpose of this trip, and was surprised to discover he did not know. Ray Marcus has been released, and Andes wants me to come. To *help*, he said, but no word as to how. It's a hell of a long journey for so indefinite a purpose.

He counted up the number of long journeys he had taken at Bobby Andes's request. This would be his fourth visit to Grant Center in a year. All this in pursuit of three men. He thought, Why I must be crazy. This is insane.

It was the vagueness of purpose this time that proved it. Each of the other trips had a specific end which made some sense. He supposed Bobby Andes had a plan, something secret, not safe to mention over the telephone. Why, he said, that's mad. It's not me that's insane, it's Bobby Andes.

They met not in Grant Center but in Topping, in a restaurant with a counter, and they sat in a booth by the window opposite the fronts of their cars parked outside. Tony's dinner was tough gray roast beef under a blanket of gravy. He faced Bobby Andes, who bent over his food, curling his spaghetti on his fork, raising a forkful to his mouth but not putting it in, putting his plate aside, leaving it untouched. Tony Hastings looked at him and said, This man is mad. Adding after a moment, So am I. Bobby Andes said, 'If it wasn't for this cancer.'

'What cancer?'

Bobby Andes glared. 'I told you, I got six fucking months to live.'

Tony Hastings stared back. 'Did you tell me?' Did he sleep through such an important message as that?

Bobby Andes was saying how it was the lawyer he got, lawyer the court appointed, named Jenks, how him and Gorman made a deal and got Ray off. A deal, politics, you take this one, I'll let you have that one.

Tony asked, 'When did you tell me about your illness?'

'It's Jenks and Gorman.'

'I don't understand what you are talking about.'

'They want to ease me out.'

'Why would they do that?'

Bobby Andes did not answer.

'Would they drop a murder case to do that?'

Yes, the case. Bobby Andes explained. They were saying the case wasn't well prepared, it was a sloppy job, slapdash, no evidence, evidence gathered improperly, won't stand up in court. According to Andes, Gorman was punishing him because the sonofabitch is scared to death to take on a case he might lose. He asked if that made Tony mad.

'I saw them, Bobby.'

'Yeah yeah yeah.'

'Are they dropping Lou too?'

Not Lou. They got the fingerprints on Lou. Make him stand trial for the whole fucking Hastings case. That's fine if you're satisfied to hold Lou accountable for crimes inspired by Ray.

'It's no good if they don't get Ray,' Tony said.

'That's what I thought you thought,' Andes said. He told how Ray got off because the only thing they had on him was Tony's word, and Jenks had scared Gorman into thinking that wouldn't stand up. And because it was *Andes's* case and Gorman thought it was time he retired and got the benefit of his cancer in Florida.

'You never told me about the cancer.'

'The word going out these days is I'm incompetent. Which Gorman would like to prove.'

'What if I spoke to him?'

Bobby laughed, haw haw. The trouble with you is this

airtight alibi Ray's got. His airtight alibi. He was with Leila Whozis, she backs him up, her aunt backs him up, what can they do?

'There's another problem, too.'

'What?'

'Get this.' According to Gorman, your identification of Ray is unreliable. Calm down, it ain't personal, it's lawyers. It's Ray's alibi, plus she backed him up. Plus, it was in the dark which increased your chances for error. Plus, you couldn't identify Turk. That's big with Gorman, you couldn't identify Turk.

'Ray was more vivid than Turk.'

'Don't tell me, I believe you. We sure could have used your friend in the truck.'

'Who?'

'The deaf man. He could have identified Ray.'

'He probably never knew about it.'

'Everybody in the county knew about it. Sonofabitch was too scared to come forward. Mind his own business, the bastard.'

'So what are you going to do?'

Well, according to Bobby Andes, the obvious way would be to break somebody down. He told how he tried that on Lou Bates, which they wouldn't let him because all Gorman would allow was polite questions. You don't break an ox like Bates with polite questions. According to Bobby Andes, Lou Bates was an idiot. He had one principle of survival, name rank and serial number. He don't know Ray, period. When Bobby told him what the guys at Herman's had said, Lou said, 'If I had a beer with him, I never knew who he was.' When Bobby suggested it wasn't fair for him to take the rap for everybody, Lou didn't know what Bobby was talking about.

When Bobby asked who was that third guy running away at the Bear Valley Mall, he don't know, was there another guy? Big stone face with a beard.

Bobby Andes set down his fork and lit a cigarette. He was enjoying his frustrations. He thought they could at least hold Ray on the holdup but now the clerk can't identify him. He quoted Gorman saying, the only thing you got is the guys in Herman's who saw them drinking beer and Hastings (that's you) recognizing him from the number on the back of his uniform after you told him who he was. And they can't use Ray's police record because that ain't done.

He looked at Tony a long time, which made Tony nervous. 'It's a question how serious you are about seeing justice done.'

He said he had George keeping an eye on Ray, so he won't get away without him knowing.

Tony said, 'What do you mean, how serious I am?'

'That's a good question.'

Tony waited. Bobby Andes put his uneaten spaghetti a little further to the side. 'Can't eat,' he said. 'Might throw up.'

'Are you in pain?'

'What time do you have? Do you have eight o'clock?'

'Yes.'

'So do I. George will be calling. He's to check me here at eight.'

'What do you have in mind?'

Bobby shrugged his shoulders.

'Can't you eat? How do you get along if you can't eat?'

He shrugged his shoulders again. 'It depends.'

'I appreciate your going to all this effort.'

'Sometimes I can eat, sometimes I can't. This place stinks.'

'Do you have any close relatives or friends?'

Bobby Andes lit another cigarette and stamped it out without smoking it. 'Let me ask you a personal question,' he said. 'Between us, okay? What do you want me to do to Ray Marcus?'

The question startled Tony, the odd wording. 'What can you do?'

Bobby Andes seemed to think about this. 'Anything you goddamn like,' he said.

'I thought you said – '

'I got nothing to lose.'

Tony tried to understand. Bobby Andes said, 'Shall I restate the question? Put it this way: how far are you willing to go to bring Marcus to justice?' He lit another cigarette.

Tony wondered, what do you mean? He heard Bobby Andes saying this: 'Are you willing to go outside the strict procedures a little?' Like wondering if that slight tremor you just felt was an earthquake.

'Me?'

'Or me.'

He looked for a clearer euphemism. 'You mean, bending the law?'

Bobby Andes explained: what you might have to do to help the law if fucking technicalities prevent it.

Tony was scared. He did not want to answer the general question. He said, 'What specifically are you talking about?'

Andes was impatient. 'I'm trying to find out if you really want this guy.'

Of course Tony wanted him. Andes was disgusted. He just wanted to know, if Tony didn't like his methods. Tony wondered, what's wrong with your methods?

Bobby Andes calmed down, took a breath, waited. 'Some of these new law school jerks don't like my procedures. They're afraid my procedures will create a scandal if Ray Marcus comes to trial, burn their ass.'

Tony felt the whiff of a different horror. 'Could that happen?'

'Not if the police stick together like they should, sons a bitches.' Deep sigh, end of the world. 'That's why I gotta know.'

Know what?

'If you're gonna wimp out on me too. If you have a congenital aversion to strong aggressive police work.'

Tony did not want to answer. He wondered, why are you asking me?

'This guy raped and killed your wife and daughter.'

'You don't have to tell me.'

Bobby Andes wasn't sure of that. He pushed the point. Law says he should be punished, but if the law can't, do you want him to go free? Does the law *really* want him free?

'What else can you do?'

'You can *help* the law. Like I said.'

Tony wished he wouldn't keep thinking of different ways to put it. He didn't want to go against Bobby Andes. He said, 'Take the law into your hands?'

'Act on behalf of the law.'

'To do what?'

Andes didn't answer. He was working his mouth, chewing, not looking.

'To do what, Bobby?'

No answer.

'Act on behalf of the law to do what?'

Now Andes looked at him, looked away, looked back again. 'What do you think?'

Two possibilities occurred to Tony. One terrified him. He mentioned the other. 'To get new evidence?'

Andes half laughed, not a real laugh. 'You think that's possible?'

'How would I know?'

The woman called from the counter. 'Is your name Andes?'

Bobby Andes went to talk on the phone. In a few minutes he came back.

'Okay,' he said. 'Ray Marcus is at Herman's. I mean to go pick him up. It's your god damn case. I have to know now. Are you willing to participate, or are you going to fink out on me?'

'Participate in what? You haven't told me, Bobby.'

Bobby Andes spoke slowly, carefully, patiently. 'I want to bring the sonofabitch to justice.' His voice had an emotional catch in it, Tony noticed. 'I'm taking him out to my camp. I want you to come too.'

'What am I supposed to do?'

'Be there. Trust me and be there.'

'Then what? I mean, what's your plan?'

Bobby Andes thought a little, as if deciding whether to say some particular thing. 'I asked you before. What do you want me to do?'

'I don't know. What do you want to do?'

'I want to bring the fucker to justice.'

'Okay.'

'So you tell me. You be the judge.'

'What do you mean?'

'What should he get? Five years and parole, hey?'

Wondering what he was being goaded to say, Tony said nothing.

'More than that, huh?' Tony stared from inside his dizziness, feeling sick trying to guess. 'I hope you're not one of these capital punishment wimps.'

'Oh no, not that.' Tony shocked cold: permission to kill

Ray, is that what Bobby Andes is asking? His voice broke as he asked once again, 'What are you going to do?'

Bobby Andes gave him a funny searching look. Then laughed. 'Relax,' he said. He started to speak, caught himself, and after a moment spoke more quietly. 'I want to take him out to the camp with us and keep him for a while. I want to work him over. Get a little rough, make him suffer a little. See what he does. Would you like that?'

Tony could imagine enjoying it. He could see the possibility like a bit of bright dust in the murk.

'It's your case, I want you to see it. You can help.'

Relieved by the soothing tone more than the words, Tony Hastings had his questions, two or three distinct and others less definite, but he saw the impatience in Bobby Andes's eyes, like fear of dying or the end of the world.

'If you can make him confess, that would be good,' he said.

Bobby Andes laughed.

# FOUR

Susan Morrow sees a new issue shaping up through the battle of euphemisms, unless it's a red herring. She doubts that, it looks like a true fish: Bobby Andes takes the law into his hands. Tony Hastings meets John Wayne. With little space left, at most five chapters, more likely four, the risk of being disappointed was never greater than now.

Meanwhile, dialogue. Susan likes dialogue, how print fastens ephemeral words to the page like flattened animals on the road, so you can go back and inspect them in their non sequitur, as when Bobby Andes says irrelevantly: This place stinks. Yet behind all this imagined Pennsylvania and Ohio stands the ego of Edward the Writer. Tony Hastings, Ray Marcus, Bobby Andes, Louise Germane, the shades of Laura and Helen, these people who have, as she imagines, some relationship to herself, all are icons of that great Edward ego, projected on a screen. Twenty-five years ago she ejected the Edward ego, clumsy and crude, from her life. How subtly it works now, soaking up her own, converting hers into his.

*Nocturnal Animals 22*

Two cars, Tony Hastings in his following Bobby Andes through the quiet streets of Topping to Herman's. A big parking lot around Herman's, which was a one-story sprawling building with a red sign in the window. The sign cast a brighter glow than the twilight and accelerated the night. Bobby came over to Tony's car. 'Wait here,' he said.

From his car Tony watched the door to Herman's while the night came on. After a while two men came out. He recognized Bobby and realized the other was Ray. They talked in the glow of the sign. Ray stood with his hands on his hips, Andes looking up to him with his back twisted. Ray made a gesture of disgust, turned to the door, changed his mind. Two policemen appeared in the door. Ray gestured. One of the policemen touched Ray's shoulder. He recoiled, then submitted while the policeman put handcuffs on him and led him over to the lieutenant's car. Bobby Andes came back to Tony.

'We're going to my camp. It's in Bear Valley. You follow.'

Full night while they drove, a three-car caravan, the police car in front, down the fast valley road. A passing car got between Tony and Bobby, then passed Bobby but dared not pass the police car, making it a four-car caravan for the next five miles.

He saw the flashing turn signal of the cars ahead and put on his own, though nobody was behind. A side road to the left, the sign read WHITE CREEK. The road went narrow and straight between two fields, bumpy, they had to go slow. Tony could make out the ridge rising ahead out of the flat valley floor. At the end of the fields the road turned left. There was a narrow stream on their right under the bluff, with woods beyond. Light ahead, a cottage in a grove next to the stream. The two cars pulled in under the trees and Tony pulled in beside them. They all got out and Tony followed them in.

'My camp,' Bobby Andes said.

They went in through the screened porch. It seemed like a crowd in the little room, and it took Tony a moment to straighten them out. There was a woman, but the others were only the people who had come from Herman's: the two policemen, Bobby Andes, Ray Marcus. Bobby Andes had a gun in his hand, and the sight of it shocked Tony like an exposed penis. Bobby was glaring at the woman. He said, 'How did you get here?'

She was bigger than he. She wore a sweater and slacks, and had a tired face. She was probably in her forties and might be a schoolteacher.

'Lucy brought me.'

'Shit.'

Ray noticed Tony. 'Hey, what's this guy doing here?'

The room had a table in the middle, a cot, a few old chairs. There was an alcove with a stove and sink, and there was a screen door to the back and an open door to a bedroom. Ray's handcuffs glittered in the light that hung from the beam. He sat on the cot.

The two policemen left. Tony heard their car going off. Bobby introduced the woman to Tony. 'This is Ingrid Hale,' he said.

'How do do, Ingrid,' Ray said.

Ingrid's look at Tony was curious. 'So you're Mr. Hastings,' she said. 'You have my sympathy.'

'Do I have your sympathy too?' Ray said.

'Shut up,' Bobby Andes said. 'You might have told me,' he said to Ingrid.

'How was I to know? What are you doing out here anyway?' Like it embarrassed her to have a fight in front of strangers.

'Police work,' Bobby said. 'I want to do some fucking police work, for Christ sakes.'

'Here? Since when do you do your police work here, Bobby?'

He was standing there white faced, as if astonished by some

inner message. 'Jesus, I'm sick,' he said. He thrust the gun at Ingrid. 'Here, hold this.'

'What?' She juggled it like fire. 'Don't give me this.' She gave it back.

He thrust it at Tony. 'Use it,' he said. 'Shoot him. I'll be right back.' Tony looked at it, heavy in his hands, wondering how it worked. Bobby went out back. They could hear him throwing up outside the screen door. Ray sniggered.

'Do you know how to use that thing?' he said.

Bobby Andes stayed out quite a while, and there were more noises. 'Jesus Christ,' Ray said.

When Bobby Andes came back, Ray said, 'This ain't legal. If this was legal you'd of taken me to Grant Center, not this fucking place.'

Bobby took the gun from Tony and cocked it. 'It's all the legal we need,' he said.

'You'll pay.'

Tony heard Ingrid Hale clicking her tongue.

'You lied to me,' Ray said. 'There ain't no new evidence. Why don't you take me to Grant Center if you got new evidence?'

Bobby Andes was studying the gun.

'I like it better here. More relaxed.'

'Seems to me you tried this trick already. If you think this guy's going to break me down, you already seen that don't work.'

'Bobby,' Ingrid said.

'Okay, you're here, you're here,' he said to her. 'You ain't gonna like what you see, but I can't change my plans on account of you.' Tony heard something boastful in the speech, like, Now you'll see what police work is really like.

'Maybe I should go to bed.'

'Maybe that's what you should do. Hey Ray,' he said. 'What was you doing up Cargill Mountain this afternoon?'

'I knew you was tailing me.'

'You got a shack up there, some gal Leila don't know about?'

No words out of Ray.

'Won't tell? Doesn't matter. I really don't care, Ray.'

'Then what are you asking for?'

'Pass the time, Ray.'

'What for? You waiting for something?'

'Time for you to think a little. You need time to make big decisions. When your whole goddamn life hangs in the balance.'

'There's nothing to think about, man. My mind's clean.'

'Say, listen to that. What would you say, Ray, if your pal Lou Bates implicated you in the Hastings murders?'

Ray took a moment.

'Who?'

'Come on, Ray, don't try that. Your only friend in the world, you know Lou Bates.'

'I got friends, you sonofabitch.'

'Sure you do, boy, you got lots of friends. What if they implicated you? What if Lou Bates confessed? You and Turk Adams and him, the whole story.'

Ray sat there, thinking.

'He's lying.'

'I don't think so. Why would he lie to implicate himself?'

Ray looking around the room.

'*You're* lying,' he said. 'If Lou had done that you would of taken me to Grant Center.'

'We'll get you to Grant Center, don't worry. Like a beer?'

'Is it poisoned?'

Bobby Andes laughed. He nodded to Ingrid Hale. 'Get us a beer, girl.' She went to the back and brought out a six-pack.

She gave beers to the three men and took one for herself. Bobby Andes opened his but did not drink. Ray drank his bringing both handcuffed hands up to his mouth. Bobby said to Ingrid, 'Now maybe you can help Tony guard our pal here while I make a call.'

She was alarmed. So was Tony. 'What sort of call?'

'Police work, right? What I gotta do. You watch him and I'll be back in a few minutes.'

'Watch him? Bobby? How?'

'Tony will guard him, won't you, Tony? Take this gun. Here, I'll show you how it works.'

They went into the alcove and turned their backs to conceal the demonstration from Ray, who sat smirking on the cot. Tony didn't want to admit how scared he was. Miserable, Ingrid asked Tony, 'Can you use it?'

'I can try,' he said.

'You must think I'm a pretty dangerous guy,' Ray said.

'You're not dangerous, crumb,' Bobby said. 'You're a cockroach. Pest control. A little exercise in pest control.'

'Don't leave us, Bobby,' Ingrid said.

'Relax,' Bobby said. 'It's only five minutes. You want we should tie him down? Would that make you feel better?' He looked at Ray. 'Okay crumb, looks like we better fasten you to something.' He looked around. 'Frame on that cot,' he said. 'Here Tony, take the key and unlock one of them cuffs, hook him to the bed frame.'

Bobby Andes went around to the side of the cot, pointing the gun at Ray to cover Tony. Tony felt nervous getting so close to Ray, who was grinning, the vicious grin he remembered, and Tony could smell the onion on his breath. He was clumsy unlocking the cuff on Ray's left hand, and his hands trembled. He pulled the handcuffs down close to the bed frame, requiring Ray to bend forward. He was afraid Ray might attack and had to remind himself Bobby Andes was protecting him with the gun.

'Christ you guys,' Ray yelled. 'You can't make me sit like this.' He was doubled over.

'Sit on the floor,' Andes said.

'Shit.' He dropped down with his back to the cot, and Tony locked the handcuff to the frame. 'How can I drink my beer?'

'Use your free hand.'

Bobby stood back and looked at him like a painting. 'That make you feel safer?' he said. She looked at him pleadingly. 'Okay,' Bobby said. 'We'll make you safer still. Tony, go out to my car and get the leg irons.'

So they put on the leg irons, and then Ray was sitting on the floor with one hand raised and attached to the cot next to his shoulder, his two feet linked together, and one hand free for his beer can, which he kept sipping from.

'That's cruel,' Ingrid said.

'Yeah, it's cruel,' Ray said.

'You want to be cruel or safe?' Bobby said. 'I'll be back in five minutes. If you have to use the gun, use it.' He went out, and they heard the car turn around and drive down the road.

Suddenly it was quiet, as if Bobby had taken away the noise. The gun was heavy in Tony's lap. He looked at Ray shackled and stretched out on the floor by the cot. He kept one hand on the barrel, the other ready remembering the motions necessary to release the safety and cock it. He thought, My God, I am sitting here with a gun in my lap. I am holding a man prisoner, my own enemy who has tortured me for a year. It's good he's shackled, for otherwise I would have to depend on the threat of this gun, which I have never used.

Ray said, 'Your guy is crazy.'

'He's a good man,' Ingrid said.

'You think he's crazy though. You're crazy too,' he said to Tony.

Tony heard the night through the screened windows, the frogs at a distance, a pond somewhere, and after a while the water in the river, close to the porch. He heard the silence spreading out to the traffic on roads far away. He remembered the anarchy of the wilderness and felt the weight of his responsibility. This now, it's all because of me.

Bobby Andes was gone a long time. Tony asked Ingrid, 'Where is that telephone?'

'Down by the gas station,' she said. She wondered what was keeping him. She got more beers from the refrigerator and gave one to Tony, who declined it, and another to Ray on the floor. She fried some eggs and bacon.

'Yay momma,' Ray said. 'You fixin us something to eat?'

They were afraid to unlock him, which made eating hard for him. He could use only one hand. He said Ingrid was a real nice lady, but he felt like a fuckin animal in the zoo.

She began tapping her foot. 'Bobby, Bobby,' she said.

'Looks like he run off and left you,' Ray said. 'You and me, the three of us, alone together.'

It was dim, the room gloomy, with only the one light, a sixty-watt bulb hanging from the cross beam. The brown cardboard walls, pictures from magazines posted with thumbtacks, wild animals, mountains, a calendar three years old. Fishing rods, a shovel, a two-man saw, stacked together in the corner. A musty smell, an old remnant of skunk. Even in the night Tony was conscious of the cavern shaped around the house by the trees, a feeling of damp woe, of rotted memory, of Bobby Andes's misery.

Somewhat later Ingrid asked Tony about his wife and

daughter. Ray was watching, listening to everything. 'We went to Maine every summer,' Tony said.

'You had a good marriage?'

'We had a fine marriage. An ideal marriage.'

'No problems?'

'I can't recall any.'

She said, 'That's very unusual.' Snicker from Ray.

She said Bobby had had a bad marriage. He played around, which his wife didn't like and eventually she divorced him. His teenage daughter committed suicide, and his son left town and hadn't been back in six years. This was where they had spent their summers in the old days.

'He told me he had only one child,' Tony said.

'That's what he tells people.'

Herself, she didn't believe in marriage. She was the receptionist in Dr. Malcolm's office, and in her spare time she was writing a historical romance. She had been coming out to Bobby's camp on weekends for about five years. She mentioned Bobby's illness, how unlucky he was. She was considering sacrificing her principles to give him six months of happiness, for she was afraid he was heading for a breakdown. He seemed so mad and fierce lately. The chief complication was Dr. Malcolm. She glanced sharply at Ray. 'It's no secret,' she said. 'They know about each other.' Ray snickered.

That makes her sound wanton. But everything about her was under control and regular. Actually, she said, she didn't care about love. Her two relationships, it was a convenience and kindness for everybody. She kept them calm, she was not a passionate type.

She said to Tony, 'I can't tell what type of person you are. Anyone who had a perfect marriage, that baffles me.' She looked at Ray. 'As for you. God knows what you are.'

'I'm just a ordinary simple fella, maam,' he said.

'I'll bet you are.'

She said to Tony, 'Do you know what he plans to do tonight?'

Tony didn't.

'Police work,' she said. 'Out here? God knows when any of us will get to bed.'

'Damn right, lady, jeez I need my sleep,' Ray said.

She ignored him. To Tony: 'Maybe *you* could help Bobby.'

'Me?'

'You're a professor, he admires your kind of people. If you could talk to him, calm him down.'

He felt sick, because he thought of Bobby Andes as helping him. The other way round had never occurred to him.

She saw his look and shrugged her shoulders.

Shackled Ray from the floor spoke up. 'Hey lady, how about helping me?'

'I want nothing to do with you,' she said.

'It's cruel. You said so yourself. I got a crick in my back, I can't move, I feel like a fuckin animal in the zoo.'

'You'll have to wait until Bobby comes back.'

'Christ, he ain't coming back.'

'What do you want? There's no way I'm going to let you go.'

'Jeez I ain't asking you to let me go. Just unlock my fuckin legs and let me sit in the chair. You got the gun. What more do you want? I ain't going no place.'

Tony didn't want to look at Ingrid, for he knew she was looking at him. He knew she thought they should undo Ray's leg irons. Probably he thought so himself, for he felt ashamed looking at Ray on the floor. It made him uneasy, though.

'What do you think?' she said.

'Let's wait for Bobby,' he said.

After a while a car approached, the light shining through the window. Reading in her chair, Ingrid muttered, 'Thank God.'

Car door outside, footsteps light on the gravel, then the screen door opened and a young woman in a red miniskirt walked in. She looked confused. Ray looked up. 'Well,' he said.

'My God, it's Susan,' Ingrid said.

The girl named Susan looked at Ray on the floor. 'What's going on?' she said.

'Where's Bobby?' Ingrid asked.

'How should I know. Isn't he here?'

'What are you doing here?'

'Leslie kicked me out again.'

Ingrid laughed. 'Well if you're willing to sleep in the woods or something.'

The woman named Susan was looking at Ray's leg irons.

'Are you playing a game?'

'A little police work here. Meet Tony Hastings and Ray Marcus. Ray Marcus is a prisoner.'

'A *real* prisoner?'

'Hi Susan,' Ray said. 'Pleased to meet you Susan.'

'Tony is a visitor from out of town. Ray is charged with murder.'

'Not anymore,' Ray said. 'They dropped the charges.'

Susan had a lot of makeup marking off the parts of her face. Her eyes were surrounded by dark color. She looked at Ray and shrank a little.

'Listen Susan,' Ray said. 'Tell your friends they can get me off the floor now.'

'What's he talking about?'

'He doesn't like the leg irons.'

Susan gasped. She had just noticed the gun in Tony's lap.

'Are you a policeman?' she said.

'Tony's the victim of the crime Ray is charged with.'

'I thought you said the crime was murder.'

'Christ, they think I'm going to jump them. They got the gun and the cuffs, and they still think I'm going to jump them.'

'Oh shit,' Ingrid said. 'Let him up, for Christ sakes.'

Tony Hastings was glad for her decisive words. He knew their precautions were excessive, and they made him feel cowardly. The only thing was to be careful. They did it deliberately, with Ingrid holding the gun at Ray's temple while Tony unhooked the hand from the bed frame, then locked the wrists together, and then released the irons. He stepped back and took the gun from Ingrid, and Ray struggled to his feet and sat in the chair.

Ray looked resentfully at them all. 'Jesus,' he said to Susan, 'they think I'm from outer space.'

'What's Bobby going to do to him?' Susan said.

'Police work,' Ingrid said. 'My God, what's keeping him?'

'Where is he?'

'Making a telephone call. He's been gone a whole hour.'

'He's crazy,' Ray explained to Susan. 'She was telling Tony here, he's out of his mind and she don't know what to do.'

'You be quiet, you don't know the least thing about it.'

'You're worried he's going to get his ass fired.'

'You shut up. You don't know anything.'

'I'm not so dumb, lady.'

'You're a monster. You're a murderer. You're a rapist. You're a *horrible* creature.'

'Don't be a bitch, lady. It ain't nice.'

## FIVE

Susan has no time for more than a passing thought on the appearance of her own name on the page or to remember that this particular Susan was named by Edward, who didn't have to do that. There's time only for a moment to savor the melancholy of Bobby's camp and think of the pervading grief in all summer places, cabins or cottages in the woods or on the shore, Penobscot Bay or the Cape in childhood, Michigan now, which is not just the memory sadness when childhood is over and the place is gone, nor the generic sadness of boarding up the windows, but sadness of the height of the season, of bright sightseeing days as well as foggy ones in the hammock, of August silence, retreat of the birds, the goldenrod, the goodbye in every greeting. The sad vanity of measuring time by summers, eliding winter and the rest of things.

Assert the present. Snow covering the car tracks in the streets. On the ice, arcs and figure eights with shrieks and music under the high roof. Henry lagging along on buckled ankles watching Elaine of Astolat's fairy ass in her short skirt sail away a hundred miles an hour into the center with the big boys. As the new cycle begins.

## *Nocturnal Animals 23*

So there was Tony Hastings sitting with a gun in Bobby Andes's camp, watching Ray Marcus on the cot with handcuffed hands in his lap. There was Susan in her red miniskirt in the wicker chair. There was Ingrid Hale fussing in the alcove. Ray was looking at Susan's legs with a grin on his face. They were waiting for Bobby Andes, wondering what had happened to him. Tony was thinking, what keeps that man prisoner is *his* belief that *I* would use this gun to kill him if he tried to get away.

Susan explained herself to Tony and Ray. 'I am Bobby's cousin. When Leslie kicks me out I come here.'

'Come any time you like,' Ray said.

She was conscious of his eyes on her thighs and she looked at him boldly. 'Hey mister,' she said. 'Who did you kill?'

'I didn't kill nobody.'

She asked Tony. 'Who did he kill?'

'He killed my wife and daughter.'

Her eyes opened. 'When did he do that?'

'A year ago.'

She looked again at the man on the cot, who was instantly different, alien or another species. In a whisper as if to pretend he could not hear though of course he could she said, 'Are you sure?'

'Of course I'm sure,' Tony said. 'I saw him do it.'

He felt shock in the room, and Ray leaned forward. 'Why, you're a liar, mister, and you know it.'

So Tony told his story again, conscious of his real audience at last on the cot, pretending not to hear, but he felt as if too much telling had made it no longer quite true.

She murmured, 'How horrible, how horrible for you.' Then, 'Are you back to normal now?'

He almost said yes, then saw the gun in his lap, in the dark strange cabin, with Ray across the room, and said, 'No.'

'No?'

He thought, I want to murder everyone in this room. No, that's stupid. He changed his mind. 'I'm all right,' he said.

She cheered up. 'What do you do for a living?'

'I'm a professor of mathematics.'

She didn't have anything to say about mathematics. He asked, 'What about you?' He had a notion she was disreputable, maybe a prostitute, and he wondered how she would put it.

'I'm a singer.'

'Really? Where do you sing?'

'Right now there are no openings. I work in the Green Arrow.'

'What's that?'

'It's a bar,' Ray said.

'It's a night club,' she said. Ray smirked.

She yawned. 'Excuse me,' she said.

'Bobby, Bobby, it's so late,' Ingrid said. She looked at Susan. 'Maybe you should go to bed.'

'Maybe you should all go to bed,' Ray said.

'You want to sleep in the bedroom?' Ingrid asked Susan.

'Sorry I can't stay, myself,' Ray said. 'I got my sweetie waiting for me.'

'Bobby won't mind?'

'To hell with Bobby,' Ingrid said.

'That's telling him,' Ray said. 'Way to go.'

'I don't want to take your bed,' Susan said.

'Use the cot,' Ray said. 'Sleep here. We won't mind.' He looked at Tony and grinned. 'Will we, Tony?' Tony remembered he hated him.

'Maybe Tony wants to sleep too,' Ray said. 'You and Tony want to lie down on the cot? I won't mind, Ingrid can guard me, okay Ingrid?'

'Don't be disgusting,' Susan said.

'Come on, baby, I know the girls in the Green Arrow. Sweet chickies. Ain't they, Susan?'

'Just ignore him,' Ingrid said. She asked Tony, 'Do you know if Bobby was planning to put you up for the night?'

'I have a motel,' Tony said.

'I can sleep on the floor if I have to,' Susan said.

'You can sleep on the cot like I said,' Ray said. 'With him. You can turn out the lights and go to town. Me and Ingrid won't mind.'

'You shut up,' Susan said. 'For your information, asshole, there aren't any chickies in the Green Arrow, I'm the *only* girl there, so you don't know what you're talking about.' She turned to Tony. 'Excuse my language. But an asshole is an asshole.'

Ray was restless, squirming in his chair. He kept moving as if to get up, and every time he did that Tony tightened his grip on the gun. He kept thinking about what this power he was supposed to have depended on. One human being with the means to hold another down: this gun, that human being. He thought, Do I remember how to use it? If I had to, could I aim well enough to hit him before he got me? If he gets up and moves around, can I threaten to kill him? And could I actually do it? And if I did it, what would be my legal excuse? The question startled him, he had not thought of it before. Obeying the lieutenant's orders, if those orders were outside the law? An act of murder to support an act of kidnapping? He thought, Why, I can't use this gun. I might as well not have it.

Again he thought: the only thing that keeps us safe is, that man doesn't know what I'm thinking. He still believes I could use it. That's the difference between him and me. As soon as he finds out, we're finished.

The dim webby cabin, he could smell the mold in the wood. Abandoned by Bobby Andes into deep trouble, which according to Andes was not trouble but a clever plan, working fine, Tony bystander and beneficiary. The difference between Bobby Andes and him. He thought Thank God for Ingrid. She sees how it is, she'll back me up. If only Bobby Andes would hurry up.

He thought, maybe we should put those leg irons back on. Maybe he should suggest that to Ingrid. If it was safe to suggest it in Ray's presence.

So thank God again a moment later when they heard another car and again the light through the window, and the car door, and voices, male and harsh, and gravel footsteps to the front of the cabin. A man with a black beard came in, the lieutenant behind him with his gun. The man with the beard was Lou Bates, Tony told himself, drawing inferences since he did not instantly recognize him. He was slouching because his wrists were handcuffed behind his back.

Lou Bates looked at everyone, trying to figure it out.

'Son of a bitch,' Ray said.

Bobby Andes gestured Lou to sit next to Ray on the cot. He stared at Susan. 'What's this, a goddamn party?'

'Leslie kicked me out again.'

He glared at Ingrid. 'Did you invite her?'

'Where the hell have you been, Bobby?'

'I said, Did you invite her?'

'She came because she always comes.'

'Is it all right?' Susan's voice was high and tiny.

Tony was wondering when Bobby would notice they had freed Ray from his leg irons.

'I had to go to town,' Bobby said. 'Had to get him myself.'

'Why didn't you tell us?'

'I didn't know. I thought George would be on duty. I thought George would bring him out.' He was full of irritation because other people were so stupid.

'This man?' Ingrid said. 'Who's he?'

'You don't want to know.'

'Why couldn't one of those other guys bring him out?'

'They weren't going back,' he said. He spoke with the contempt of a man talking to someone who had no business being there. He stood in the middle of the room looking around at the crowd, his face pale and full of disgust. 'Jesus, I'm sick.' He sat down on the wicker chair. The look on Ray's face was watchful and curious. Bobby never did notice Ray's legs. He calmed down deliberately and looked at Susan. He said, 'I'm sorry to be unhospitable but I'm doing some police work here. I wasn't figuring on visitors.'

'Mr. Policeman – ' Ray said.

'I count on you to maintain the confidentiality of what you see. I may have to send you women into the bedroom later on if you don't mind.'

'Mr. Policeman, can I go to the bathroom?'

'Oh shit.'

'Yeah, shit. That's right, Mister Policeman, and pretty quick too.'

Bobby snarled. 'Get up,' he said. He led Ray out the back. They heard them clumping across the leaves in the back.

Susan looked questioningly at Ingrid and Tony. Ingrid raised her eyebrows. Lou Bates stared at the floor. Finally Susan turned to him. 'Can I ask who you are?' she said.

He didn't answer. She repeated her question, and he still

didn't answer. Tony said, 'That's Lou Bates. He was the other one who killed my wife and daughter.'

Lou raised his eyes and looked gloomily at Tony, then back to the floor. Susan said, 'Oh. I think I begin to get it.'

Ingrid had a book. 'You better read,' she advised Susan.

After a while Ray and Bobby came back. Ray's handcuffs were off now. He sat on the cot next to Lou, and Bobby sat in the wicker chair. Ray looked at Ingrid and said pleasantly, 'What you need, lady, is more lime out there. It don't smell too good for the women and children.'

'Shut up,' Bobby said. He turned to Susan and said, 'So, can I trust you?' He was finishing the point he had been trying to make before Ray's shit interrupted him.

'Who, me? Sure, I guess.'

'Hey,' Ray said. 'This don't sound legal to me. All this confidential shit, that don't sound good at all, mister.'

'Ha,' Bobby said. 'You worried about legality, are you?' His lips were the same color as his cheeks, he was breathing heavily, and he grinned. 'I told you not to worry about it.' He leaned back in the wicker chair and looked at them as if enjoying the sight.

Tony looked at them too, Ray and Lou, the same Ray and Lou, prisoners here because of him, paying for what they did to him, since what happened last summer in the woods had not ended then but was still unfolding in ways he never imagined.

'Okay you guys,' Bobby said.

'Hey Lou,' Ray said. 'What did you tell this guy?'

'I didn't tell him nothing.'

'He says you implicated me in the murder of this guy's wife and kid.'

'Shit man, that's what he told me about you.'

Ingrid Hale clicked her tongue. She turned her back and read her book fiercely.

Ray laughed, meanly. 'You think he was trying to play a trick on us, hey?'

Lou looked at Bobby, outraged, shocked. 'You're supposed to be the law, man. What kind of bullshit is that?'

Bobby Andes laughed. 'Fuck off,' he said. 'You fellas got anything to say to each other?'

'What's to say? You told us a bunch of lies.'

'You ought to be ashamed of yourself, an officer of the law,' Lou said. He sounded really aggrieved, disillusioned.

'Let that be a lesson to you.'

'What?'

'The lesson is, everybody in this room knows what you done, so it don't make the slightest bit of fuckin difference who implicates who. I don't give a shit what you tell me.'

Nobody said anything.

'I *know.* That's all I need. Got that?'

Ray said, 'So what are we doing here?'

'*That's* what you're doing here.'

'What?'

'Because I know what you done.'

'I don't get it.'

'You will. I ain't got anything to lose. Consider that.'

'You threatening us?'

Bobby Andes laughed again. The laugh was sickly and choked and nasty. 'I'm dying of cancer but I expect you to die first.'

'Don't take it out on us, man.'

'We're going to have a party.'

Ray looked uneasy now, uneasy. 'Man, you better watch it,' he said.

'Tell you something, babies. You thought you were free,

Ray, but look at you now. Here you are. Imagine that. Jeeze I feel sorry for you.'

No answer.

Bobby Andes stretched himself, as if he had a belly ache, a kink in his middle. 'You're gonna be kind of sorry you bothered a guy with womenfolks in a car. You may prefer to die, guys. You're kind of like garbage, you know, you kind of stink. Skunks, yeah, that's you. Not exactly live skunks, more like dead skunks.' He was twisting and twisting.

Tony Hastings was embarrassed though Bobby was speaking for him, saying what he thought Tony was thinking. But Bobby was ill.

'What's the matter, Bobby?' Ingrid said.

He looked at Ray Marcus and said, 'Have you ever had the stomach flu? Have you ever had the stomach flu on top of cancer of the insides?'

Ingrid whispered, 'Bobby?'

Bobby Andes to Ray Marcus: 'Don't you grin at me you fucking bastard.'

Ingrid to Bobby: 'Maybe you ought to lie down a while, Bobby?'

Bobby Andes to Lou Bates, 'You're dead, you son a bitch.'

Ingrid touched Bobby's shoulder.

'You ever had a bullet in your gut?'

He took deep breaths. She brought a wet washrag and put it on his forehead. 'Ah shit,' he said. He shoved it aside and turned to Tony.

'I'm thinking of killing them now,' he said.

'Killing them?' Jolt for Tony, the two men too, who stiffened.

'I ain't quite made up my mind. Do it now or catch them by surprise later on. You know what the law demands. They think they can lawyer their way out of it, but on that point they're mistaken, the death sentence has been passed, it's only a question of when it will be executed.' He looked at Ray and Lou. 'You know the meaning of that word, don't you, guys? "Executed," it means carried out, like when they carry out the body after the electric chair. I wish I could tell you your mode of execution, Ray my man, because it's much worse not to know, but I'm afraid I can't.' To Tony again as if to explain, while the two men listened. 'You see, if I let them go, it'll be rough on these poor guys, not knowing how it will come. The police are all around, they have a busy schedule of work. Ray could get killed resisting arrest, for instance. Or breaking into a jewelry store with some guy he thought was his pal. Coming home to his house late at night, he might get shot by a burglar in the kitchen. Who knows? No telling who you can trust, no telling at all.'

'Be careful mister, you got witnesses in this room.'

'You talking about my ladies, man? They know what they're seeing, don't you, gals?'

All for Tony's sake, who felt irrationally ashamed, wondering what Bobby Andes hoped to gain by this scary talk. Wondering how Bobby knew it wouldn't blow his case against Ray Marcus in any court of law.

Lou with his wrists handcuffed behind him was twisting his shoulders back and forth. 'Feeling uncomfortable, son?' Bobby said. He went over, unlocked him, patted him on the shoulder, fatherly. Now both men had their hands free, with Bobby grinning at them through his sickness.

He went back to his chair. Conversational, to Tony: 'I've been making a study of torture.'

Tony heard Ingrid breathing.

'These guys are good at it, I hear,' Bobby said. 'But they're amateurs. I've been studying legal torture. What governments use, which is more efficient than private torture, like what guys like these here perform on women and children.'

'You'll pay,' Ray murmured.

The possibility hit Tony, if Bobby had actually given up on a legal solution, if he really was intending to execute his own remedies. Which made Tony wonder what to do if that were the case. If he should intervene – if he had ever intervened in anything in his whole life. To intervene he would have to know what he was trying to stop. Tough talk, aggressive police work? Bluster, intimidation, psychological tactics. What would he propose instead?

'In government torture,' Bobby said, 'there's supposed to be a purpose. The purpose is to get a confession. That's what they have to say, the ostensible purpose. Do you guys know what *ostensible* means? The real purpose is different. The real purpose is to make them wish they was dead.'

The trouble with intervening was that Bobby was riding a plan like a horse, and no cautious question about legality or charity could stop him now.

'Nobody gives a shit about confession. The great thing about torture, it gives you a maximum awareness of your natural instinctive death wish. How's that for a definition, Tony?'

So Tony said, 'Bobby.'

'What?'

Tony didn't know. If Bobby was merely talking, Tony would feel like a jackass.

'What should we do with them, Tony?'

'I don't know.'

Bobby Andes was thinking it over. He looked at his gun, weighed it, picked it up and aimed it experimentally at Ray's head. Ray ducked, then sat straight. Bobby Andes cocked and uncocked it, aimed again, put it down. He looked a long time at Ray and Lou and Lou and Ray and then got up. He winked at Ray and handed his gun to Ingrid. 'Here, hold this.' She handed it back and went into the kitchen alcove. He handed it to Susan, who held it in her fingertips with astonishment. He went to the back and opened the closet door and squatted down, looking for something on the floor.

Ray leaned back on the cot with his hands behind his head while Lou sat on the edge, and Tony with his gun in the straight chair watched. Ray snickered. 'You scared, Lou?' he said. He tickled Lou in the ribs. 'Cut the fuck that out,' Lou said.

'He ain't nice, that man of yours. He's gonna get in big trouble when he grows up,' Ray said. He watched Bobby's back as he put his old fishing tackle box on the table in the alcove.

In the other wicker chair the girl named Susan, who had no last name, handling Bobby's gun as if it were a turd, was trying to keep its cold metal from touching her bare white thighs. In the alcove Ingrid was banging around. 'I didn't know I was going to guard a prisoner,' Susan said.

They watched Bobby take something out of the tackle box and hold it up, examining it. He got up and took a rusty sickle out of the closet, felt the edge, put it back and brought what looked like an old automobile battery back to the table. Seated with his back turned, he held up a long piece of wire. He cut something with his knife, then held up the wire to make a loop, then leaned over and scraped something metallic with his pocket knife. He had fishhooks and pieces of wire scattered around him, and Tony could not see what he was doing.

Ingrid was sloshing water in the sink. They heard the tin dishes bang. Susan squeaked. The gun had slid onto her thighs.

'I wonder if I could use this thing if I had to,' she said.

Ray sat up.

'It's a pretty dangerous weapon,' he said. 'You gotta be careful how you handle something like that.'

Ray was thinking about something, Tony could see that. He was looking at Lou trying to communicate, but Lou sitting there gloomy didn't notice. Bobby glanced around, then back to his work. Bent over the table he made a grinding sound.

'Can I go to the potty?' Ray said.

'You just went.'

Ray got up. 'Watch it,' Tony said.

'It's okay, okay, just stretching my legs.' He went to look at the magazine pictures tacked on the wall.

'Sit down,' Tony said.

'Aw jeez, I need to exercise.'

'Sit down.'

'Yes boss.' He sat down.

At the table in the alcove Bobby turned around and looked at them. He had a knife and a pair of wires in his hand. He turned back to his work.

'Better do what the man says,' Bobby said, his back turned.

Ray said, 'Did you ever shoot one of them things?'

Tony did not want to answer.

'I bet you never did.' He was talking quietly, but not too quietly for Bobby to hear.

'Hey Tony. If you shot me what excuse would you use?'

'That's my problem, not yours.'

'This ain't the law, this is kidnapping. If you shoot me that ain't a police action, that's murder.'

Tony chilled, what he had hoped would not occur to Ray. Which would take the gun away from him. He wished Bobby would finish what he was doing.

'Where do you teach, professor?' Ray said. He got up again. 'Let's go, Lou.'

'What?' Lou said.

There was Ray, moving around to the side, along the wall toward the door, 'Let's go, move it!'

Lou looked at Ray, blankly.

'Sit down,' Tony said. 'Bobby!'

'Come on you jackass, it's time to go,' Ray said.

Tony jumped up. He tried to cock the gun and block Ray from the door. In the alcove he saw Bobby Andes stand up in the shadow. 'Shoot him, Tony,' Bobby Andes said.

'Let's go, let's go.'

'You crazy, man? That's a gun he's got.'

'Move man, move.'

Standing in front of the door, Tony got the gun up and pointed it. 'Stop. *Halt!*' he said, while Ray came right at him, and he ducked aside because he was afraid Ray would grab the gun out of his hands. When Lou saw that he jumped up too, and Susan screamed.

The door caught Ray, who fumbled with the catch and broke out. Now Bobby moved, Tony saw him rush forward, grab Susan's hand, heard him say, 'Gimme that,' saw the inner door slam into Lou's face, heard Ray's feet running off the screened porch, saw Lou push the door out of his way and run, and Bobby rushing by Tony, shoving him aside and shouting, 'Now I got you, bastards.' Then a great explosion just outside the door threw all his perceptions into chaos.

A bomb, he thought, thinking the cardboard ceiling would collapse. He saw the faint blue smoke, smelled the powder, saw the gun in Bobby Andes's hand held up as he jumped off the step running after Lou. That was Susan who was screaming. He saw her, she had picked up a carving knife, while Ingrid held the dishpan full of soapy water cocked and ready to throw.

Outside another explosion, then another. He ran out to the porch, saw the man standing on the path with hands extended aiming the gun, looked and saw one man running along the river's edge. One more shot while the man kept going and disappeared down the path by the river, behind the trees. Then Tony noticed the other man lying on the grass near the river.

There was Susan on the porch beside him, gasping, and Ingrid wiping her hands on a towel. There was Bobby Andes on the path, small and fat, tucking in his shirt. He was looking down the river to the woods, where the man had escaped.

'Get the keys,' he said. 'We gotta catch that guy.'

'Wait, Bobby,' Ingrid said.

Tony's car keys were in his pocket. The man on the grass was Lou. He was groaning, trying to get up, his hands on the ground, but he couldn't make it. He was looking at them, calling. 'Somebody help me, please.'

Ingrid went into the house and came back with a towel. Bobby Andes was staring down the river or thinking.

'I'm hurt, man,' Lou said.

'It's no use,' Bobby said. 'We'll get him later.' He looked at Tony. 'Christ. Why didn't you shoot him?'

A quick answer jumped into his head, 'That's your job,' but he couldn't say it and couldn't think of anything else instead. With the towel in her hands, Ingrid went out across the grass to where Lou lay. 'Stay away from there,' Bobby said.

'He's injured. We've got to look at him.'

'Get back here.'

'Snap out of it, Bobby, and get dressed. We've got to take him to the hospital.'

'Be quiet.'

'He could die while we wait.'

Transfixed, thinking about something. Suddenly Bobby Andes moved. 'Stand back,' he said. He walked over to Lou and shot him in the head.

One of the women said, 'Mother of God.'

Go back over that. There was Lou on the ground, sobbing from the pain, looking with pleading at Bobby Andes striding toward him like a soldier. There was the executioner's gun pointing at him, the shocked face and the man hiding his head in his arms trying to roll away. Then the explosion and the body like a jumping bean, falling back with a kick of the legs, then limp.

Susan cried like a child.

There was Bobby, nudging Lou, who would have to be dead, leaning over to look at him, then back at the others on the porch or at something above their heads. He raised his gun, pointed it at them, and fired again. The wild shriek of total terror was Susan, running inside.

'Shut up,' Bobby said, 'I'm not shooting at you.'

He held his belly as he hobbled back to them, leaning over, gun hanging in his hand. 'Go on in,' he said. 'You look like a bunch of idiots.'

Wherever he was aiming that last shot, what he actually hit must have been the door spring, which was hanging loose and vibrating next to a torn piece of screen.

# SIX

## *Nocturnal Animals 24*

They stood in Bobby Andes's camp while the echo of catastrophe died in the woods: the girl named Susan in her miniskirt, Ingrid with a dish towel, Tony Hastings with his unused gun, all in shock by the table. Bobby Andes full of police work fixing his pants, holding the gun he had used. Lou Bates outside on the grass with a bullet hole through his brain.

'Shit,' Bobby said. 'What happened, Tony, gun wouldn't work?'

The rage Tony wanted to feel was smothered by the shame of not knowing what he was supposed to do, so he said nothing.

Bobby looked at Susan. 'Sorry I scared you. I saw a bat.'

'A bat, Bobby? You were shooting right at us.'

Andes's face changed. He put his gun on the table and went out the back door. They could hear him heaving like a seal. He came back. 'Christ of all fuckin times to be sick.'

He sat down at the table and took deep breaths. 'Got to move,' he said.

'Bobby,' Ingrid said, 'there's that man you killed out there.'

'Give me time.'

She looked at Tony and Susan, they all looked at each other.

'Bobby? What are we going to do?'

'It's all right,' he said. 'It's under control.'

'What are we going to do? You killed that man.'

'Right. He tried to run away.'

'You deliberately killed him.'

'He was trying to escape.' He looked at her. 'What's wrong?' he said.

'You shot him a second time. You shot him in the head.'

The room was still, everyone looking at him, the sound of peeping frogs once more down the river. He ran his hand across his head, opened his mouth to speak, changed his mind.

'Why did you do it?'

'Because I didn't get him the first time. Jesus.' He felt in his pocket and brought out his car keys. 'I've got to go.'

'Go where, Bobby?'

'Telephone call.' She touched his shoulder, he brushed her off. 'Don't touch me, I'm all right.'

'Can't you send Tony?'

This alarmed Tony, but Bobby looked as if she were crazy.

'Tony can't do it,' Bobby said.

'Can't do what? He can deliver a message to the station. What more do you want?'

'I want to catch that bastard when he gets out to the road.'

'Oh no, Bobby.'

'Oh yes, Ingrid. I have to catch that bastard.'

'And leave us here by ourselves?'

He stood up, straightened himself, walked to the door. She cried out. 'Bobby!'

'Relax,' he said. 'Tony's got a gun. If he can remember how to use it.'

'There's that man lying out there.'

'Leave him lay. Don't touch him. Stay inside and hope no early morning fisherman trips over him.'

He went out. They heard the car go. Ingrid said, 'Damn him to hell.'

Susan asked, 'Was that *legal*, what he did?'

'Shooting him?'

'Is a policeman *allowed* to do that?'

'He was trying to escape. However,' Ingrid added. 'That second shot in the head. There was no need for that.'

'Will he get in trouble for that?'

'Also.'

'What?'

'He had no legal grounds for holding the other man.'

'You mean Ray?'

'That was against all rules,' Ingrid said.

'Will that get him in trouble?'

'I don't want to think about it.'

'Maybe if we don't tell.'

'They'll know,' Ingrid said. 'The wounds in the body will tell. The question is, will the buddies rally round?'

Tony's shock was turning rancid.

'What was he trying to do?' Susan said. 'I mean, when they find out, won't it ruin him?'

Ingrid's half laugh. 'When who finds out?' She said, 'I don't think he cares. I think he decided if the District Attorney wouldn't go after him, he'd do it himself.' Ingrid trying to figure Bobby Andes out. 'What I don't understand is, how he could have been so careless.'

'Was he careless?' Susan said.

'Fiddling at that table. Expecting Tony to stop them. That's not like him.' She looked at Tony. 'I guess *you're* glad that man is dead.'

He couldn't think about it, distracted by the question of what Bobby expected when Ray made his dash to escape. The death of Lou Bates seemed unimportant, as if he had ceased to be Lou Bates. It had no satisfaction for Tony, no more than had the death of Turk. Time had redefined the crime, and the only criminal who mattered was Ray. It was all Ray and Ray alone, and once again Tony had been afraid and let him go.

'Are you sure he's dead?' Susan said.

'He was shot through the head,' Ingrid said.

'He might not be dead though. Maybe we should go see.'

'He's dead. No doubt about that.'

'I think someone should look at him just in case.'

'Not me.'

Not me either, Tony's thought repeated when she turned to him. They stood in the door and watched while the policeman's young cousin whom he and Ray had both considered a prostitute but who seemed to be rather only a kind of child in her miniskirt went out with the flashlight and gingerly approached the dark shape by the river and watched while she crouched down courageously and studied him, her knees pale in the black. They saw the spot from the flashlight as she moved it over the man's body and saw her hands touching his face. When she came back her face was wan. 'His eyes are open,' she said.

'That's what they do when they die,' Ingrid said. 'They open their eyes but can't see.'

Things go sour. Food spoils, milk curdles, meat rots. In the dim light of the camp there's this feeling of accident and breakage. The death of Lou Bates was not a right death. Tony wondered if he had caused it by having failed to stop Ray and Lou with his gun. But the only way to stop them would have been to shoot them, which would have made him rather than Bobby the killer, and that would have been worse. Therefore it wasn't his fault. The reason for his dumb rage burst into light: if Bobby had intended him to be the executioner of Ray and Lou. The question was intolerable. Whatever went wrong, he insisted, he was only a witness, not an actor.

Susan yawned again. Tony remembered how he walked through the woods and along the roads without sleep a whole night until he found a farmer getting up in the earliest dawn.

'You want to go in the bedroom, lie down?' Ingrid said.

'I can't sleep with him out there,' Susan said.

'Me neither,' Ingrid said. 'Bobby'll be back soon.'

'Will he? I thought he was going to try catch that guy.'

'If he does that, I'll kill him.'

But Bobby Andes was already back. They heard the car in the driveway, the sweep of its headlights through the window again, the car door. They saw Bobby Andes striding up to the cottage, fast into the room, transformed.

'That was quick,' Ingrid said. 'Are they coming?'

'I got to go to town,' he said.

'No, Bobby, not again.'

Notice the change in him, leather face, no debilitating liquid sickness now, only the harder more permanent kind.

'Wickham's got the phone. I got to see Ambler myself.'

No panic, but urgent. Everything under control, but effort needed to keep on course. No catastrophe if we keep our heads.

'Before I go,' he said. He looked around at the three of them, as if waiting for their attention, though he already had their attention. 'You need to know what happened tonight.'

'What happened?'

'What happened here. What you saw.'

'I saw what happened,' Ingrid said.

'Did you?' He gave her a look.

'Oh,' she said. A silence, queasy.

'You want us to lie?' Ingrid Hale said. 'Please, Bobby, don't make us lie.'

'You don't want to lie? You want to tell the whole truth,

nothing but the truth, so help you God, everything you saw tonight? That what you want?'

She looked miserable. Tony was full of palpitation. She said, 'Oh Bobby, dear.'

Bobby dear had droopy bloody eyes, his mouth gaped like a fish for air. It always had, but Tony had not noticed it before.

'I don't give a shit,' he said. 'I thought you'd *like* to have a story. If you don't want one, the hell with it.'

She slumped in her chair. 'All right. So what story are we supposed to tell? Are you going to tell us?'

'That was *Ray Marcus* who shot Lou Bates. Shot him twice. Once in the body, once in the head.'

'My God,' Ingrid said.

'Shot him because Lou had agreed to testify in court.'

Quiet while they think this over. Ingrid gave Tony a desperate look, help, help, though he avoided it.

'That doesn't make sense,' Ingrid said.

'It makes all the god damn sense you'll need.'

Tony was trying to visualize Ray Marcus shooting Lou Bates.

'You want to know how he did it?' Bobby said. 'You do want to know, don't you? You can't just have Ray popping up suddenly with a gun when he's a prisoner here, right? You want to know?'

'You'd better tell us then,' Ingrid said.

'I'll tell you. He wasn't a prisoner. I mean he was here but he left. He left after we had a conversation and I dropped him off at the road on my way to pick up Bates. Only he didn't go home. Or he went home and got his gun, or got a gun somewhere and hitchhiked back, and that's when he did it. Ambush. Lay in wait outside the cabin, shot him as I was taking him into the house, caught me by surprise, pow pow.'

'You've got it all figured out,' Ingrid said.

'It's enough.'

'It's ridiculous.'

'Naw it ain't.'

'You can't get away with it. Can you?'

'What's to get away with? I got Ambler, I got George. All we need is you guys to agree, not tell more than you need.'

'Perjury?'

'Jesus, girl. Think of it as the potential in the situation. It would have happened, given enough time.'

'Come on, Bobby.'

'What do you mean, come on? I'm offering you scandal-free days for the rest of my life, whatever that may be. If you think that's perjury, turn me in, I don't give a shit.'

She looked at Tony, at Susan. 'Can you go along with this?'

'Me?' Susan said. 'What am I supposed to do?'

'You're supposed to say that Ray Marcus person wasn't here,' Ingrid said.

'He left before you came,' Bobby said.

She got it. 'Oh. And then he came and shot the other guy with the beard?'

'That's right. If they ask you, that's what you saw. Only, wait, you didn't actually see him. You didn't see the guy with the beard either. All you heard was shots as I was bringing the guy with the beard in from the car.'

'That's what I'm supposed to say, huh?'

'That's what you're supposed to say.'

He seemed relieved and pleased with himself. Tony, thinking if I object to this I destroy Bobby Andes, was scrambling through his mind for questions he could be asked on the witness stand.

Ingrid said, 'He'll deny it.'

'His denial ain't worth shit. He denied killing Tony's folks.'

'He'll go to the police and report it.'

'He's not that dumb.'

'He'll go to the police and tell what he saw. He'll tell everything, Bobby. How you kidnapped him and the handcuffs and how you killed Lou.'

'Nah, he won't.'

'How do you know? If it was me I would.'

'He won't because he knows they would arrest him for killing Lou. He knows because he knows me and he knows my friends and he knows you three are witnesses. That's why he won't go to the police. But if he does go, that's what he'll find. He'll find out no one believes him.'

'It's so cynical, Bobby.'

'What's cynical? Don't argue with me. If that's cynical, give me an alternative. Tell me the non-cynical thing to do.' He was melodramatic, full of opera.

As for Tony, full of woe, at fault and to blame for everything, he was groping around in the empty spaces of the story he was supposed to tell, looking for its questions. 'Bobby,' he said. 'If Ray Marcus killed Lou Bates, when did he leave here?' More. 'Where did he go?' Still more. 'How did he get his gun? How did he get back here?'

'Let me worry about that,' Bobby said. 'He left here when I left. I took him in town. I took him in town, yeah, because I didn't want to do business with Ingrid here, that's how it was. God knows what he did then. Got hold of a gun. Hitchhiked back this way. Don't worry about it.'

He was looking at them like a sick scoutmaster. Have you got it now? Can I leave it with you? Are the gaps plugged?

'Let me recapitulate,' he said. 'Shall I do that? Yes. So I brought Ray. When I saw Ingrid here, I took him away again. You waited. Susan came. You wondered where the hell I was. After a while I came back. As I came up to the house with

Lou, bang! Two bangs. You ran out and saw this guy lying on the ground, the other one running away. Simple, right?'

Tony thought how galling to have Ray Marcus on the right side of the law against him.

'Don't worry about Ray,' Bobby said. 'He's liable to get killed resisting arrest. Yes?' To Ingrid. 'Did I shock you?'

She didn't say anything.

'I have a job to do, and I have to find ways to do it.'

No one said anything.

'Shit. You're all so fuckin honest. You too, Tony? Your wife and daughter murdered and you sit here splitting hairs?'

'Bobby,' Ingrid said, 'is this how you always work?' She looked as if she had never seen him before.

'You criticizing the way I do my job?'

They stared at each other. After a moment he yielded. 'No, I don't usually do it like this.' He sounded reasonable now. 'No, I never did it like this before.' Regretful.

'You're a stubborn bastard, Bobby,' Ingrid said. 'Why can't you just say you lost control of a prisoner? Then you lost your head and shot him. Will they kill you for that?'

Bobby thought about it. 'It's not so simple,' he said at last. 'I don't lose control of prisoners. I prefer my version.'

Tony was thinking about the hostile officials who would be cross-examining him.

'I'll explain it to Ambler,' Andes said. 'He'll take care of it. You probably won't have to say anything at all.'

He rubbed the gun with a handkerchief and went to the door. 'Be right back.' They watched him from the porch. He went by the body of Lou where it lay, shadow like roots of a tree, and on down to the river where he flung the gun into the water. When he came back he said, 'If you're worried it's not the truth, think of it as the intrinsic truth. What happened is what would have happened.' Then, 'Tony, I need your help to catch Marcus.'

This scared Tony, and again Ingrid objected. 'How can you catch him? He's in the woods.'

'If he's in the woods we track him with dogs. If he gets out of the woods, he'll hitchhike. So we catch him before he gets a ride.'

'He could be anywhere.'

'No he won't. There's only two roads he could get to before morning. If we get out there quick enough.' He looked at Tony, Tony full of horror. 'If you go in your car and I in mine.'

'Hunting for Ray?'

'Relax.' It was not a laugh. 'I want you to go to George Remington's house. Wake him up and tell him we need his dogs.'

'Do that yourself,' Ingrid said.

'God damn it, woman, I've got to see Ambler while he's still on duty.'

'Why Ambler?'

His look was one of those secret things. 'I'd rather report to Ambler than to Miles.'

Bobby Andes went to the table with a piece of paper. He drew a map. 'Here Tony. Bang on his door until he wakes up. Give him this note and tell him I want his dogs. Tell him a man got away and a man got killed but don't say anything until he hears from me. Then come back here.'

Ingrid said, 'Leaving Susan and me alone with him out there on the grass?'

'I have no choice.'

She didn't say anything, but he heard it anyway. 'Fuck you,' he said. 'Let's go, Tony.'

Obedient Tony got up, feeling horrible, and at the door

Bobby turned around and made a speech. 'The next time you see me I'll have the guys. I'm gonna tell them how Ray killed Lou. If you don't like it you can tell them any fucking thing because I don't give a shit.'

He saw Tony trying to hand him his useless gun.

'Keep that, if you see Marcus.'

'Am I likely to?' He had to tell himself, being in the car there was nothing to fear.

'If you see him, pick him up. Stick his hands through the front and back windows and handcuff them together.'

Using the gun which he had not been able to use.

'Where do I take him?'

'Here. Leave him in the car until we get back.'

'What if he tries to run away?'

'Shoot him.'

Tony looked at him.

'Self-defense,' Bobby said. 'Shoot him in self-defense.' He turned to Ingrid as if she had spoken. 'It's only a suggestion. He can do what he likes. If he needs to shoot him, do it in self-defense, that's all I'm saying.' He patted Tony on the arm. 'If worse comes to worst, stay put. We'll find you.'

Tony Hastings and Bobby Andes went out to their cars. Before they went, Bobby tried to have a farewell scene with Ingrid. She turned away and then submitted. Tony got in his car. Bobby came over and leaned on his window. 'How do you like that?' he said. 'We got the bastard with the beard, that makes two. The one with the teeth, we'll get him now, you'll see.'

Trapped Tony saw his urgent last chance taking shape in words, a protest, Don't make me tell that lying story, but he was too afraid of the violence of Bobby Andes's scorn to be direct and instead what he said was, 'Are you in trouble?'

'I don't know. I don't give a shit.'

He sat in his car motionless against an overwhelming resistance. He watched Andes get into his car and start up, lights, then pause, a shout, 'What are you waiting for?'

'After you,' Tony said.

As if not trusting him, the man waited for Tony to start his engine, then drove out. But still not trusting, stopped at the turn and waited for Tony to move. As Tony backed out, the headlights swept across the grass and displayed the body lying by the river, looking small, the gray checked shirt, the black beard and white throat turned up. He wondered why he felt no gratification in that death and what had spoiled his fury and righteousness against the other. The clarity of the night stunned him. He had never left a dead man on the ground before.

## SEVEN

Susan Morrow is running out of book. Two, three chapters left at most. The gun goes off like a bomb on the page, and everything swirls down a funnel toward some disastrous end.

Violence thrills her like brass in the symphony. Susan, who is well past forty, has never seen a killing. Last year in McDonald's she saw a policeman with a gun jump a guy eating a sandwich. That's the size of violence in her life. Violence happens in the world, in the parks, ghettos, Ireland, Lebanon, but not in her life – not yet.

Knock wood, knock knock. Safe insured Susan lives on the verge of disaster because everything she knows has happened, whereas the future is blind. In a book there is no future. In its place is violence, substituting thrill for fear, like the thrill in a roller coaster. Never forget what's possible, it says, if you, lucky Susan with secure home and family (so unlike the world), should happen like Tony to meet something vicious in the night. If you had the gun, would you use it any better than Tony?

Edward is coming, so is Arnold. The more the book shrinks, the closer they come, like tigers. The character named after her is a ninny. Susan Ninny, it hurts her feelings. She has no spare feelings to be hurt just now, and she reads on.

## *Nocturnal Animals 25*

Tony Hastings saw Ray Marcus on the mountain road to George's house. He took shape from the darkness in the flash of Tony's headlights on a curve, man walking on the shoulder, gray shirt, jeans, reflecting buckle, turning to look, and Tony did not realize who he was until the man was again in the dark behind the car, though the possibility of seeing him had been on Tony's mind from the start. Seeing him, he thought, that's not Ray because that would be mind over matter, and then, after the flood of light had left the bald forehead and narrowed jaw and face, it was too late to stop. Tony's instinct was to hide his face, requiring an explicit assurance to himself in words that there was nothing to fear, he being in the car and it too dark for Ray to make him out. He drove on, only then remembering he was supposed to capture Ray with that gun he had.

Going on up the next curve, he wondered if he should stop and go back and realized if he did the man would run into the woods. Therefore the real reason why he had not stopped was not fear of Ray but that the place was not propitious. He could not have stopped on the curve back there, jamming his brakes and backing up, without giving Ray the alarm and letting him get away. Maybe he could turn around further on and catch him from the other direction.

The road started to descend, and just as he was thinking the curves looked familiar, he noticed something white in the woods over the next curve and recognized in the dark, unlit, the trailer, the horrible deathbed trailer. He had not realized Bobby's map, which he had memorized, would take him on this road. It shocked him, followed by some chilly thrill of wanting to stop, ghoul, but for his errand and Ray Marcus approaching on foot from the other side of the crest.

He drove more slowly now, still thinking about why he had not stopped to recapture Ray. He did not like to think what Bobby Andes would say, cowardice, sloth. He wondered if it was possible to capture him from a car at any place on this road. The curves, the woods, the night. On the other hand, knowing what to expect, having the gun, being prepared. He was Bobby thinking, Too many excuses. He decided to do it, yes, rectify the cowardice, what he owed. The question was when? Now or eventually. Whether he'll disappear if you don't do it now. On the other hand, there's no place for Ray to go on this road, it'll be a long time before he gets to another. The question was whether to interrupt his errand to George, so as to catch Ray, or go to George first. He didn't want to have to catch Ray all by himself, but that did not have to be the reason. He would go first to George because how could he explain his prisoner while talking to George?

Then there was a better reason. He was not a deputy, it wasn't his job to catch fugitives. More than that. The police themselves had released Ray Marcus, so it wasn't police work at all. Nor had Tony Hastings murdered Lou Bates, it was Bobby Andes did that. Tony Hastings was not Bobby Andes. Repeat that. It wasn't his fault Bobby had kidnapped Ray. It wasn't his fault Bobby had shot Lou Bates. Up to now, he was a bystander, a witness, but not implicated. He hoped he was not implicated. But if he tried to detain Ray Marcus on his own, that would make him accomplice, accessory.

Catch him yourself, he said. Don't involve me in your dirty tactics. A surge of anger, a certain joy, words rising. Don't hook me in your terminal rage. Don't crash your fatality on my head. Astonishment to see how much Bobby Andes took for granted. Assuming everyone made the same connection between grief, loss, and revenge. Assuming no one cared how the man died so long as he died. Assuming no one minded complicity in murder to avenge murder. Assuming everyone was as desperate as he. Tony thought, it's my tragedy, who do you think you are?

They would say, We'll hang your murderers, but we might hang you too. Detectives would probe his story for discrepancies. Courtroom lawyers would cross-examine him. Judges would ask why he allowed himself to get involved. Prosecutors pushing beyond the first excuse would search for the active conspiracy. Bystanders, strangers, and former friends would look for the even worse not yet revealed. In the solitude of the car he spoke, God damn you, Bobby. For a moment Bobby Andes was as unpleasant to him as Ray Marcus. For a moment only, for the thought shocked him, since it ignored the great evil done him and who was trying to pursue that evil and burn it out. Never allow yourself to forget the difference between Ray Marcus and Bobby Andes. Which restored to mind his debt to Bobby Andes, who for Tony's sake was now jeopardizing his name and his career. It didn't make Tony like him, but it made him feel ashamed. If he betrayed Bobby Andes now.

The darkened house just passed on the left must be George's. He backed up and drove in the driveway, a white house without lights. The dogs barking in back would be the dogs he had come for. He remembered other sleeping houses a year ago when he had passed afraid to stop, to be a stranger at a rural door at night. He thought if he could get past the danger of knocking, George would recognize him. If they challenged, he could yell, Bobby Andes sent me.

Repeat the message: He wants your dogs over at his camp. Now, in the night, a man got away. The man himself – Tony just realized this – the man is no longer in the woods, the man is on this road a mile or so back, coming this way. So what do you need dogs for?

The absurdity of the message, Tony Hastings wondered what to do now. Parked here in George Remington's driveway in sudden embarrassment, what to say if George wakes up? Or what to do instead? Do you go back to Bobby and say, I didn't wake George because I saw Ray Marcus on the road, no need for dogs? I didn't pick up Marcus either, but I can tell you where he was.

He remembered George was one of the police who had helped Bobby pick up Ray. Maybe it was all right to tell him. The man you helped catch got away. Bobby wanted your dogs, but since the man is right down the road now, you can recapture him yourself.

A light came on upstairs. A head appeared, silhouette, shadow, hair, no face. A female voice, 'Who's out there?'

Tony called from the car. 'I'm looking for George.'

'What do you want with him?'

'Message from Lieutenant Andes.'

A short silence. He thought, I'll ask George to come down, not to shout across this space. Bobby sent me, the man got away, I won't say anything about shooting Lou. The woman in the window said, 'He ain't here. He's working the night.'

'All right. Thank you.'

Thank God, he thought. Then he realized what faced him now, and the stupidity of his relief. Without George. He started the car but hesitated to back out because he couldn't think what to do next. Two things, the only possibilities. Either he drove back to the camp (passing and ignoring Ray Marcus on the road) and waited there for Bobby to return with his men to pick up Lou, at that time to tell him I saw Ray Marcus on the road an hour ago but didn't pick him up, he's probably gone now but that's where he was. Or he drove back, looking for Ray so as to stop and point the gun at him and make a threat convincing enough to persuade him into the car, putting his hands through the two open windows handcuffed together so that he could announce to Bobby when he returned to the camp with his men: I got him for you.

He drove slowly back. The gun lay ready on the seat. He searched the farthest reach of his headlights up the road looking for the first sight of a walking man. He did not know what he would do when he saw him, it was in the future, unrevealed, as unknown as someone else's choice, or as if he were someone else, a stranger.

The previous image of Ray on the road had been the quick flash of a slide upon a screen, glare of light without color. Standing there, watching the car go by without fear, not hitchhiking but not realizing either that he might be pursued, for if he had wished he could have disappeared into the woods well before the approaching light reached him. Tony remembered himself watching the car's lights, how they swung around, how they came at him, how he had to jump into the ditch. Here they were again, a year later, and now Ray was the hunted, Tony the hunter, and even the car was the same.

He passed the little white church and knew the trailer would appear in a moment and realized this was the first time since the original night he had been on these roads by himself. He imagined having the freedom to revisit alone and from the safety of this distance the places which had scarred his mind so deeply. He was not free yet, though, he was still on Bobby Andes's errand, though no longer sure what the errand was, and Ray Marcus was approaching along this road. That was the main thing, Ray Marcus approaching on the road. He wondered why he hadn't met him yet, he ought to have met him by now.

He saw the curve where the trailer would appear, which for the first time would not take him by surprise. Then it was there, he looked at it hard, and then, after checking to make sure Ray Marcus was not now coming around the curve, he stopped. He saw the dark window which had been lit before with a print curtain. He remembered inside with Bobby and George, where he had slugged Ray, how small it was, the brass bedposts on the little bed, the stove, the trashbox with newspapers. He wondered if he could look inside again now. But it might not be empty, someone might be living in it, someone might be in there. But no one was there because no car was parked. Then it occurred to him, Ray Marcus was there.

The possibility Ray Marcus was there, only a possibility, he said, call it rather not an impossibility. Say only, it was not impossible Ray Marcus was in there. For if Ray had continued walking from where they had passed before, they should have met again, well back down the road before now. He could have picked up a ride, but he had not been hitchhiking when Tony had passed. Almost certainly Ray Marcus was in the trailer. He would have arrived a few minutes after Tony had seen him and slipped inside to rest. It would explain why Tony had not met him again.

If he was there, he was probably looking out the window at the car. Tony picked up the gun on the seat. He fixed the safety so it wouldn't go off while he moved about. He got the flashlight from the glove compartment. The chances of Ray's being in the trailer were slight, Tony just wanted to take a look at it because he was by himself, because he had never seen it by himself. Or else, he wanted to check out Ray, make sure he wasn't here. If he was, he had his gun.

With the gun and the flashlight, he got out of the car, making as little noise as he could. He slipped around the front of the car, into the ditch and up to the front end of the trailer. Pebbles scraping around his feet, he stopped, waiting for silence. He heard the distant roaring of mankind being civilized, but nearby nothing, only the wakeful stillness of the woods in the night. If

Ray was watching, Tony had his gun. There was no way Ray could have acquired a gun of his own. If Ray stopped here to rest, he was probably asleep. Tony said, if Ray is here I will capture him. The reason I am doing this is to help Bobby Andes. Thinking again, Bobby Andes is helping me. Some other reason. He looked for it, this debt he owed. He told himself, it makes no difference if Ray did not kill Lou Bates, or if his arrest tonight was not legal, because he killed Laura and Helen, which I know.

He crept through leaves around the front of the trailer to the door. He thought, probably the door is locked. In that case I shall not pursue this further. I shall assume the trailer is empty and go back to Bobby's camp. If I don't meet Ray on the road, which seems likely now, I can report how he eluded me and there was nothing I could have done. Unless, if the door is locked, I might look with my flashlight in the window.

The door was not locked, the latch yielded. A moment's alarm, too late, as he felt his fingerprints go onto the latch, which would have messed things up if this had been a year ago before they could take the fingerprints placing Lou and Turk here with the crime. He took the flashlight out of his belt with his left hand, the gun still in his right. He thought, if Ray is inside the door, waiting to jump. He cocked the gun again, held it up, nudged the door open with his side. He turned on the flashlight, swept its beam across the room, which was empty. He noticed the light switch by the door, switched on the light, and saw Ray Marcus asleep on the bed.

Who rolled over suddenly, covered his eyes, turned, squinted at Tony, sat up. 'Christ,' he muttered. He fell back on his elbow.

'You,' he said. 'Where's your pal?'

'What pal?'

'Ganges, whoever.'

'Andes. He's not here.'

'Your cop friends. Where are they?'

'They're around.'

'Are they here?' He sat up and pulled back the curtain on the window, tried to look out.

'It's just me,' Tony said.

'Just you? With that fucking gun? What the hell are you doing here?'

'Looking for you.'

'Me? Aw Christ, what the hell for?'

'You know.'

'Aw shit.' He ran his hands through his mostly bald head. 'I was asleep, man.' Tony waited. 'What happened to Lou?'

'He was killed.'

'What? That sonofabitch killed him?'

'He's dead.' Some odd shame prevented him from confirming it was Bobby who killed him, a shame Tony felt no obligation to feel.

'That's big trouble for your friend, you know that?'

'He's not my friend,' Tony said, wondering why he said it.

'He ain't? Ain't that interesting?'

'Let's go,' Tony said.

'Go where?'

'I'm taking you in.'

'In where?'

'Back to the camp.'

'You ain't taking me anywhere, mister.'

'You're coming with me. Come on, now.' He jerked the gun.

Ray laughed. 'You think that's going to make me go?'

Tony cocked the gun. Ray got up and came toward him. For a moment Tony thought he was obeying, then he saw differently. 'Stand back,' he warned.

'Relax,' Ray said. 'I ain't going to hurt you.' He turned to the door. 'I'm just taking my leave. So long, old buddy.'

'Stop,' Tony said. He thought, desperate, it can't happen again. He thought, resolve, I'm different now. He pointed the gun at the door, in front of Ray. There was an explosion and a flash and a violent force jerking his hand up. He saw Ray stop, yank his hands back like a burn. He saw the torn aluminum frame of the door jamb where the bullet must have hit.

He saw Ray looking at him with surprise. 'Well,' he said. 'You missed.'

Tony Hastings felt a thrill. 'I wasn't trying to hit you,' he said. 'That was a warning.'

'Warning. Okay. May I go sit on the bed, sir?'

'Come on, outside. Let's go to the car.'

Ray turned and went back to the bed, where he sat down.

'I said, let's go.'

'What's gonna make me?'

'I just showed you.'

'If you shoot me, what good will that do? You'll have to carry me.'

'I'm not afraid to shoot you,' Tony said.

'Yeah.'

He did not move. Tony waited, and he did not move. Tony said, 'Let's go now,' and Ray opened his eyes wide, shrugged his shoulders, spread his palms out wide. Tony cocked the gun, and he clicked his tongue, tsk tsk. 'I'm not afraid to shoot you,' Tony repeated, hearing the strain in his voice, and Ray did not move. Tony thought. He pulled up the little straight-backed chair, straddled it backwards resting his chest on the chair back, and said, 'Well, if you'd rather wait here, they'll be along after a while.' Thinking that was true, they would look for his car when he didn't show up, and they would find it here.

Then wondered if that much of a concession was a mistake.

Ray said, 'You want me to wait for them?'

'You wouldn't have to wait so long if you came in the car.'

'I don't seem to want to do that, do I? Listen mister, I think I'll be going now. It's been nice talking to you.'

He got up and headed for the door again. Tony said, 'I warned you. Watch out.' His voice was turning into a scream. 'I don't want to shoot you, but if you try to get away, I swear I'll kill you.'

The strange voice stopped Ray, who put up his hands, okay okay, and went back to the bed. Tony thinking, if I can't make you go, I can make you stay, and another thrill of power.

They sat looking at each other. Ray said, 'Listen mister, why does a nice guy like you keep such crummy company? That Ganges Andes fella, he's a bloodthirsty crook. He kills people. If I go back to him, he's going to kill me, just like he did Lou. You wouldn't do that to me, would you?'

Tony thinking, he's right about Bobby Andes. He said, '*You* kill people.'

'Aw shit.'

'Don't you shit on that,' Tony said. 'That's why I'm here. That's why you're here.'

The annoyance in Ray's face, like something inconvenient he'd rather not talk about. Tony enjoyed seeing that look.

He said, 'There's no point denying it. I *remember* you.'

'You got a cigarette?'

'I don't smoke.'

'Nah, of course you don't.'

Looking at him, staring at him, after a moment Ray said, 'They had it coming.'

'What? Who?'

'Your fuckin wife. That kid.'

The leap of Tony's heart, after all these months, a whole year, news, news at last. 'So you do admit it. It's about time.'

'You got me wrong,' Ray said. 'That was an accident.'

'What was an accident?'

'Your wife, yeah. I remember your fuckin wife.'

'My wife and my daughter, whom you killed.'

'Take it easy man. An accident, like I say.'

Wait. Hold back your joy, husband your energy. 'So. What sort of accident?'

'Listen mister, I know it's your wife and kid, and I sympathize with your loss, but that don't excuse how they treated us.'

'How *they* treated you?'

'They asked for it,' Ray said.

Well now. That's good. That calls for joyful uncorrupted rage. Contain it, though, steam to drive the cylinders, not swoosh out the stack. Hold the voice down, still: 'Exactly what do you mean, they asked for it?'

'You want to know? Nah mister, you don't want to know.'

'You tell me just how you think they asked for it.'

'They called us vile things.'

'They were right.'

'They was full of suspicion and dirty thoughts. Mister, they was set against us from the start. They didn't give us a chance. They thought we was crooks and murderers and rapists from the moment they laid eyes on us. You saw that daughter of yours when we fixed your tire. They acted like we was the scum of the earth. When we got in the car, they thought it was the end of the world, like we was gonna slit their throats and fuck their dead bodies. I tell you mister, I got a certain pride how people talk to me, and there certain things I don't put up with.'

Slow and easy. Tony said, 'Their suspicions were justified.'

'They brought it on themselves.'

'You are murderers and rapists. You murdered and raped them.'

'Let me tell you, man, when someone accuses me of something, that's an insult, it gives me the right. When Leila accuses me of screwing Janice, by God I screw Janice. If your fucking daughter thinks I'm a rapist, by God she gets raped.'

'They were right to fear you. Everything they feared came true.'

'Because they fuckin asked for it.'

'They were right you are the scum of the earth, because you are the scum of the earth.'

'You're a fucking mushroom, man.'

'You have no rights. You lost your rights when you killed Laura and Helen.'

'I have as much rights as you do.'

'You have no rights. I've been waiting a year for this.'

'Yeah?'

Tony Hastings knew this pleasure of the gun in his hand and the right to insult which it gave him was a treacherous and dangerous power, for every additional insult would have to be backed up by his willingness to use that gun. He was proud of himself for running that risk, the courage he was acquiring, minute by minute.

He said, 'Let me tell you something. Nobody gets away with what you did to me.'

'They don't?'

'You came after me, that was a mistake you'll never forget.'

'You're scaring me.'

'You ruined my life, you'd better be scared.'

'Well gee, if I'd a known I was ruining your life – '

'I mean to make you suffer. I mean to make you remember,

the reason for your suffering is what you did.'

Tony thought, I sound like Bobby Andes. Ray did not look impressed. 'How do you propose to do that?'

He thought about that, a flaw in his strength, he did not know the answer. The power was only for now, the two of them together here, he with the gun. He considered how to extend the menace, protect his pleasure. 'I'm turning you back to Andes.'

'That won't work,' Ray said. 'They've already decided there's no case.'

How to make it dire and frightening. 'Andes has other plans for you.'

'It's Andes's own ass from now on.'

Probably true. True also realizing this orgasm of power was based on an assumption he had not made, namely, that he was going to kill Ray Marcus. But there was also an ecstatic notion that he had now been liberated to do so, though he did not know where that idea came from. This feeling he had a right, it had been given to him. Or even a duty, which gilded the right and made it an orgy. He looked back, trying to find it: where did that liberation come from which would change the killing of Ray Marcus from a murder to a right or duty?

He remembered Bobby Andes saying, Kill him in self-defense. He doubted that was it.

He thought, Tony Hastings, professor of mathematics. Not the right thought for moments like this.

He thought, Is Tony Hastings professor of mathematics willing to accept the sympathetic but scandalous publicity and possible detention for a crime of passion everyone would understand?

Ray was studying him and said, 'So why don't you just kill me, man?'

'I'll kill you if I have to. You think I won't?'

'Come on man, you don't know nothing. It's fun to kill people. You ought to try it sometime.'

'Fun? Yes, it would be, for you.'

'Fun, right.'

'You found it fun to kill my wife and child?'

'Well, yes, I did. Yes, that was fun.'

Fun? Tony heard the word. He gathered himself together and expressed shock. 'You sit there and tell me it was fun to kill my wife and daughter?'

'It's a acquired taste,' Ray said. 'It's something you gotta learn, like hunting. You gotta get over the hump. You gotta kill someone before you know what it's like.'

Tony was experiencing a sensation like a dazzling light.

Ray kept talking. 'My pals Lou and Turk, they didn't get it. They were scared shitless when your folks died. Shitless. They thought they was going to be charged with murder. It takes some people longer to catch on than others.'

'You don't deserve to live,' Tony said.

'You ought to try it, Tony. Kill somebody, I guarantee you'll want to do it again. You're no different from nobody else.'

'Is that why you did it?' Tony said. 'Because it was fun?'

'Sure. That was why.'

At that moment, Tony felt an explosion of what he thought was disgust but was really joy. The light was blinding, and it lit clearly the difference between himself and Ray, how simple it was. The fact was that Ray was wrong, Tony was not like his notion of everybody, he belonged to a different species of which a savage like Ray was completely ignorant. It was not that Tony was inhibited or asleep to the joys of killing, but that he knew too much, had too much imagination to be capable of such a pleasure. Not that he had not yet grown up to appreciate such joys but that he had grown out of them as a natural part of the process of maturation. The possible fun of killing had been trained and cultivated out of him by a civilizing process of which Ray had no comprehension, and Tony was full of fierce and vengeful contempt for that lack of comprehension. It gave him a luminous clear feeling, where he had hitherto been murky and uncertain. He felt confident. He felt right, knowing he could trust his instincts and feelings. He felt invigorated, and in this exciting mood he made a decision.

He said, 'Okay Ray, enough talk. It's time to go.'

'I told you, I ain't going nowhere.'

They sat there a minute. Tony cocked the gun again. 'Why don't you just leave then?'

'You'll let me?'

'I didn't think it mattered whether I let you or not.'

'That depends on whether you can shoot that gun or not.'

'I can shoot it.'

There was a look from Ray, and Tony saw he had lost his confidence, he had seen the change in Tony.

'Maybe I'd better not leave then.'

'In that case, maybe you'd better go out and get in that car.'

'I ain't gonna do that.'

'Then you just want to wait until they come and get you?'

'Maybe I will leave, now that you mention it.'

'I'm not going to let you.'

'Then I'd better stay.'

'Go ahead and leave. I dare you.'

'I don't think I will.'

'I think you ought to at least try.'

'I think maybe it's safer just sitting here.'

'I don't think that's so safe.'

'You don't. Maybe you're right.'

He stood up. 'Maybe I will go.' He took a step forward, watching Tony's hand with the gun, stopped, stepped back.

'You'd better not.'

'That's what I'm thinking.'

'You don't know what to do, do you?'

'I know what I'm doing.'

'I didn't shoot you the other time. That was Bobby Andes. So what makes you think I'll shoot you now?'

'Just to be on the safe side of things.'

'You think I've changed, do you? You think I'll shoot you now?'

'It's a dangerous weapon. You have to be careful around dangerous weapons like that.'

'The safest thing for you is to come out to the car with me.'

'I see no need of that.'

'You're scared of me. You're really quite frightened.'

'Don't overrate yourself, man.'

'Why don't you go, then?'

'I think I will.'

'What's keeping you?'

He looked Tony in the face. He began to grin, the insolent grin of recognition Tony knew so well. 'Why, nothing I guess,' he said, and stepped forward again.

Toward the door, with nothing in his way. Tony felt his lungs freeze, himself paralyzed and all his courage gone, failure and humiliation the rest of his life. Meanwhile, the gun went off. He heard the yell, 'Ow! you sonofabitch,' after the explosion, which knocked the gun in his hand up bang against his forehead as the chair tilted and he fell over backward. There was Ray roaring down on him like the world, holding something, and time only to cock the gun again before the sun exploded.

# EIGHT

The sun explodes, so does the book. Susan Morrow stops a last time to appreciate, reading almost over, only one chapter left. Dorothy and Henry are upstairs, having returned from skating just when Tony put his fingerprints on the door latch. She heard them stomping on the porch, calling good bye across the snow, then in the vestibule breathing and giggling. Now they are talking upstairs, Rosie too, probably a rehash.

Again Susan finds the screened porch in her mind, the one in Maine, the path and rocky steps by the boathouse, the still harbor with a mirror afternoon sheen across to the trees. Dying, like her mother and father. Like Bobby Andes. Like her jealousy. Like Edward's writing. Like this book.

Edward is coming, so is Arnold. Susan, for no reason at all, is full of dread.

*Nocturnal Animals 26*

The trailer was open to the woods, its walls gone, its roof propped on stakes to make a shelter. He was under a picnic table, and Ray had escaped down a stream bed, and others were looking for him because they knew Tony could not. The people who had been fussing over him had disappeared, the picnic bench was on his chest, he couldn't push it away, he thought if he rested he would be all right.

The sky beyond the trees was a dome of darkness weakening into light, dim green. Beyond it was another dome which he could not see, world within a world. It was the inside of an eyelid the size of a world, but he lacked the strength to open it. This is dream, he said.

There was no sky and no eyelid, however, and it was no dream. It was total dark, and the picnic tables and trees were inventions of thought. He knew that sometimes in a dream you wonder if it is real, but in waking life there is never a doubt. He knew now. He was awake, with something on his eyes like a bandage. He could not see, but it was no dream.

He remembered the trailer, Ray coming after him, the sun bursting. He was lying on a floor, the back of his head against a wall, his right arm crowded against a bulky object. Something had fallen on his legs. Something else was pushing his head.

He could not feel what was on his eyes. He raised a hand from the floor, a move he could make, moved his hand toward his eyes, then stopped, frightened. It was no bandage. He did not want to touch his eyes, afraid what he would find there. He wanted to know, am I in the darkness or is the darkness in me? If Ray had turned out the light, could it be this dark? He tried to test, look for the window, the door, but he did not know how to look, something was missing in the forward part of his face, a blank space, wires cut. He heard the news whispered in the back: I'm blind, which in younger years would have been the worst of all possible news.

He moved his right leg, it was okay, his left leg too. The object lying across his legs was the chair, he remembered falling backwards. He raised his knee and shoved it aside. He wondered what Ray had done to his eyes, whether he had blinded him with a blow to the head or had attacked them directly, fingers or knife or fork, torn them or stabbed them with a pain he was yet to feel. He wondered why Ray had not grabbed the gun and shot him dead. He wondered how much time had passed, how far Ray had gone by now. He would have taken my car, Tony said. If he had gone. If he was not sitting over there now watching and waiting for me to wake up so as to torture me.

He felt too heavy and leaden to be frightened by that thought. Even the blindness did not frighten him yet, though he knew a moment was coming when it would rip him like a rake. He felt cold, shivering. His insides rose, gorge, he turned his head to heave but nothing came.

Tony Hastings knew time had passed but he had no memory of it except the scraping where his eyes had been. Now he felt the gouges burning, holes dug in the front of his face with fish hooks in them. The pain was a loud noise, he could not think, wonder, calculate, the only words were Stop This Now. Still unable to move because of something on his head, he banged his legs and hips against the floor. He shoved his hand into his pocket for his handkerchief, too small, tore off his necktie, rolled it up, put it gingerly to his face but it was not enough. He pulled his shirt out of his belt, tried to tear it, could not, remembered obscurely dish towels above a sink, and after a long resolve forced himself to move despite the threat of a headache like Zeus out of the sky. No headache could be as bad as this though, and thereby he discovered he could get up. He staggered, leaned against the wall, bumped into some huge object at his feet, found the sink, felt above it, the soft edge of one dish towel, then the other, grabbed them both, crumpled them, touched them lightly to the holes in his face, then pressed hard and soft to keep out the acid air.

The pain was deep and permanent but no longer a flame. He found the chair with his feet, lifted it up and sat in it, keeping the towels on his eyes to keep it out. Not knowing if he had eyes or sockets, not daring to feel and find out, nor if Ray had gouged him or merely smashed him hard in the eyes with his fist or if it wasn't Ray at all but the gun going off too close to his face. Someday someone would examine him and tell him. Wet streams and crusted riverbeds on his cheeks.

He thought, Am I sure it's both eyes? He took the towel away from first one side, then the other. The air was quicklime. The second edition of the news came screeching: I'm blind. Not dead, blind. His worst childhood fear. The rest of my life, blind man, grope. Green, yellow, trees, mountains, ocean, red blue and magenta shades, tints of violet.

Looking ahead, the question, Can I endure it? Thinking, could he learn braille? Would people read to him? A seeing eye dog. A white tipped cane.

On the chair, himself as tragic. Chosen for catastrophe. The bad things that can happen which won't happen to you. The third edition of the news – I'm blind – was the melancholy fulfillment of a long downward process, his fate confirmed. He thought woefully, the life and career of Tony Hastings, mathematics, Louise Germane. Louise Germane and the blind man. Instead, unlucky fellow.

He heard a car on the curve, like some old myth of danger. What he needed was help. They should come looking for him. If they missed him when he didn't return, it wouldn't be much longer. He tried to remember what the ugly thing was that darkened the recent memories of his friends.

Then he realized that if Ray Marcus took his car, no one would think of looking here. He would have to rescue himself.

He would have to grope his way out of the trailer and up to the road. He would have to stand by the road with the bloody towels on his eyes and hope a driver would see his distress and stop. He would say, Help me to the state police office in Grant Center. There was a reason not to go to the state police in Grant Center. Bobby Andes, he was on the edge of remembering something. He felt around on the floor and found his necktie which he tied around his head to bind the towels to his eyes. Wondering, night or day? He listened and heard the cool distant whistle of a bird, two clear notes, and again the fortified distant roar of mankind being civilized, so it must be day.

Every move exhausted him as if he had been kicked in the belly. Force himself. Which way the door? He turned, and his foot caught against whatever it was on the floor, big. Like a bag of earth, he remembered feeling something like that against him when he was lying there. He felt down, touched heavy cloth containing something hard, an arm, a shoulder, a person.

'Ah,' Tony said. 'You.'

This would be Ray, then, and he had not got away. From the shoulder, he felt for the head and recoiled, cold skin. He lifted the arm and let go, heard it fall, thump.

So I killed you, Tony Hastings whispered.

He had bought something with his blindness.

To make sure he was dead, Tony forced himself against revulsion to touch the head again, feel around the eyes, up to the bald front. The touch shocked him, and he allowed his hand to rest a moment on the brow, the hair of the eyebrows, the shape of the forehead, liberties he could never have taken before. The devil had a skull like Tony's. The devil had guts and organs, charted in an endlessly replicated geography like his own, like all of us, making it easy for doctors, who would find the same things wherever they looked.

He wondered how he had killed him and if Ray had had time while dying to reflect and understand why. But from the talk they had had just before, he realized there was no way Ray would understand, no way he could grasp what he had done or see what Tony saw, neither the crime nor the punishment. The only understanding would be what Tony could imagine for him as he went, the figure of Tony's imagination, suffering in Tony's imagination. Eventually that could be plenty, a tremendous satisfaction, later when Tony was himself again, though at present he felt nothing, and the only Ray was a dead body.

He tried to resurrect his hatred so as to enjoy this death by imagining Ray dying slowly. Bleeding to death, not so much pain as weakness and helplessness and knowing he was dying. But his hatred and vengeance all seemed remote, dead feelings of no interest now. He remembered Ray's boast about the pleasure of killing and his own imagined superiority, and he wondered if Ray had blinded him to make him pay for that superiority. Blinding him because he wanted Tony to be conscious of something too. Refinements of revenge.

He felt around for the gun. His hand discovered a cold place on the floor, sticky, crusty, Ray Marcus's clotting blood. He started back, banged his head on the table. He tried to get up, put his hand on the table for support, found the gun there. Think about that, Tony. That means Ray Marcus found the gun before he died. Then watched himself bleed to death.

He didn't want to stay in the room with the corpse. He put the gun in his pocket, forced himself up, and tried to find his way around the obstacle, prodding with his feet. The stickiness on the floor seemed to be everywhere. He stumbled against the bed where it shouldn't be. He found the wall, the stove in the wrong place, he rearranged it, found the door. Cautiously he stepped out, but despite his care there was no ground. He dropped, landed hard against tree roots, for he had forgotten the trailer door had no step.

Head aching from his fall, pain returning, he waited a while to recover. His belly ached from where he must have been kicked. The air was moving sweetly, it was warm, he could feel the sun on him. He would try to find the car. He thought if he went downhill he would end in the ditch under the curve and could climb up to the shoulder. He would stand by the road and when he heard a car step out to wave. The ground scrambled beneath his feet, he slid and fell again. Held by branches, he grabbed them, staggered over roots and mossy rocks and tangled limbs. He kept going down, longer than he should. He was on bare rock and slipped again, lost his footing and landed in water. A cold stream ran around his ankles.

He was so tired he sat down in the water. His clothes soaking cold made his middle ache, he couldn't stay there. After waiting a moment for breath, he decided to retrace his steps. He tried to climb up but the bare rock wouldn't have him, he stumbled upstream and then managed by reaching out for saplings to grab and pull himself up by. He came to what seemed like a grassy spot. He could feel the sun which he couldn't see. He had no idea where the trailer or the road were. His strength gone, he decided to rest until the sound of a car could give him a clue.

After a few minutes one went by. It was closer than he expected, off to his left and below in the direction from which he had come. He thought, I'll sit in the sun and wait here. Close enough that when they come, if they don't already see me, I can call out. Up here, you guys. He didn't know whether it was shock from having been blinded or the kick in the belly, but he felt faint, like spots before his eyes if he had eyes.

He thought, Now we're square. You took my wife and daughter and blinded me, and I killed you. That's three to one, but he could accept it as the additional price he had to pay for his pretensions. His ego and vanity, the comfort he took in his name and title, which cost something, quite a lot, evidently. Right now they meant nothing, but at a later date doubtless they would again.

Similarly he anticipated the plans he would make later for a future restored by blindness, as if he had not had a future during the last dark year. There would be an interval of preparation and learning. He would be granted a leave by the university to learn how to change his living habits. New ways, how to study, how to prepare classes, how to teach. Where to live. What to do about clothes, food, hygiene, all the details, which he could see ahead like a mess of trees on a mountainside becoming distinct as he approached. He could see himself on the campus, on the streets of his neighborhood, with his black glasses, his cane, perhaps his dog, known to everyone as a story: Tony Hastings blinded by the man who killed his family. The black glasses, hiding the eyes not there, would spread the legend.

He was not afraid of the police. For them too, he thought, the blinding exonerated him. Not to claim self-defense as Bobby had said, how could he claim self-defense when he had the gun? He thought he would tell them what actually happened. It would give him a good feeling to tell it. I found Ray Marcus in the trailer, asleep. We had a conversation. What did you talk about? What if they asked what you were doing with that gun? What if they said you were trying to provoke Ray to attack?

Which reminded him of Bobby Andes. Was he still obligated to say Ray killed Lou Bates? The possibility sickened him, but he thought his blindness excused him from having to think about it, and he did not think about it.

The day dragged on, he felt the sun shining on his head,

the temperature rising, the day getting hot. The early birds silent now, the woods still at midday. He thought, I can wait.

Sitting there under the blind dome, Tony Hastings felt the light through his skin. He reconstructed without eyes the place where he sat: a clearing with sunbaked yellow grass dropped down in front of him into small trees beyond which were the trailer and the curve of the road with his car parked on the shoulder. He grew big trees in the other directions with an oak near by and a rising slope of woods beyond. As clear as seeing, absolute knowledge, he did not know where it came from.

Bravado then. Give it a test. He picked up the gun. The oak tree was to his left, he would hit it with the gun. Target practice for a blind man, it made him laugh. He cocked the gun, pointed it. Fire. That horrible loud explosion knocking his hand back again. The silence of the violated woods returned after the echoes, the endless midday went on and on.

Then the roll of the earth brought the sunlamp directly on his blindfolded face. It must be afternoon. He was obsessed by the thought that his body was identical in all its formal features to that of Ray Marcus. But when he tried to stretch, his body resisted as if tied to the ground. And his unique wounds were already old and familiar, permanent endurable pains, and he had been a blind man most of his life. Never eaten a meal. Never had to pee. He discovered his pants were chilly wet as if he had peed without realizing it. Another effect of the shock, he told himself. The reason he did not go back down to the road was the steepness of the slope, which his imagination saw. He would wait until the police came and helped him down. They would come when Bobby Andes reported his failure to return. If no one else thought to look on this road, George Remington would see the car on the way to his house. There was no reason to be alarmed by the long drag of the day. It's not forever.

Maybe he had been asleep. He heard voices, footsteps on gravel. Words, not loud, he couldn't distinguish. Then, 'What's it doing here?'

'Are you sure that's it?'

'Where'd he go?'

He heard a louder harsh male voice, intoning, numbers, a squawk – police radio. They had come at last. He raised his head, held still, listened.

The police radio squawked on and off, bursts. The live voices stopped.

Suddenly one: 'Hey Mike, *Jesus Christ.*'

Feet scurrying, gravel loosened. 'Holy cow!'

They had found Ray Marcus.

He could not hear what they were saying.

'Look, bloody tracks.'

'See where they go.'

'Stay here.'

He heard crashing in the brush below. Blind Tony Hastings as quarry, stretched on the ground not knowing if he was visible or not, took the gun by his side and cocked it as a precaution. The police are your friends, he said.

Someone shouted. 'It goes on down, I can't see where.'

The other. 'Forget it. We'll wait for the others.'

'Call it in, will you? Tell Andes.'

And Tony still not knowing what Andes had told them about who killed Lou Bates.

A voice said, 'Probably bleeding to death in the woods.'

Tony Hastings was lying on his side, head propped on elbow trying to listen, not knowing if they could see him if they looked up. The police radio kept spattering. He couldn't make out what it said but guessed the men were reporting their find. Then on the radio distinct: 'Andes here.'

'Marcus, not Hastings?'

'Are you sure of that, god damn it?'

He thought, they will bring dogs to follow his bloody footsteps. Like a fugitive. They will train guns on me, and if I don't obey swiftly, they will kill me. I killed Ray Marcus, who was unarmed.

Remember the headlights approaching in the woods and hiding in the shadow of a tree so as not to be seen, and the voice trying to find him calling, Mister. I don't want them to see me when I can't see them, he said.

You'll have to come out sometime, they said. I'll wait for Bobby Andes, he said.

He heard them walking around below, not their voices. Then nothing. Almost silence, a long time. He knew they were there because the radio was going, though the volume had been turned down, he could hardly hear it. Either in the car or in the trailer with the body, if he were they he would prefer to wait outside. Maybe they were outside, sitting on the shoulder smoking cigarettes. He heard bird songs again, the two clear notes, chickadee, pewee. He felt the retreat of the afternoon sun, some cooling breeze. A woodpecker telephoning a tree. The distant ceaseless sound of traffic, the Interstate somewhere bearing families and commerce and thugs through this countryside from all the other countrysides.

The leash tethering his belly to the trees was getting uncomfortably tight. It was silly hiding here like a fugitive. Tony Hastings knew that. He didn't intend to be a fugitive. If he had any guilt, he had reconciled himself to it. He had not forgotten his plans and his conversation with himself a few hours ago. It's time, he said. Wake up, you can't stay here forever.

Still, he waited. Preferring to let the others arrive, if Bobby Andes were among them. If Bobby Andes could find him first and give him the latest news on the death of Lou Bates before someone else should ask. It was not long now. The cars drove up, he heard their feet, their radios, voices, exclamations. He heard Bobby Andes, 'Where the fuck did he go?'

Here is what happened. He wanted to get up and call, Hey Lieutenant, Bobby Andes, look up here. As he turned he rolled over the gun which he had cocked earlier. He groped for it with his hands, found it, and put it in his left hand so he could push down and raise himself with his right. He had just got one foot under his body and started to push up when the gun went off. The whip slammed into his gut, the sound he hated came later. *Damn!* he said, why did I do that? For a moment he thought he had shot himself.

What a recoil, he'd forgotten how hard it could kick, it knocked him flat. If it was a bullet through his gut, he'd be dead. He was on his back, face up to what should have been sky. The blow of it tightened the rope around his middle, worse than before. He tried to work it loose. He tried to move, but the rope was tightening, holding him down. If it was a bullet, it had missed his vital parts, it wasn't as if he was dying, but it was pulling through him, it was dragging him on the ground. My God, he said. If that's what it was. He thought, Why did I do a stupid thing like that? If I'm bleeding to death. The rope was tied through his middle, holding the broncos in the corral so they wouldn't spill out, but they were bucking pretty hard. Field mice were slipping out under the lower bars.

If this was really the big news, he wondered why it didn't seem more important. He thought, Would a bullet feel like a rope? It would feel like what it feels like. He groaned, recognizing. So, he said, here comes another life for Tony Hastings. This would be a lifetime of dying. It would stretch from past to future dominated by one fact, a bullet through his belly. Though you get used to everything, he had no interest in anything else.

A long time afterwards he was aware he had long ago heard a voice saying, 'Jesus, what was that?' You would expect the police to round up the cattle set loose by the rustlers pretty soon, wouldn't you? Yet they did not come. It was a long time before they did not come.

If they did not come: a remnant of brain suggested he should be thinking about dying, he should be giving it his full attention. Tony Hastings dying, think of that. He ought to be more surprised. Vaguely he remembered things he had wanted to think about when he died, but he couldn't remember what they were. At least he ought to figure out why he had died. The kind of question others would ask, how it could have been avoided, what he should have done differently. Must be he got his left and right hands mixed up. If he had meant to lift himself by the right hand against the ground, but had pushed down instead with the left, which was holding the gun in his gut. Pressure of finger against the trigger, in the confusion of groping for the hard ground through his soft belly. A neurological mistake, caused by the shock of being blind, though he should have been used to that, having been blind so long already.

It occurred to him if the police got up here in time they might save him. If having heard the shot they scrambled up through the brush, they could call an ambulance on their radio. It didn't seem likely. He heard no signs of them.

It occurred to him they would find his body and think he had committed suicide. It seemed like a logical conclusion, they would not be surprised. He wondered what motives they would attribute to him. Probably (they would say) he did it because he could not tolerate being blinded on top of all he had lost. (They would not know he had reconciled himself to that.) Or perhaps he was so obsessed with the crime committed against him and the need for revenge that when Ray died he had no further need to live. (They did not know about Louise Germane waiting for him – if she would take him blind.) Or else (underestimating his cynicism and his cowardice, those all-important qualities) it was his idealism: his inability to endure the self-knowledge forced on him by Bobby Andes and Ray, whereby he too was revealed with no moral advantage over his enemies except what he retained from the fact that they started it. More likely (not knowing how cheerfully he had reconciled himself to waiting) they would simply attribute it to impatience with pain and dying: having realized not only that he was blind but that he had been shot by Ray and was bleeding to death, he couldn't take it any longer. It was too much for him and he cracked. It was unlikely the cops would call his death an accident.

He really didn't want to die, and he wished they would hurry up. Meanwhile the rope through his middle explored him, it mapped his territory. The organs in his middle included, though he did not know exactly which was which or where each one was, the liver, kidney, spleen, appendix, pancreas, gall bladder, and miles of intestines, large and small. He tried to think what else there was and regretted he had not been on more familiar terms with them while he lived.

The only definite thing he knew was this: he was free to continue his trip to Maine. After all this time, more than a year. The police told him this when they arrived at last, standing by the door congratulating him as he got into the driver's seat and strapped himself in. The seat belt was tight around his middle. They shook his hand. Wished him well. Told him the route, estimates of how long it would take.

And so he had gone, and now he was driving fast with a little of the cowboy and the baseball player still in him, almost singing for the joy of it, and in no time at all he was there. He saw the summer house at the end of the road, down the slope. It was a big old-fashioned two-story house with gable windows and a porch. All the windows and the porch were screened, it was covered with screens. He drove down the drive and onto the grass, and saw them in the water waiting for him. He walked down the grass to the water's edge.

'Come on in,' Laura said, 'we've been waiting for you.'

'What took you so long?' Helen said.

He asked, 'Is it cold?'

'Pretty cold,' Laura said, 'but you can bear it.'

'It's better after you've been in a while,' Helen said.

They were standing up to their necks so he could see only their heads. The water was flickering blue and white like sweet milk in the afternoon light, and the fuzzy pine islands out in the bay shimmered with summer joy.

He stepped into the water, icy around his feet. Laura and Helen laughed. 'You've been away too long,' Laura said. 'You're all out of shape.'

He looked back up the slope to the house standing on the grass, high and spacious and beautiful. The screen door on the screened porch was propped open, and two of the screened windows on the second floor were open, he did not know why. He thought how good it would be to return to the house after his swim, to walk up the grass and go inside and sit in the big empty pine-smelling rooms and enjoy the warming up after the chill. Then they could talk, all he remembered that he wanted to tell them. He wanted to tell her about her arms swinging as she walked up to the house. He wanted to ask if they had ever quarreled. He couldn't remember and he hoped not. He wondered if he was ever jealous, he thought probably not, and if she was jealous of him, he hoped not, for he did not think he had ever given her cause. He wanted to tell her he remembered the blueberry field and something after that, he had forgotten.

But not yet, first there was this. Only their heads were above the surface, laughing and encouraging him, as he moved gingerly in the bitter cold water step by step toward them. It was hard to move, while they waited with such generosity and welcome he could hardly bear his happiness. With all his strength he pushed on, while the ice kept rising. It rose from his ankles to his knees, from his knees to his groin and groin to hips. It seized him freezing around his belly. It crept up to his chest, it covered his heart, it clutched his neck. Then still rising still freezing it reached his mouth and filled his nose and closed his burning eyes.

# NINE

The book ends. Susan has watched it dwindle before her eyes, down through final chapter, page, paragraph, word. Nothing remains and it dies. She is free now to reread or look back at parts, but the book is dead and will never be the same again. In its place, whistling through the gap it left, a blast of wind like liberty. Real life, coming back to get her.

She needs a silence before returning to herself. Absolute stillness, no thought, no interpretation or criticism, just a memorial silence for the reading life that has ended. Later she'll think about it. She'll put things together, make sense of her reading, and decide what to say to Edward. Not yet.

There's a shock of terror in the return of real life, concealed by her reading, waiting to swoop down on her like a predator in the trees. She dodges it – not yet for that, either. The kids upstairs, who came back in the middle of the last chapter: it's their time now. She hears them laughing and squealing. She puts the cover on the box, the box on the shelf, checks the rooms, the front and back doors, turns off the lights, starts up.

They are all three on the floor in Rosie's room, Rosie in her pajamas. Dorothy's and Henry's faces are unnaturally red.

'Hi, Mama,' Dorothy says. 'Guess what?'

'Henry's in love,' Rosie says.

He is grinning, triumph overruling embarrassment.

'How exciting,' she says. 'Who with?'

'Elaine Fowler,' Dorothy says.

'That's news? Why, Henry's been in love with Elaine Fowler for the last year.'

Rosie looks disappointed. Henry mumbles. 'This is different.'

Dorothy says, 'It's moved into a new phase.'

'A new phase. How wonderful.'

'What did you do this evening, Mama?' Dorothy says.

Susan Morrow is startled. 'Me? Why, nothing. I finished my book.'

'How was it? Good?'

She's not ready for that question. But she's back in the real world, where it's time to discriminate and be responsible. 'Sure,' she says. 'It's good enough.'

Later, her mind loosens and the book liquefies. It's impossible to say when. Maybe when she's in bed, the house dark. More likely earlier, subliminally when she closed the house or while talking to the children. It's impossible to pin her thought to a time or unfold it in a sequence.

Still conscious that some frightening reality has been planted in her mind, she postpones it still, to dwell longer in the book. She remembers her pang for Tony in the last sentences like a stab of personal grief. The sharpness fades when she thinks about it, as such things do. The water scene at the end reminds her of something. But does she understand why Tony has to die? She looks back, sees the path leading to death, its shape through the woods. He was on the way to Maine, he gets there in the end. She likes the ending better than she expected to, but has no idea if it's right, or whether it resolves the questions raised. That requires recollection and thought she's not ready for, if she'll ever be, for now she's not even sure it matters. If she asks Edward, he'll think her dumb.

Forgetfulness follows the trail of her reading like birds eating the Hansel and Gretel crumbs. The path from the beginning is obliterated with weeds. It has buried the bodies of Tony Hastings's wife and child and will bury Tony too. She tries to remember things. Helen on the rock fifty feet down the road, poor kid. Helen as Dorothy, as Henry too. Ray the weasel, where did he come from? Remember Tony miserable looking up the slope to Husserl's: what made you name the neighbor that? Tony, man of postures, she's ashamed of her superiority as she sees him flip from one stance to another, looking to clothe a burning body when it was the icing water he needed. Susan as Tony.

She knows that mountain road as if she had been there herself. Sees it with the same clarity blind Tony saw the tree he shot. The clearing, the mannequins, the trailer by the curve in the road. And Tony staggering over the bulky body of Ray. But around such spots as these the acid burns, the pages crumple.

There's a feeling of loose ends hanging, but she finds it hard to remember. She wonders what happened outside the story. Back at the camp: what tale did Bobby finally tell his men? Did they buy it? Would it matter? Louise Germane, left behind and forgotten, it's just as well for her.

The house in Maine with its porch and screens looks like her house, which Edward visited at fifteen and again when they were married. All those screens. She sees Tony looking at it in his dim archetypal blindness, and she feels meanings around her which she cannot see. She wonders if they are real or only her imagination and how long it will take her, if ever, to know.

She wants to talk, she doesn't want to talk. What can she say? She's ashamed to tell Edward how blind she feels. If readers could simply applaud and writers bow. She can do that. She can applaud, she can honestly tell Edward she liked his book, and that's a relief. Postpone the critique. She had fun and felt regret when it ended. That will please him. Would you recommend it to your friends? Depends on the friend. Would you recommend it to Arnold? Sure she would. It would serve him right.

The secret fright she keeps dodging in her mind somewhere: that's her private problem. It has nothing to do with the book.

# AFTER

# ONE

Arnold is coming, and then Edward. Susan Morrow is tense enough to take her breath away. She feels the contempt of each for the other as if for herself. Arnold thinks Edward a failure, always has. When they last met, years ago by accident at a play in Chicago, Arnold bought Edward a drink. He slapped him on the back, talked of cultural values and judged him effete. Edward ignored Arnold's objections to obscurity in art, avoided the contemporary, changed the subject to baseball, and judged him simple.

She does the work of her day, kids to the dentist, groceries, with plans to meet Arnold at O'Hare in the evening. Frightened by what Arnold may be bringing home to her, the possible terrors, she turns her mind to Edward, who comes tomorrow. The critique he expects from her, the questions he expects her to ask, which she has postponed.

She'd rather leave the book where it was last night, to act untended in the sub-basements of her mind, but for Edward she'll form an opinion, what she liked and what she didn't. Adjectives. Questions that will organize her reading for tentative answers. To Edward's question – what's missing from his book? – she has a mischievous reply.

She meets Arnold at O'Hare in the evening, trying to be glad to see him. Kisses him, takes him by the arm, Arnold the Bear, who always looks disoriented in public places, with his graying beard, his bushy brows, worried about his baggage, distracted by thoughts. Preoccupied. By what, Susan does not know. He does not tell. She waits for his unwanted gift and holds back the urgent questions that are driving her crazy.

She drives him home on the busy expressway. As if nothing had happened, he talks of meetings, people seen, lectures attended. Describes the interview with the Cedar Hall Institute. Chickwash, what an honor for him, if only his mother could have lived. He expects the invitation within a week. She remembers his promise to discuss it with her before deciding anything, but he seems to think they've had that discussion already. If she reminds him, he'll say he thought it was settled. She fears what other news such a reminder might elicit.

Instead she mentions Edward's forthcoming visit. She describes Edward's book as she drives but can't tell if Arnold is listening. She talks in the blast of wind around the car windows, he not saying anything. She speaks of her plan to invite Edward to dinner. Tomorrow night. Since Arnold doesn't hear that either, she repeats. Oh excuse me, he says. You'll have to do without me, I've got to work tomorrow night.

That night Susan Morrow has sex. With her own Arnold, in their own ways, with their twenty-five year history. She wasn't expecting it, his fatigue, her irritability, whatever is distracting her. A feeling of grievance, sorry for herself, all the sacrifices she has made. His neglect of her adventures, like the latest, this book of Edward's, as important to her as Arnold's New York adventures are to him: his total indifference. So she's not expecting it and is halfway through the trapdoor to sleep when he puts his bear paw on her in his intimate privileged way bringing her violently back.

Back to an old world of bodies at night, featuring her nipples, throat, hips, and abdomen, along with his sweaty ribs, hairy legs, armpits and beard. Also their mutual tongues, and eventually his vulnerable fat thrusting sausage in the dark wet sensitivities under her pelvic arch. She forgets her grievances with a relieving yelp, approving her policy to be faithful and true whether in Chicago or Washington, while everything else disappears, including Edward and Marilyn Linwood. Or does not disappear. She's thinking about them while Arnold rocks away, wondering how they would like each other. Afterwards, he (who? Arnold, of course) puts his head on her shoulder and moans: Forgive me, oh forgive me. There there, she says, like a mother, patting the back of his head, not daring to wonder what he wants to be forgiven for.

The next day she waits for Edward. His card said he would stay at the Marriott, but there was no specific plan to meet. She expects him to call and will invite him for dinner then. Excited and nervous, all morning and part of the afternoon she waits. Meanwhile daylight drains the glow from Arnold's night. As it usually does. She's annoyed by his disregard of Edward. The official dogma for twenty-five years, that Edward is of no importance. She wishes Arnold would read his book. She wishes it as if she wrote it herself. The idea grows: to capture Arnold by the book, send him too through the woods with Tony, let him suffer the shocking loss and the uncomfortable discovery, enslaved to Edward's imagination for the three days or whatever it requires.

But Arnold would say, this Tony Hastings of yours in this book by Edward, your Tony Hastings is a wimp. That's Arnold's language, how he would put it. He'll say: I appreciate what Tony goes through, but what's wrong with this man who can't protect his family or control Ray even when he has the gun? That's just the kind of hero your Edward would make up.

It irritates her though she's the one inventing and making Arnold say it. Mistrusting his motives as she invents them, saying, *You* would never let Ray's thugs get me, would you, Arnold? Nothing like this could happen to you, because you wouldn't let it, is that what you want me to believe, my hero? She sees how the sneer at Tony's maleness intends to certify and augment his own, though her particular recollection of Arnold's maleness from last night is parched, lost in the memory of stroking his head and saying, There, there.

Her thought is full of rancor. She tries to correct for that, in fairness. In fairness, she too was bothered by Tony's lack of backbone, which explains how she can invent Arnold's critique. Don't do that, Tony you fool, she would say. But never thought of complaining to Edward, because she knew his reply: that's what he's supposed to do. If she understands that, Arnold can too. Arnold should understand Tony's dilemma with the gun. To have it and be unable to use it: for Susan that's real life, unlike the movies, where the mere display of a gun by anybody confers the powers of God. Susan in the cabin in that situation would have been no more able to use the gun than Tony was. She should praise Edward for that, but hesitates, if the thought contains more than she knows: if in that flash of Tony the Wimp, there's a spreading reflection of herself.

Well, Arnold would deny that. Patronizingly perhaps, he would assure her: Tony and you, Susan? There's no resemblance in the least. I know my Susan. If Ray and his pals attacked your children, you'd fight in ways polite Tony never dreamed. You'd jump and grab him by the throat, bite, kick, pluck his eyes. There's no way you'd let a thug hurt yours as Tony does, as you well know.

Right, Susan knows. She knows her Susan.

## TWO

And she waits. She looks forward to seating Edward at her table, serving him dinner, joined by her children without Arnold. To talk about his book. Also, without apology, to say a conciliatory thing or two, like how far behind she has left the old wrangle. How free her mind is now, how friendly at last, how glad she would be to renew him as her oldest friend, to whom she can speak of things her husband can't know. Don't misunderstand. This is not an infidelity she contemplates. It's not the compensation for Linwood her husband secretly wishes she would take. It's only a freedom to talk in a place where she can say what's in her head, without secrets.

All this from reading Edward's book, though less from the book itself than from the return of its author. To confess to Edward what she can't confess to Arnold. The new Edward, who grew up and gained the wisdom to write his book. This Edward would understand why what Arnold thinks her greatest virtue is no particular virtue to her. He would know what it's like not to use the gun.

Sometime in the afternoon getting late she wonders: maybe he isn't going to call. Jolted, she calls the hotel. It's after 3:30, if she wants him for dinner, they'd better get in touch quick. She leaves a message at the hotel desk, call Susan. Asks the clerk when he arrived. Yesterday afternoon, maam, the clerk says. Yesterday? He's been here since *yesterday*?

She considers driving into the city (letting the kids have pizza by themselves), going to the Marriott to catch him when he comes back. Too frantic. Better to cook dinner as planned, with enough for Edward when he calls. She blames herself, stupid. Later, during a time in the preparations with nothing to do but wait for the stove, she has twenty minutes to sit at the kitchen table and think. Time to change course, reverse, shift guilt-in to anger-out. To sizzle with the stove. Why should *you* take the blame, Susan? He's free to call. Not to call is a snub. Raise that to insult: three evenings she spent at his request reading his novel in good faith, with so much effort preparing what to say, and he didn't care enough to call.

Such thought is a furnace, it converts everything, including the novel itself. A fiery question: Why did you send it if you don't want to discuss it? That he could send it out of spite had not occurred to her.

She eats with the children, tries to join their chat as if nothing were on her mind. By the time they are finished, it's obvious: it was not her neglect that caused her to miss Edward. Setting her up for the snub, he's given her a startling new view of himself.

Out of the forgotten she remembers how bitterly he resented her failure to appreciate the dignity of his writing. Like blinding, he said: your attitude blinds me. Evidently he's angry still. Unforgiving twenty-five years later for an offense equivalent to blinding, and the novel his revenge.

The novel as revenge is preposterous, but the idea won't go away. In what sense is it revenge, how is its punishment supposed to work? Figure that out. An allegory? She denies the charges. She has not blinded him, hurt him, destroyed his life, has done no damage whatever – as the novel's own achievement proves. At the kitchen sink with the dishes, she can resent too, resentment bites her lips demanding gesture and breakage, requiring her strongest efforts for self-control.

Her anger depends on how she phrases it, feeding on the language by which she defines Edward's affront, like this: his novel as hate. His favor as trap. Her right to read censored. It gets away from her, what she's angry about, proving to be other than she thought. It comes down to this: the strain, the sheer strain. The strain of maintaining fairness through the humiliation of being wrong. The strain of ignoring love and hate so as to read dispassionately for three sittings. The strain of entering his imagination, of being Tony, only to be kicked out as impertinent. The strain of ignoring the strain, and then to be snubbed.

Irked. Of course, the message may not have been delivered. At 9:30 she calls the hotel again. Edward is still out. She leaves another message. After eleven, she hears the car turn into the garage, Arnold returning late. The thought of what he brings is too horrible to think, and she hurries upstairs, preparing quickly while he eats his bowl of Wheaties in the kitchen, to be in bed and asleep before he comes up so she won't have to talk to him. The necessity for this makes her fume. As she gets into bed (closing out for good the possibility of meeting Edward) there's a conflagration of shame all through her mind. A vast image of the world moving, tectonic plates shifting, spreads out like solitude.

Susan as idiot, such a ninny. She lies in bed wide awake, no trapdoor down tonight – it's shut tight – the floor solid and bitter, thoughts racing and raging. Scolding herself for what she was imagining a few hours ago. She sees herself, fatuous gullible Susan, Arnold's healthy-faced skier, sentimental as a puppy-dog, leaving messages for Edward like an abandoned lover, like a groupie, begging for the right to talk, about what? His book, or was it to complain about Arnold? How could she be so foolish? How could she complain about Arnold to a stranger like Edward after all those years when she has scarcely dared complain to herself? Where could she begin? What would she tell him? What would Edward care? How understand? What is there to understand?

She hears Arnold in the room, in the dark. Shuffling, bumping, grunting, snuffling. The bed sags under him. She smells him. He thumps, snorts, turns heavily over, bumps her as he turns again, making no concessions. She holds still, refusing to be waked, holding her breath to tell him: if not asleep, she's not there either, nowhere to be found.

He has been with Marilyn Linwood. She decides it is true, she thinks it deliberately, lets her mind dwell, turns her imagination to it, visualizing everywhere, New York, Chicago, her apartment, the patient couch in his office, Washington, Chickwash. Does this in direct violation of the mental discipline she adopted three years ago that would enable her to accept the status quo. Enough of that. If she can't tolerate the imagining, she has no right to the status quo.

The absolutely terrifying question has returned to her mind, and again she can't face it. She wonders why he is thrashing and sweating so enormously like a guilty conscience, what's on his mind? She can't think about it. She thinks of those two snuffling together. Talking about her. Protecting her, poor Susan. Let Susan protect herself. She thinks of Arnold's pension plan and annuities, which will start paying off some fifteen-plus years from now, for which she is still the sole beneficiary, the children following after. She plans to remain the sole beneficiary, she *intends* that. She'll insist on that.

She turns in the dark to face Arnold, opens her eyes, looks

at the big empty shadow where he is, to think it like a murder weapon, an arrow, a dart. Arnold the bigamist. He'll move them to Washington or he'll commute on weekends, or worse. Must I take this? Susan asks Susan. You have no choice, they say. You're past the time of revolt or denial. Your husband's career, they say.

What if she refuses? What if she says, I won't do it. I won't move to Washington, nor will I be left behind. I refuse to let you run away from us. I assert myself, your wife. I assert myself selfishly, Susan the bitch.

She sees Marilyn Linwood advising Arnold what to do, just as Susan advised him about mad Selena twenty-five years ago. Using the moral authority she had over him, his natural dependency upon her. She sees how little authority she has now. What happened to it, where did it go? How galling, if she has forfeited it to Linwood. She sees herself in a long vista over years surrendering everything to the project of pleasing him, as if that were her job. Her feminist friends would be surprised how far she's defected from her own politics, defender of all women's rights except her own. What authority could she exert if she dared? She pays the household bills, will Linwood take that over too? Abjectly she waits for Linwood's message, Arnold's gift, held back for as long as she keeps quiet and makes no wrong move. Censored, blackmailed, contained and jailed by the danger of saying a wrong word, a small complaint that would give Linwood the right to take charge.

So she tries a strange word on her silent lips, the word *hate*. She's afraid to use it, lest it commit her to a drastic revolutionary life. Is she strong enough for that? Among her vows when she split with Edward was never to split again. A foolish vow. But it's no mere vow that holds her now. It's the institution, departments and physical plant, an institution no less real than Chickwash: Mommy, Daddy, and the Kids, Inc. If Susan torched the corporation, where would she go? How could she escape blame for arson at this time of life?

Arnold is asleep at last. Deep, oblivious, stupid. Though she's afraid to think hate, she does let herself think him stupid. The thought allows her to relax, dim some of her anger, feel a little sleepy herself. How corrupt I am, she thinks. That thought startles her too, she didn't intend to think it. How surprising to think that what Arnold always required of her might be considered corrupt. Yet she must have known it before, considering how automatically the thought calls to mind a catalogue of cases. Her argument with Mrs. Givens, a memory symbol, emblem, token of discomfort: Mrs. Givens over coffee daring to tell Susan the Macomber rumor, that it wasn't the nurse's fault but the doctor's, too fast, smug, cocksure, etcetera. And Susan reflexively scolding her, blaming the hospital, condemning the lawyer, relying on Arnold's version of what had happened. How surprising that Susan's integrity could be compromised by the noble virtue of loyalty, or whatever it is she has.

The sleep door opening, as she begins to slide she's vaguely aware of Tony in the vicinity. Her temper has cooled. Once again she has forgotten the question that terrified her. She sleeps tentatively and then deeply, and in the morning her anger is an empty space, a mold like the holes made by bodies in the ash at Pompeii. She no longer imagines that Edward deliberately snubbed her, and she's surprised how wrought up she was about Arnold. In the cold daylight it's easy to persuade herself that if she keeps her peace, he'll stand by her, and to dismiss her pain as a flare of selfishness. Easy, too easy. She knows it's too easy, she knows there's something not to be dismissed in what she has seen, but that's for another time, for quiet reflection and deep thought, which can wait. As for Edward, she should have sent her message earlier. She never knew the purpose of his visit nor his obligations nor his schedule. At nine she makes one more call to the hotel. The clerk says Edward Sheffield checked out at seven. Maybe she's disappointed, maybe relieved. She refuses to resent it. She'll assume he didn't call because he came back too late last night and didn't want to disturb her family at an uncivilized hour.

Yet it seems as if something has happened that could change everything, if she's not careful. Through Tony, through Edward, she's had a glimpse. Never mind, not now. For civilization's sake, she'll write Edward a letter. She'll gather her critique together, trim it into tight clear sentences and send it. She writes through the day. The desk is at the window by the bird feeder, devastated by a flock of English sparrows. The snow on the lawn, so clean and white yesterday, has begun to melt, and chunky patches of brown earth show through the holes. The walk to the garage is muddy. The sidewalks glisten with moisture. She hardly notices any of this, so busy is her mind clearing the way to Edward.

She says all the things she planned to say. She praises the book's good qualities and criticizes its flaws. She tells how it made her think of the precariousness of her sheltered life. She confesses her kinship to Tony, writing as if that were a problem solved. She rhapsodizes: While civilization oblivious to him roars in the distance, Tony lies dying, hiding from the police who should be his friends, as he hid earlier from his enemies. Dies, joyfully believing a story which is not true. It gives him comfort, but it's not true, while death and evil rage around.

Edward says, So tell me, what's missing in my book? She replies, Don't you know, Edward, can't you see? The thought sidetracks her into irrelevance. What's missing in *her* life? She wonders if she'll ever see Arnold in the old way again, even if it's not hate. She feels the power of habit pulling her back, as it has for so many years. Looking out at the emerging dirt-brown winter lawn, believing she's still thinking about the letter of forgiving praise and criticism she'll write, or else about how to make herself stronger with Arnold, with more self-respect, Susan Morrow begins to dream. The rowboat in the harbor, she has the oars, Edward lolls in the stern, dangling a hand in the water. The house with screens is behind him, over his head. Behind her and around are the pine islands and cottages. He says, 'The tide is taking us.'

She sees that. She sees the shore behind him moving sideways to the left.

He says, 'If we drift much further it will be hard to get back.'

She knows that. She knows how much further they have to drift and how hard they will have to row.

'If we fell in do you think we'd drown?' he asks.

The question surprises her, the shore doesn't look that far away. But the water is cold in Maine, and they are not good swimmers.

'I don't know if I could reach the shore or not,' she says.

'I know I couldn't. You're a better swimmer than I.'

'You must learn to relax, let your head go under. Being tense makes you carry your head too high and that wears you out.'

'If I fell in could you rescue me?' he asks.

'I'm not that good a swimmer.'

'We'd have to call them.'

'What could they do? We have the boat.'

'They'd stand on shore and watch us drown.'

'How terrible. Imagine them standing on the shore and watching us drown.'

Dreamily she sealed her critique in an envelope. Then, remembering his failure to call on his visit, and all the things she had been unable to ask, such as why he had sent her the manuscript and what made him write such a book, and what was the real reason for their divorce, she snapped out of it and tore the letter up. Instead, she dashed off, without thought, the following note, which she later went out to mail, also without thought.

Dear Edward,
I finally finished your novel. Sorry it took so long. Drop me a line if you want my opinion.
Love, Susan

She wanted to punish Arnold too, but the only thing she could think of was to make him read the book. He would do that if she insisted, but she doubted he would see anything.